THE COST OF KILLING

A DERRICK DRIVER NOVEL

K.A. BROWN

TACTICAL 16 PUBLISHING

The Cost of Killing

Copyright © 2024 by KA Brown

First Edition

This is a work of fiction. Names, characters, places, and events are either the product of the author's imagination or are used fictitiously. Any resemblance to actual persons (living or dead), events, or locations is entirely coincidental. No references made are intended to represent (and neither should they be inferred to represent) reality.

Published by Tactical 16 Publishing

Colorado Springs, CO

www.Tactical16.com

ISBN: 978-1-943226-95-5 (paperback)

ISBN: 978-1-943226-94-8 (hardcover)

CONTENTS

PROLOGUE

WHEN A CERTAIN KIND of person reaches a level of wealth that it seems limitless, some will allow their minds to turn to other things that are difficult to obtain. Power often becomes their next challenge to conquer. Failure to achieve power through honest attempts does not deter some who would do this, but instead, drives them to deeper, darker, more nefarious lengths to find and possess this elusive goal of power.

Sometimes they endeavor alone, other times they seek those with similar agendas. Loyalty is not a concept they embody; hidden agendas and back-stabbing are the norm in this world, with each of them out for their own best interests. Wars have been fought simply at the behest of those with the funding and the desire to have others distracted from their shady dealings and their plans of dominance.

While many have no concerns for their actions, the worry they should have now is the retribution coming from those they have wronged and not prepared for...

1

THE ODOR of antiseptic cleaner mixed with a bit of perspiration filled the air, the lights were low except for a bright light that shone down on him. Pictures of strange drawings filled the walls wherever his eyes wandered. He tried to lay perfectly still. The needle jumped up and down, perforating his skin with every stroke. Tiny droplets of blood and ink would occasionally push to the surface and be wiped away by a small clean cloth. The artist pushed forward with no attention paid to the small amount of blood. It was normal.

Occasionally, she would ask, "Are you okay?"

"Yes, I'm fine, keep going," he replied, as the pain made him wince occasionally. He thought of his promise, "I won't stop," he muttered under his breath.

The artist glanced at the drawing that was sitting to the side of the skin that was her canvas. The background of a Celtic circle was nearly complete. Other shapes had also been outlined on her client's arm. The needle would soon begin to puncture those lines and push ink into the skin as well. Only a temporary reprieve from the constant feeling of being stung by a thousand small bees came when the artist stopped to clean the needle or change colors.

Derrick endured the pain, convinced this was the first small step in his obligation to seek justice for Shannon, a penance he must pay for surviving the incident that killed her. The outline showed a shamrock positioned on the Celtic circle; a dagger pushed through a skull was layered on top of the shamrock. Blood dripped from the end of the knife as it protruded from the skull. Two small roses filled the skull's eye sockets and gave the appearance of glowing red eyes. Below the graphic tattoo was a Latin inscription: *donec debitum solvit. Till the debt is paid.*

The artist continued several hours more, till the image was complete. She wiped away the excess ink and blood and then applied a protective ointment and wrapped the tattoo in plastic.

"Keep that on till at least tomorrow. Don't scratch it, and keep applying that ointment when you remove the plastic," she advised in an almost motherly tone.

Derrick paid his bill and left a sizable tip to show his gratitude for the amazing work, then he left with the first tattoo he had ever gotten. This was for Shannon, a promise that he wouldn't stop until those responsible were dead or brought to justice. He preferred dead.

———

THE SINGLE-STORY CLAY and sand structure baked in the sun all day, now it released that stored energy into the cantina like the inside of an oven. Anyone seeking reprieve from the evening heat had come to the wrong location. A layer of sand covered the floorboards inside, as a testament to the desert-like environment that surrounded the cantina. Sweat glistened on the skin of the patrons, slightly matted by a thin dust that hung in the air like smoke. Two men sat tucked into a back corner of the little cantina. They were fidgeting in their chairs and drawing figures in the dust on the table to cover up their anxiety over this meeting. They glanced around the room, eyes darting rapidly from one person to the next, afraid they might be recognized and reported to the government.

While their goals were noble for the people of this land, they were treasonous to the current government. They sat waiting for a meeting that believed could change not only their lives, but the course of their country. A singer performing a familiar tune, would help provide cover for their anticipated conversation. He was late, and they were beginning to grow concerned not only for his tardiness but for their safety. The first man gazed around the cantina; his clothes were now evidently wet from his perspiration, he continued to fidget in his seat and had started writing swear words in the dust on the table.

"We need to get out of here, he's not gonna show," his voice trembled as he spoke. His partner's face was expressionless, just staring at the door, summoning the will to endure the risk a bit longer.

"I am afraid as well my friend, but we must remain exposed for just a little longer. Our country is depending on us," he responded to his compatriot.

The mere suggestion that they were conspiring to revolt could have them beheaded in front of their families and their bodies placed on poles in front of the central government building, to serve as a blatant deterrent to others who might be considering similar crimes.

They waited another half hour before they decided it was time to leave.

One of them raised his hand to attract the attention of a server walking by. "Waitress, our check please," he asked quietly.

While they were waiting for the waitress to return, an extremely tall man ducked in through the hanging beads that passed as the inner door to the establishment. He slowly gazed around the room and upon seeing the two men standing over in the corner, he quickly moved toward them, his boots scuffing through the thin layer of sand. He held out his hand to the men, neither reciprocated. "That's okay, I know I'm late. I do bring the benefits you've been wanting though," he said with a smile and the bravado of a used car salesman.

After waiving off the server who was returning, the men returned to their seats joined by their guest.

The tall man spoke softly. "You've read the proposal from your benefactor, by accepting this money you are agreeing to work within the timeline we've laid out, and that you'll coordinate your attacks to maximize the benefits to your financier as well." The two men looked nervously at each other, they understood that their path to revolt was being financed to allow their benefactor to accomplish things that he needed to be hidden from the public, and that their war for freedom would likely be just a distraction to the rest of the world.

The two men stood up and this time they shook hands with the tall man—for them the meeting went well. The two turned and left quietly from the cantina, doing their best to go unnoticed. Outside as the tall man promised, the two men found two large duffel bags. They grabbed the bags of untraceable funding and disappeared into the city.

———

THE TALL MAN exited and found himself brushing against the bodies of people crowded into the area outside the cantina. It was dusk and the lighting was minimal at best. He wasn't worried about crime though; he was only worried about becoming lost. He needed to get to his next meeting.

Barry Klinger was known as a facilitator and for the right price, he could arrange almost anything. In this case, his fee was higher than normal. He had worked for this client for a long time and even considered him a friend, but this time he was arranging a war, one that would serve mostly as a distraction from his client's political manipulations.

Barry headed directly to his next meeting with The Royal General of Milekistan, a title that the leader bestowed on himself after a military coup seven years ago. Since then, the General had been living like a king at his country's expense. Barry's driver navigated the car up one of the few paved roads in the country to a beautiful sprawling estate. The landscape was manicured and watered by sprinklers even as the people in this country struggled for fresh drinking water. This did not escape Barry's notice as they drove closer to the meeting; he hated himself for the next part he had to do.

The residence resembled a small hotel or a castle. Stone walls and large glass windows were the things that stood out at first, but the more one looked, other oddities emerged, things that were out of place in this country. Ivy grew up the walls, small red flowers blooming from in the ivy. It truly was a beautiful sight. The entire estate was like a Hollywood set, fabricated to present a specific impression.

During the ride, he considered how he was playing both sides against each other. He chose not to dwell on the moral implications, as it was causing his stomach to hurt. His task was to orchestrate a bloody conflict that would enthrall the media and consume the public's attention. When he arrived, he was escorted inside to the General's office. Ornate sculptures from around the world sat on pedestals, fine art hung on the walls between the windows, and a large bookshelf behind the desk looked as though it held a thousand books. As he was ushered into the private study, a short thin man stood up from behind the desk.

Barry felt the hairs raise on his neck, a response much like a dog's when it senses danger. He took a deep breath and almost gagged; the air was mixed with a sweet smell of some flower and the sour scent of curry and body odor that emanated from the General himself.

"Royal General, thank you for meeting with me," Barry forced out with a smile.

Barry reached out and shook the little hand that belonged to such a diminutive man, as if they were buddies reunited. He was amused at how small this overbearing man really was.

As he shook hands, the Royal General watched as his hand disappeared completely in the grasp of his visitor. Intimidated, he rapidly snatched it away. He motioned for Barry to sit in a chair positioned in front of the large ornate desk. Barry chuckled to himself as he realized that the General's desk was raised to give him the appearance of having more stature over his guests.

"You said you can help me with the threat against my power," the General stated as a question more than a statement.

Visions of choking this little man till his head exploded were running through Barry's mind. He looked around the room as he talked, afraid too much eye contact would betray his hateful feelings toward the General.

"Yes sir, I can. I have some information I am sure will be of great value to you," Barry reassured him while appearing to look around and admire the art.

The General stared at him as if sizing him up for a suit. Looking him up and down and ultimately trying to gaze directly into Barry's eyes. Barry met the gaze only briefly.

"I suppose you should give me this information then, Mr. Klinger," the General said with a snide growl in his tone indicating this was a precursor to a threat.

"Oh, Mr. General I plan on it, however, I need a small gesture from you first," Barry said, meeting the General's tone with one of equal authority.

The General's eyes flashed with anger. "How much do you want?"

Barry quickly reframed his statement. "General, I am not looking for money, only a simple assurance from you on how you will use the information."

The General continued to stare as if he was looking past Barry and blurted out, "You will not dictate how I will use this information in protecting myself and my position!"

His voice had risen nearly to the point of cracking while he was responding. Barry thought quickly. He was losing his grip on this conversation. The General was known for his quick and exceedingly violent temper.

"General, I promise you may use the information as you see fit, my client only asks that your actions coincide with a timeline that benefits him as well. After all, he has spent a considerable amount of money to uncover this information," Barry responded in a diminutive tone.

As quickly as he became aggressive, the General deflated. He seemed to be content with Barry's request and reasoning. "Okay let's have it," he asked.

Barry laid out the timeline for the General, who agreed to it in writing, pending his validation of the information. The meeting finished, Barry wiped his brow as he exited, relieved to be able to escape the presence of such a dangerously insecure man, secretly hoping the rebels would destroy him. As he rode down the long-paved drive on the way out, he thought about his client and the deal he just secured. *He will be happy.*

———

TWO DAYS LATER, Barry was waiting for his next meeting. There was a hacker his client had asked him to locate and solicit to help with his plan. Barry had a bit of trouble locating this man, because this person was intentionally trying to hide. Now that Barry had found him and arranged a meeting, he was excited to finally put a face to this man who made his job so exceedingly difficult. The hacker was dressed like anyone who would be in the park. He wore a hat pulled low over his dark sunglasses, no electronic devices at all, and an oversized hoodie over sweatpants and sneakers.

Barry sized him up, using his displayed caution as a baseline, it made Barry look over his shoulder as well. This guy was obviously worried about being followed or found. They sat on a bench in the public park. Kids and dogs ran around freely, some of them with their parents or guardians watching from close by. The cheerful noise of playing children or the occasional bark of an impatient dog provided acoustical cover for their conversation.

"How did you find me?" the hacker half whispered, half hissed.

Barry studied him a second longer. "You were not an easy person to find."

The hacker stared coldly back at him and responded quietly, "I make myself hard to find. The fact that you found me, means I must have missed something. Make this fast. What do you need?"

Barry took a minute to relay a greeting from his client. "George Avail says hello, and he needs your assistance."

He noticed the hacker's demeanor relax slightly, but not completely.

Barry continued talking, hoping the hacker was relaxing a bit, "You are needed to hack into these specific locations," he finished with as he handed over an envelope.

The hacker reviewed the contents of the envelope, mumbling to himself as he read.

Barry stared at him. "Are you sure you understand all the instructions laid out in there?" he questioned, referencing the letter.

"I'm good, this is a complex hack, but I can do it. I will need to assemble a team to get it done," the hacker responded.

Barry understood the implications and handed over a duffle bag full of cash.

"This should get you going, there will be more when you acquire the content as directed."

The hacker grabbed the bag, and abruptly stood up and said, "I'll be in touch, don't look for me again. Only call me on this." He handed Barry a card with the number to his encrypted burner phone.

A group of teens passed by shouting at each other and being generally rowdy. Barry looked over at them—when he looked back, the hacker had disappeared into the park. He smiled; he considered Tinker just an ordinary person, no military or spy training. It was impressive to him that someone like this could be so effectively elusive. "Well done."

2

ELSY HAD GONE from a cybercrime police officer to the CEO of the fastest-growing cybersecurity firm in the US in less than two years. Elsy had become the television morning show's favorite person after they discovered her involvement in uncovering Lileth Waller's attempted presidential assassination. It didn't take long before the calls from prospective employers started to pour in from all over.

Instead of taking any of those lucrative offers, she decided to capitalize on her current fame and opened her own company, Cold Assassin Cyber Security. Within three months of opening, she had needed to hire twelve employees to keep up with the demand. Even as the media hype waned off, her reputation grew exponentially within the cyber community. She had become the new 'go-to girl' in this community. Elsy's new company was always growing, and was known as a great place to work, but all employees were provided one extra incentive on being hired. It was a cash bounty for information leading to the location of a hacker known only as, "Tinker."

———

ELSY SAT in her office looking out the window that framed the city from eighteen stories above. She mused at the view for a moment, and then turned back to her desk. She tapped on the keyboard of her computer and then leaned forward for a retinal scan to verify her identity. In just a few milliseconds the computer sprang to life displaying numerous windows that Elsy had left running when she was last at her desk. She popped open one screen and studied the numbers. She grinned a little and thought, *that should help a bit.* She was looking at an account she had set up for a dead man. Only he wasn't dead, and only her and a limited number of other people knew that. She opened another window and typed into an encrypted texting app, sent the message, and then closed the app. She knew it would be a while till she heard back again.

Now her attention turned to the search she was running 24/7 on multiple platforms. Her search for Tinker, the hacker who had almost bested her but still managed to escape without a trace during the Waller case. Elsy was sure that Tinker had more information than had been uncovered by the FBI. As far as they were concerned, the Waller case was closed with Lileth Waller's death. The screens showed data that hinted at different data points she was searching for. Today more information came in that looked promising. She printed the information and slid it into a folder, a trick to prevent data loss she had learned from a friend who was once a detective where she worked in Boston. She also sent a copy to her phone, that way she'd always have the info with her if she needed it. The data suggested that the man she had been hunting, might be right there in Boston with her.

Elsy wasn't afraid of Tinker; she was intrigued by him and hungry to know the secrets he hadn't shared yet. She took the elevator down to the parking level and headed for her Audi Etron GT. It was a fast car and had the features of a normal Audi, except that it stood out with its bright white paint with electric blue racing stripes and dark tinted windows. Elsy exited the garage and headed for the coordinates indicated by her computer search. She had a Canon DSLR camera on the seat next to her, as well as a high-powered pair of binoculars, in her handbag was a Springfield XDS 9mm.

She circled the block where the GPS coordinates led her to, an old brick building which was located on a slight corner in the middle of the block, with an alley running off the corner behind the building. After her second loop, she parked about a half a block away on the opposite side of the street. She used the binoculars first and surveyed every inch of her target building.

———

GEORGE WIPED a bead of sweat from his brow with his silk handkerchief as the condensation around his glass dripped over his fingers and onto the white tablecloth. Although they had fled out of caution, this island had turned out to be a wonderful break from the day-to-day grind in the States. From his veranda he could easily see the ocean, and the breeze was exactly the right amount to keep the sun from making it too hot to be outside. The cloth covering of the pergola and the small potted palms provided sufficient cover and shade to truly make it feel like paradise. A twelve-foot-wide set of glass doors separated the spacious deck from the house, and when they were all opened, it was like the whole house was open to the island. George glanced out to see his daughter Linda emerge in a bright pink bikini with a white mesh sarong tied around her waist.

"Good morning, daughter," he proclaimed it as if he were king of the island.

Linda smiled and held her drink up towards him. Her glass had also started to perspire from the ice. A few drops made the journey down her arm toward her elbow. Linda laid down on the chaise lounge. Her spot was in the direct sunlight, and she flung her now blonde hair over the back as she snuggled into the chair where she felt comfortable.

"So, what's on the agenda today, father?" she asked with a whispery, almost uncaring tone to her voice.

"Do you still *keep* an agenda?" he responded with a sarcastic tone.

Linda laid in her chair basking in the sun, content despite her father's slight chide about work. Even with her father's continued desire for control of whomever they could, Linda couldn't remember ever being more content than she was here on the island. To herself she thought, *I hope we stay here forever.*

She felt a little guilty for thinking it, and yet she was experiencing a freedom she had never known. The idea of sharing these thoughts with her father made her queasy, so she turned her mind back to the sun and her tan.

Linda had laid in the sun for about an hour when she heard her dad talking on the phone.

"Okay thanks Barry, you've given us immeasurable assistance. It will not be forgotten when this plan is complete."

George said goodbye and ended the call. Linda looked from the lounge at her dad who was standing a bit inside the open door to the house.

"Sounded like work," she said playfully. "I guess there is an agenda."

Her father grinned lightly and spoke.

"Nothing too important, just some groundwork I'm laying ahead of time."

He then refilled his drink and moved to a chair under an umbrella out on the deck. He smiled at his daughter and pulled a linen fedora down over his eyes and relaxed thinking to himself.

"This plan needs to work, if it does, we will restructure power as the world knows it…" Thoughts of his plan bounced around in his head as he sipped his drink in the lounge chair.

———

BOREDOM WAS STRUGGLING to distract her; Elsy had watched the building for several hours. She had taken pictures with the camera that were automatically sent back to her office computer and would be analyzed by her software.

"Time to change things up," she decided.

She looked around as she checked her mirrors for traffic and exited her car. The street was littered with loose garbage, bits of paper and plastic that swirled in the corners before bursting up into the air only powered by the occasional breeze. Elsy watched, momentarily distracted. She shook her head and regained focus on the task at hand. As she walked toward the building, she reached into her handbag and retrieved a pair of sunglasses.

The sun was not overly bright, but these sunglasses were made with a special coating and electronic enhancements that allowed her to locate possible electronic surveillance equipment. As she approached the target building, she scanned the area, both the building itself and everywhere she could see that would have a view of the building entrance. Elsy felt an exhilaration as the evidence seemed to point to this being the location she was searching for. She discovered several possible surveillance cameras and stopped out of the cameras' view angles. The presence of the elaborate surveillance equipment made it feel that she probably had the right building.

Feeling that her excitement might cloud her judgement and not willing to sacrifice her perceived upper hand yet, she retreated to her car. "Time to regroup." She drove slowly back to her office, evaluating her options to proceed.

———

TINKER SAT BEHIND multiple computer screens. Each had different information or images displayed on it. A total of nine screens offered him continuously updated information on his ongoing searches and hacking programs. Since his impromptu visit from an employee of his former boss, he had been on 'high alert' in his mind. Although it seemed his former employer wanted his assistance on a project, he was not convinced that it wasn't a ploy to draw him out and kill him.

The only problem was whenever he thought about that rationally, he realized that he was already found, and someone would have killed him if that was the goal. He moved the mouse to select one of the nine screens and move the image to a much larger screen that hung behind him. Tinker swung his chair around to look at the image displayed on the screen. It was a large building in Boston. He was preparing this to be his next base of operations. His servers had already been moved in and were fully operational, he once again had the ability to hack any server he chose, even those belonging to companies that repeatedly claimed to be 'un-hackable'. A claim many were forced to make by the nature of the data they processed.

Tinker fast forwarded through hours of video looking for any sign this area would be compromised before he made his final move. As he watched the video, he saw an Audi Etron drive by. He stopped the video to look at the car. It was bright white with dark-tinted windows. He stared at the car for a few minutes. He then resumed his review, all the while thinking about the car. *That is the most awesome car on the market. I must get one of those.* This made him think of his latest offer from his old employer. *The payday from that job will allow me any car I choose.* After finishing the last twenty-four hours of video, he was satisfied that his new place of business was secure, and he made the arrangements to finalize his move. "Boston, here I come."

———

THE UTV BOUNCED around like a rodeo bull under a cowboy. Tree branches slapped at the passengers as they passed through them. The path was not exactly made for any type of vehicle and was actively protesting their presence as they drove on it for the second time today. The guns and equipment in the back were securely strapped in place, but the driver and his dog were left to do their best to retain their seats while they navigated the path. It wasn't an overly long walk between the cabin and the private shooting range set deep in the woods, but Derrick secretly liked the rambunctious drive, and he was sure that Killer did too.

As a cop, Derrick had always remained extremely proficient with his martial art and firearms skills by training continuously. These skills were even more important now that he was dead and seeking justice from those responsible. Finally, the trail gave up trying to make them pay for their trespass against it, and the forest opened to the smooth field path that led the rest of the way to the cabin. Derrick pulled the UTV into a large cover that also housed his van. He unloaded his cargo and he and Killer headed for the house.

As he prepared lunch for the two of them, the smell of tuna and onions had his eyes watering. Killer sat licking his chops waiting for the tuna juice to be poured atop his kibble. Derrick smiled; he had no doubt which one of them would enjoy lunch the most. Derrick opened his laptop to check emails and check his notes regarding the whereabouts of the Avails. He glanced over the news headlines on the web. *China lends helping hand to smaller countries.* He scanned the next smaller headline, *President Harrington refuses to attend world financial forum.* And then a smaller headline caught his eye, *Twentieth US food processing plant burns to the ground.* Derrick read a little bit more out of curiosity, according to the article, no government agency was too concerned about this. He wrinkled his forehead as he read it. "*I'm* concerned, why isn't our government?" he thought. He didn't have time to read further, since he had other things to attend to.

3

DERRICK DABBED the lotion on his new tattoo. *Tattoos don't move,* he thought, *and neither do dead men.* He needed to find a way to fix that. It had taken a while to track the Avails' movements around the globe, but now he wasn't able to get to them. He was limited by no passport to travel legally and not enough money to do so by other means. He knew the Avails were on a tropical island in the Caribbean, and this caused him mixed emotions of anger and even jealousy, making him even more determined to make them pay for their past crimes against him and others. He checked his email, hoping for something good to think about.

He had two messages, both a few days old. The first was from an old colleague that was now one of the few friends that knew he was alive. Just seeing the name caused him to feel a warmth inside, since she had known Shannon as well. He read the message,

"Good day old friend, I hope all is well.

Today the department started archiving the old files and undercover IDs from an old detective that is no longer with us. I happened to secure one such ID that you may remember. The background, bank accounts and passport are all valid as well as the social security number associated with it. A brown manila envelope containing these items should be delivered to the cabin PO Box within the next couple of days, I hope this helps return you from the dead.

Love, Donna."

Derrick read the email twice, tears welled in his eyes. He knew she was risking her career for him. He sent a reply thanking her immensely, hopeful he could thank her in person soon. He reread her words, *return from the dead.* When this package arrived, he would finally be able to. Derrick almost didn't open the second message, afraid that it would be bad news. He cautiously gazed upon the contents as if he could shield himself if it were the bad news he expected. He recognized the name of another work contact who had become a close friend after they were both targeted by assassins that were sent by the man he was now hunting. Elsy wrote,

"Hey Buddy,
I'm sure you might be a little short on cash by now, so I funded an account for you. The card should arrive any day. The pin is the name of your dog. Text me back if there is anything I can do for you. I hope all is as well as it can be. Love ya.
P.S. I got the name and account number from Donna."

Derrick turned away from the screen. A tiny drop of moisture trickled from his eye down his left cheek. He wiped it away in a swift but effective motion. He would soon be unfettered to hunt his prey. Time to prepare for a trip to the islands. Derrick was about to be reborn.

———

THE MINIVAN PULLED into the alley behind the building. In preparation to inhabit this building, construction was done to make it fit his wishes. The street's main entrance only offered access to the business side of the building; Tinker rented out to several legitimate clients who had nothing at all to do with his endeavors. The construction made the rear entrance the only access to his area and it was secured with extreme biometric security measures.

Tinker walked in the back door; inside his body size was measured against an electronic measurement stored inside. His weight was matched to a file associated with his facial image, and then a retinal scanner was opened for him to match his retina to the one on file. After all those security measures were verified, a latch was heard unbolting and a hidden door opened. Tinker stepped into a hallway only illuminated by a red light. He moved ahead until the door behind him closed and latched. He stood in front of what looked like a full-length mirror.

"Aren't you a beautiful thing?" he said slowly and deliberately.

The mirror slid away revealing an elevator. Tinker pushed a button for the floor he wanted and then entered a code on the keypad. The door closed and the elevator rushed to its destination. When the door opened, Tinker felt like he had arrived in his version of heaven. The only problem was that he didn't travel upwards. Tinker knew that many people like to occupy the highest floor in a building they own, but he was the opposite —he had created his area two levels below the surface. He smiled; he had a 'lair' like any dark hero.

———

THE DRIVE from the cabin to town was about thirty minutes in the UTV, a ride Killer was enjoying immensely. Derrick parked in front of a small general store that also serves as the town's Post Office. Killer waited patiently guarding the vehicle. As he entered, Derrick was greeted by a store clerk behind the counter. "Hi, D. How are you doing today?"

"I'm fine. Thank you for asking," Derrick responded, smiling politely.

The young redheaded clerk had always been friendly and although he never remembered Derrick's name, he remembered it started with a D, so that's what he called him. Derrick went into the back to the Post Office area and checked his PO Box. No envelope—instead there was a note that said to see a counter person for mail. Derrick took the note and headed for the postal counter. As he approached, he could see the postal worker, an older man named Donald, was thoroughly involved in a conversation about fishing at the lake with the town sheriff, another older man named Hank. Hank and Donald continued with their conversation, oblivious to Derrick waiting in line. Suddenly Donald stopped mid-sentence and exclaimed,

"How long have you been waiting, boy? You can push this old stump out of the way and get up here."

Hank stepped aside and assessed Derrick as he stepped up to the counter. "You're out at the old Driver cabin, aren't you?"

Derrick was surprised. This was the first person to ask about him or the cabin.

"Are you the brother to the detective that was killed over in Boston?" the sheriff asked.

Derrick smiled politely and said, "Just a close relative."

He collected his package from Donald, excited about the possible contents. The sheriff seemed content with his answer, and returned to the conversation about fishing the lake. Out in the UTV, a nagging question came to his mind as he ripped open the package, "So, who am I?" Killer sensed his demeanor and matched his excitement, prancing around on the front seat furiously wagging his tail. Clipped to the top of the file inside was a Massachusetts driver's license. The name Derrick Dunn was listed on it. This brought back memories. He knew this person well; he had become him for thirteen months of undercover work. A cover that was never blown and as a benefit, had no criminal record. Derrick smiled. Donna had done very well; he was now alive and free. He looked at the rest of the documents. Elsy hadn't just handled the financial part, she made sure he would be set for quite a while.

———

LINDA LAID out on the lounge chair, a drink on the table beside her and a paperback novel rested alongside her on the lounge. She thought about her current life and how she had lived until now. She knew she had crossed many lines to get to this point. She knew serious crimes had been committed to allow her this lifestyle. These were things she had never allowed herself to think about before—for the first time, she felt a sense of remorse over the previous actions committed by her or her father.

Now she laid out in the sun, considering the possibility of leaving that all behind and living this new life. A life of maintaining her tan, enjoying the beach and salty air, the tropical cuisine and entertainment. For the first time, she found herself enjoying people being around her. She had never enjoyed socializing with anyone, but the people on the island were genuinely friendly and inviting. Unbeknownst to her father, she had attended several events at local nightclubs in the tourist areas. She was starting to desire this life over the one that had been arranged for her. She was longing to make connections with people, instead of just using them.

Linda had a question that many teenagers ask, but one that had never plagued her until now.

Who am I?

On a much deeper note, and well beyond her moment of existential curiosity, she wondered if any real chance existed to allow her to become anyone else.

———

TINKER SAT amid his newly created world. His area was elevated like a king. Not only did this environment placate his ego, but it also gave him a sense of security he had come to need. While it was enclosed with glass walls so he could always view his kingdom, the walls were made so that with a touch of a button, he could turn them from clear to a grayish-white color that couldn't be seen through.

From his desk, he could look across the room at his computer servers all located behind a glass wall in an environmentally-controlled room. These were his tools of the trade, tools that allowed him to pry into areas he didn't belong to, access secrets that he shouldn't know, and ultimately to change things that shouldn't be changed. Tinker studied the screens that were broadcast through the glass walls that surrounded his office. It was another new technology that he chose to enjoy. The money from his former boss, now his new employer again, was perfect timing.

Despite being one of the world's best hackers, someone had found one of his largest bank accounts and drained it, something he had done to countless others. He was afraid it might have been some law enforcement agency, so he chose to abandon it instead of risking exposing himself even more. That made this move perfect timing. Now he was looking for a new identity to assume. Several possibilities popped up on his screen, he carefully evaluated each of them. *Who am I?* He wondered as he shuffled through the possible identities.

———

ELSY SAT ALONE in her office contemplating the recent events regarding her prey. She thought of how close she had come in the past, even discovering and then depleting one of his bank accounts. The money she happily used to fund her friend's new identity. This time she was even closer. That thought caused her both excitement and trepidation. She was excited to be here, so close that it was almost inevitable that she would finally catch him. Nervous because she was close enough that she might catch him.

"What if I do catch him? I'm not a cop anymore."

She took a few moments to contemplate what her next move would be. She realized she would have to send someone other than herself to investigate the building. Around the room were her trusted employees. She trusted them all to do their jobs and be loyal. This was another level completely. Her eyes came to rest on Tulia Pretense, one of her longest employees. Not only was Tulia a great employee, but she had also proven herself already to be completely dedicated to the company and Elsy.

Elsy wondered if this would be the right course of action. She knew she could potentially put Tulia in danger if she somehow spooked her prey. Elsy knew firsthand that people that tangled with this hacker sometimes ended up as targets, and some were killed. She closed her eyes and played a hypothetical scenario of Tulia playing spy for her. It ended with Tulia being chased down on a back street and struggling for her life against a would-be assassin. She opened her eyes to the reflection of her face on a dark computer monitor. She stared intently for a few seconds.

Who am I? She pondered as she thought of recklessly sending an employee to potential danger.

"I need to re-evaluate this whole thing."

———

GEORGE AVAIL LOOKED at the drink in his hand and then glanced out to the veranda where his daughter was sunbathing. Indeed, he had never seen her so content, possibly in her whole life, apart from the few years while her mother was still alive. There was no part of him left that had fatherly instincts—if there were, he suspected that he would want her stay here forever, enjoying the downtime in the sun.

Unfortunately, he had already set plans in motion that they would need to deal with soon. They had several politicians to speak with, as well as the head of one of the United States' largest political organizations, all for the Avail family to maintain the global position they needed to control certain members of the US political leadership. Leading from behind was his specialty. With several outspoken and seemingly unintelligent new candidates running for office, George found the perfect opportunity to insert himself and his money to gain influence. His new approach was to simply control those already elected rather than control an election.

He had plans already in motion to make this happen. While his daughter was resting comfortably soaking in the sun, he returned to the inner sections of the home to make some phone calls. He dialed the first number to a candidate from Massachusetts—a newcomer who wasn't being challenged by a conservative. This candidate had painted the incumbent Democrat he wished to replace as a 'DINO', stealing a version of a phrase given to Republicans who voted like Democrats. The phone rang twice before it was answered.

"Hello, this is Alexander Ernest Cortega," the voice on the other end responded. "Who is this?" he queried.

George thought about that. "Who am I? I can be either the worst or the best thing that will ever happen to you. Give me ten minutes and you will agree," he responded.

4

ALEXANDER PONDERED the phone call he received. He had never considered that anyone would find his hidden past. Now he was offered the choice to be exposed or be funded by someone who would offer money to promote his campaign. The trade-off was unrestricted access to Alexander once he was in office. He didn't need to think about it. He looked over his daily social media posts, maybe one hundred views. If the world knew his secret, he would top a million, but that wouldn't help his campaign.

If he accepted this offer, that would all change. He would have a campaign office and staff to run it. That would include a real public affairs person to handle and direct his public image. Deep down he knew he didn't have a choice. He wanted to be mad, even furious over this situation, but in the end, he was simply resentful that someone else held this power over him.

"I wanted to make a mark for the public to see, so what if it was someone else's mark," he mumbled.

In his campaign he positioned himself as 'the champion for the oppressed'. In his current ads, he claimed that his competitor was 'just an old white guy that helped create modern oppression'. A move that earned him quite a few threatening letters and emails, with many calling him a reverse racist. Alexander was ready to make the call; he never really had to even think about it.

———

GEORGE WOULDN'T BE SATISFIED with one new politician on his take—he needed a full stable of them. He had been building his stable for quite a few years. Some of whom he shared with other interests that were more global. These compromised politicians included two from Connecticut and a couple from New York. As for California, so many of them were secretly planted to fill those positions. He needed a couple from red states, or at least who were considered Republicans. He searched his contact list. He already had Senators from Utah, Maine, and Alaska. He even had a Senator from Georgia that no one suspected. He thought their past voting records might give their corruption away, but it was accepted as DC politics.

George had learned from his previous failures; his last plan had been defeated, he believed, due to its massive overreach and that it had required too much human interaction before implementation. He also knew that many of his key actors last time had faced a crisis of conscience that led them to make errors that ultimately caused his plan to fail. He considered his own conscience; nothing bothered him about the things he had done to get here. This time he would gather his minions using guile and ingenuity; he would use a universal motivator, greed, but also compelling background information he had uncovered on many of them.

He was more than willing to use his money to simply buy the politicians he needed, but he hoped to soon have a new information source that would greatly assist his endeavors to ultimately get control of the White House. He knew that he would have a bit of an uphill battle simply because President Harrington was doing a great job. His approval rating kept going up despite the media's influence against him. People were slowly starting to use multiple sources to determine the real story behind every evening news report. While the mid-terms had given Democrats a near even split in the House, he still wanted the Senate and the White House. He realized a major distraction would be needed this time, not only to obfuscate his actions but also to change what everyone was talking about. He wasn't just hiding his plans from the government.

———

DERRICK LOOKED at a pile of papers scattered across his dining table. He had satellite pictures of a villa located on a tropical island. They showed the streets and building around one large villa that was circled in red on the largest of the images. Derrick had located the Avails a few months ago with the help of Elsy and some strong detective work. Now he was trying to figure out how to get to them, to fulfill his promise of revenge and still get away and return to what he had of a life. He glanced over and smiled at Killer who was curled up on his bed on the floor. Derrick felt a pain in his chest realizing that his intentions were changing due to this dog. When he started his mission, he didn't have any concern for his own survival. Killer had been abandoned when he found him, and they saved each other. He would never let Killer be abandoned again.

As he reviewed the images and weighed his options, he realized that he would probably encounter other civilians that he would need to subdue or otherwise incapacitate. He looked away from his plans and thought of his promise to find justice for Shannon. The more he thought about killing the Avails, the tighter the knot in his stomach would get. He felt like he had the angel and devil characters sitting on his shoulders, pushing him in opposite directions. Rationally, he justified his desire to kill the Avails because that's what they deserved. After all, they had been responsible for possibly hundreds of deaths. But intentionally hunting and killing another human, regardless of their prior acts, went against everything he had ever believed as a police officer. But then again, they took all that from him. The potential collateral damage he might inflict if he rushed into this without a concrete plan also weighed on him.

He pushed his emotional turmoil aside and went back to studying the pictures and reading as much about the island's police response, laws regarding murder, and any other pertinent information he could find. Knowing where they were was the easy part; taking them out and getting out without hurting anyone else was the part that required all the planning.

———

ELSY STARTED her day with several client meetings. Clients that all had letters like CEO, CFO and COO after their names on their business cards. She was generally the youngest person in the room and almost always the only woman. This made her smile—they all usually had one of two similar reactions when they met her. Either they had an image of her in their minds already and said something like, "Oh, you look nothing like the pictures of you in the papers," or they didn't even know who she was and were surprised by her appearance. Some even went as far as to mistakenly ask, "Is your boss going to be joining us?"

Elsy usually smiled and responded, "No," in those situations.

Sometimes the client was offended by that and would threaten to leave if the 'Boss' couldn't speak with them. When that happened, Elsy would stand up and apologize.

"I'm sorry, but I don't think your business would be a good fit for my company."

She never said it angrily, on the contrary, she found it generally amusing to watch the faces of these arrogant men change to shy and defeated when they suddenly realized their error.

With her morning meetings over, Elsy turned her mind back to her concerns about locating Tinker. Overnight her software confirmed that his code was emanating from the building she identified. She did some hacking of her own to pull up the building plans associated with that site. The public records showed it as a mixed-use office building with six floors above ground and three sub-terrain levels. It also showed recent permits had been pulled for renovation, but they were not able to be found.

———

IN HIS OFFICE, the 'king of hackers' sat at his desk. He was still having difficulty picking his new identity. *Maybe it was too many choices,* he thought. His eyes were always drawn back to the same name, a name he was forbidden to use. He wasn't even sure why he didn't delete it. But deep down he knew why—it was his real identity, the name he was born with, the life he left as a teen, a life he never wished to return to. Despite all of that, he still couldn't delete the folder. Joshua Hanson would live another day. He smiled at the thought of a king sparing the life of a peasant. He looked back at his other choices, and *Martin Brennan* stood out to him. "Welcome home, Martin," he whispered to the screen. "We suddenly have a lot in common."

He selected individual files and sent them to various printers that were located strategically around his office. A few minutes later he had a registration for his vehicle, a driver's license, and a social security card, all in the name of Martin Brennan. "Welcome to your kingdom, Martin," he announced to himself as if speaking to another. Tinker sat back down. He had work to do, and having a real ID would help him complete it. He started reviewing the applicants that were applying to help him complete the task for Mr. Avail.

He had put out a call for talented hackers on a dark web message board that many hackers used, and in two days he had almost a thousand interested parties. He hoped that maybe he could reconnect with a few of the hackers that made up his old crew, but most if not all of them had abandoned the field after their close call with law enforcement not too long ago. Since every application was digital, he wrote a quick program to eliminate anyone who asked, *how much?* He also eliminated anyone who asked, *will I be hacking? Is it legal?*

"These were all hackers, why the heck would you expect it to be legal?" He said out loud as he added the line to his code. With the code written, he added all the applicants to the batch and engaged his new filter. About ten seconds later, it was done and had reduced the thousand plus down to four hundred and two. Tinker stared at the screen. *This is BS*, he thought. He stood up and decided he need to get some fresh air and check out his new neighborhood. He left through the same way he entered, as it was the only way in or out. As he emerged into the sunlight, he donned a pair of sunglasses but still had to wait for his eyes to adjust. The smell of pizza drifted in the air. Martin raised his nose in the air as if to inhale the scent. *That'll work,* as he started toward where he believed the delectable aroma was coming from, he realized one thing.

"Damn, I should have added a door out the front. This is a long extra walk." On the way, he called his contractor to make some changes.

———

GEORGE READ the electronic report on his computer. He wasn't quite sure what to make of it. He had people in various levels of government and law enforcement and other helpful positions staggered around the world. All of them were tasked with assisting him in any way they could, but also helping to keep him safe. Today he received a report that said someone had pulled satellite images and building reports about the villa they were living in. George wasn't sure what to make of it. The report didn't include *who* pulled this information, only that someone had. For all George knew, it could simply be the buyer he had beaten out when he purchased the villa. Even still, his cautious side was telling him to get more info on who acquired the information, and why.

He looked outside and saw Linda was in her now usual spot. To him, it seemed the only thing that changed with her from day to day now was her bikini. Today it was bright yellow and a little too small for his taste. *I've finally gotten the teenager I never had,* he thought. He went back to his desk, picked up the phone, and dialed a number from his contacts. He pressed the call button and waited as the phone followed his command. A few seconds later, the ringing stopped and a man's voice said, "Good afternoon, Mr. Avail. What can I help you with today?" George proceeded to tell him of the report he received. "Can you figure out who gathered this information and why?" Barry listened to the request and responded with, "Yes sir, I'll get on that right away. I don't think it should take too long. Would you like me to arrange for additional security for you and your daughter until we know more?"

George thought about that for a moment. "No I think we'll be all right for now. If you find something that contradicts that, you let me know right away." Both ended the call and George returned to the window to look at his 'teenager'. He smiled and took another sip of his drink. *This will have to end soon,* he thought, as he switched to the financial section of the paper he had shipped in every day. The Chinese yuan was drawing closer to the value of the US dollar. This was a new development he would have to investigate. His financial planners hadn't forecasted this for him.

––––––

DERRICK DECIDED he needed a break from his planning. He gathered all the documents he had strewn around the table and filed them neatly in a big folder. He took the folder and placed it in a hole behind his chair that was hidden by two boards. He didn't know why he felt like he should do this, but he did it anyway. With all of it picked up and hidden, he grabbed the keys for the UTV and called Killer.

"Come on boy, let's go for a ride."

Killer's ears perked the second Derrick started to speak, but it wasn't until he said *ride* that Killer sprang to life and started prancing in front of the door, waiting for Derrick to meet him. They both jumped into the UTV and headed for town. This time they drove past the General Store and continued a bit farther down Main Street. They passed the local diner where there were still a couple of cars out front. He pulled the UTV into a parking lot set back a bit further from the street. The building looked much like an old barn, with weathered wooden siding and not many windows, though the neon signs that adorned the whole front kind of betrayed what it was.

One of those signs illuminated the words 'Nik's Bunker Bar' and underneath was a kind of playful printed warning, "This is the barrel, you're the fish!" It was a way to let patrons know what they were walking into. Derrick parked the UTV, and he and Killer headed for the bar. Derrick skipped the main entrance and walked along the side to a patio area. The sign over the door read, "Nik's Bunker Bar, where attitude is always on tap." A waitress delivering drinks to another table noticed the pair and smiled.

"Hey D, oh and Killer my favorite man, grab any open table. I'll be back in a second."

Derrick glanced around and got a few waves or head nods from the regulars. He responded similarly and sat at a table near the back of the patio. Killer laid down underneath, happy to be out with his best friend. As Derrick waited for the waitress to return, he allowed his mind to think of how he ended up here so far. He thought of Baller Quinn and the other hitmen that were dispatched to kill him and others. Then he thought of Shannon. He smiled as he recalled an image of her sitting across from him at a diner, kinda their first date. He realized that the waitress named Nicole was returning and that he was wearing a big smile as she approached.

Nicole coyly smiled back and said, "I think you're a little too old for me D, but I'll still take your order."

Derrick laughed at her veiled flirtation. "Okay, well that's the last time I smile in front of you then."

He ordered a beer and some boneless wings with sauce on the side, that way he could share them with Killer. Nicole continued her flirtatious banter as she walked away to enter his order. "Too old, but you're growing on me..."

Derrick watched her walk away when he felt a slap on his back.

"How are you feeling, brother?" was the greeting as a man slid into the seat across from him.

Derrick didn't even have to look up to know who was joining him. Nik was the owner of Nik's Bunker Bar, and Derrick had known him since they were kids. He was also the only person outside of Elsy and Donna that knew his real identity and why he was hiding in the small town. Nik smiled and handed him an ice-cold beer in a can.

"It's on me."

Derrick looked at the can and smiled. *Greek Freak*, the beer, was named after Nik. He did videos on social media under the name Greek Freak, and a small brewery had made the beer to honor Nik's work with veterans. Nik had never given him a beer he didn't like, and this one was no different. Nik produced a second can, and they opened them at the same time, seeming to amplify the *tshheeet* sound. The two talked for a bit about what each of them were dealing with in their lives. It made Derrick feel helpful to listen to Nik unload a bit, and it was nice to have someone he could talk to.

After several beers, a little food, and a great conversation with what could honestly be described as his only lifelong friend that knew he was still alive, Derrick winked at Nicole before he got up to leave, and she smiled back. Killer ran over to get some love from her before they left, and she obliged by ruffling the fur atop his head. On his way out, Derrick noticed a local artist painting a new sign on the wall. A sign with her business name, 'Killustrate it', was displayed by her work. He stopped for a minute to appreciate the sign she was painting and its inscription.

"The beer is cold, the wit is sharp, and friends are family."

"So true," he said, thinking of the love he had for this place.

5

IT DIDN'T TAKE LONG for Barry to find out where the information had gone. The IP address he tracked belonged to some guy up in New Hampshire. Despite every tool he had at his disposal, he couldn't associate the IP address to an individual, and that kind of bewildered him.

Who doesn't have a social media presence with selfies everywhere? This concerned him. Barry pulled up a contact list on his computer, he searched for New Hampshire. Only one name popped up, so Barry dialed the phone number.

"Jason, it's Barry Klinger, I need you for a quick reconnaissance mission in New Hampshire, do you have any time?"

Barry waited for an answer to come from the man on the other end of the call. It suddenly dawned on him that he hadn't spoken to Jason Paul in a long time. Despite Barry's epiphany, Jason knew exactly who he was.

"Ya I'm available, what exactly do you need?" Jason asked.

"I need you to do a little reconnaissance work and get some surveillance photos. If you can check out the inside of the place without getting caught, I need to know if there are any signs of planning anything against the Avails."

Barry finished up his instructions for Jason and sent him his retainer via a cash app on his phone.

———

GEORGE WAS AWAKE EARLY and watching world news. Among the top stories was a war brewing in a small country most people probably never heard of before. George was quite aware of where this country was, and he was not happy with the news. This was too early for this story to be picked up. He called to one of his house staff and said he wasn't feeling well, when they arrived, his face was red, and he complained of an instant headache. Without warning, he dropped the glass from his left hand and said his vision had started to blur, then he collapsed into the chair that was behind him. The house staff member witnessing his collapse immediately called for an ambulance and Linda. Seconds later, George was surrounded by more staff and his daughter. He waived the staff away so he could speak to Linda. "Listen, get Barry and tell him to fix Milekistan, they're starting too early."

His words were mumbled, maybe even slurred a bit. Linda's hands were trembling out of concern for her father's health, but she understood his message.

"I will take care of it. Just relax and hold on, the ambulance is on its way," she said with a quiver in her voice.

While she had been raised to push her emotions aside when working, she couldn't help but worry about her father's condition. Involuntary tears pushed through her icy emotional wall and forced their way down her face. Within minutes an ambulance arrived, and paramedics took George away to the hospital.

———

LINDA WANTED to follow the ambulance right to the hospital, but she knew she had been given an important task to complete first. She wiped away the tears she was unaccustomed to—she blamed the sun for melting her a bit on the inside, she headed into her father's office to search for Barry's number. Seconds later she was waiting while the phone was ringing. Barry reached for the phone, kind of shuffling his hand cautiously across the nightstand. He found his phone and held it to his face. "Hello," he said in a deep scratchy voice. The phone rang again while he held it to his face. Barry pulled it from his ear and peered at the screen.

He slid the bar at the bottom that said 'answer', and he tried it again. "Hello," he said in the same voice as before.

"Barry, is that you?" Linda inquired, not recognizing his voice.

Barry cleared his throat and sat up in bed, it was still dark outside. He didn't recognize Linda's voice as well because he rarely spoke with her, his mind was in full gear now. Once he realized who he was speaking with, he assumed there was a problem. "Yes, it's me. What's wrong?"

Linda almost broke down. The severity of her dad's potential condition was weighing heavily on her. "Dad may be having a stroke, he is in the hospital, but said I had to relay a message before I went there." Barry listened carefully. When Linda had finished relaying the instructions, he responded.

"I'm sure your dad will be fine, he's a strong man. Tell him I will handle all of that, I'll leave this morning. It will probably take a couple of days to arrange a meeting with both parties. I'll let him know when it's done." He finished up with, "You take care of him and yourself."

Linda ended the call; she rushed into her room and threw on clothes on top of her bikini of the day.

———

GEORGE WAS TREATED like royalty at the island hospital. Linda burst through the door to his room, and the doctor turned quickly to see what was going on. The doctor told her they identified a possible small stroke and immediately treated him to counteract the symptoms he was having. It was too soon to talk about any lasting effects, though. Linda looked at her father hooked up to monitors and an IV. Her face was drawn and pale despite her tan, evidence of her concern. The doctor calmly told her that they were confident that they had acted in time and that George would have little to no permanent damage. He will have to reduce the stress in his life and change his lifestyle.

Linda almost laughed and blurted out, "There is NO chance of that."

She pulled up a chair in the room and waited for several hours while her dad was monitored and taken occasionally for one test or another. Each time the prognosis got better. Finally, she had a moment to talk to her dad after the nurses indicated that his mind was no longer altered.

"Dad, how are you feeling?" she asked.

He responded in a tired voice, "I'm ok I guess, feel like I was hit by a bus." He smiled and added, "I highly recommend skipping this ride."

Linda smiled back but it was more that he was returning to normal than due to his wisecrack. "I handled that other thing you wanted. Two or three days to complete," she said.

George gave her a questioning look and asked, "What was that honey, what did you handle?"

Linda gave her dad a mean stare and thought it was too soon for jokes like that, then she became a bit scared, seeing the sincerity of the question on her dad's face. She pushed the little red button hanging from his bed. A nurse appeared after only a few seconds.

"Isitnormalforhimtoforgetimportantthingsfromthismorning?" Linda blurted out, almost as a single word.

The nurse stepped back and asked her to slow down and repeat the question. Linda took a deep breath and realized that she had verbally vomited on the poor nurse.

She started again, this time purposely and slower. "I'm sorry, my dad seems to be forgetting some things from this morning, I'm worried if that is normal or not?"

"I will have the doctor come in and talk to you," the nurse said, as she smiled at Linda then turned and walked out.

———

BARRY'S PLANE touched down on a small runway made of dirt. Clouds of dust billowed up as the plane taxied toward the only structure on the edge of the runway, a small building that could only be described as a hut. It had a large round tank marked what he assumed was 'fuel' but written in the local language. The tank was bigger than the building itself. A local with a Jeep had been pre-arranged to take him into town and he had already sent word to his rebel contacts that they should meet him at the usual place.

The road into town was bumpy and extremely dusty. Barry wore a cloth over his mouth and nose so that he didn't inhale dirt for the whole ride. He certainly wasn't worried about anyone following them; the cloud of dust behind their Jeep was so thick it would probably stall another vehicle. The Jeep slowed as they approached the town. Barry instructed the driver to pull over before they reached the center of town. He paid his driver with a substantial tip included and asked that he be available later.

The driver looked at the money and shook his head affirmatively in an exaggerated motion. "Yes, yes," he said and then shook his phone in the air. "You call me, you call me." Barry grabbed his backpack from the Jeep and disappeared into the center of the small town. Cautiously, he made his way toward the bar that would be used for the meeting. He took a table at a tea house across from the entrance to the bar. He sat in the corner obscured by a potted palm and a few other patrons. He wanted to make sure this meeting was only between the invited participants.

———

A FEW TABLES away at the same tea house, another man was also intently watching the bar's entrance. He had received intel stating there would be an important meeting today involving two rebel leaders and another outside influence. He had been in this area for six months pursuing this, and this was the first time he had actionable intel that may produce something. He sipped his tea and surveyed the area. His sunglasses took video of whatever target he pointed them to. It was then transferred via his sat phone to his agency for facial recognition and analysis.

Simon was hopeful for the first time. He just had to force himself to be patient. He took his glasses off to rub his eyes which were irritated by the small sand particles that were constantly swirling through the air. They were only off for a second. By the time he was putting them back on, a voice in the earpiece he was wearing was saying. "Simon, take your glasses back off and point them to the corner behind you to the left," Simon knew enough to resist the urge to turn and look. He did as he was instructed. "Great, leave them for a minute." Again, he followed the instructions being offered through the miniature communication device. The device relayed the voice again.

"Holy dog poop," the voice chirped. "This is our guy."

Simon noticed an active increase in the man's voice as he spoke.

"Simon, That's Barry Klinger! It's got to be him."

Simon reached down and replaced his glasses to his face. In his mind, he was jumping up and down and screaming, *hot damn! This is it. Finally.*

Externally, he was sipping his tea and casually looking around, internally, he had to regain his mental composure. He would still need to catch him with the rebels to have a case to pursue.

———

JASON PAUL SAT in the woods watching the cabin, occasionally making notes in a small notebook. He had seen the resident come in and out several times but found no discernible pattern that he could exploit yet. This morning was the second day that he sat and watched from his hiding spot. This was a curious case; he hadn't heard from Barry in a long time. Then he offered this job as if it was the most important in the world.

Jason sipped his coffee from a thermos. The target was exiting the building. He was carrying several long bags to his UTV. After two trips to the house, his target emerged with the dog and headed for the UTV. Jason watched as the dog headed for the UTV and then suddenly stopped in his tracks. Jason held his breath for a moment as the dog peered intently in his direction, his nose in the air.

———

KILLER SNIFFED at the unusual scent he picked up and started towards the woods out in front of the cabin. Before he reached the source of the scent, he perked his ears and spun his head to the call.

"Killer, come on buddy, time to go."

Killer immediately discarded the scent and ran back to the UTV, leaping in and occupying the passenger seat in one jump.

———

DERRICK NAVIGATED the UTV over the rough terrain back to his shooting range. He unloaded his cargo onto the bench he had assembled and prepared the weapons he would train with today.

The course he built was set up with different colored silhouette targets. To force himself to make instant decisions, he had created a playlist of color commands that would alternate randomly. As he went through his course, the media player would call out colors for him to target.

"Red, blue, red, green, green, yellow, red." This was the best way he could keep trained and sharp with his weapons on his own. It wasn't perfect, but it worked well. He would cycle through weapons and perform reloads as he went through the seven stations he had built. He started and finished each training session the same way. Kissing his hand and touching it to the laminated picture of Shannon he had put on the bench. Motivation always appeared when he reminisced what had been ripped from his life.

"Don't get too comfortable, Avails. I'm coming for you soon," he whispered as he withdrew his hand from the picture.

6

LINDA WATCHED INTENTLY as her father was assisted into their home by medical personnel.

"I'm okay, I don't need this pampering like I'm a child," George kept repeating.

"Father, let them do their jobs. You had a stroke, and they are here to assist you until you are fully recovered," Linda scolded him with a compassionate tone.

She knew that this would put a large portion of her father's current activities on her shoulders. "I guess my suntanning days are going to be severely limited for a while now," she moaned.

George looked at her with a bit of a smirk. "It's about time."

Linda wasn't amused by his snide remark. "You picked a hell of a way to force me back to work," she replied, suddenly losing some of the compassion she had been feeling.

She turned and left the room as the attendants were helping George into a multi-position hospital bed that had been delivered shortly before his return to his home.

———

THE HOT WATER cascaded over her body. It fell like a sheet over her head, matting her hair to her face as it ran down around her neck. The water separated and merged numerous times as it plummeted over her chest, then down across her stomach and eventually found its way to the drain via her legs. Linda desperately needed this moment of relaxation and hot water. Due to being at the hospital with her father, it had been two days since she had showered. She wasn't in any hurry to finish washing and step out. In her mind the shower wasn't just rejuvenating her body, it was healing her soul.

Her mind played over her dad's stroke and the call he had her make; she was so concerned about him during this event. She was at a crossroads for herself. While she had felt a duty to pick up the responsibilities of her father while he was rehabbing, she had been recently dreaming of a different life for herself. The concept of heading back into the dark world her father had raised her in, no longer appealed to her.

Suddenly the shower seemed cold despite the steam escaping over the glass door. She finished washing and stepped from the shower to dry off. As she got dressed, the bikini stayed on the dresser—instead she opted for a light summer dress. It was yellow with small flowers in a pattern on it. Small straps were tied on her shoulders, her breasts hung freely underneath, something her father would disapprove of. This was her one act of rebellion for being forced to abandon her sun worship.

Linda didn't care if this was normal business attire for the people she would be dealing with. It was appropriate for her location, and she wasn't ready to give that up yet.

MARTIN BRENNAN, aka Tinker, was on his daily pilgrimage to the local pizza house around the corner from his office building. He had found them by smell right after he had moved into his new accommodations. He knew better than to be predictable, but the pizza was a weakness of his. He would do his best to alter the time he would go and to change his route, but that was almost an effort in futility. After all, his departure and destination point always remained unchanged. Today he had the feeling that he was being watched; it unnerved him. He spent his trek constantly looking over his shoulder and surveilling his surroundings. He was so unnerved that he almost walked right by the pizza shop.

"Oh, sorry," he muttered as he nearly walked into a patron that was exiting.

"Just watch where you're going, moron," was the Bostonian's reply.

Martin entered and was greeted by the counter person.

"Good afternoon, Mr. Brennan. Your pizza will be out shortly."

"Thank you," he said while looking around.

Martin handed the girl his credit card which displayed his fake persona.

The girl returned the card with no issues, and Martin waited patiently for his meal.

Pizza in hand, he quickly returned to his office still with the feeling he was being watched. There he consumed his meal and continued the work he had been tasked with. He sent a message to Barry via the secure phone. *"I'll need more financing. This is a big job."*

———

DURING MARTIN'S trek for lunch, he had been under observation the entire time. A serious telephoto lens provided this opportunity while staying out of the perceptible range of Tinker's security cameras. Elsy had expanded her trusted circle and asked one of her employees to perform this surveillance. Dillan Pratt was happy to help, and was enjoying the ability to be out of the office and still not have to deal directly with other humans. He had picked coding up as a child and now he loved it for allowing him to avoid direct human contact. This new assignment may be as good.

As Tinker entered his building, Dillan used the screen of the camera to check the quality of the pictures he had taken. "They all came out good," he thought. He set the camera down and grabbed a sandwich from his cooler, he unwrapped it and then opened a small bag of chips to go with it. "You can't eat a sandwich without chips," was like a mealtime rule for him. Despite having his lunch, Dillan remained vigilant in his surveillance.

———

DERRICK FINISHED his training for the day and was picking up to head back. Killer was now running around chasing scent after scent. This was their clean-up routine. While Derrick practiced his weapons training, Killer would remain in the UTV, curled up on the front seat. When training was over, it became Killer's time to play. Derrick would pick up slowly to allow Killer more time to run through the woods pretending to hunt. This was good for them both.

———

JASON PAUL HAD CREPT up to Derrick's cabin. He checked the door for locks he might have to pick. It was unlocked, and opened with a simple turn of the knob. He entered and took in the modest accommodations. A part of him was slightly envious of the simplicity. The cabin, despite its rundown appearance from the outside, was immaculate inside. It smelled of smoke from the fireplace and old pine. Paul was overwhelmed by the feeling these smells created for him. He briefly stopped with little regard for the stealth he should have been using as he absorbed the atmosphere.

He was taking it all in, as memories of his childhood hunting with his dad entered his mind. A noise out in the woods snapped him back to reality. He sped up his search for anything that might look like the surveillance or target package that Barry had asked him to locate. The only thing he found was an old magazine clipping with a picture of George and Linda Avail. The noise was getting closer, and Jason knew his time was up. He made sure anything he had disturbed was replaced as he found it, and quickly exited to the woods for cover.

———

SECONDS AFTER JASON'S DEPARTURE, Derrick and Killer pulled up in front of the cabin. As usual, Killer leapt from the vehicle and continued his 'hunting'. Derrick collected the contents of the UTV to put away. Killer suddenly alerted on a trail. Derrick noticed the change in his actions. Killer immediately started to pursue the new scent. Without knowing exactly what killer was onto, Derrick could only think of the skunk they had seen in the area recently.

"Killer," he yelled. "Cut it out and get back here."

The dog initially ignored him and inched ever closer to Jason, who was hiding in the brush.

Derrick yelled more forcefully, fearful of a skunk interaction with the dog, "Killer, come here now."

The dog stopped his pursuit and returned to the now open door of the cabin.

———

JASON WAITED ten minutes from the last time Derrick exited the house before moving. The entire day was mostly an effort in futility as far as he was concerned. He rolled out of the brush and started to get up when he noticed he wasn't alone. He was face to face with the worst-case scenario he could think of—the business end of a skunk. It was too late to retreat and too late to change the skunk's direction. A distinct hissing sound and an overwhelming pungent odor surrounded and permeated his skin and clothing.

"Are you fucking kidding me?" he hissed, trying to still be silent.

He ran, coughing and spitting, abandoning his cover before the skunk tried again.

———

BARRY WANTED to wrap this up and leave again. He hated this area of the globe.

"Too much heat, too much sand, and too much war and betrayal," he thought to himself.

After seeing his contacts enter the cantina, Barry casually stood and scanned the area. Although nothing struck him as out of the ordinary, he had the sudden feeling this might be a trap. He ducked into the cantina for his meeting. He approached the table, and both men were ready to argue with him. Before he was even greeted by their waitress, the men started to state their position as if he would have no say. Barry remained silent and listened, waiting for someone to bring him a drink before he would start to talk. A young boy with an apron around his waist appeared and took Barry's order while his two associates refused the offer of a drink on his tab. The waiter returned and Barry started to talk after their waiter disappeared.

"You have failed to adhere to our agreement, this is a simple warning. Follow the timeline you were given, or your financing will be cut off and your position will be given to your opposition." Barry said this with a straight face even though he was secretly rooting for the rebels.

Both men stared at him wide-eyed. One of them spoke.

"You wouldn't do that, that would destroy the rebellion."

"I don't care about your rebellion, I don't care who wins, you are serving as a distraction to the world when it's needed, nothing more. If you can't do that, then you and your rebellion are not needed. Do what you agreed and how you agreed to do it. I won't be back again, and it'll be too late for you by then." Once again, Barry delivered this lie with a straight face.

Barry stood and chugged his drink. Then left the cantina and returned to the cab still waiting for him.

———

MADAM FELSDER RECALLED the conversation she had years ago with George Avail. She had needed his help at the time to ascend to her current position, and she might have told George a bit too much that night to sway his vote in her direction. If he remembered the secrets she shared, that could be a problem for her. She called an assistant into her office. "Get Mr. Bittersmith, I need to speak with him."

———

LINDA HEARD her dad's private line ringing; she picked it up.

"This is Linda, who am I speaking with?"

"Hi Linda, It's Barry. I believe the problem you were having is now fixed. I'll be headed back to the States now to handle a few other things personally. I'll be in touch."

Linda said goodbye and hung up. "That was good news," she said to her dad who was watching from his hospital bed restlessly.

Linda had put his phone out of his reach intentionally. She didn't want him getting any calls that might get him worked up again. She leaned over and kissed him on his forehead. It was a new feeling to see him as a weaker version of himself. She didn't like it. She left the room and headed to wait outside on the gazebo. A guest of her father would be arriving soon.

————

ALEX CORTEGA HAD BEEN surprised when the travel arrangements arrived in his mail. He wasn't given a lot of time to plan or make excuses for his absence either. The trip on the private jet had been a first for him. He was treated like royalty the whole time and it continued through his arrival at the small tropical airport. There he was greeted by the driver of a limousine that was now taking him to meet the silent benefactor that had given him a real chance in this next election.

He watched from the open window of the limousine as they approached a small, gated community. The limo passed through the main gate and traveled down the narrow road lined with palm trees and vibrant local flowers, and then pulled into the arched driveway of a large sprawling villa. From what Alex had seen on the way in, this was the largest by far. The driver opened his door and retrieved his small bag from the trunk.

"If that is all, sir?" He extended his hand.

Alex frantically reached for his wallet. He always used cards these days, he wasn't sure if he even had any cash for a tip. He found a twenty he kept for emergency.

"Thanks for the ride," Alex said as he slipped the driver the twenty in the traditional fashion as he shook his hand.

"Thank you, sir. Have a good day," the driver said while giving a slight nod.

Linda had appeared on a walkway by the corner of the main house.

"Good afternoon, Mr. Cortega. Please follow me."

She turned and walked down the path leading behind the house.

Alex grabbed his bag and quickly walked to catch up to his host who wasn't willing to wait for him.

————

THE NURSE WALKED in to check on Mr. Avail. George was sitting upright and seemed agitated.

"What can I do for you, Mr. Avail?" she asked.

"Get me my damn phone," he demanded; his agitation was evident in his tone. The nurse quickly retrieved his phone and was going to mention that Linda wanted him to keep from getting excited, but based on George's current attitude she opted to remain silent on that issue.

"You can leave now," George said as she handed him the phone.

She smiled a fake smile at him and complied with his demand.

GEORGE LOOKED through his missed calls and messages. Most were items that could be held off for a bit, one however made him sit straight up. "It's starting," he mumbled in a thoughtful tone, and then pressed play on the voicemail.

"Good afternoon, Mr. Avail, Harold Bittersmith calling. You must reach out to us as soon as possible to resolve a small issue the Council has become aware of. If we do not hear back soon, we may be forced to find an alternative solution. Good day."

As the message ended, George's face became vibrant and full of color. His demeanor became invigorated, like a young man who had been challenged to a fight. He thought about his plan. Did she know?

THE GAZEBO WAS SURROUNDED by bright-colored flowers and other tropical plants that erupted from clay pots set around the structure. It provided shade from the hot sun and a steady breeze thanks to a fan mounted in the ceiling. There was a small table and two chairs that were now occupied by Linda Avail and her father's guest. This meeting felt different to her, more as if she was acting a role than living it. She felt their island stay had changed her in ways her father would never accept. Despite her reservations, Linda started right in.

"Mr. Cortega, I see your campaign is off to a booming start due to the influx of capital that you received," she stated without any sign of emotion.

"Yes, I am thankful for that. The ability to bring on the needed staff and compete head-to-head with my competition is so immensely beneficial." Alex responded quickly, showing that he was uncomfortable being there.

Linda studied his mannerisms and subconscious movements while he spoke. She could see he was nervous.

"So, Alex. Is it okay if I call you Alex? Don't answer, I'm going to call you Alex. So, Alex, you do know that the money you received is because you've agreed to assist my father from your elected position when you win?"

Before Alex answered, a member of the house staff appeared and set a tray on the table that separated them.

"A cool drink for you and your guest, Miss Avail." The attendant stated and then disappeared as fast as they had appeared. They all knew the danger of overstaying their welcome when serving the Avails.

Linda continued the conversation that would normally have been handled by her father. She handed him the envelope containing the evidence from his past and watched as the color drained from his face. His eyes opened wide, and a small gasp involuntarily escaped from his mouth. "How— where— my God. You can't let this out!"

Linda almost felt bad for him. Even though she had participated in this very scenario multiple times in the past. She would have to bury her newfound feelings about this. They had the evidence and he had taken their money, and both were very well documented.

———

JASON PAUL STOOD in the shower for the third time. He had tried numerous concoctions to remove the skunk smell. It seemed after the latest round of tomato juice and dish soap that much of the smell was gone. He was hoping to mask whatever was left with deodorant and cologne.

He decided he would charge Barry a hazard fee for this major inconvenience.

7

LINDA OBSERVED as their new political puppet was ushered back into the limo for his return to the States. She would be happy to inform her father that things had gone as expected. Her movement was quicker than normal as she bolted up the stone steps that led to the main level terrace. She longed for the lounge chair that she had spent so much time in as of late. Though it seemed to beckon her, she would not be able to accommodate that urge until later.

She entered the home and proceeded to her father's room. She sensed something was not right as she approached and saw his door wide open. Her father was not in his bed. She shouted for her father's caregiver as she searched the home for her father, but he was nowhere to be found.

———

ALEX HAD SLIPPED into the back of the limousine to find he was not alone, an older gentleman he had never seen before was sitting across from him. Neither man said a word. The car sped along to the airport. When it stopped, the driver opened the door, and Alex's co-passenger exited first. As Alex started to get out as well, the driver put a hand on his shoulder and said, "Not yet."

Alex did as he was instructed and sat back down. He watched as the other man disappeared from his view. The door was shut, and the car started in motion, this time when the door opened, Alex was at the main terminal for international flights. The driver helped him out and handed him his bag and a ticket for a public plane. Alex looked at the ticket. First class. *Not a private jet, But I'm okay with it,* he thought as he found his way to his seat on the aircraft. The flight attendant brought him a drink, and he couldn't help but wonder who the man was that got the private jet today.

———

DERRICK SAT at his table looking over the property layout. He would write on sticky notes and attach them where he had questions. He looked at Killer, who was waiting by the door.

"I know you want to go find it, but I can smell that skunk too and I don't need that scent in here."

Killer turned back to him with a tilted head and cocked it back and forth as Derrick was speaking. He responded with a quiet bark.

———

THE CREW OF THE AVAILS' private jet had been expecting the easy job of transporting another Avail political puppet back to Washington. Just before he was scheduled to arrive, they received a call from Mr. Avail himself.

"Please have my jet fueled and ready for a trip to France. Make all needed arrangements. I will arrive in an hour or less."

The crew was standing outside the plane waiting as their boss arrived. The level of scrambling they had completed to meet his requests was not evident by looking at any one of them.

"Good morning, Captain. Good morning, Ginger." George only offered his greeting to the captain and his chief flight attendant. They each responded with a similar greeting and smiled as he entered the plane.

———

GEORGE WAS CAUTIOUSLY excited about this trip. He had been avoiding the previous invitations of this group for specific reasons, but this trip was a different type of invitation—it was more of a veiled threat. He pulled papers from the small satchel he had brought with him.

He had made notes on what to say to shield his actual intentions. He was still buying elections in smaller, less media-covered areas, and helping put district attorneys and judges that were aligned with their vision in office. This should look like business as usual. He would highlight these actions to prove to the Council that he was not faltering from the plan set out by the Global Council. He was ready to stand his ground.

He also needed to make sure his underlying plan was not discovered. If it was, he would not return from this trip.

———

LINDA WAS CONCERNED for her father. The fact that he disappeared without telling her, made her consider darker possibilities. She dialed a number on the phone. After a couple of rings, it was answered.

"Hello, this is Dr. Brindle, to whom am I speaking?"

Hello doctor, it's Linda Avail. I'm curious if you've seen my father today?"

The doctor pulled the phone away from his ear and paused as if wondering what to say next.

"I haven't, is there something I should know?" he asked.

He was fishing to find out what she knew.

Linda thought his question was odd and became more frustrated.

"Tell me what you know," she countered.

The doctor knew this day would come; though he thought it would take longer.

"Okay, but it's probably better if we meet in person to discuss this."

Linda was caught off guard by that response, "How bad could this be?" she wondered.

"Where do you want to meet? It must be now!"

The doctor hadn't expected this level of aggression; however, he knew better than to push back.

"I'm at the golf course. I'll meet you at the club as soon as you can get here," he responded, not even considering delaying her.

Linda accepted that and hung up. She called for her driver and headed out the door.

As she was helped into the car she mumbled, half to herself and half to the driver, "If things don't start making sense around here soon, I'm going to lose my mind!"

———

THE DOCTOR WAS WAITING for her when her car pulled up. He stepped over and opened the door for her.

"Miss Avail, I have a private area that we can speak in. Please follow me."

Linda exited the car and followed him to a small private lounge that the club had for just these reasons. The room was furnished with four overstuffed leather chairs and a big round coffee table set between them. The doctor stopped and offered the choice of seats to Linda. She settled in and he chose the chair opposite her. He started right in before she could ask any questions.

"I must admit, you must be a better detective than I assumed. I hadn't expected to have this conversation for a few more months. To satisfy my curiosity, how did you figure it out?"

Linda was confused by the doctor's words. She decided the best thing she could do would be to steer the conversation back to where she wanted it.

"Well, when he was missing from his bed, that was a pretty good clue. Please just tell me what you know," she asked.

The doctor eyed her up, it was evident to him that she knew enough. He also knew he didn't want to incur her wrath either.

"I'll start at the beginning, a few months ago your father came to me with a proposal. He offered me a large sum of money if I could make it look like he had a stroke. At first, I was adamant against it, but then he said he was losing you as a daughter and this was the only way to draw you back. I know what that feels like. My daughters pulled away from me after the divorce and now I hardly ever get to see them. I'm sorry we used this subterfuge on you. Your father thought it was the only way."

Linda sat silently stunned. For a second, she wondered if she was having some type of coronary incident herself.

"This is a lot to process. So where is my father now?" she asked.

Dr. Brindle stared at her with a blank expression. "How would I know?

The sudden realization came to him that he had spilled a secret that Linda had no clue of.

"That's all I know. Isn't that enough?" he asked.

Linda regained her composure. She realized her dad was not in any medical harm by missing, just the danger he'd face when he saw her again.

"Doctor, thank you for your time and all this information. I'll decide whether I report you to the island medical board later."

The color drained from the doctor's face. He hadn't expected that.

———

DERRICK WAS MAKING final preparations for his trip. He knew it could be a one-way journey, so he had made plans with Nicole, the waitress at the bunker bar, to watch Killer while he was away. Killer loved her, and Derrick was pretty sure it was a mutual feeling for them both.

Derrick wasn't looking forward to the first part of his expedition. He would have to drive roughly twenty-six hours to get to where he'd meet his ride to the island where the Avails were hiding in plain sight. His pal Nik had hooked him up with an old army buddy who now flew a small plane out of the Miami area. Derrick was told not to ask any questions about any other cargo on board and the ride would be free, without questions in return.

Derrick hadn't paid much attention to the snow that was piling up as he gathered his items for his trip. When he stepped outside, the snow was already up to his ankles and coming down hard. Derrick cleared the snow off the van and let it heat up as Killer ran around in circles jumping in and out of the snow. He hopped in the van and Killer assumed his normal spot as copilot in the passenger seat. He moved the shifter into drive and the van moved about two feet and then started to spin.

"Arggg, this can't be happening now!"

Derrick turned the van off and pulled his supplies back into the cabin.

He pulled up his bank account on the computer. He had plenty of money for a new vehicle.

"I guess it's time," he said, looking at Killer.

Derrick hopped into the UTV. It had four-wheel drive, and the snow wouldn't be a problem for it. Unfortunately, he couldn't drive that all the way to Florida.

———

THE DEALERSHIP WAS empty as Derrick pulled in with the UTV. No salesman rushed out to meet him, so he drove around slowly, looking at the used cars on the lot. He spied a nice-looking 4x4 pickup and started to head toward it, and that's when he saw it. It was parked behind a box truck that had blocked it from his initial view. That was it, the new ride for him and Killer.

Derrick got out and examined the entire vehicle, it had everything he wanted and more. He smiled at the price on the window tag. It wasn't high, but he still would negotiate. He jumped back into the UTV and drove up to the sales office. As he approached the door, this time a salesman met him and opened the door. After exchanging pleasantries, Derrick pointed out the window.

"Tell me about that orange Jeep," he asked.

The salesman led him over to a counter where he retrieved a set of keys.

"Let's go for a ride," he said, ushering Derrick outside to the Jeep.

Derrick opened the door and used a grab handle to jump up into the Jeep.

It was raised and had larger than normal tires. It also had custom accessories all around. Front and rear bumpers had been replaced and rock rails were added as well. This Jeep was built to play. Derrick inserted the key and turned it as the engine roared to life.

"That's a five-hundred horsepower HEMI." The salesman shouted over the engine being revved up by Derrick.

They went for a ride in the snow. Derick couldn't resist spinning the Jeep around in an empty parking lot, the salesman just simply responded, "If you break it, you still have to buy it."

They headed back to the dealership. After some negotiations, Derrick handed over his fake IDs and a check for the total amount of the vehicle. When he left, he was the proud owner of a new orange Jeep and had a brand-new registration under the name Derrick Dunn.

———

ELSY WAS GETTING CLOSER. She was now positive that Tinker was set up in the building she had been observing in Boston. She was still concerned with using Tulia and Dillon to assist her with this. She knew how fast this could turn deadly, but that thought kept her feeling exposed for all of them. She looked over the pictures Dillon had sent her. The reoccurring trip to the pizza place was her best opportunity to verify who Tinker was. She took his image and ran it through a facial recognition program. She knew the kind of talent she was up against, so this program was based on internal images she had scrubbed from all federal and global criminal and driver's license databases. She could run the scan and never use an external source. Nothing for the hacker to be alerted by.

It took about twenty minutes. Now on her screen she was looking at Martin Brennan. She absorbed the information in his background as if she were consuming who he was. As she was studying his background, she noticed something very odd. Martin Brennan had been inactive for almost ten years and suddenly became very active again.

"It's a friggin alias," she said as she slapped the desk in front of the monitor. The shockwave caused coffee to jump from her mug and splash on her keyboard. "Grrr, give me a break."

Elsy cleaned up the mess as Tulia entered her office.

"We now have the complete current building schematics," she said as she approached the desk.

Elsy looked up at her. "Anything useful or different?"

"Oh yes, quite a bit," Tulia exclaimed, excited to show her boss what she had discovered. She laid the blueprints out across the conference table and pointed to a section near the bottom of the print.

"He had the whole sub-basement remodeled and cut off from the rest of the building. There is only one way in and out, and it uses multiple biometric security points to gain access."

Tulia continued by flipping pages and moving her hand to another section, indicating the network connections and power for the underground facility.

"I think he has a server farm on site this time. The whole system is shielded and protected from almost anything but an interior attack. His cabling is encased in twelve inches of concrete." Tulia concluded her presentation. Elsy studied the prints; she loved the challenge.

"This is excellent Ms. Pretense. Well done."

Her cell phone rang. The caller ID announced it was Harlem.

"I should take this." She blew Tulia a kiss and proceeded to answer the phone.

8

THE JET TOUCHED **down** in a small private airport in France. The normal procedures for entry had been skirted due to a sizable donation to certain officials who handle these things. No official record of the landing or their presence in the country would be documented.

A black car waited for George as he exited the aircraft with just one small bag in hand. Hopefully, this would be a short stay. The driver of the car greeted him saying, "Welcome to France, Mr. Avail," and then handed George a black hood.

"Sir, if you would please put that on. I've been asked to keep our destination a secret."

George was ready to demand that he be treated like any other Council member, but decided against it. Instead, he complied and donned the hood. Surprisingly to him, it smelled very nice. He had expected it would smell of vomit and perspiration, like the hoods he had used on others in his past. The car began to move, and George relaxed back against the seat. The ride was bumpy and quite curvy as they proceed to their destination.

After about forty-five minutes the ride slowed and then came to a stop. As the warmth of sun through the car's window suddenly disappeared, he surmised they had entered a garage of some type. George was helped from the car. He listened and used his other senses to find clues to his location—he felt dirt beneath his feet and then brushed up against walls that were made of stone blocks. Not much help in this part of the globe.

———

MR. BITTERSMITH MET him in the doorway that opened next to the car.

"Come with me, Mr. Avail," he said as he removed the hood.

George reached up instinctively to straighten his hair and then complied with what seemed as much an order as an invitation.

They climbed a narrow stone staircase and Harold opened a heavy wooden door at the top. They stepped through into a much wider hallway with heavy timber floors and stone walls. It had the feeling of an old castle. Harold continued to lead George down the hallway to another heavy wooden door. This time Mr. Bittersmith knocked before opening the door.

"Bring him in," said the voice from the other side of the door.

For the first time in a very long time, George was not the top dog in the room. He felt uncomfortable; he held an ace but was slightly concerned that they already knew his secret plan. *But how?* he thought as he tried to regain his superior attitude.

———

"GOOD AFTERNOON, Mr. Avail. Thank you for responding so quickly to our invitation."

George knew it was just a threat, not an invitation, but he remained silent.

"Come, have a seat." The speaker from end of the room pointed to a single chair at the end of a long table.

George looked toward where the speaker was. There was light coming from tall narrow windows to the right, the light, however made it even harder to make out the faces of what he counted were a total of seven figures seated at the other end. The light illuminated a haze in the air, causing a veil effect that obscured everything beyond it.

"Please sit, we have a bit to discuss." The voice was firm but not aggressive.

George complied and took a seat. He was aware that Mr. Bittersmith was standing directly behind him.

The woman at the other end of the table started to talk.

"Mr. Avail, you are a member of this Council, are you not?" George shook his head in the affirmative.

"Very well. George, it has come to our attention that you may have plans to meddle in areas of Council interests outside of the United States. While I know this organization has agreed to let you manage our interests in the United States, it's also my understanding that you agreed to verify your actions would not disrupt our global operations beforehand. Am I correct?"

George once again nodded his head.

"I'm sorry George, I will need a vocal answer this time." The firmness in the speaker's voice had increased.

"Yes ma'am, that was the agreement," George answered.

George could hear a hushed discussion taking place at the end of the table, though he was unable to discern their words.

"George, I'm going to ask you some more questions now. You must answer these questions accurately and honestly. We will know if you lie, and quite frankly, that will change the nature of this discussion."

George shook his head up and down again. "Here it comes, they know," he thought.

"Words, please," the speaker directed.

"Yes, I understand. No lying. Accurate statements," George conceded.

"Excellent, let's begin. Did you orchestrate a coup in Milekistan?" the speaker asked, with a bit of disdain in her voice.

George didn't answer immediately. He wasn't expecting this line of questioning. He felt his skin flush, and a wave of relaxation swept over him as he realized this was his plan working.

"No and yes ma'am. The revolution was coming either way, I am just utilizing the inevitable turmoil in that country as news cover for other actions in American politics."

George heard some movement and discussion once again. A few voices were suddenly louder, allowing George to realize they were not speaking English. He concentrated on keeping his composure and his story straight. Despite his last stroke being a fabrication, he didn't want to have a real one now.

"Mr. Avail, is Milekistan in the USA?"

"No ma'am, it is not."

"Then why is it that you feel you have a right to meddle there without our consent? Do you not understand that we have a specific plan in place ourselves regarding our global goals? Even a slight disturbance can cost us the timeline, financial gains, or even the goal of our operations."

As the questioning continued, George began to feel more in control again, comfortable that they were unaware of his actual plan. Adrenaline started to surge in him as he regained his feeling of dominance.

He continued the charade. "I'm sorry, the war is already coming. I just want to control the media narrative and timeline."

"We are aware that indeed, yes, it is coming, however, it is not only the timeline you altered. You provided weapons and intel to both sides, thereby increasing the carnage, essentially forcing the media to jump to provide coverage. Isn't that true as well?"

"Yes ma'am, that was the intent."

Without any further discussion the speaker stated, "Okay George, you are free to go for now. No more actions outside your own country or we will revoke our allowance for you to operate as our envoy there."

George stood up. "Thank you, ma'am. I'll end the operation immediately."

The next statement shocked him.

"There is no need for that yet, you will supply us with your timeline and keep us informed."

He sensed that there was more to them being gracious towards his plan in Milekistan than what they said. As George turned to leave, he was given one more piece of information.

"By the way, Mr. Avail, you have someone that may be plotting your demise. We have not identified them yet, but we have intercepted many information transactions that all point to you. I would watch your back."

Mr. Bittersmith took him by the arm, as he turned to leave, he saw a face he remembered, and the voice he had been speaking with, returned to his memory. Madam Felsder was exiting through a side door. He smirked. *If she only knew...*

George was led out the same way he was brought in, hood and all. Back at his plane, he was very ready to leave France and return to his island. Once airborne, he made a secure call. The phone rang until voicemail picked up.

"Barry, I need to enhance my security immediately, and did you ever find anything about that guy in New Hampshire? Please get back to me immediately." George hung up after leaving the message. The attendant brought him a glass of bourbon and offered a cigar. He accepted both. He took a sip of the bourbon and then a long drag on the cigar. Despite the potential threat, he was content that the Council was unaware of his true intentions.

———

DERRICK STARTED to pack the new Jeep for his trip. He didn't need a lot, but knew he might need some extra travel supplies as well. The rear bumper of the Jeep had two gas cans mounted on it. This would help him avoid a lot of gas station stops during the trip down to Miami.

Bright orange Jeep or not, he wanted to be as inconspicuous as possible. He had already dropped Killer off with Nicole and had closed up the cabin for now. He was hoping this whole trip would take three weeks or less. He also hoped he would make it out alive, but had made peace with the thought of if he didn't.

———

ELSY REVIEWED the new data she had been given. One of her employees had cracked part of Tinker's network. She was staring at the large deposit he had recently received. Was he back in business, and if so, could it be from the Avails' accounts? She was suddenly exhilarated by the prospect. Time to do some digging.

She glanced at her watch; she had the nagging feeling that something important was happening soon. Something that she might need to stop due to this new information. She remembered and grabbed her phone and started dialing. "I hope I'm not too late," she said out loud to only herself.

———

DERRICK STARTED his Jeep and the large engine roared to life. As he reached down to put the Jeep in drive, his pocket started to vibrate. Instead of moving the gear selector, he pulled his phone from his pocket.

"Elsy, are you calling to wish me a good trip?" he asked as he answered the phone.

"You know I'm not a fan of what you're doing. No, I found something I want to show you before you go, can you detour through Boston?" Elsy pleaded with a sense of urgency in her voice.

Derrick was shaken by her request. He hadn't been to Boston since… well, since he died! He contemplated her question.

Elsy sensing his hesitation responded, "I know it's a big ask, but this is big news. I hope it might be an option for you. One that might preserve your soul."

"I'll be there. I can't run from the past forever," Derrick replied in a contemplative tone, then he hung up and put the Jeep in gear. "Slight detour," he thought.

———

AS THE JET touched down and taxied up to the hanger, George could see Linda standing outside waiting for him. He could tell by her body language and the look on her face that she was not happy at all. He assumed that it was just that he had flown off while she thought he was sick. He was about to find out differently.

Linda was more mad than she could ever remember her being in her life. While standing there waiting for her father to return, the breeze had blown her sundress up numerous times—she didn't attempt to stop it because she never even noticed. She was consumed by the pain and concern her father had set upon her, all just so he could manipulate her. She had been planning what she'd say ever since her meeting with the doctor. This was it—time for a new Linda to arise. The door opened and the stairs unfolded from the plane. The co-pilot exited first and positioned himself to assist Mr. Avail as he exited the plane.

George looked at his daughter. "Thank you for meeting me, I know you must be concerned."

"Father, you have no idea what I am. Get in the car," Linda stated angrily, with a slight quiver in her tone.

George wasn't sure what to make of his daughter's attitude or the meaning of her statement. He got into the car as she so strongly suggested.

————

DERRICK'S DRIVE to Boston would take a few hours from where he was. As he drove, he ran his retribution plan through his head. Security had been lighter than expected throughout his entire planning stage. He had made his plans based on that, and hoped it would mean he could quickly accomplish his objective and retreat unseen and unnoticed. His mind drifted to Elsy's call. What could she have found that would convince him to forsake his promise to Shannon?

————

LINDA WAITED till the divider screen was fully up between the driver and passenger compartments, then she exploded.

"You faked your stroke? Are you fucking insane?" The veins in her temples were visibly pulsing when she spoke. She rarely swore, however; this seemed like the perfect opportunity to try it out.

George lost all the color from his face; this is not what he expected. Before he could say a word, Linda continued.

"I'm done. I suggest when we get back, you take your business dealings and head back to the States. I will stay here and contemplate my future and whether you will be a part of it. I can't tell you how incredibly small and useless you've made me feel with this betrayal."

George stared at her, unsure of what to say. As he opened his mouth, she cut him off.

"Just don't, I'm not ready to hear any excuses yet. You'll only make this worse."

She turned away from him, and the rest of the ride was in silence.

————

BARRY LISTENED TO HIS VOICEMAIL. George Avail was requesting security. This was a new one for Barry. He had never in all his years of dealing with George heard him even remotely alarmed. He picked up the phone and called his guy in New Hampshire.

"Jason, do you have anything for me?"

"Yeah, a larger bill than you were expecting, I got sprayed by a friggin' skunk."

Barry suppressed the urge to laugh, he could tell by Jason's tone he wasn't in a laughing mood. "I mean about the guy in the cabin, do you have an ID or proof he was after the Avails?"

"I couldn't find an ID, and the only thing related to the Avails was a magazine clipping about both of them," Jason reported.

"Pretty big coincidence though. Can you do a deeper search and see what you find, maybe a safe or something where he's keeping documents? I'd like an ID on him," Barry requested.

"I'll see what I can do. I'm not kidding, you're paying me triple now!" Jason stated firmly.

"Okay, find me something and I'll make it four times. Is that fair?"

"That is fair, I'll be in touch," Jason agreed as he ended the call.

As the call disconnected, Barry was already dialing the next.

The phone was answered by a receptionist.

"Blackheart group, how may I direct your call?"

"Hello, it's Barry Klinger for Mr. Forsythe."

"Stand by Mr. Klinger, I'll put you right through."

Blackheart Group was a private military and security contractor agency, considered by some to be the best in the world. By others it was a private army doing the illicit work of billionaires.

"Barry, brother, to what do I owe the honor of your call?" was the greeting as his call was transferred.

Barry smiled. Eric Forsythe was a former special forces officer turned businessman, and he excelled at both.

"Eric, I need a security force for Mr. George Avail and his property. I'm thinking six men for the property, and a four-man follow team for Mr. Avail."

"When do you need it?" Forsythe questioned.

"Yesterday, but since that's not a real option as soon as you can get them airborne, I'll take it," Barry responded, his gratitude evident in his voice.

"No worries brother, I got you," Eric stated.

Eric didn't just talk like this—it's how he operated, what he believed. He viewed Barry as his brother. After all, they had spilled blood together on foreign soil...

67

———

SIMON LITTLE LISTENED to the conversation, his tap on Barry's line was paying off. He now had a name for the possible financier of the coup in Milekistan.

9

TINKER HAD REBUILT his hacker staff. While only three were from his original group, the new hires were equal to or better than the ones who didn't return. They had cracked the entry code to the servers requested in less than forty hours. Now they were trying to completely rewrite the system code to give them anonymous live access to storage files across multiple platforms that had been outlined by their employer. These systems utilized artificial intelligence that made it difficult to maintain their intrusion, because it reacted in real time to defend against their unauthorized presence.

Essentially, he was writing code to create an open back door to the artificial intelligence that was used by certain platforms to identify users subject to subliminal programming. George Avail's plan no longer needed a mutation to control how people thought, they were already being manipulated by these platforms. Tinker's group's code would be seamless and perfect. Mr. Avail would have full control in any area where the hack was applied.

The code writing was going extremely well, and Tinker decided to try his remote access portion on a machine that Mr. Avail had paid an employee of a certain social media company to make available online.

As Tinker was reviewing the code interaction with the machine, he noticed something peculiar: he was not alone. Another entity was using their own code to gain access. Tinker started recording the other hackers' moves and the code they were using.

He spoke into a speaker on his desk. "Have Deidra come here immediately."

Out on the floor of his hackers, a computer screen flashed a quick message. A young girl with bright orange hair in a ponytail stood up. She moved quickly toward Tinker's location.

Tinker looked away from the screen as Deidra entered. She was like a force of nature; she was hard to ignore when you were near her. He started talking before she said anything.

"I found a competitor in our workspace, I need you to track this other hacker with the test site, grab as much of their code as you can, and see if you can identify them. I have an idea if they turn out to be another hacking group."

"Okay, is that all?" Deidra asked.

Tinker looked at her over his screen, "Yeah."

She disappeared as quickly as she came in.

———

THE RIDE back to the estate was silent. George knew better than to poke at Linda while she was angry. She had never been this angry at him for as long as he could remember. This was a new level for her. He wasn't sure how to console her about his actions.

As the driver assisted them from the car, Linda peered at her father.

"You'll find I took the liberty of packing for you. I had the Arlington property brought back online as well. A full staff has been hired and they're awaiting your arrival. Don't call, I'll call you when I'm ready," she stated as she exited.

Linda turned and walked away without giving her father a chance to respond.

George stood still, completely blindsided by his daughter's reaction to all of this. He had hoped his charade would ignite her passion again, but this was not what he expected. She still didn't have any idea of the greater dangers that potentially existed.

"Sir, can I assist you inside?" The driver's question stirred him from his trance.

"No thank you, I'll be fine. I was just thinking about a few important things," George responded as he headed inside to gather his luggage.

Apparently, he was going back to the States.

———

DERRICK NAVIGATED the Jeep through the winter storm. It was unusual for a massive snowstorm this late in the season, but not unheard of. The weather in the northeast liked to mess with its residents as often as possible. The larger tires and the V8 engine were both a blessing and a hazard. It went wherever he pointed it; it didn't always want to stop well, though. Derrick had to be careful driving and always be ready to maneuver due to another driver's ineptitude. Boston was getting closer. Not only could he see it on the GPS, but he could feel it in his chest. The loss of Shannon festered inside him—right now, it was flaring up with intensity. He called Elsy with the Jeep's handsfree option.

"Hey, I'm about forty-five minutes away. Do you still have a spot for me in the garage?"

"Yes, I do, I'll see you in forty-five minutes. By the way, I have even more to show you now."

Elsy hung up without elaborating on her last statement. Derrick's curiosity peaked. He stepped a little harder, as much as he dared, on the accelerator.

———

JASON PAUL HAD SEEN the Jeep leave. He knew it was the man from the cabin driving it, the only thing he wasn't sure of was where the dog was. He loved dogs and didn't want to end up in a situation where he might have to hurt one to escape. The snow was coming down quickly, which meant his tracks would disappear in a few minutes. The van was still in the yard, and he could see the UTV in the shed. Jason decided he would walk right up to the door and knock. He rapped on the door and listened. Nothing. No movement, no barking, no anything. He tried the door handle; this time it was locked. Jason took a few minutes to pick the lock and then entered the cabin. He quickly scanned the room for cameras or motion sensors, he didn't see anything.

"Time to get to work. Where would you hide stuff?" The words were almost inaudible; he was thinking out loud.

Slowly and methodically, Jason moved through the small cabin looking for a safe or hidden space that would allow for documents to be stored. He searched for anomalies in the way the building appeared, scratch marks on the floor for no reason, seams between boards that looked unusual.

After about an hour of searching, he was sure nothing existed. As he reached down to grab his coat from the chair, it yanked against the table. Right in plain sight he found two boards that ran along the wall, hidden by the table's placement. Jason pulled the table away from the wall and yanked on the boards. They pulled away and the documents stored inside spilled out onto the floor. Jason knew right away he had found what Barry needed.

———

BARRY'S PHONE RANG AGAIN, He had only hung up with his security force leader seconds ago. They had informed him that they had landed on the island without incident and were en route to the island villa. Security would be up and operational within the hour.

Barry read the caller ID his phone—it was Jason Paul. He hit the 'decline' button; Jason would have to wait. Barry started to scroll to Mr. Avail's number when his phone rang again.

"Don't be so impatient Jason, I'll get to you shortly," he glanced down at the screen, and it wasn't Jason; Mr. Avail was calling him. He answered.

"Barry, I need to amend the security I requested. I am going to the Arlington property. I will need additional security there as well."

Barry was surprised by this.

"Okay sir, I'll get right on it. I do have a four-person shadow team for you that will be at the villa shortly. When do you intend to head to Arlington?" Barry queried.

"As soon as they can get here. The jet is already prepped," George responded impatiently.

"Yes sir, I'll have them meet you at the hanger." Barry hung up. "What the hell is going on?"

He forgot all about Jason's call.

SIMON LITTLE REPLAYED the conversation over and over. While neither the US government nor the CIA had an official position on the pending war in Milekistan, they did quietly hope for the rebels to win. They couldn't publicly say that, however, due to the trade and military agreements they had negotiated with the General. The issue the CIA had was that someone other than them was doing the manipulation. This had become much more of a global problem for them ever since the US government's involvement in social media was discovered.

The FBI had been discovered using social media and mainstream media to suppress certain stories related to previous administrations. The biggest hit was when it was discovered that what was commonly called an *insurrection* was executed directly from a CIA PsyOps plan. It was even known which politician accessed the document and put it in motion. Unfortunately, that was one of the stories the FBI managed to use its weight to bury.

All that this meant to Simon was that he had to deal with more entities operating in his sandbox than ever before. He now had a name to pursue quietly. He didn't want to interfere as of right now, but the end goal was to facilitate the rebel win and take over. Having a person to blame for this was a better scenario than he could have asked for.

The recording ended. "Dear Lord, thank you for Mr. George Avail," Simon smiled as he feigned a prayer.

DERRICK PULLED into the driveway of Cold Assassin Cybersecurity. He was stopped inside the driveway by a guard in the gatehouse.

"Derrick Dunn for Elsy Davenport, she's expecting me," he advised the guard.

"You made good time Mr. Dunn, just follow the drive around to the back, you'll see the garage entrance," the guard said as pushed a button and the gate lifted.

"Thank you, sir, have a nice day," Derrick responded.

The guard smiled, "You too."

The orange Jeep navigated the driveway to the parking garage. As he pulled up to a heavy chain-link style door, it started to open automatically.

Derrick parked the Jeep. When he got out and turned, he was startled by a woman standing in from of him.

"Good afternoon Mr. Dunn, My name is Tulia, and I am Elsy's assistant. If you would follow me, I will take you to her."

Derrick did as he was asked. He couldn't help but admire what Elsy had built in such a short time.

They entered the elevator and Tulia used a key fob to grant access to the buttons. She pushed the button for the top floor, and the elevator rushed them upward. The door opened and Elsy was waiting for him. She stepped forward as he exited the elevator smothering him with a bear hug. He hugged her back with a similar effort; it was good to see her. Elsy led him back to her office. There were only a few offices on this floor and a large open area in the middle between them. Couches, hanging pod chairs, and other forms of comfortable seating filled most of the area. People were located sporadically throughout the maze of furniture.

"I'm impressed with what you've built here, Elsy," Derrick praised.

She looked over her shoulder at him as they entered the large glass cube she called an office. "Keep it up, I love flattery."

Tulia was still walking along with them.

"She does, it's how I get a raise every year," she smiled at Elsy and left the room, closing the door behind her.

Derrick took a minute and absorbed the presence of his friend.

"Geez, you look great. But what's so important that I had to detour my mission?"

Elsy smiled at his attempt to veil his displeasure with the short compliment.

"I found the Avails' bank accounts," she waited for Derrick to grasp what she meant.

"I found ALL their bank accounts. You remember how I funded your new life by stripping that hacker of one of his accounts?"

Derrick shook his head yes.

"I am confident I can do that to every account the Avails have. For them, this would be a fate worse than death. I can leave them destitute; they'd lose everything. They'll wish they were dead."

Derrick thought about what she was saying. He knew one thing: he made a promise to Shannon to make them pay. This might work, as they would lose the thing they loved most as well.

"How long will it take?" he asked, uncertain if he could wait for long.

"I'm guessing it would take me two weeks to set everything up, so we have a place to move it all to. After that, it would take about twenty minutes to execute."

Derrick considered her timetable.

"Okay, you start. In the meantime, I will fly to their island and start surveillance, just in case my way wins out."

Elsy realized that was the best offer she'd get from him.

"That's reasonable, just stay in touch so I can keep you updated," she asked.

Before Derrick could get up, Elsy asked him another question.

"Do you want to stay for dinner? I haven't been out since Harlem returned to Virginia."

"Sure, I'd love to. What did you have in mind?" he said, realizing he hadn't eaten all day.

They started to make their plans, briefly pushing more important issues to the back of their minds.

————

WHEN GEORGE ARRIVED at the hangar, four men in dark suits and sunglasses met him at the car. Two men walked on either side and the third flanked him. The fourth checked his luggage and then instructed the attendant to stow it on the plane. Safely on board, one security member met with the pilot while the other three took positions around the cabin. They were out of the way, but each had access to Mr. Avail from a different angle.

George was quite impressed with their professionalism. He suddenly didn't feel as vulnerable as he had all day. The plane lifted off as the lone security member returned from the cockpit and was seated. He sat directly across from George.

————

JASON PAUL COULDN'T BELIEVE the level of intel that the occupant of the cabin had on the Avails. He was sure this is what Barry had been looking for; however, Barry had declined his call and hadn't called back yet. Jason had a simple rule—you hang up, you call back or we don't talk anymore. As he waited, he began to photograph and catalog all the information he found. The only thing he didn't find was anything that provided ID on the occupant of the cabin.

He wasn't too worried though; he saw the van outside and it had current marker plates. He was sure there would be papers related to the owner inside. As he continued to go through the documents, he found a notebook. It was all handwritten inside. He couldn't help but start to read.

These people will have to pay for killing Shannon, there will be retribution.

After reading a few lines, he started to jump pages.

The assassins that killed Shannon are dead, and yet I still feel no comfort. According to the evidence I collected in the bar and the conversation I had with the Avails' man; I am completely confident that they are the ones ultimately responsible for her death. THERE WILL BE JUSTICE!

Jason noticed how the last part was all capitals and it was repeatedly traced over. He started to question his involvement in this case. This man was on a journey of retribution, against an untouchable family that had taken his love without a second thought. Jason knew what he'd do— exactly what this guy was doing. He tossed the notebook back into the wall, along with any other indicators of motive. He would give Barry the documents that pointed to a pending attack, but the personal notes would stay in the wall. As he was packing things up, his phone rang—it was Barry.

"Took you long enough to call back," Jason stated with obvious irritation.

10

THE BLACK SUV drove down the long cobblestone driveway. The estate was recently landscaped, and the main house was brightly illuminated. Every few seconds, a guard could be seen walking in the shadows along the perimeter fence. The SUV pulled up in front of the house. Two men stepped forward and took positions in front and rear of the passenger door. The one in front reached out and opened the door. George Avail stepped from the vehicle and was escorted inside. It had been a while since he called this location home.

The staff was in the foyer to greet him and welcome him home, and he nodded as they offered him a welcome. The security teams disappeared as the front door was closed behind him. His house concierge stepped forward.

"Welcome, Mr. Avail. You have a guest waiting in the sitting room."

The concierge led the way, opening the doors to the sitting room and closing them after George entered.

———

GEORGE COULD SEE his guest sitting in front of the room's large fireplace. George knew who his visitor was without even seeing his face. The way he towered in the room, even while sitting, gave it away.

"Barry. I'm surprised to see you here, but I'm also glad. Things are heating up."

Barry stood to greet Mr. Avail. He understood to some people, this might have been interpreted as an attempt to intimidate simply due to his height. George didn't see it that way.

Barry spoke slowly and softly, "Sir, I'm afraid things might be worse than you imagine."

"Okay Barry, have a seat and we'll have a drink and discuss whatever this is," George stated in a voice that was slow and quiet. He was tired due to a full day of travel and stress. He was sure nothing Barry had to say would surprise him at this point.

"Sir I spoke to my guy up north, he found evidence that someone is indeed tracking you. Luckily his plan seemed centered on your villa in the islands."

George quietly responded, "My daughter is still there, and she won't take my calls. You must contact her and warn her."

"Sir, I've already put the villa guards on high alert and added extra security staff for you. You should have noticed an added layer of protection here as well," Barry advised him.

George sat back down, not completely relieved but satisfied those precautions had been taken. He decided he needed to share the rest of his concerns with Barry.

———

"BARRY, a larger entity is at play here as well. It was through them that I was warned about a possible person looking to harm me. They gave no details, and it's possible it could be one of their agents and they are just toying with me."

"Agents? What kind of group are you involved with?" Barry questioned.

"A powerful one. Imagine a group made up of one hundred people like me, some even backed by governments of countries that do not exactly love the USA. That's what I am facing." George calmly informed him.

Barry was contemplating Mr. Avail's situation. He realized that he was involved in a much more serious scenario. It was starting to make sense why they were unable to find the identity of the man in the cabin.

"Sir, I'm going to go and investigate a bit for you. I'll let you know what I find out."

"Thank you, Barry. Also, you can't say anything to anyone about what I told you. If you do, they will kill us all."

George's final statement to him was so matter-of-fact, it even made Barry feel cold.

———

LINDA WAS CONSIDERING CALLING her father. The security force that had shown up unannounced had just doubled in size, now they were giving her a hard time about even going outside.

"Ma'am, you just can't walk around and be an easy target," one guard had said to her.

Linda ignored him and did what she wanted.

She had planned on returning to the sun goddess role she enjoyed before her father's betrayal. Now she was afraid that even her tanning routine would be ripped away from her.

Instead, she picked up her phone and dialed.

"Hello, Ms. Avail. How can I help you this evening?"

Barry knew exactly what she was calling for. This would be a challenging call.

"Mr. Klinger, please get your damn security people out of my house and tell my father I'm fine and I'm safe. I don't need a babysitter because he is untrustworthy," Linda demanded into the phone.

Barry wasn't sure what the last part was about, but he knew it would be more difficult to convince Linda to keep the security because of it.

"Linda, I can honestly tell you that you need it. A credible threat has been discovered against you and your father," he implored.

"Credible from where—you saw the evidence, or my father told you it existed?" she questioned.

"I have seen evidence, yes, Ms. Avail," Barry responded, hoping to sway her.

"Be precise, Mr. Klinger. Did the evidence you've seen *say* I was in danger?" Linda continued his interrogation.

"No, but it was an awful lot of surveillance for a fan club," he said, giving in to her obvious resentment.

"Alright then, here is my compromise. I noticed two women are on your security force, they may stay, everyone else must leave."

Barry knew he was losing this negotiation.

"Ok, Ms. Avail. I'll make it happen."

Linda was satisfied, she now can go back to laying in the sun tomorrow, without any guards eyeing her up.

———

DERRICK AND ELSY were enjoying dinner in a nice restaurant in Boston. Although he once had worked in the city as a detective, he wasn't overly concerned anyone would recognize him. He now sported a full beard and much longer hair than he ever had during his whole career. The thing that overcame him at dinner was that this was his first night out with someone other than Killer since Shannon had been murdered. The thought of that ignited the fire that Elsy had spent all day trying to extinguish.

Elsy sensed his slow change of demeanor during dinner—she knew he was thinking of Shannon.

"Hey bud, I'm sorry if this brings up bad memories, I was just hoping you could start making some new ones with friends."

Derrick looked up at her. She had truly become his little sister. It does feel good to know someone still loves and cares about you. Elsy made sure Derrick knew that every day since they had reconnected.

"I'm sorry," Derrick started. "I have been lousy company as usual. You're right, I was thinking of the last time I went out with Shannon."

"Derrick, you don't have to apologize, I want you to know you are loved and I don't want you to get hurt chasing the need for vengeance," she said the last part quietly as she leaned into the table towards him.

"You may be my little sister, and I couldn't live without you. But I made a promise I must keep. I even got a tattoo."

He said with a smirk as he pulled up his sleeve to show her.

"Oh my God, that's beautiful! Did you design it?" Her excitement was evident.

"Thank you, and yes I did," he said quietly.

"What does it mean?" Elsy asked.

"It means I made a promise, and I won't stop till it's completed."

Elsy already knew what it said—she could read Latin as well as four other languages.

"What does the phrase mean?" she pushed.

Derrick didn't see her trap coming. "Till the debt is paid."

"Is that the promise you made her?" She continued.

"Yes," he said tentatively, realizing she was setting him up.

"Excellent, that means we can settle the debt my way, and still honor your promise, right?"

Derrick was taken aback by Elsy's mental jiu-jitsu.

"Ah, uh, well I guess," he stammered.

She smiled brightly across the table from him. Without a word, she returned to eating her meal. She had handled him, and both knew it.

Derrick was still looking at her. He felt played a bit, but was willing to give her one shot.

"Elsy, one try, wipe it all out, or I do it my way. That's the deal, okay?"

She gazed at him, still chewing a mouth of food. She swallowed it and replied.

"That's fair. I won't let you down. So where to now? I'll need a little time to get everything in order."

"I'm still gonna head down south, maybe I'll hold up in Florida for a bit before I head to the islands."

"I'll make you a reservation, I have a timeshare down there. I'll book you a month in Orlando. Close but not too close, and it's a great place to unwind. I think you could use that."

They stood on the sidewalk after dinner. The air was brisk, and they could see the steam from their breath. Elsy stepped forward and squeezed Derrick in a hug. He returned it.

"I love you… like a brother," Elsy said in a soft voice.

"I love you too, lil' sis," Derrick responded with a smile.

He leaned over and kissed her on the forehead.

"Thank you for everything. You have been a lifesaver," he told her, his gratitude evident as he said it.

"We're a team. It's kinda self-serving," she said, trying to downplay her efforts.

She held his arm as they walked back to her building. She tried to get Derrick to spend another day in the city, but he refused. "Thanks again for everything, but it's time for me to move closer to where I need to be," he said as he headed back to the Jeep.

Elsy watched as the bright orange Jeep exited the garage and headed out for the highway.

———

TINKER WAS happy with the new direction he was going in. Having a scapegoat for this AI hack would be a new safety net he hadn't originally anticipated. They continued to test their programming; it performed flawlessly. He was ready way ahead of schedule.

He hadn't heard from Barry or Mr. Avail since his request for additional funding, and he wasn't sure what he should do next. He had another target in mind, and decided to spend some time on an old hunt. "Where are you, Miss Cyber Cop?" he wondered. Deidra walked up to his open door and knocked on the frame.

"Come on in," Tinker invited. "Did you find out who we're up against?"

"Yes sir, and I don't think you'll like it," Deidra said with a grimace on her face.

Tinker had been leaning back in his chair with his feet up, now he sat upright and gave his sole attention to Deidra.

"What did you find?"

"It appears it's the Chinese government and possibly other nation-state actors. So far it seems they are completely unaware of our collecting their coding."

Tinker thought for a moment.

"Okay, we know our end works like we need it to. Switch to passive monitoring. Let's not tip our hand."

"I got this," Deidra said as she disappeared again.

Tinker now pondered this new twist. This latest news caused him to feel hot and flushed. At first, he wasn't sure why. He didn't think of himself as a patriot, but the thought of other countries secretly messing with American media kind of pissed him off. That surprised him.

———

SIMON HAD BEEN SPENDING ALL his time trying to build a case to have the FBI grab Barry Klinger. He was sure that Barry was tied up in the coup starting in Milekistan and that he was being funded by the billionaire George Avail. He just didn't have any direct proof of either, just some vague conversation that could be construed in several ways. He hated the endless paperwork whenever he needed help from the FBI. There was much less paperwork in the CIA—less paper trail that way.

He typed up the conversations he had recorded, and he added the surveillance from the cantina on the border of Milekistan. He felt he was building a solid reason for Barry's detainment and questioning. If his request was granted, he would receive temporary Federal Marshal credentials to assist in the arrest while on US soil. He double-checked everything. It was as good as he could make it. He hit 'send'.

———

LINDA AWOKE to the sun rising. She had heard some commotion during the night, but hadn't tried to see what it was. As she strolled from her bedroom to the kitchen area in her robe, she noticed the absence of the security guards. One lone female guard sat at the island in the kitchen as she walked in. Linda almost felt inadequate as she gazed at the guard's smooth dark skin, her bright brown eyes, and her silky jet-black hair. *She's like an ebony god,* Linda thought as she gazed at the guard. Her thoughts were broken as the guard spoke.

"Good morning, Miss Avail," the guard greeted her in a formal tone.

"Good morning to you, I'm glad to see the others are gone. Is it just you or is the other female guard I asked for here also?"

"For this morning it's only me. The other officer will be on during the evening and night," was the guard's reply.

Linda never thought about shifts when she demanded only the two female guards stay.

"Okay great. Do you have a name, or should I call you number one?" Linda casually asked as she sipped her morning coffee.

"My name is Ebony Godd, ma'am," the guard responded.

Linda snorted and almost spit out the coffee, recalling her earlier impression. "You're serious?"

The guard stared at her and responded, "I am. My parents were young, and my father thought I was dark like ebony when I was born. So, here I am."

Linda felt bad for laughing, it just caught her off guard.

"I'm sorry Ebony. I didn't mean to be insensitive. It truly seems appropriate, you're a beautiful woman."

"No worries, ma'am, and thank you for that compliment," Ebony conceded in a much less formal tone.

"Still, I should be better. So, I plan on sitting out on the deck most of today. I would appreciate it while you are here as well, if you put on a suit and pull up the chair next to me." Linda invited.

Ebony declined as graciously as she could,."Thank you for that generous offer, ma'am but I don't think I could properly protect you in that scenario."

"Okay I get it, but stop with the ma'am. Please, call me Linda."

The guard shrugged.

"Okay, Linda."

Linda slid open the door leading to the deck, placed her coffee on the small table, and hung her robe on the back of her chair. She lay down in the direct sunlight. She was back in her happy place.

———

THE MAN PEERED through the binoculars; he had a very clear view from his location. There she was, soaking up the sun. Linda Avail would have no idea she was being surveilled from there. He switched from the binoculars to the digital camera with the telephoto lens. He zoomed right up on Linda; he snapped a couple of pictures. *She is a very attractive woman,* he thought. He snapped a few more pictures and went back to a computer set up on a desk in the room. He made some notes and saved them to the daily log he kept. It seems she was back to her normal routine of sleeping, drinking, and sunbathing.

He went back to the camera. As he looked through the viewer, Linda was removing her top. He was tempted to snap a few extra photos, but he did not. This was an important assignment, and he was a professional— teenage antics had no place here. He did, however, take another look through the camera.

11

DERRICK HAD BEEN in Florida for three weeks already thanks to Elsy's generosity. He was doing what he promised he—giving her time to find another way to make the Avails pay without him becoming their executioner. He sat on the screened porch of the timeshare unit. They were much like a real home, having a complete kitchen, living room, and laundry, as well as two bedrooms and baths. He felt like he could easily live in one of these. Today he planned to go to the pool for a little while. Elsy had been right about that as well; he needed a little downtime, and this place was built for it.

He checked his phone for messages and then donned a swimsuit he had purchased after he arrived. Even in March, the temp was pushing eighty-five degrees.

———

THE ROOM WAS DIMLY LIT, and faces could hardly be seen. A lone voice was speaking in a panicked tone, but in the language of his country. After listening to the report, his direct supervisor became similarly panicked. The translation of their words became.

"Sir, it looks here like someone has detected and manipulated our code."

"Who? How would they have known to look?"

"Maybe the machine was a trap, sir?"
"This is not acceptable."
"So now what?"
"Fix it!"
"Sir, fix it how? We don't even know where it came from."
"Find out and fix it. Otherwise, you know what your fate will be."

The young Chinese military programmer just stared at his screen. The alternative to finding a solution would probably mean death. In his mind, he could see the local paper headline, a young soldier dies unexpectedly of natural causes. He shuddered and started combatting the code that had put his life in danger.

————

GEORGE CONTINUED to work on his plan. He kept funding the campaigns and the control of votes for key candidates in tactical positions, even though this had nothing to do with his current plan. The use of purchased politicians and outright cheating still worked, but when President Harrington was elected it became apparent that the people could still overwhelm their manipulation of the system.

Now he had a new plan that was a combination of his old plan, modern technology, and psychology being used in unison. He had media distractions and multiple ways of manipulation being set up for this coming election. No longer was he looking to control the voters—his plan was to directly control most politicians. He had no illusions about defeating President Harrington, as he was still polling in the sixty percentiles.

————

ELSY MOVED HER 'TINKER TRACE', as she called it, to her main monitor. Tulia had noticed something strange going on and suggested she look at it. Sure enough, there it was—a strange line of code that was continuously transmitting. She started to record the code. After she felt she had captured a significant amount, she ended the recording. She started to pour over the code and dissect it. It was strange. It was almost as if it were two tracking codes fighting for dominance over a piece of information. She looked even deeper at it. That's exactly what it was!

She wondered if she could identify either of the end users. This felt like it was important—she felt a strange urge to look even further into it. She used an app on her computer to call Tulia and Eric into her office. When they both arrived, she asked Eric to close her office door.

"I want you two to work together on this." She showed them the code she had recorded. "I want to know who the players are. I assume one is Tinker, but I want the identity of who he is sparring with as well as what they are sparring over."

Eric asked the first question, "How soon do you need this, should we drop everything else?"

Elsy knew he was just asking for clarification.

"I want this information as fast as you can get it without exposing us. We must remain outside of their periphery. We need distance from whatever is happening." A chill ran down her spine as she said this, her mind alerting her to an unseen danger.

Tulia shook her head in agreement and then stood by Eric. Before she could say a word, Elsy knew what she was thinking.

"Tulia you take the lead, Eric work with her and get this done for me."

"Yes, boss," they both answered in unison.

They left her office to accomplish their new assignment as soon as possible.

IN THE CORNER office of a high rise somewhere in France, A woman looked at an email.

Madam, I agree with your assessment, I also am not one hundred percent sure he was honest. I believe it's in our best interests to have a coercion plan in place should his real intent become exposed. I was thinking maybe his daughter may be a suitable motivator. Let me know. I will have a plan for you as soon as I hear back from you. Also, Milekistan may not wait for his timeline; things are escalating once again.

She reached for a glass of cognac that had been placed on the desk in front of her. She swirled the liquid around in the glass, taking in the aroma before indulging in its taste. As she brought the glass to her lips, she considered the email. "George, what is your end game? Are you planning on betraying me?" she pondered. He was the only one that knew of her own plans regarding the Council.

The liquor was well-crafted and had excellent flavor and body. She took another sip.

She pulled her keyboard closer and typed a reply email. *Send me a plan.* She hit 'send'.

———

AFTER WEEKS of the cat-and-mouse paperwork chase with the FBI, he finally held the arrest order for Barry Klinger. He knew Barry was currently in the US, but hadn't been able to locate his direct whereabouts. Simon was getting perturbed at the difficulty of nailing down where Barry was. He decided to force Barry out of hiding. He made a phone call.

"Hey buddy, I need a favor, I need a special pizza delivery to an address in Arlington. Make it obvious enough that they'll find it, but not so much they think we wanted them to. Thanks."

He hung up and texted the address to the same number.

On the other end of the call, a CIA technician started prepping a pizza box for a special delivery. He was using a slightly older piece of equipment that was out of circulation, but was still current enough to not give away their plan—after all, this little spy gadget was probably about to get stomped on. It did still work, however, so maybe it might even provide a little help in its martyr quest.

———

DERRICK SAT BY THE POOL. There was music playing on the resort's speaker system. It was an eclectic mix of pop and rock from the past twenty-five years. He leaned back in his lounge and let the sun beat on his face, imagining Shannon sitting beside him in the little red bikini she used to tease him with. His mind remembered every inch of her body, and he let his memories wander through the good times they shared. As his memory trip ended, and the remorse for not being able to save her reappeared, he lifted his sunglasses and wiped a lone tear that had formed and started to run down his face. He looked around to make sure no one was staring at him.

Standing, he removed the glasses and set them on the table beside him, then got up and jumped into the pool, simply ignoring the sign that displayed *No Jumping!* The cool water felt good just as the memories of Shannon had also felt good. For the first time in a long time, these thoughts weren't swallowed up in anger. *Maybe Elsy will have a better way,* he thought as he dove under and swam as far as his breath would let him. He resurfaced and felt refreshed, not just his body but a bit of his soul as well. After getting out and drying off, he decided it was time to call and check in on Killer. He dialed Nicole's number.

———

THE PIZZA DELIVERY van was stopped at the gate of the sprawling estate. Guards refused to let it down until the order had been confirmed. A guard in the shack picked up a landline and waited for someone to answer.

"Hey, I got a pizza delivery here for the main house, did someone order pizza?" the guard asked into the line.

"I have no order for a pizza delivery," was the only reply.

The delivery driver saw where this was going and decided to improv.

"What the hell man? Not again! I get this shit all the time. Little douche bags send me all the way out here for a pay-on-site order."

The guard gave him a slight smirk.

"Awe that must suck man. Sorry, you'll have to leave though," the guard said, sounding amused.

The driver tried to reason with him.

"Sure, it's funny to you. I am out of the pizza money and a tip. Any chance you guys wanna buy a pizza? It's still hot."

"What kind is it?" the guard asked.

"It's pepperoni, bacon, and sausage with onions and mushrooms."

The guard's eyes widened.

"How much?" he asked, obviously interested.

"How about, thirty? Pizza and tip."

"Okay, that pizza smells incredible," the guard said, digging into his pocket for cash.

The driver handed over the pizza and made a quick U-turn and sped away, pocketing the thirty dollars for himself. He wondered if the hungry guards would even notice the bug.

———

THE PHONE RANG at the estate again. This time, the guard at the shack seemed more excited.

"Sir, we found something in the pizza box. You should come to check it out. I don't think it's prudent to bring it to you."

The guard who answered in the estate was the officer in charge of the security team. He first wondered why they had pizza; it was against company policy to have food from an unsecured source while on duty. Second, what could be so concerning about a pizza box?

The OIC was driven quickly out to the gate in a UTV reserved for his current assignment. As the UTV approached the shack, the guards were all waiting outside. He could hear music playing loudly from inside the shack.

"What the hell is going on here?" the OIC demanded.

The guard who had called him stepped forward.

"Sir, it's my fault. When that pizza guy was here, he tempted me with an incredible pizza, and I was hungry, so I violated the policy," the gate guard confessed.

"That's for later, what is the concern that you insisted I come here for?" the OIC questioned.

"Well sir, as we were eating the pizza, we noticed something funny about the box. When we investigated, it turned out it had a listening device embedded in it," the guard informed him.

"We immediately turned the radio up and then exited the building. I called you from the portable phone," he continued.

The OIC contemplated this news. It was obvious someone was trying to infiltrate the estate. He went inside to look at the bug. It was hidden very well until the pizza sat in the box too long and the soggy cardboard gave its location away. He found a glass jar with a lid under the desk in the shack. He picked up the bug and dropped it in and screwed down the lid, taking the evidence with him as he returned to the UTV.

"Back to the estate," he told the driver.

He looked at the other guards standing around.

"Get back to your posts. No more pizza, and turn down that damn radio," he shouted.

The UTV driver spun the vehicle around and raced toward the main building.

————

THE CIA TECH knew the moment the bug was discovered. They wouldn't get any intel from it, but they hoped it would still serve its purpose to motivate Mr. Avail to call Klinger. The tech used the secure building line to make a call.

"It's me, the bug was found and is in play. I hope it goes the way you want."

Simon took the call and listened. His Hail Mary pass was in the air, now he'd just have to wait and see if it was caught. He went back to the tap on Barry's phone to wait for a call.

————

GEORGE OBSERVED THE DEVICE, not quite sure what it was. He questioned the guard standing in front of him.

"Is it still active?"

"No, sir. I disabled it before bringing it inside," the OIC answered.

"So now what? What does this mean?" George questioned.

"Well sir, based on the reason you hired us, I'd say it's evidence that someone else knows you're here as well. It might be time to initiate whatever contingency plans you have," the OIC informed him.

George just stared at the Guard. *Did he even have any contingency plans?* he wondered.

"I need to call someone; you can go now. Thank you for bringing this to my attention," he said with a wave of his hand in dismissal.

The guard left. He knew who Mr. Avail was going to call, but he was an employee and did as he was instructed.

———

THE PHONE WAS RINGING. He looked at the number—this was it. He used another phone to send a text as he was listening. The text said, *Teams on standby, we will have a location shortly.* Simon continued to listen; the phone rang again.

"Come on, pick it up already!" he encouraged.

Simon looked around when he realized he was speaking out loud. Either no one heard, or they didn't care. The ringing continued. No one answered, and the voicemail picked up. Technically the tap warrant did not cover voicemail, but Simon didn't care; that just meant it wouldn't stand up in court. He wasn't worried about that.

A message was being left. *"Barry, where are you? I need you right now, something has come up, and I need to know what my contingency plan is. Call me back immediately!"*

Simon could tell their pizza trick had worked perfectly on that end if only Barry would cooperate. He dialed another number. Deacon Shoop, an NSA agent, answered.

"Deacon, it's Simon, I need a favor."

"Well hello to you too, is this line secure?" his friend chided.

"Yes, it is. I need some recon video from your DC satellite," Simon almost pleaded.

"What DC satellite?" Deacon responded on cue.

"Don't play games with me brother, you know I know," Simon's tone was escalating.

"Okay, say such a thing did exist, what would you need?" Deacon asked, being coy.

"I'll send you an address, I need surveillance for the last 24 hours and going forward for the next two days. I also have a target vehicle I'll send you. This is an instant alert project, and I have authority for this request," Simon said, now taking a more official tone.

"Okay, okay, settle down. Don't go getting all 'Mr. Official' on me just cause I'm bustin' your stones; I owe you a few you know," Deacon reacted.

"I'm sorry. This is a big deal for me," Simon lamented, as he sent the address.

"Alright, let's see what we got here, okay okay okay, yup that's it. Come to Papa," Deacon muttered as he worked.

Simon listened as Deacon mumbled to himself while he searched through the satellite data to find what he was looking for. The satellite captured all the DC area in super high resolution twenty-four hours a day. It was a top-secret project because it recorded everything. Most Americans under its view would most likely consider it an invasion of their privacy if they knew how much this satellite could see with its multiple camera filters and other gadgets. They would be truly appalled.

After a minute or two, the mumbling stopped.

"All set, I captured everything you asked for. I also set up a live link for that segment, I sent it to your secure cell. Enable the link and you'll be live. The previously recorded images are in a desktop folder on your agency computer already."

"Deacon, thanks buddy, I owe you a big one," Simon said.

"Yeah right, you owe me like a hundred big ones. Let's grab a beer when you get a minute," Deacon responded.

"You're on. Take care buddy," Simon agreed.

Simon hung up. While he was uncertain of Barry's current location, he wasn't giving up on finding him.

———

BARRY SAT on the bed looking around the room. The bed was clean, but the bedspread was probably as old as he was. The walls had needed a new coat of paint for a very long time. Even the light from outside was filtered through a layer of something as it struggled through the window and the thin curtains.

This was not the normal accommodation he would use while staying anywhere. It's not that he was above it—he had slept on the ground without cover many times before—but now he was able to afford and appreciate much nicer accommodations. The text he received had taken him off guard. It was a simple message from an unknown source.

They're on to you. You better run and hide.

He wasn't even sure who it was, or if it was real. Life had taught him not to discount such cryptic messages. Barry had chosen to follow the suggestion from the unknown sender; he left his electronics in his 'better' hotel room and just grabbed essentials in a go-bag when he relocated here. He took six cabs and three Ubers in random order, along with walking a total of about four miles to get to the motel. His path here was as untraceable as he could make it. He paid for the room in cash under an alias. He purchased a burner phone from a convenience store a bit down the street. He had seen the call from George Avail as he was leaving his room, but he didn't answer it, afraid it might be bugged. Knowing George wouldn't call unless he needed something, Barry knew he needed to call him back.

———

"WHERE ARE YOU? I HAVE A PROBLEM!" George screamed into the phone when the anonymous caller turned out to be Barry.

"Sir, it seems I have a bit of a problem myself. I have been warned that I'm being targeted. I am in the process of trying to discover who, but I wanted to make sure I kept you shielded."

Barry's answer seemed to sway George's irritation.

"Who is after you? Does it have anything to do with who is trying to bug my house?" George inquired.

Barry was taken by surprise by the latter part of the statement.

"Wait what? What is this about a bug? Please save it. I'll come to you. Alert your security that I'm coming, and I will be on foot when I approach, and I won't be using the main gate. I will use 'Pineapple' as a security word," Barry stated.

"Okay, I'll wait to see you. Why pineapple?" George asked, suddenly curious.

"It's my favorite fruit and means 'welcome,'" Barry said, his smirk almost audible.

12

THE CHINESE KNEW the key to winning against America was to subtly control its people. Manipulating the output of social media through its AI algorithms in a few key areas would be enough to even swing an election. It had been done before, and the American people did little about it besides fight amongst themselves.

Now however, it felt as though China might be fighting against someone else for the same prize: control of these machines. Ping Zi had been coding against these subtle attacks for twenty hours straight. He stepped away to gather his thoughts and grab a coffee and smoke a cigarette. Smoking was allowed inside many buildings in his country. He laughed at how such a "free" country like America told its people where they could even smoke. He tried to push the code from his mind while he enjoyed two of his favorite things in the world.

Instead, the questions of *who* and *why* replaced the code. Who would battle them so completely for control of these machines, when it seems that their intentions were aligned to the same final result? Why would someone else want to control these same AIs? Iran wanted to diminish the power President Harrington had exerted against their country, Russia wanted to sow disinformation, both were China's subtle allies.

While in the past there were presidents too weak to stand up against these countries, Harrington was not one of them. His outspoken demeanor, combined with military experience and a level of diplomacy not recently seen, meant he held not only the American people's affection but also many in the global arena were enamored with him as well. This all gave him incredible authority to deal harshly with any country that moved against the US, with very little global pushback. Ping finished his cigarette and stopped to grab another coffee to bring back to his terminal.

———

DEIDRA WAS CODING as fast as she could. The computer power she had at her disposal was immense, but sometimes it just came down to the code. She could tell that she was in a code battle with another advanced coder. She was also starting to notice something from her childhood. A Chinese influence on the coding—though she had abandoned it as she grew as a hacker, she still remembered it from when she was first taught to code by her friend who had immigrated from China. She was sure she had just figured out the *who*.

This was not good; she ran to Tinker's office. He wasn't in, so she looked at her watch. It was hard to keep track of time in a bunker with no windows. *Pizza time.* Frustrated, she knew she'd have to wait until he returned.

———

ELSY FELT her stomach twitch it was time for lunch. She remembered a small pizza place near Tinker's building. She decided to stop in for a slice or two. She was sitting in a booth when a man walked in and the staff greeted him by name. "Good afternoon Mr. Brennan, your pizza is all ready for you."

As soon as Elsy heard the name, she realized he matched the pictures her assistant had taken. She pulled out her phone and acted like she was using the camera to check her face. She snapped a half dozen pictures of the man she had been hunting ever since his attack on the Boston precinct she used to work in. She was excited, but sat quietly in her booth while he exited with his pizza. From the window, she was able to watch him walk back to the building and, surprisingly, go through the front.

Elsy remembered the blueprint; it showed no front entrance. "What have you changed, Mr. Brennan?" she whispered.

"Good afternoon, see something I can help you with ma'am?"

The waitress startled her.

"I'm fine thank you. Oh, wait. Do you know if that man who was here was Martin Brennan? He looks familiar to me, and I used to know a Martin Brennan," Elsy questioned.

"Why yes that's exactly who that is," the waitress was excited. "If you want to leave your name, I'll make sure he gets it. He comes in here every day, same order."

"Oh goodness, no. I'm sure he wouldn't even remember me. Either way, I'd rather surprise him. Does he work or live around here?" Elsy asked quietly, trying to be subtle.

"I know he works in that building; I think he might live there too," the waitress said, she started blushing a little bit as she was pointing. "I went in one day and tried to find which floor he was on, but no one knew who I was talking about. He is a handsome man, isn't he?" the waitress gushed.

Elsy knew she had an in with the waitress now.

"I'm not competition, if that's what you're worried about. He was just a friend a long time ago," Elsy continued her ruse.

The waitress seemed to relax a bit, happy to have someone to talk with.

"So, here's the thing, I followed him a couple of times trying to work up the nerve to ask him out. The first few times he went to the back of the building and a guard was there. I watched him look closely at the wall before a door opened. I don't know where it led to. I thought it was very 'Bond-sh', if you know what I mean?" the waitress said in a hushed voice.

Elsy shook her head encouraging her, "Go on."

"Lately, he goes in through the front, there is a large painting on the wall in the lobby behind where the elevators are, the painting slides to the side and there's a room behind it. That's all I know. It kinda scares me that maybe he's not as nice as I want to believe he is," she conceded.

Elsy felt the need to console the waitress.

"I'm sure he's fine. Probably another over-cautious businessman," she lied.

The waitress smiled. "Anything else I can get you?"

"Just the check, please," Elsy said, moving her finger in a check motion.

———

TINKER RETURNED to the office to find Deidra sitting with legs crossed on his floor. He assumed she was meditating, so he walked right past her quietly and set his lunch down on a table next to his desk. He turned to a small refrigerator next to the table and grabbed two cokes from it. Meditation time was over. He gripped the tab of the can and opened it with a loud *phsstt* sound. Deidra opened her eyes.

"God, you're predictable. I figured out who we're up against. You're not gonna like it."

Tinker lifted his head up from the pizza box.

"Why, who are they?"

"They…" she hesitated for effect, "are the Chinese military."

"What? Why are they hacking us?" he questioned.

"Well technically, they're hacking the social media AIs, and we happened to be doing it as well," Deidra responded.

Tinker realized this was information that Mr. Avail would want.

"Keep them at bay, until I verify what our client wants to do. And make sure you keep us anonymous. They don't play nice!" Tinker advised.

———

BARRY'S ABANDONED phone was ringing again, and it went to voicemail, Simon listened.

"Hello, Mr. Klinger. It's Tinker. I need to speak to Mr. Avail about the project he ordered. It has expanded into other unexpected areas. I need direction on how he'd like us to proceed. Get back to me ASAP. This is a very fluid and dynamic situation, and most likely dangerous as well."

Simon immediately started to search for Tinker in their database, it didn't take too long. Tinker was known to multiple law enforcement agencies as a high-level hacker. "What was Mr. Avail up to?" Simon wondered aloud.

He pulled up an electronic CIA request form on his computer, *Request for video and audio surveillance of a suspected criminal/terrorist target*. He now believed he had enough to get a wiretap authorization for Mr. Avail. He was excited that his case was finally coming together and moving forward.

BARRY HADN'T TRIED to check his messages yet. He had a feeling he was being surveilled electronically, and that is how he was tipped off. He knew to keep himself informed and ahead of whoever was targeting him; he would have to check in. He decided on a course of action. He left his little motel room again and went for a walk. He strolled to an underpass walkway that wasn't too far away. The concrete and steel might force the phone to grab a tower that wasn't the closest to his call.

He leaned in against the wall in the tunnel and dialed his own number. At the prompt, he entered his code for voicemail. He used a notepad to record anything pertinent and any numbers that were left. He became concerned after Tinker's message. How were so many things spiraling out of control so quickly? This was not a coincidence; it was time to start going on the offense.

He used the burner phone to make a quick call.

"Eric, it's me. Can you let all the officers stationed on Avail Security know that there seems to be an ongoing movement against Mr. Avail? I'm not sure where it's being directed from, but it's widespread on multiple levels. Increase the external coverage of Ms. Avail as well. Maybe see if you can get them closer without her knowledge."

The head of Blackheart security immediately put his friend's request into action. Security would be on high alert.

Barry snapped the burner phone in half and tossed in a little stream flowing alongside the path. He pulled another from his pocket and activated it.

MADAM FELSDER WAS READING another report on *the Avail situation,* as she had started to call it.

We reached out to the facilitator to let him know he was being surveilled. I'm quite sure doing it anonymously spooked him quite a bit. Mr. Avail is still moving forward with his plans, however, there has been no current contact with either side in Milekistan. It now appears that our friends the Chinese may be standing in the way of part of Mr. Avails' plan.

I suggest that we watch their involvement closely. The daughter is under surveillance by not only us but by her father's security team as well. Currently, she thinks it's just her two female guards assigned to her. She has not attempted to facilitate any of her father's plans and seems content to just lay in the sun. We did identify the computer hacker that they are using and his location. End of summary.

She set the report down. The addition of a hacker to Mr. Avail's deception bothered her. *What is his real intent? We may need to encourage him to rethink his actions.* She glanced out her window at the beautiful evening in France. Her mind turned to an evening a long time ago. She remembered a conversation she had with a much younger George Avail, a conversation where she shared too much to win his confidence. This was now her biggest regret. She was convinced that George now intended to use that info, and that his daughter must know as well. She shut her computer and called for her driver—it was time to go home.

————

DERRICK WAS on the way back from the pool when a man bumped hard into him on the way to the elevator.

"Excuse me," Derrick said sarcastically.

The man turned and started to shout at Derrick. "Why don't you watch where you're going you fucking oaf!" This was the first time he had encountered such an arrogant person during his stay. The man reached out and pushed Derrick back, still shouting obscenities at him. Derrick had an instant surge of adrenaline. He felt his face turn red and he went directly into fight mode, a feeling he had been repressing well until this minute. No one had been accidentally foolish enough to challenge Derrick up until this point. Before he knew what he was doing, he had the arrogant prick pinned by his throat against the nearest wall.

"I think you owe me an apology," Derrick hissed in the man's face.

The once arrogant loudmouth was suddenly no more. His personality shrank in front of Derrick like a sponge drying in the sun.

"I'm sorry, I didn't mean it, please don't hurt me." Derrick started to relax his grip as the anger started to subside. It was only then that he saw a little girl staring at him. Ashamed, he thought it was the little girl's father that he had attacked. He started to release his grip as the little girl ran up toward the man.

Instead of crying and begging Derrick to release the man, the little girl sprinted forward and kicked him as hard as she could right in the shin. The man in Derrick's grasp shrieked.

"That man broke my doll and threw it in the trash because of the noise it made, thank you for stopping him."

Derrick looked at the girl and then at the man still in his grasp.

"I'm sure he intends on paying for the doll, doesn't he?" Derrick encouraged the man.

The man shook his head as much as he could. He released his hands that had been ineffectually gripping to Derrick's wrist and reached for his wallet. He pulled out a twenty-dollar bill. The little girl laughed at the offer.

"More than that."

The man increased the payment by another twenty.

"More," she ordered.

"All I have is a hundred," he managed to squeak out.

The girls stepped forward and grabbed both twentys and the hundred.

"You can let him go now," she said as if Derrick worked for her.

He released the man who crumbled to the floor. It was then Derrick realized the man had urinated himself.

"Just go," Derrick ordered.

The man climbed back up and slowly disappeared from the area.

Derrick was impressed by the little girl.

"You're pretty smart for a… how old are you?" He asked.

"I'm nine, and yes, I'm very smart for my age. Everyone says so," she confidently responded.

"What's your name?" Derrick questioned.

"Katrina Shoal. My friends call me Trina. You can call me that too. What's your name?" She asked in return.

"I'm Derrick. Nice to meet you, Trina."

"Thanks for your help," she shouted as shook his hand and then ran away.

Derrick felt the crumpled paper feel of something she had left in his hand and laughed, forty dollars.

She shared her windfall. He hit the elevator button again, this time without incident. Derrick smiled at the confidence this little girl had, he smiled even broader when he realized she paid him forty dollars for his assistance.

————

TULIA AND DILLON were working hard on monitoring the stream anonymously. They had been reviewing the strange coding when Dillion noticed something.

"Hey, I'll be back in a minute, I want to go verify something."

He was only gone a few minutes when he returned with a smile on his face.

"I knew I'd seen that coding before. Back before I started here, I was doing some Blackhat stuff for some alphabet agencies. I was counter-coding against the Chinese Government. The point is, this is their coding. The other entity is China."

Tulia looked up at him.

"We need to let Elsy know. This is even bigger than she thinks. My guess is we'll have to loop in the FBI or some other agency."

Dillion told her to go, but Tulia refused.

"This is your find; I'm not stealing your thunder. I'll keep making sure we stay hidden."

"I'll be back as soon as I can and let you know what she says," Dillon said as he left their workspace and headed over to Elsy's office.

————

ELSY WAS STILL MONITORING the facial recognition software running on the pictures she had taken of the man she believed was Tinker, aka Martin Brennan. She knew Martin was an alias, so that was really of no help to her. The use of the front door by Tinker was also on her mind.

"Would this man have been lazy enough to compromise his own security to facilitate getting pizza every day?" she wondered.

Dillon was at her door, preparing to knock.

"What's up Dillion, did you find something?"

"Yes boss, we sure did, and it's big."

Elsy motioned for him to come in and close the door.

"What did you find?" she asked.

His lead-up had dramatically raised her curiosity.

"We know who the other group is, it's not good," Dillon answered.

"Well tell me, don't make me ask. Who is Tinker's group sparring with? And why?" she queried.

"We're still working on the why/what part, but the who is the Chinese," he continued.

"Individuals, or the government itself?"

"Looks like government code," he responded.

Elsy took a minute to process that last unexpected part.

"China? You're sure?" she asked.

"Yes, ma'am, we are," he stated.

Elsy shot him a cold stare. Dillon knew immediately why he got the stare.

"I'm sorry boss, I didn't mean to say that," he was referring to the word 'ma'am', which Elsy had let all her staff know she hated.

She smiled a bit at his instant shame of the slip-up.

"Good work, now carefully try to find out what they're doing," she instructed.

Before he could turn to leave, Tulia showed up. She just whipped open the door without knocking, and her excitement was visible in her whole demeanor.

"Elsy, I know what they're doing, or at least what they're trying to do."

She didn't wait for anyone to respond, she kept talking.

"They're hacking the AI systems of the major social media platforms."

13

MADAM FELSDER HAD SPENT the previous night considering her options about George Avail and his secretive plans. While she was agreeable that they both were trying to manipulate political outcomes, she was not sure that Mr. Avail's plan was succinctly in line with the Global Council's plans to move forward. Globalism could not be a sprint —it needed to be a marathon so that citizens, especially American ones, wouldn't become alarmed at the centralization of power. Her bigger concern, however, was that George might be trying to usurp her own plan, one that she was not quite ready to exploit.

She had made up her mind. George would be given explicit direction, and if he chose to comply all would be fine. If not, other measures would be utilized.

———

IT WAS STILL dark at this time of the morning. Barry used the darkness to sneak onto the estate using paths that lead through the woods surrounding the property. He was almost to the main house when he encountered his first guard.

"Halt! Or I'll shoot, this is private property!" the guard commanded him.

Barry hoped his message had been relayed properly.

"Pineapple!" he said loudly.

"What did you say?" the guard questioned.

"PINEAPPLE!" Barry said louder.

"Mr. Klinger, is that you?" was the guard's reply.

"Yes, now please let me pass. I'm on a timetable here."

Barry started to head for the main house when he realized, his whole interaction with the guard took place out in the open, with no trees or other cover.

"Damn, I'm gonna have to make this fast," he thought.

He didn't know who was after him, but he knew it was probably some government agency, and that they had access to satellites. He couldn't be too careful right now.

When he reached the side door to the house, he found it unlocked. He opened it and stepped inside. He was immediately confronted by three armed guards. "Pineapple," he repeated.

"Thank you, Mr. Klinger, we will still need to search you before we let you in any further. I hope you understand, we still need to do our jobs appropriately."

Barry nodded.

One guard lowered his weapon and stepped forward to pat him down. Barry remained still, cautious not to trigger a muscle memory defense of the guard. He informed the guard he was carrying a weapon.

The guard finished the pat down and removed the single pistol Barry had concealed in his back holster.

The guard looked over the pistol.

"SIG huh, nice gun. I will hold it for you during your visit. You get it back when you leave," the guard told him.

The guard removed the magazine and racked the slide, removing a bullet from the chamber. He left the gun with the slide racked back and the bullet and mag separate. Before he could put it in a lock box, Barry stopped him and demanded his weapon back—he felt this wasn't the right time to be unarmed. The guard hesitated and looked to the other guards with him, one of them nodded and Barry took possession of his gun again. He placed the lone bullet in the chamber before releasing the slide then he reinserted the magazine.

Barry returned his weapon to his holster; he was now good to go meet with George.

———

GEORGE WAITED, wearing a robe and slippers, as the man he had been waiting on entered the room. It appeared security had awakened him when Barry was discovered outside.

"Barry, what is going on?" George questioned.

"I'm sorry George, I don't know. I received an anonymous text telling me to run and hide. I did as I was instructed."

"Is someone after you, or me?" George asked nervously.

"I don't know that either, sir. I've reached out and increased your security both here and on the island. That's all I can do until I get more intel," Barry informed him.

"Do you think it could be the Council?" George asked cautiously.

"It could be anyone with money and power. I feel this may be a government agency, though," Barry surmised.

George was growing concerned.

"I've avoided government scrutiny my whole life, I'm not about to let it get me now."

George picked up the phone and dialed an asset he had helped get into office every year for twenty-plus years. It rang for a bit before it was answered. The voice was scratchy and sounded annoyed.

"Hello, who is this, how did you get this number?" the man asked, irritation evident in his voice.

"Good morning Senator, George Avail calling."

It took about twenty seconds of silence before the Senator seemed to wake up and grasp who he was on the line with.

"George, do you know what time it is?"

"Senator, I'm aware of the time. Listen closely. I need you to use your considerable network of agency contacts to see if I or any of my associates are under investigation by a government entity. Something is going on."

"George, I'm not sure I can do that, it would seem inappropriate for me to make such a query," the Senator stated.

That response caused George's face to turn red, and his anger started to rise.

"I put you where you are! I'm not asking. Get this done now. My backing can disappear as fast as it showed up. Not to mention if I go down, it won't be alone!"

"Okay you don't have to make threats. I'll find out who's looking at you and your friends. Give me twenty-four hours."

"You can have six hours. This needs to be handled quickly. I cannot sit around if I'm exposed," George ordered.

The Senator knew six hours would be tight—he was going to have to wake people up himself.

"I'll call you in six hours. Goodbye, I now have a lot of work to do."

The Senator hung up.

George was unsatisfied, he was not accustomed to waiting.

"Barry you'll have to make yourself at home here for the next six hours. We should have an answer by then if these buffoons are worth all the money I've spent on them."

Barry thought about it; secure house, secure property, and he had snuck in. This was about as safe and hidden as he could be.

———

SIMON WAS AWAKENED from sleep by his phone vibrating on the nightstand. The alarm to wake up was still a few hours away. The screen indicated he had a new video to see. As he played the video it started in night vision. He could see the shape of a human with a green tint running through the woods towards the Avail estate. After crossing the fenced perimeter, the subject encountered a guard on patrol. At this point, the video switched to a proprietary type of camera image. Even in low light conditions, the camera was able to give a clear picture of the subject.

"Ahh Barry, I knew you'd come!"

Simon called the team on standby.

"We have a go. The subject is at the Avail estate. The warrant is active."

He jumped in his SUV and headed out; he was twenty-five minutes away if he drove like he meant it.

———

TINKER WAS CATCHING SOME SLEEP. He had been smart enough to build sleeping pods into his design when he refitted the basement of this building. Each pod was a little mini apartment, with a small bathroom and a shower, and in the main area was a bed tucked into the wall, along with a small tv built into the opposite wall.

Deidra had decided she needed to rest; it had been almost thirty hours since she had last slept. She coded a software trigger to notify her if anything dramatic changed with the programming she was monitoring. It was nearing sunrise, something she couldn't see from her basement location. She was awakened by a noise that sounded like the red alert from the TV show *Star Trek*. She scrambled to find her phone and shut it off. A message on her phone flashed. *Destructive code introduced!*

"Oh shit! That's not good."

She jumped from the bed and ran down the hallway to the main coding room. Almost no one else was present at this hour—maybe two other coders, engrossed in whatever they were working on. She ran to her workstation and started reviewing the code. She was ten minutes into the review before she realized she hadn't even put her pants on. Coding in her underwear wasn't unusual for her when she did it at home. It didn't faze her now either. She dove into the code and located the destructive code designed to wipe them out.

"Oh, you Chinese are sneaky little bastards!" she muttered under her breath.

She was sure this would happen again unless she found a stealthier way to insert their code into the programming they were doing. She thought for a moment. The easiest way to spot another's code was identifying the code accents, which were similar to linguistic accents. Deidra started to write code the way her friend had taught her many years ago. This is how she would hide from them—simply by blending in.

———

PING ZI WATCHED as the competitor's code started to disappear line by line. His attack program appeared to be working. This was excellent news for him. His supervisor was already on his way to review his progress; the timing couldn't be better. He also was sure he had found the proximal location of the other hackers. His supervisor would be most pleased about this,

Before the code had finished disappearing, Ping felt a hand on his shoulder.

"Did you resolve the issues of yesterday?" his supervisor asked.

Ping stood, turned, and faced his supervisor.

"Yes sir, I am attacking their code as we speak. It seems they are not as prepared for defense as they should be," he said.

"Don't be arrogant soldier, that is a sure way to defeat," his supervisor chastised him.

"Apology, sir. I only meant that the code to remove them seems to be working," he replied.

"Let's hope it does, keep watching it to make sure," the supervisor moved on.

Ping sat down like he was deflated into his chair. He needed sleep.

———

MADAM FELSDER HAD BEEN WAITING for the opportunity to discuss her concerns with George Avail. She was waiting for the time difference to make her call more likely to be taken. Before that time came, an assistant entered her office.

"Madam, we have the rest of the intel on the man we believe is hunting Mr. Avail."

"Let me see it," she said, extending her hand.

He handed her a file that she immediately opened and began to leaf through. "Is this everything?"

"It's all we were able to find up to this point. As you'll see in the file, we know he is in Florida right now. We're not sure why, but he is staying in a timeshare unit rented by an Elsy Davenport."

"Is he accessible?" she asked.

The assistant knew what she meant.

"Yes, we have a plan in place. We've secured local assets to make it happen whenever you give the order."

"Make it happen. Don't leave any loose ends," she ordered.

"Yes, Madam." The assistant left to send orders to the assets in Florida.

She gazed out her window. "Another thing I can hold over his head," she said, thinking of Mr. Avail.

―――――

DERRICK'S SLEEP had been restless last night. The incident with the arrogant man and the little girl fired up memories and feelings that he thought he was controlling. He left bed feeling unrefreshed and went to the kitchen and made some coffee. The machine's clock showed six fifteen in the morning. He stepped out on the screened balcony and sipped it while looking out over the pool area. He noticed the little girl from last night, as he looked closer, he saw her talking to the man from last night as well.

The man was grabbing her arm aggressively. Derrick couldn't hear them talking from so far away, but assumed the man was demanding his money back. He started to feel rage again. He watched—as the girl pulled away and left the man standing alone, Derrick settled down. He hoped he wouldn't run into that man again; next time he might not be so kind. As Derrick watched, he was sure the man had seen him and then walked away. About ten minutes later, someone knocked on his door. He used the peephole and saw Trina standing outside, he wondered if she was there to get the forty dollars back.

He opened the door, and she was crying.

"Hey, what happened? Why are you crying?" he asked.

"I'm sorry I'm sorry I'm sorry." She repeated.

From the hallway, two men rushed into his unit, The unseasonable coats they wore were unzipped, and Derrick could see the grip ends of pistols in shoulder holsters.

Without conscious thought, he pushed the girl aside into the kitchen area as the two men rushed him, the first one pushing him back towards the living room. Derrick sensed the first man reaching for the gun in his shoulder holster. He adjusted himself to grab the man's hand—as he reached for the gun, he pushed his right leg back and pushed back against the man's attack. He then used his left knee to punch through the man's left knee at the same time.

A crack and a small yelp let him know his strike was effective. Using his right hand to secure the weapon, he used his left elbow to land a severe strike to the man's face, breaking his nose, while his right hand stayed on the weapon. He then wrapped his left arm around the man's neck front to back, and following the motion created by the knee strike, Derrick pulled the attacker's head down and slightly to his right to keep him subdued.

Through his peripheral vision, he could see the second attacker grabbing his gun from his holster and starting to raise it towards him. The first assailant's momentum was altered with the strike to the knee, and the attacker was sinking and turning toward his right. Derrick used this change in direction to allow the holstered gun to naturally follow the fall and be directed at the second attacker.

As the attacker in his grasp was still attempting to control the weapon, Derrick used his right hand to operate the trigger. Even though the gun was still holstered, the bullet erupted from the barrel of the pistol. The second attacker never had a chance to complete his aim or fire his gun as the bullet struck under his cheekbone and fragmented up through his skull. His eyes instantly turned red, and a mist of blood escaped through his mouth and the bullet hole; there was no exit wound. The man suddenly stopped and dropped to the floor like a drone when the power stops.

The first attacker started to fight harder. The knowledge of his partner dying so quickly sparked his desire to survive. He tried desperately to regain control of his weapon. That hope was crushed as the pain of his trigger finger snapping rushed through his hand and to his brain. He was no longer in charge.

Derrick had ripped the gun from the man's hand so quickly and violently that the man's finger almost tore off as he took possession of the weapon. The gun had jammed after being fired from the holster, but Derrick cycled the slide to clear the jam and turned the gun on his attacker as he slowly backed away. As the situation slowed down, Derrick realized that this was the man from last night. The whole thing had been a setup.

"Trina. You alright?" Derrick called out.

Derrick could hear her crying.

"I'm okay. I'm sorry though," she said miserably.

"It's okay, just shut the door and then stay back there." Derrick ordered.

While the gunshot had been suppressed, he wasn't sure if the rest of the noise would go unreported. He looked at the man now sitting on the floor in front of him. He was trying to hold his finger in place while blood ran through the fingers of his good hand. He glanced over at his partner—no doubt he was dead, dark crimson blood was dripping from his mouth and pooling on the floor.

Derrick gave the man an evil grin, his attacker just stared back at him.

"I told you we shouldn't meet again, why are you trying to kill me? It's obvious you're on someone's payroll. Who is it?"

The man fidgeted, blood dripping from his nose, he blew it out onto the floor causing a spray that covered the area in front of him.

"If I say a word, I'm dead," The man said.

Derrick pushed the suppressed pistol up against the man's forehead. "You're dead if you don't."

Derrick felt that deep inside this man was the coward he so easily pretended to be on their first encounter.

The attacker sat there quietly. Derrick pushed the pistol harder up against the man's forehead.

"Talk, your time is running out," Derrick pressured.

"It won't matter, they'll kill me anyway. I failed in killing you and the girl," the would-be assassin mumbled.

"Why me and the girl?" Derrick grilled.

"You were the primary target, she's only collateral they didn't want," the man finally said.

"So, you'd kill a nine-year-old because she helped you?" Derrick angrily probed.

"I'd kill my mom if they told me to, at least I'd know it would be quick. If I refused, they'd send someone who would take their time," the attempted killer continued.

"Who is 'they'? Why do they want me dead?" Derrick continued his interrogation.

"I'm working for the Council. They are huge, bigger than one government, bigger than most governments. If they want, you dead you will be." Now he was crying through his answers.

Derrick contemplated the man's statement. Why would this group want him dead? It didn't make any sense. Unless the Avails were part of that group? But still, how would they know he was coming for them?

Derrick tied the attacker up and started to gather his things. Trina was still laying on the kitchen floor, afraid to get up. Derrick had his duffle filled and grabbed a few drinks from the fridge and tossed them in as well. He returned to the attacker.

"I'll send someone in for you after I've had time to disappear."

"Please don't, just kill me. If I'm found dead, they won't think to harm my family," the man cried.

He could see the fear in the man's eyes as he made the request. Derrick took the pistol and removed the mag. He ejected all the bullets except the one in the chamber. He wiped the gun down well, replaced the mag and set it on the table across from where the man was sitting. With a broken knee and finger, he wouldn't try to get to it and waste the one bullet to shoot at either of them as they left.

Derrick grabbed Trina from the floor. They exited the unit, and he led her to the outside stairs; he didn't want to be trapped in an elevator right now. As they were headed into the stairwell, Derrick heard a muffled *pop* sound. There would be no witnesses to what happened when the police arrived.

14

WORD CAME QUICKLY that the hit on Mr. Avail's potential assassin had failed. She was not happy about this at all.

"I thought we hired only the most proficient people in the world. What happened?"

Cornice Felsder was irate. She was not used to being disappointed.

Her assistant shared what he knew so far.

"Both men were killed, the police are ruling it an accidental shooting and suicide. Their running theory is that these two were looking for the occupant when one accidentally shot the other while trying to draw his weapon. They are looking for the unit occupant who they believe may have witnessed the shooting."

"*Putain de merde*! Make sure those two morons are completely wiped from our systems, link them to the American mob, loan sharks, or something."

The Madam was seething, she had even resorted to swearing in French. Today was spiraling quickly. She still had to call George Avail and push him around.

"That better go well," she thought to herself.

———

GEORGE WAS PACING, the six hours allotted for information about who was after him or Barry was driving him crazy. He checked his watch; it was only thirty minutes since the call. "I can't stand this waiting," George whined.

Barry had worked with George on and off for two decades. Not once in all that time had he ever seen George Avail this jumpy. Something had him off his game. One of the estate's staff entered the room.

"If you'd like, the chef has prepared breakfast in the dining room. Perhaps that would help you wait in more comfort."

"Who said I was waiting for something? Are you eavesdropping?" George erupted on the staff person.

"I'm sorry sir, I just saw you pacing all morning, I just assumed you were waiting on something, I am so sorry for my intrusion," the staff member said apologetically.

George calmed down as fast as he erupted.

"No, I'm sorry that was uncalled for. I have a lot on my mind," George conceded.

George now felt that breakfast was mandatory as a gesture to show his repentance for the outburst. Good staff was hard to find, he didn't want to lose anyone due to his overreaction.

As they stood and headed towards the dining room, security came rushing into the house.

"Sir, it's the FBI, they have a warrant, they're coming down the drive now as we speak, you must use the emergency exit."

George froze in place.

"The FBI? I pay for their protection; how can this be happening?" George asked angrily.

The guard, who intentionally ignored the 'paid for them' part, shared more information.

"Sir, I believe they are here for Mr. Klinger. You both must go now, or this will get ugly fast."

"Don't shoot anyone, obstruct peacefully until we're offsite, but no violence. Understood?" George ordered.

"Yes sir, no violence," the guard repeated back.

Two other guards approached and escorted George and Barry to the rear of the estate. They took an elevator down underground.

———

DEIDRA FINISHED HER CODE. It was now subtly embedded in the Chinese code. Whatever they chose to do, China would now take the blame for it.

Tinker had slept through her fight to save their code. He had no idea how close they came to both being discovered and located. Tinker strolled into her coding area.

"So, how's it going D, are we all set yet?"

Deidra was suddenly angry at her boss. She hated being called D, and he had no idea how hard she had worked with only a couple hours of sleep to advert the threat they had been facing. She bit her tongue.

"I managed to slide us in beneath their radar sir, I think we're good," she said flatly.

"Awesome, do you wanna grab some breakfast with me?" he asked.

Deidra looked at her phone. It was eight thirty a.m. "Sir, I've been up for hours."

"And this is my thank you, I know a place that serves the best breakfast," he pressured.

She knew what he meant. It was the only place he ever went. She knew he'd be back and leave with a pizza at lunchtime. *How is he not three hundred pounds already?* she wondered.

"Sure, let's go," she yielded.

Tinker held out his hand to help her up from the floor where she sat when coding. He then led her to his secret route to the pizza shop.

———

TULIA AND DILLION were watching as Tinker's code took control of the Chinese code without their knowledge. They traced the location of both parties. Tinker's were super hard to nail down and the computer was still following the breadcrumbs it was leaving. The Chinese, proud of their abilities and fearful of no one, allowed their geographical location. Elsy had them hard copy every bit of information they uncovered. It was time to call a friend.

———

PAULA NEWLY HAD ADVANCED QUICKLY since the Lileth Waller case. She was one of the FBI's golden girls now. She hadn't heard from Elsy Davenport in quite a while, but she was aware of her superstar status in the cybersecurity world. Seeing Elsy's name on the caller ID surprised her.

"Elsy Davenport, is that really you? How does such a big shot have time for us lowly public servants?"

"Good morning, Paula, it's been a while, I'm sorry for that. It seems we've both been busy though. I hear you are the new AIC in New England now." AIC meant Agent in Charge.

"Wow news travels fast, I only got here two days ago."

"Unfortunately, this is not a social call. Can we meet? It seems I have what may be another big case for you."

Agent Newly immediately thought of the last 'big' case. It wasn't big, it was gigantic. It was life-altering for all involved.

"You have my attention now. When would you like to meet? My schedule is open for the next two days then I get extremely busy."

"How about now? I'm here in Boston as well. What I have needs your eyes on it as soon as possible."

Paula felt a tinge of apprehension. Not about meeting Elsy, just because if Elsy was anxious, she was smart enough to be as well.

"Nine thirty, Blarney's pub?"

The pub was also a restaurant with a good coffee, plus that would give her forty-five minutes to get there.

"I'll be waiting. Bring your laptop," Elsy said as she disconnected the call.

Paula just sat at her desk for a minute. "Could this be starting all over again?" she wondered.

DERRICK DROVE FOR ABOUT AN HOUR. Trina sat quietly in the front seat. He had offered to take her home or drop her off anywhere. That's when he found out she was homeless and not in the 'system' yet. Her parents had been killed in violence in Atlanta and she ran away to live with her aunt in Florida. Her aunt turned out to be a drug addict and tried to sell her. She had been on the street hustling ever since.

When the man Derrick fought with the night before had approached her and offered her five hundred dollars to distract someone, she jumped at the chance. She had ad-libbed the part about the doll to get some extra cash out of him. She knew he wouldn't break his cover. Later though, he caught back up with her. That's how she ended up at his door.

Derrick pulled off into a state campground in the Everglades. He had prepped his Jeep before leaving New Hampshire with camping gear. Luckily the first sleeping bag he got was too small for him, so he had to buy another, and both were still in the Jeep. He set up his tent and both sleeping bags. He pulled out the cooler he purchased and set it at the back of the Jeep. He threw some wood in the metal fire ring provided at the campground and minutes later he had a fire going. His whole life was now even more complicated—something he didn't think possible.

———

SIMON WAS FURIOUS.

"He was here when we hit the gate! Where is he now?" he screamed, shouting in the face of the supervising officer of the security guards.

"Sir, I'm telling you, we haven't seen this 'Mr. Klinger' you speak of, and Mr. Avail left two days ago," the guard calmly answered.

Simon had walked the whole house, he saw the uneaten breakfast, it was still warm when they entered. He could tell they had been up in the library based on items left in there.

Where had his quarry gone? Who alerted them? Barry would not escape, and now Mr. Avail has added himself to his list. Simon called for another agent.

"I need this room checked and I want this line processed. I want to know every call in and out for the last forty-eight hours," Simon ordered, pointing to a phone on the table.

The agent shook his head and added, "Yes sir, right away."

Simon punched the couch cushion. He was still furious.

"Take them all into custody!" he shouted to the FBI agents. "Someone knows more than they're saying, that's obstruction."

———

THE ELEVATOR STOPPED and the doors opened. George and Barry were hustled to a small SUV waiting in the underground tunnel. The second the doors were closed, the vehicle accelerated forward, driving at a speed that made the rear seat occupants nervous. The driver showed no emotion and seemed as if he had rehearsed this drive a thousand times before. They were in the tunnel for several minutes driving at a high rate of speed. Then the driver began to slow the vehicle. The area up ahead was lighted. Barry looked to see what was coming.

The tunnel widened and they pulled past a similar-looking vehicle to the one they were riding in. They started up a ramp and found themselves inside a residential garage. They heard a strange buzzing squealing noise as the floor behind them rose and sealed the tunnel. The garage door in front opened and the car pulled out and headed in the same direction as it did every morning for the last four years. Not one neighbor would see anything suspicious at all.

———

AS THE POTENTIAL war in Milekistan was starting to heat up, Certain global leaders started to see a chance to be the hero of the situation. The Prime Minister of Germany started to make speeches about how it was the responsibility of the world to avoid this crisis. Others soon rallied around this opportunity to get their names in the press.

Not one of them cared about the actual outcome, they just wanted to see their beautiful faces on the television every night. Almost every one of them had elections coming up in their own countries. The leader of China even took to the press to condemn the US for not standing up to the radical rebels who were undermining the Royal General of Milekistan.

———

MADAM FELSDER ANSWERED her phone after it rang three times. By the caller ID, she knew who she would be speaking to. The caller spoke in Russian, and she answered back in perfect Russian as well.

"Good morning to you too, Mr. President. What do I owe this esteemed honor of your call to?"

She knew exactly why he was calling, but also knew he was a man who needed his ego stroked to be pliable.

"Ah Madam, you know full well why I am calling. Have you spoken to the others yet?" the Russian President asked.

"Luckily for me, you are the first. I am sure the others will reach out soon," Cornice answered.

"Many things are in motion, what is the situation with the American billionaire? Is he under control?" he continued to question.

"He has been spoken to. We are waiting to see if he will need additional encouragement or not. There is a plan in place already should the latter be required," she informed him.

"Ahh very good. It seems you are fully in control, as always. Perhaps we should meet for dinner to discuss the finer details," the Russian invited.

"Thank you, Mr. President, for such an incredible offer, but I'm afraid I can't afford the distraction that would create."

She detested the Russian President but played this game every time she spoke with him.

"I understand Madam, I'm afraid I have that effect on many women. Perhaps when this is done, we may enjoy each other's company," he pushed.

"Yes, perhaps then. Good day, Mr. President," she politely suggested.

She disconnected his call. She knew full well it would deteriorate from there if she had not. Many times before, these calls resulted in pictures of himself being forwarded to her by the President. Those were things she could never unsee.

———

SIMON HAD agents searching the entire residence looking for a hidden safe room. He could tell by the satellite imagery that no one had left the compound. After about four hours, the electronic search crew called him.

"Sir, come to the rear of the structure, we found something you'll need to see."

Simon ran to the rear of the house. In a back hallway, he found two agents standing in front of a wall. They were staring at a screen on an electronic device.

"Sir, there is a room or a closet behind this wall, we just haven't figured out how to open it yet."

Simon grabbed the radio.

"Someone brings the estate manager to the rear hallway. Now."

About a minute later two agents showed up escorting the manager to them.

"How does this open?"

"What open? I don't know what you're talking about."

Simon slapped his hand against the wall, it made a banging noise that echoed down the hall.

"We know it's here, either you tell us how to access it or I bring in a demo team and we disassemble the house until I find what I'm looking for."

The manager contemplated the options, and he glanced at his watch. Seeing the time, he relaxed.

"Okay, yes. See that switch there, move it to the center and hold it there."

An agent reached out and did as instructed, and the wall pulled back and slid away. Right in front of them was an elevator. Simon pushed a call button, and the motor could be heard very softly spinning.

"Where does this go?"

"Well, I've never seen it, but I'm told there is an underground tunnel system below us."

Simon and several other agents entered the elevator. They knew this was a tactical disadvantage if they were being waited on below. Two agents held shields and stood in front, the others, including Simon, were well armed. The descent started.

———

ELSY WAS at the restaurant a little earlier than the time they agreed to. She had become hyper-vigilant regarding safety in the last year. She now suspected almost everyone and everything as a potential threat. She didn't view it as a fear, but more a mindset of preparation. She checked for all the exits and took a mental picture of all the guests in the restaurant. She then chose to wait at the bar where she could watch the entrance until Paula arrived.

It was only a few minutes until the familiar face appeared at the hostess desk. Elsy hopped from the bar and ran over to the hostess desk, drink still in hand. The two women hugged and were shown to a table in the corner Elsy had requested. Elsy went right to the point and filled Donna in on everything. After all the information had been shared, Donna said something that took Elsy completely off guard.

"Elsy, please hold on to all of this, the whole FBI is currently under orders to ignore any social media complaints until after the election. This order comes from Congress itself. I'm sorry, but I can't help. "

"But this is a foreign country that is successfully hacking into the major social media AI servers!"

"Elsy, I love you and I wish I could say more. Please let this go. Now let's have some dinner and forget about this."

Elsy looked at her in stunned disbelief.

"Okay, I'm going to need another drink."

15

THE ORANGE JEEP didn't even stand out in the campground. It was one of at least six other orange Jeeps he saw when he had pulled in. This allowed them to stop a bit more securely. Derrick was still aware that they might be located there, but figured this would at least buy them some time.

He woke before his new young ward, but he hardly slept at all. Even with the attempt on his life and the plan he had already set in motion to enact his retribution for Shannon, his biggest concern was now the little girl still sleeping in the tent. He tried all night with no success to create a reasonable strategy that would keep her safe.

Derrick rekindled the fire in the pit and was making a pot of coffee in a percolator made for camping. He pulled the eggs and bacon he had purchased at a convenience store from his cooler. It only was a few minutes of the bacon sizzling and the distinct aroma drifting into the tent before Trina appeared.

"Is that bacon? I love bacon but I haven't had it in a long time."

"Well, today's your lucky day," Derrick said, grinning.

Trina gave him a sad look, "I haven't had one of those in a long time either."

She hesitated for a second and then continued, "So, what are you going to do with me? You could just leave me here. I can take care of myself…" she said, looking as pathetic as she could muster. "Or you could take me with you, I am an asset, I'm super smart and I have skills," she said, changing her look to a big bright smile.

Derrick wasn't sure how to take her, but he couldn't help smiling at her sales pitch though. He was surprised her choice seemed to be to stay with him.

"Why would you want to stay with me? I am a trouble magnet," he suggested.

"Well, you're also a trouble destroyer, and trouble seems to follow me as well. I think we make a good team," Trina responded.

He smiled. "Well, let's have breakfast and we can talk about it."

Derrick finished the bacon and quickly fried the eggs. They sat quietly and consumed all the food Derrick had made, including a bottle of orange juice he had purchased with the other items.

After they finished, they cleaned up together. Trina worked extra hard to show she was valuable to Derrick. When all was cleaned up and packed away, they sat and talked. Derrick asked Trina to tell him the whole story about how she ended up on the street, right up to how she became associated with the men who tried to kill him. She told him everything, including that she was really thirteen and was just short for her age. She pretended to be a nine-year-old because it was effective at making people pity her instead of being wary of a homeless teenager. Then she thought it was her turn for answers and started to question Derrick.

"Why did those men try to kill you?" she asked.

"I don't know, I have never seen them before," Derrick answered her.

"Who is the Council?" Trina questioned.

"Well, that is the question, isn't it? I have never even heard of them before. I don't know why they're after me, and now you," Derrick replied with a blank look.

"So, what's gonna happen to me?" she said with her most serious look.

Derrick looked at Trina with compassion but uncertainty.

"I'm still trying to figure that out. You've kinda changed my plans," he quietly said.

Derrick finished his talk with Trina and told her he needed to make a call. From the stuff he bought at the convenience store, he pulled out a phone. It was pre-activated, so all he had to do was turn it on and use it.

———

THE AGENTS MET no resistance in the tunnel. As they started to explore, they realized it ran for as far as they could see in both directions. The teams split up and started off on foot. After walking for over a quarter mile, Simon and his team came into an area where the tunnel widened. As they investigated the area, they noticed framework that looked like a large lift of some kind. There were stairs located on the right side of the tunnel based on the direction they had approached from.

Simon radioed the other team what they found and started up the stairs. He pushed up on the lid of a trap-style door he found at the top of the stairs; it moved easily. He was in a room with bits of light shining in from the outside. It only took a second before he realized it was a shed. He walked out the front to find himself in a residential neighborhood less than a mile from the Avail estate.

———

THE SMALL SUV sped on the back roads leading from the suburbs it had escaped from. It arrived in a more congested area and proceeded to blend in with the morning rush traffic. For all intents and purposes, they had disappeared. George and Barry sat quietly in the rear seat until they merged into the local traffic jam. George spoke first.

"So, driver, what is the plan? Where are we headed?"

The driver glanced in the mirror at his passengers.

"Sir, I will drive you to the designated location. That is the extent of my orders."

"Okay, where is this designated location, how long till we are there?"

"A few more hours, sir. I'm not allowed to divulge the location until arrival."

George looked at Barry, who had been silent up to this point.

"So, what is the deal with you and the FBI?" he asked, giving up on the driver.

Barry turned from the window he had been looking out to look directly at the man who was probably responsible for his troubles.

"George, I guess that it probably has to do with you. After all, I do things that aren't exactly legal at your behest."

They both stared at each other. George knew he was right.

"It's not like I'm your only client, though."

Barry laughed at the deflection of guilt.

"You have been my only client for the past ten years. Back then I was contacted by your man Bryce. Now it's directly by you."

The senior Avail thought of the man who had disappeared. Bryce had been an integral part of his world and then vanished. George didn't believe Bryce was still alive.

———

ELSY HAD HEARD of the shooting at her timeshare resort. The silence from Derrick had her even more concerned. Her worry was intensified when she realized there was no longer a police report able to be found in their system. All references to there being a body at the scene were now gone. The news was even reporting that the call and report had been an elaborate hoax.

Elsy knew better—she had played this kind of game before. Someone with a lot of power had gone after Derrick, and she needed to know if he survived. Almost on command, her phone rang. Elsy grabbed it off her desk; the caller ID showed it was not a number she recognized. She was about to cancel the call when the thought that it could be Derrick jumped into her mind.

"Hello?" she answered inquisitively.

"Thank God, I reached you. You will not believe the things that are happening down here."

Elsy was instantly relieved by Derrick's voice.

"What *is* going on down there?"

"That's a long story. Listen I know you gave me too many favors already, but I need another. Can you call Harlem, and meet me in Virginia? There's something I need to show you."

Elsy was stunned by his suggestion. She and Harlem had been working on a long-distance relationship, but she hadn't seen him in over three months. They both had become so busy at work.

"Uh okay, what's going on?"

"Not now. We're already headed for Virginia; we should be there in eleven or twelve hours. I will tell you what I know then."

Derrick hung up before Elsy could ask any more questions. Still, one played over in her head.

"We're? Who are 'we'?"

———

LINDA WAS in her normal location on the deck, and after much harassment, Ebony finally gave up on her uniform and joined Linda in a bikini on the deck area. Despite laying out under the sun, Ebony always had a short-barreled rifle within her reach and her pistol tucked into a bag right next to her chair. Linda had her chair fully reclined, and Ebony's chair was upright. One was worshiping the sun and darkening her tan, the other was on alert and feeling exposed, and possibly inadequate to perform her job if necessary. The second guard came outside to tell Ebony something.

Ebony looked up at her as her mouth opened, but no words came out. Instead, just tiny red droplets seemed to be released that covered her and Linda. The scene was surreal for a second as the lifeless body collapsed to the floor. As her training kicked in, Ebony rolled to the floor and grabbed for her rifle. She then sprinted to Linda, telling her to move to the house immediately. Linda was oblivious to the chaos now surrounding her. Ebony flinched and stumbled as a burning sensation tore through her left calf. She didn't look down, but instead pushed and pulled Linda into the house as two more distinct thuds could be heard hitting the ground around her.

"What is happening?" Linda demanded.

"Ma'am you need to listen and do! No more questions if you want to survive."

Now inside the house, the gunfire quieted. Ebony was sure there would be more people coming. She grabbed her phone and sent the distress text to her employer; she knew there was more of her team not too far away. She dressed her wound quickly, which luckily was not too deep and did not contact the bone. She could still operate near full ability despite her injury. She slid her uniform over her bikini and put on her boots and a gun belt. She felt like herself again.

———

DERRICK HAD HUNG up with Elsy, and he had a plan for now. His vengeance would have to wait some more. He quickly glanced at his picture of Shannon. "Sorry babe, you'll need to wait a bit longer."

"Who's that?" Trina questioned.

Derrick turned to see the inquisitive eyes of Katrina staring at him, waiting for his response.

"Someone I made a promise to, someone I loved."

Trina seemed to accept that answer at face value, but her questions were interrupted by a *pop pop pop*, heard from elsewhere in the campground. Derrick knew the sound; he walked out to the edge of the road looking toward the direction that the shots came from. The other orange Jeep. He could see a dark-colored SUV blocking the driveway for the site where it was. Three men were tearing the site apart. He knew what they were looking for!

"Get in the Jeep, now!" he yelled to Katrina.

She complied without a single question; she was familiar with what those sounds were as well.

Derrick turned the key and the modified V8 engine roared to life. He had no idea where the back way out led to or even if it would let them out of the park, he just knew it was their only option right now.

———

THE SUV with George and Barry had driven around for hours since it left the Arlington estate. The rear seat occupants were now getting a bit anxious to get to a destination—at this point any destination would work.

George called out to the driver, "Do you have a plan besides driving aimlessly around for hours?"

"Yes sir, there is a plan in place, and I am following it," the driver answered.

"Where are you taking us?" Barry inquired.

"As I stated earlier, I'm not allowed to discuss that information while still in transit. I can answer more questions when we get there."

"So, when will we get there?" George pushed.

"We are almost there, sir," Tte driver replied.

A few minutes later, they turned into the driveway of a small house in Virginia Beach. The house had a great view of the ocean, but was smaller than the ones that Mr. Avail was usually accustomed to. There was no staff waiting to greet them, only some gardeners who looked more interested in the neighbors than the plants. Barry knew what they were; they were only disguised as gardeners to placate the neighbors. Glad to be free of the car, they quickly entered the home. Inside they were greeted by the one staff members that had been cleared to be there. She would be the maid, cook, and whatever else, for the duration of their stay.

———

MADAM FELSDER WAS LIVID. Her face was red as could be, she reread the reports on the three separate subjects she had issued orders on.

"Who do we have on this?" she demanded from her assistant.

"Madam, we have deployed our best people in each area respectively."

"Well, it sure doesn't seem that way based on their results, does it? Which is the most likely for us to recover and succeed on?" she asked, hoping she could salvage at least one of her orders.

"Probably the daughter. While she was able to avoid our man's bullet, she is still held up at that location. We have a team en route as we speak."

"I want live updates, if we can keep her alive and capture her, I think that will be more useful to us in the long run," she stated.

"Yes Madam, I will pass that along," her aide acknowledged.

"What about the others? Mr. Avail and the other guy?" she questioned.

"Avail disappeared with the FBI on his trail. Our contacts will keep us updated on that. The other guy we believe has been neutralized according to our team in Florida. They did not find the little girl though," he reported.

"Tell them to keep looking. She's a loose end we don't need," she ordered.

16

THE ROYAL GENERAL slammed his hands down on his desk. The glass of whiskey and his lamp both shook visibly from the impact.

"Why must I wait for the American to tell me when I can defend our country against these rebels?"

His second in command sat across the desk from him in a large brown leather chair.

"Sir, I am unfamiliar with the deal you made, but I would think the protection of your command would supersede any such deal. I say we act now and act swiftly. The rebels are gaining support amongst the softer countries in the world. Soon, we will be the bad guys."

The Royal General's eyes flashed with anger.

"Gather my command staff. We must devise a plan to counter these rebels. I want to know where all their money and weapons are coming from!"

The General's phone on the desk beeped. He hit a button and responded with a voice that betrayed his level of displeasure at being disturbed, "What is it that couldn't wait until I finished this meeting?"

"Sir, there is a foreign diplomat here to see you, he says he has an offer to extend your power."

———

HAVING HAD a night's rest that was long overdue, both Barry and Mr. Avail awoke early the next morning. The smell of coffee and pastry wafted through the house. The lone house employee was earning her keep.

"Barry, I feel we have neglected our plan participants long enough. You will need to reach out to all parties today to reaffirm our agreement," George instructed.

"Yes sir, I was thinking the same thing. The Royal General can be quite difficult if left unsupervised for very long," Barry agreed.

The two took the time to enjoy the homemade pastries that accompanied their coffee. It was a simple breakfast by both of their standards, but satisfying and delicious, nonetheless.

"Please check in on the General today," George urged.

"I will sir. For the rebels though, I will have to travel there again," Barry reminded him.

"Whatever you need. Just be careful, I think we have disturbed the Council and I have no way of knowing what they'll do."

As Barry headed off to make some calls and possibly travel arrangements, George picked up the newspaper that had been left for him.

Another massive fire takes twenty-sixth food processing plant in Indiana.

"Twenty-six, what's up with this?" George wondered to himself. He didn't understand the subtlety of the slow attack being perpetrated on America.

———

AFTER THE TWENTY-FIFTH FIRE, President Harrington asked Congress for an investigation into all the food processing plant fires. Congress told him they would see if there was anything to investigate. In less than a week, their intel committee stated that it was all coincidence and nothing to be concerned with. No investigation would be required. The President then went to his homeland security advisor, who told him the same thing.

Despite their dismissals, President Harrington could not shake the feeling that more was going on than he could see. With the report of this latest fire, President Harrington decided to act. He made a call to the FBI and requested a visit from an agent he knew he could trust.

———

DERRICK AND TRINA were tearing through the dirt roads out of the campground at dangerous speeds. He didn't know how long it would take, but was concerned that the men who attacked the other orange Jeep were probably after them and would soon realize it. Their head start was their best advantage. Derick stopped quickly to look at a real map. Quickly he plotted a route that would take him to I-95 near the Florida/Georgia line using all back roads. It would take longer, but would help keep him from being a sitting duck in traffic.

He looked over at Katrina; she didn't even seem phased.

"Are you doing okay?" he asked.

She had a matter-of-fact expression on her face.

"Do you think those guys were there to kill us?" she questioned.

Any doubt Derrick had about what she knew so far was completely wiped away.

"Yes, probably. You seem to be handling this pretty well," he said, surprised by her calm.

"I'm not scared. I've seen you in action—besides I've got skills as well. You don't survive on the street like me without learning how to defend yourself," she stated firmly.

Derrick navigated the Jeep onto its first paved road in a while. He looked for a gas station as he drove. Having to stop made him nervous, but it had to be done.

———

EBONY TOSSED A BAG AT LINDA. "There's clothes your size in there, put them on now!"

Linda was out of her element; she no longer felt in control of anything. As she lay on the floor it seemed like her world was spinning with no way to stop it.

"Listen to me! Get those clothes on right now. People are coming to KILL us, and we need to move."

Linda forced herself to act. She pulled on the clothes over her sun-worshipping attire and never even thought about the fashion of what she was donning. As she started to pull the laces tight on the shoes, she noticed it was a uniform much like Ebony's. Ebony grabbed her by the arm and low-walked to the stairs leading to the lower level. This level was below grade in the direction of the sniper, so it would give them better cover for a short while. Ebony checked her phone, she had a text. A single word, *Received*—help was on the way.

———

A SMALL TOYOTA truck drove up the driveway at the villa. The two men in the cab were closely watching the house for movement of signs of danger. They didn't see anything, which had them more concerned. When they stopped, three more men emerged from the bed of the truck where they had been hiding themselves from the view of any nosey neighbors. All five men carried suppressed rifles and pistols. They wanted to go as quietly as they could, hoping to accomplish their mission without alerting the authorities.

They split into three groups, one group of two going upstairs from the outside, one group of two going upstairs from the inside, and the single man holding the accessway to the lower level. They moved with a well-rehearsed accuracy and a methodical approach. They did not underestimate their opponent. They needed their prey alive; their entire group was aware that not taking a kill shot would increase the probability that at least one of them could be downed or killed.

———

EBONY HAD TAKEN a hiding spot with the cover that allowed the two groups to bypass their location and head upstairs. While she did not have a suppressor for her pistol or rifle, she did have a combat knife that would be quieter than any gun. It just required more stealth, and potentially more danger, to use quietly and effectively. She was still holding out hope her team would reach them soon as she handed Linda a piece of paper.

"If things go bad, get out and run. Get to that address; they'll know who you are and get you off the island," she said.

Linda read the address, memorized it, and then tucked it into her bikini top beneath her shirt.

"Now get down and stay down, until I tell you otherwise or you see me go down."

She handed Linda a gun. "Do you know how to use this?" she asked.

Linda shook her head yes.

"Good, don't use it unless you have no choice. It will give away your position," she instructed.

As Linda secured her hiding spot, Ebony moved into position to silently attack the single member of the attack squad. She moved swiftly and without any noise—her prey never knew the danger he was in until it was too late. From a dark corner, she sprang onto him like a tiger. She drove her knife deep into his neck, severing his carotid artery. Blood immediately gushed out of the wound as she removed the knife and plunged it between the plates of his body armor, piercing his right lung.

In an effort to stave off this vicious attack, the man bent over and tried to throw Ebony from his back. This resulted in him collapsing to the floor with her on top. With a final and probably unnecessary blow, she struck the last time with her knife at the base of his skull, using both hands to drive the blade through his spinal column and severing the brain stem. The body stopped moving. She withdrew her weapon and re-sheathed it. She checked the suppressed rifle the man had dropped. It had a full mag and one in the chamber.

She held the weapon in a low-ready position. Satisfied that her attack was as quiet as it could have been, and now armed with a suppressed rifle, she turned to get Linda. Instead, to her surprise, she was facing the second two-man team. One of the men raised his weapon towards her, she dove behind a stack of boxes that were to her right. She heard the suppressed weapon fire at her as she moved. The boxes were suddenly jumping as if they were alive. Ebony returned fire blindly; she only had one mag in the gun, thirty-one rounds max. She felt her odds diminishing.

As the gunfire continued in her direction, she felt as though she was suddenly punched in the gut with a hot iron poker. It struck right below her body armor. She felt the area with her hand, it was warm and sticky. She knew what that meant. One of the bullets found a path. One last thing to do.

"Linda, run!" she yelled at the top of her lungs.

She heard two loud *pops* and then nothing. She waited.

————

LINDA APPEARED AROUND THE CORNER, pistol in hand. As Ebony came into her view, she saw the blood.

"You're hit, let's go before the other guys get here." Linda helped Ebony to her feet.

Ebony was surprised to see her attackers both downed with head shots. She pointed to one of the dead man's rifles.

"Grab that and those mags on his belt."

Linda was like a new person compared to when Ebony had left her. She was suddenly in charge again. As Linda helped Ebony toward a large sedan parked in the portico, they could hear the other two team members calling out to their partners. They got to the car and Ebony looked at Linda.

"Thank you for saving me, but you must go now, get to that address, they'll get you safe. I'm gonna buy you some time."

Linda knew exactly what that meant.

"Let's both go," Linda pleaded with her.

Ebony now started to show signs of blood loss, her face was getting pale, and her skin was sweating profusely.

"I wish I could. Please, go. Let me finish my job," Ebony stated firmly.

Linda hugged her briefly and turn and got into the car. As she drove away from the villa, she could see flashes of light as Ebony and the last two attackers exchanged gunfire. Linda drove away as fast as she could.

————

THE ROYAL GENERAL took the call from Barry.

"Good evening Mr. Klinger," he did not account for the time change where Barry was calling from.

"Good evening to you as well, Mr. Royal General," Barry replied.

The General didn't want to be bothered by small talk. "So, what do you expect me to do for you today, Mr. Klinger?"

"Since you want to get right to the point, I am calling to make sure we can stay on our timetable. This is most important to your financier," Barry reminded him.

"Ah, see that is why life is unpredictable. I have received new funding that comes with little to no requirements for me. I'm afraid, Mr. Klinger, that your influence with my regime is over. It is probably best if you remain out of my country as well."

The call ended abruptly; Barry was dumbfounded by this unexpected turn of events.

What the hell is going on? he wondered.

———

THE CHINESE AMBASSADOR sat in front of the Royal General as he ended his call.

"Mr. Royal General, China will be a great friend to Milekistan for your loyalty to our agreement. As soon as you put an end to this uprising, China will help build the power plant you need for your whole country to have prosperity."

The Royal General stood and extended his hand. "Tell the Great Leader that I am most happy to be his new ally."

The two men exchanged goodbyes and the ambassador exited.

The General called his aide back into the room.

"China has agreed to our demands and will build us the nuclear power plant to power our entire country. We must end this war with the rebels. We will not negotiate. We will exterminate. Please send this message to our troops. The time to push forward is now. I have abandoned the deal with the Americans. He no longer has any value to us." The General said this like he was giving a victory speech.

———

PAULA RETURNED to her office the day after the dinner with Elsy. She was bothered that Elsy had actionable intel that she was barred from pursuing by a new department directive. Paula's inquisitive side took over. She pulled the document regarding this order up on her computer screen. Who would order such a thing, she wondered? First, she re-read the document, it clearly prohibited all agents not specifically designated from pursuing any social media tampering related cases or leads. It went as far as to list the penalties for failing to follow the document, which were up to and including termination without notice.

Paula scrolled down to see who authored this seemingly contrary-to-the-law document. Instead of a name of a superior, it contained a number. She was more perplexed now than before; she didn't even know what the number meant. How could a document of such monumental importance carry so much weight without even the name of a single superior on it?

There was a knock on her office door; her assistant was standing in her doorway.

"Ma'am, the White House is requesting your presence for a meeting with the President," her assistant informed her.

"The President himself? Do we know what about?" Paula queried.

"No ma'am. I was just told to schedule your flight and accommodations," her aide replied.

"So, when is this meeting?" Paula asked.

Her assistant reached out with a bag.

"Your bag is packed here, The flight leaves in twenty minutes. Your meeting is upon arrival," the aide said.

Paula continued to be surprised by the direction today was going in.

"Thank you," she said as she took her bag packed by her assistant.

"The car is waiting, ma'am," her aide advised.

Paula exited her office unsure if she had everything she needed. She hated being rushed.

17

THE BLACKHEART RESPONSE team arrived to find a mess. Two of their personnel were down, one dead and one in critical condition. They also found five dead members of an assault team. What they failed to find was their client. Daniel Wright was the supervisor for the response team. He ordered his team to secure the premises and conduct a thorough search for the primary asset. He also called for a medic helicopter to grab his downed agent. Ebony Godd had suffered numerous gunshots and severe loss of blood. Daniel knelt beside her, unsure if she could hear or answer him.

"What happened here?" he asked.

Ebony weakly grabbed at his pant leg. "She went to extraction." These were the last words she spoke.

Daniel moved to allow his team medic to start the process of trying to revive her. He worked at it for twenty minutes while awaiting the helicopter. Revival was not possible due to the amount of blood she had lost.

———

LINDA REALIZED she knew very little about the roads on the island. She had driven for five minutes and decided to pull over to activate the GPS with the address Ebony had given her. While she was pulled over, she saw several cars fly by headed in the direction of the villa. She wondered if any of them were friends or more attackers, intent on harming her or the guard who saved her.

She resisted the urge to turn around and go to try to help her. It was an urge she was quite surprised she had. She knew Ebony's wound was severe and most likely would have already killed her. Going back would accomplish nothing and belittle Ebony's sacrifice. With the location locked in, Linda put the car in drive and raced off toward what she hoped would be security and freedom.

———

THE SECOND WAVE attack team showed up too late—the Blackheart team was already onsite.

The lead car radioed in for directions. "Security team already onsite with perimeter locked down. No visual on the target. Please advise."

The radio was silent for a few seconds. "Do you think the primary is still on site?" was the reply.

"Sir it's unknown. It appears that casualties were suffered by all members of Team One." The second team leader responded.

"Understood, stand by for orders."

"Standing by."

A minute later their orders were delivered. "Team Two, you are a go for assault, we must have hard intel on the status of the primary. When the status or capture is verified, you should retreat with primary if possible."

"Understood."

The Team Two leader called his men together. "We are a go, securing the primary target is our only goal, we fight our way in, grab the girl and get out. That is the only objective. Is everyone good? Let's go."

The team of eight men was separated into two groups of four. The first group would engage the Blackheart soldiers, the second would do their best to get in undetected and find Linda. The first group initiated contact, a third Blackheart agent went down, and the response was instantaneous. Blackheart soldiers swarmed the four-man force.

Five minutes of sustained gunfire later, the four-man team was eliminated. The Blackheart leader called for an immediate sweep for others. The other half of Team Two was located trying to breach the rear of the compound, and another firefight ensued. The attackers had their orders; it was far better for their families if they would die fighting, than to turn and run. The second half of Team Two fought fiercely, but the Blackheart force was better armed and more prepared. In the end, all the attackers were neutralized, and Blackheart suffered an additional two lost agents.

————

THE PLANE RIDE was short from Boston to Washington. Paula was greeted by a Secret Service agent on the tarmac where the small jet taxied to. Her only luggage was the small overnight bag that had been packed for her and the laptop bag she brought from her office. She was rushed to a black sedan, where the agent ushered her into the rear seat and then jumped into the front. She had barely fastened her seatbelt before the car lurched forward and sped towards the White House.

A million thoughts were rushing through her mind, and not one of them was even remotely close to what the President wanted. The car pulled up to a covered private entrance and she was escorted inside by more Secret Service agents. Despite her being with the FBI, she was asked to leave her weapon with the agents during her visit. She handed it over and was given a voucher by an agent sitting at a little desk in the hallway. She was then searched with a metal detector before being led on to her meeting with the President.

————

LINDA ARRIVED at the address she was given by the agent; the house looked almost abandoned. Quietly as she could, she opened the car door and walked to the house. She was still dressed in the guard outfit she had been told to wear. She had left the rifle she picked up in the car, but she still had Ebony's pistol tucked in her waistband. Out of nowhere, she thought about how comfortable the bulky black boots she had been given were. She tried to peek through the windows, they appeared to be blacked out with paint or something.

Taking a deep breath and slowly letting it out, she took her left hand and rapped on the door three times, her right hand firmly gripping the pistol behind her back. She could hear some movement inside. The door whipped open, Linda saw an arm extend which grabbed her and pulled her inside. The door slammed behind her. It was quite dark inside and it took a bit for her vision to adjust from the bright sunlight that was outside.

Before she could draw the pistol, it was taken from her by an unknown person. She heard some people talking quietly, but she couldn't make out what they were saying. Two things she did hear though, "Blackheart" and her name. She had been led to a chair and politely asked to sit while also being gently pushed into it. She wasn't sure if she had found a way to freedom or another trap. As her vision started to adjust, she could see the outlines of at least five people.

"Are you going to help me get off the island?" she asked.

The outline closest to her moved up to her face. She could see him now. He had a beard and dark hair. The skin that was uncovered around his face was weathered, like an old seaman.

"Miss Avail, we will most certainly get you off the island. Right now, we are awaiting instructions to verify our route is safe. Unfortunately, the accommodations will not be up to your normal standards. There is a bathroom here, and a bag of clothes in the bedroom. I suggest you shower and change. It could be a while before you get the next opportunity to do so again."

Linda listened to every word he said and let each one sink in. She stood up.

"Which way to that shower?" she asked almost casually.

A younger female came over to her and said in a soft voice, "Follow me Miss Avail, I'll show you where everything you need is. I'll also make sure none of these degenerates try to spy on you."

The other men in the room started to laugh.

Linda was sure there was some inside joke, but she wasn't privy to it.

She simply said, "Thank you."

———

GEORGE SLAMMED HIS PHONE DOWN.

"What is going on?" he shouted.

There wasn't anyone there to answer him. All morning he was trying to verify the things he had put in place to make sure his operation would go as planned. The problem was, people who he thought he "owned" politically were refusing to assist him—and in some cases, they wouldn't even take his call.

This was unprecedented in his lifetime of political manipulation. As one of the richest men in America and the world, he had always achieved his goals by manipulating others. This operation was not going that way. He knew he was working with a global entity, but he never dreamed that they would act on their aspirations to take over the American government. Political manipulation had always been his domain. In his mind, this was an act of war. He just didn't know where or how to fight back. He called the assistant of the house.

"If Barry is still around, I need him back here immediately," he ordered.

"Yes sir, I will locate Mr. Klinger and inform him of your wishes," the assistant said.

———

ELSY BOARDED HER COMPANY JET. The destination had already been confirmed with their flight plan. The crew was prepared for her arrival. The flight attendant took her bags and stowed them, while the captain spoke with his passenger briefly.

"Welcome aboard Miss Davenport, we are ready to go if you are?" he informed her.

"Yes Captain, let's get there as soon as possible," Elsy replied.

The captain relocated to the cockpit and moments later was heard on the jet's intercom.

"We are cleared for taxi, please make sure your seatbelts are fastened."

Elsy cinched her lap belt a little tighter; she didn't like to fly. But sometimes it was required by the client or by circumstance, and this was one of those circumstances.

After the sudden feeling of being sucked into her seat, the jet rose effortlessly into the sky. Elsy relaxed a bit and withdrew her laptop from its bag beside her.

She logged into her company's system remotely. This gave her the ability to see in real-time what was going on with the issues she had been dealing with.

———

DERRICK AND KATRINA sped along back roads and smaller town roads as much as possible. He was surprised by the number of seemingly back roads with a fifty-five mile-per-hour speed limit. His trip to Virginia Beach was going to take longer than expected, though. Elsy would be there way before him. He was pretty sure that would be good for both her and Harlem. It had been three hours of driving, and they still weren't out of Florida yet.

The good news is that they hadn't seen anyone following them or trying to kill them yet. Even with the big engine in the Jeep, gas would last okay—he had filled up the two gas cans he carried on the back as well. That would make his fuel stops unpredictable for anyone who was trying to follow them. The one thing he was trying to locate now was some food and a bathroom appropriate for a little girl.

———

TINKER HAD COMPLETED another portion of his assignment and was awaiting contact for payment. In all the years he provided his service to his current client, he had never once been late with a payment or contact regarding the job. Today marked three days past the agreed contract date. Tinker checked his screens again. No law enforcement chatter, no death notices, not one thing regarding his client that would explain what was going on. He became afraid that once again, he might be in jeopardy and would need to run. He liked this spot—it was easily his most favorite, he would fight to protect this one. He looked around the room at the people he now employed. His eyes settled on one. "I will fight for her as well if it comes to that. She's too good at what she does to leave defenseless," he murmured to himself.

Meanwhile, he kept up the search, hopeful that his client would call with his payment.

———

HARLEM POSADA WAS at work when his phone rang. He smiled at the caller ID. He turned to his partner.

"I'll be back in a second, I need to take this."

He accepted the call.

"I was just thinking about you. You must have read my mind," he said into the phone.

"I'm in Virginia Beach, I'll see you soon. Something is going on with a friend of mine and he asked for our help. I said yes," Elsy informed him.

Harlem had been hoping for a much more personal response, after all, it had been about three months since they last saw each other, and the calls were becoming less frequent as well. Long-distant relationships were difficult.

"Okay, yeah, anything you need. I can't wait to see you. Do you need a ride from the airport?" hHe asked, hopeful she say yes.

"I have a car here now; I'm looking forward to seeing you as well. I'll be there in about thirty minutes," she answered.

Elsy hung up, leaving Harlem's head spinning. That was a lot of unexpected information.

Harlem looked at his new partner. He wondered if he was that inept initially when he worked with Beckett Swede, his old partner who retired. He called to his rookie detective, "Let's wrap this up. I think we have all we need for now."

———

BARRY HAD BEEN STANDING on the lawn making calls when the house help found him.

"Mr. Avail has requested that you come inside and meet with him immediately," he was told.

"Okay, I'll be in shortly," Barry responded.

"I don't think he is in the mood to wait," the assistant told him.

"Damn it, okay let's go," Barry conceded.

Barry was concerned to tell George what had occurred on the call with the Royal General. He was also afraid that this might not be an isolated incident. His gut was telling him they were being attacked from all sides.

George was inside the home office on the computer, a place he was not normally associated with.

"George, what's going on?" Barry asked as he entered.

"Sit down. I'm afraid while we thinking we were the puppeteers, we were actually the puppets," George informed him.

George was typing frantically on the keyboard. He'd hit 'enter' and anxiously await the results. This went on for a few minutes until he turned to Barry to give him his full attention.

"I have unwittingly put myself in a very bad position. I believe a government member of the Council may be acting against us. The headlines in the news indicate a plan they have been pursuing for many years. I fear we may have missed the writing on the wall," George extolled.

He took a long deep breath and slowly let it out.

"We may have been compromised by a more powerful player," he added.

"Sir, tell me exactly what is going on," Barry pleaded.

"While you were contacting the Royal General, I reached out to what I thought were solid contacts that I had purchased a long time ago for assistance. To my surprise they rejected my calls, only one accepted the call and then told me that I needed to stand down. I was quite disturbed, so I picked up the paper to calm my thoughts regarding these betrayals. It's all right here—it's been here the whole time, and no one is looking anymore.

Our food supply is being bought out or destroyed, our farmland is being sold off to foreign countries, multiple countries are moving away from the dollar as their backup currency, and our infrastructure is being hacked daily. This was a plan China submitted to the Council years ago; they were asked to table it until a later date. It appears now may be the later date. We are in a war with China, and no one even knows," George was obviously disturbed.

His face was bright red, and he was starting to sweat. Barry encouraged Mr. Avail to take a moment to calm down. He wasn't sure what had gotten his client so agitated, but the story he had woven was concerning.

"George, let me see what you have, let me look at it objectively and see what I think," Barry suggested.

George handed him the paper along with the notes he had scribbled across it.

"Go ahead, Mr. Know-it-all," George chided him.

18

THE IDENTITY of the man killed in the campground had just been delivered. A new young aide had been the one chosen to bring her the bad news. He approached her quietly, full of fear—and rightly so. She was highly unpredictable when she was angered. The information he carried was sure to anger her. He stopped at her desk; her back was turned to him.

"Ut'hm. Ma'am, here is the document you requested," he said quietly, with audible fear in his voice.

She turned and eyed him up,

"You're new. How bad is it?" she asked.

"I haven't read it, ma'am, I was told to deliver it to you," he said, hands shaking.

"Those cowards. Do you know why you were asked to deliver this to me?" she asked with a smirk on her face.

"Not really ma'am, they said it was part of being accepted and that everyone had to do it," he relayed to her.

"Sit down, let me tell you a story," she encouraged him.

The aide sat down; he was more scared now than when he walked in. He had heard the stories, but did not want to repeat them to her.

"Young man, they are afraid of me because bad news angers me, Sometimes I lash out, sometimes most violently. I am assuming this report contains bad or extremely bad news," she said, pointing to the folder.

He shook his head affirmatively.

"The last time I got such bad news, I reached down to this drawer and pulled this out." As she was saying it, she reached into her desk drawer and retrieved a Walther PPK pistol.

I then proceeded to point it at the bearer of the bad news and pulled the trigger, it made an awful mess, and it took them two days to clean it all up," she said matter-of-factly.

The aide sat completely still, the color slowly disappearing from his face. He started to wonder if this was his last day on Earth. Why did his fellow workers hate him so much?

As if reading his thoughts, she continued.

"Do not think your fellow workers don't like you; they only like themselves better. Each of them was afraid they might die—the same fear you're having now. That will not serve any purpose today, so you may go. I won't open this till you're gone," she promised.

The aide sprang from the chair, turned to go, and realized his leg had fallen asleep. What was supposed to be his first step toward freedom was his introduction to the floor instead.

In the main area, his coworkers were watching to see how it would turn out. They saw her retrieve her gun from the drawer, they saw him get up to run, and then the poor guy face planted right to the floor. They were all sure she shot him. Not one of them considered why they hadn't heard a shot.

After a second, the body moved, and as he started to get up, they all stood awaiting a kill shot. It never came. The aide stood up rubbing and shaking his leg. Even giggling as the pins and needles feeling sent a nervous tickle up his leg. From the doorway, he could see what appeared to be the whole staff looking at him. All of them had eyes and mouths wide open. He laughed and then walked as fast as he could before she changed her mind.

———

PRESIDENT HARRINGTON CALLED Paula into his office; his Chief of Staff was the only other person present.

"Good morning Paula, Welcome to the White House. What we're about to discuss is what I believe to be an issue of National security." He offered her a seat and a coffee and then continued, "Numerous fires have occurred in food processing and distribution plants all across this country. Ever since I lost Congress in the midterm election, they have been fighting my desire to investigate these fires. It seems they may have a hold in the FBI as well. I've heard rumors that you've been prohibited from looking into certain cases until after the election. I am appointing you as a special lead investigator for these processing plant fires. I need to know whether they are just coincidence, or a quiet attack on American food suppliers," the President finished.

"Yes sir, I will do my best. May I have the latitude to bring on a few investigators that I trust to assist in this investigation?"

"You may have whatever latitude you need to get to the bottom of this. You should try to stay under the radar as much as possible though. I feel this is more than a partisan issue that I'm fighting against."

"Thank you for your trust in me, Mr. President. I will do my best to unravel this mystery for you," she said. As she met his gaze, there was something else in his eyes as well; she looked away.

Paula shook the President's hand, the thoughts in her head made her blush ever so slightly. *How could he still be single?* she wondered. She took the envelope containing his Presidential Order that authorized her actions with her as she was escorted to the same place she entered. She retrieved her gun and her small bag and went out to the same car that was still waiting for her. As the car was pulling out, her cell phone rang.

"Hello, this is Agent Newly."

"Agent Newly, this is the office of the Director. We are calling to verify your new orders. You will report to the Virginia FBI offices to conduct your new investigation. You have been assigned a remote private office located in Virginia Beach. I am texting you the address."

Paula hung up and smiled. "Back to Virginia Beach; this will be fun."

LINDA WAS SHUFFLED into the rear of a passenger van. It had darkened windows that kept anyone from looking in. They were taking her away from here, and hopefully to safety. The drive was short and when the door slid open, she was looking at a small plane with twin engines.

"Your ride to the States, ma'am. We know it's not up to your normal standards, but this way will keep your location and destination secret longer," the driver said.

"I'm grateful for all your help. Does anyone know how Ebony made out? Did she get to a hospital?" Linda asked.

The look on the man's face answered her question.

"Oh, my God. She died?" Linda inferred.

The driver assisting her into the small plane answered solemnly, "I'm sorry to say, yes ma'am."

Linda secured herself in her seat and the twin-engine Cessna taxied down the runway and lifted off. She thought about Ebony. She wasn't sure anyone had ever sacrificed anything willingly for her in her entire life up to this point. She still had no idea who was after her or why, but she was grateful to be alive. Hopefully, she would be able to contact her father and get some answers.

———

BARRY WAS WORKING on a laptop he had just acquired, and George was on his cell phone with a black notebook by his side. They were both trying to piece together the real facts behind why they were suddenly targeted and were now being ignored by the very people George had placed into office. The answers they were finding were all starting to point in the same direction. There was a much bigger player involved who wasn't aligned with Mr. Avail's current plan. George looked at Barry after setting his phone down.

"It seems, my friend, that we are being replaced by an extracurricular player. My guess would be the World Council is making a move against us. I think we need to find out why that is," George said, still keeping his actual plan from even Barry.

"I concur with your assessment. I also think we need to be careful. The Council will not hesitate to remove us or those we love to facilitate their goals," Barry agreed.

"I should reach out to Linda and warn her," George said, as if it had suddenly occurred to him.

"Sir, she's with the Blackheart guys, I'm sure she couldn't be safer. Besides, they would call if there was an issue," Barry stated.

As if on cue, the phone that George had placed on the table started to ring.

He snapped it up quickly. "Hello."

"Hello Mr. Avail, we had an incident at your villa. Your daughter is safe and being relocated as we speak. There was an exchange of gunfire with a group that we are still trying to identify. We killed thirteen of them, but we lost four good agents. I thought you'd like to know your daughter is safe," the caller stated.

"When did this happen, and where is Linda now?" George asked calmly.

"Sir, it happened several hours ago. We were unable to reach you at first due to your changing phones. Your daughter is en route to your location. We are also sending you more guards for your protection."

"Can I speak to Linda; does she have a phone with her?" George inquired.

"No sir, she's on a plane right now. She should touch down in the States very soon."

George hung up the phone. In all his life, he had never been on the victim side of any scenario. He was angry.

———

DERRICK HAD BEEN DOING his best to make good time headed towards Virginia. The whole part of sticking to back roads wasn't the fastest route. They had been driving for several hours now and Trina needed a break— and so did he, if he was being honest. They pulled off into the parking lot of a little diner somewhere in South Carolina. They headed inside, and Trina went straight to the restroom. She had been asking Derrick to stop for the last thirty minutes. Derrick waited for the waitress to show him a table and then called to Katrina when she exited the lady's room.

"You good now?" he asked her.

"You try holding your pee forever, see how you feel," Trina responded with a slight irritation in her voice.

The two checked out the menu. It was a large selection for such a small restaurant. Trina was the first to decide.

"I'm gonna have the double bacon cheeseburger with loaded cheese fries and a strawberry shake," she announced triumphantly.

Derrick slowly lowered his menu and peered over the top at her.

"That meal will weigh more than you," he harassed.

She grinned.

"Well, then I guess I'm gonna double my weight," she said, as if it were a fact.

They ordered their food and Derrick watched as she devoured the whole meal she ordered. When the straw made the sound indicating her shake was gone, she asked Derrick if she could get one for the road.

"Sure, get us both one. I'd like a coffee shake. I'm going to use the restroom while you order, okay?"

"I got it, large coffee shake," Trina repeated.

The waitress came over and Trina placed the to-go order. When Derrick returned, he noticed two men sitting in a booth by the door. Neither of them had ordered anything, and both seemed to be very interested in him and Trina. Derrick checked the bill on the table. He tossed down enough cash to cover it and the tip. Katrina pointed at the now empty table.

"We gotta wait for our shakes, silly," she said.

Derrick was about to tell her they'd have to go without them when the waitress appeared with a paper bag with both shakes inside.

"Here ya go dear, you folks have a nice trip to Florida," the waitress offered.

Derrick gave her quizzical look.

"Uh yeah, thank you," Trina responded.

Trina winked at him. On the way to the Jeep, she opened the bag.

"You can never be too careful with who you talk to, and always check your order before you leave. She got it right."

Derrick glanced over his shoulder; the two men were still in the diner. They were watching him and Katrina walk to the Wrangler. Options were spinning around in his head: do nothing, probably a bad move; attack first, also a bad move. Derrick decided on a third option: set a trap. He grabbed Trina gently but firmly by the arm and led her away from the Jeep.

"Follow my lead," he whispered.

Trina understood what Derrick meant. She didn't resist or react, she stuck to his side. Something was about to happen.

————

THE TWO MEN had been trying to watch the orange vehicle but without being obvious. The man and girl in the diner appeared to match the description they were looking for, but why would they be headed back to Florida? They watched as the two exited the diner and headed for the parking lot. Only they weren't headed for the Jeep. The two men grabbed their menus to look less suspicious. Suddenly their potential prey was gone from sight; they laid down their menus. The orange Wrangler was still there, but no one else in the diner fit the description they were looking for. The taller one of the men dropped a hundred-dollar bill on the table as they both left the booth and headed outside. The tall man was obviously in charge as they walked from the diner.

"Let's find those two. We need to wrap this up and meet up with the other team to help them out," he said to his shorter partner.

Quietly they walked through the few cars in the parking lot. The neon sign on the road and a streetlamp were their only illumination. The tall guy pulled a pistol from his waistband. It was fitted with a light that he turned on. The second guy followed his direction. As he led the way, the tall guy wondered if maybe they were about to murder another innocent family like it turned out they did at the campground.

As he pondered his previous errors, he never noticed the quiet movement behind him or that his partner was swiftly and silently rendered unconscious. By the time he realized he was alone, it was too late. He turned in time to see a large wooden branch level with his face moving right at him. He didn't have time to duck or raise his arm. He was airborne briefly and unconscious before he struck the ground.

————

"OOF, THAT HAD TO HURT," Trina gasped as she watched the man go down.

She grabbed at her face in a sympathetic gesture to what had occurred.

"Here, take his keys and find their car," Derrick instructed her while he was tying up the tall man.

Trina held the fob in the air and hit the lock button. A large black sedan chirped its horn and flashed its lights.

"Open the trunk," Derrick instructed.

Katrina complied by hitting the trunk button on the key fob.

Derrick dragged the first man over and tossed him in the trunk. He was already starting to moan a bit. He would wake up soon. Derrick went and retrieved the second guy and carried him over to the trunk as well. He tossed him in on top of his partner and slammed the trunk closed.

"Now what?" Trina asked.

Derrick looked at the cash he had swiped from both men. It was just shy of three grand.

"We're running because of them. They might as well finance us," he smiled and winked at Trina as he said it.

She laughed, because she approved of his way of thinking.

———

THE PLANE LANDED with no issues. It was a small runway and barely had any resemblance to an inhabited area. There was an SUV waiting by the fuel building the plane was taxiing towards. She could see the lights of a housing community along a lake when they were landing, but she wasn't sure how close it was now. After the plane stopped and the cabin door opened, a man stepped from the SUV and opened the rear door. Linda was rushed from the plane to the SUV.

"I'm sorry ma'am, but we still have a long drive ahead of us to get you to safety." Linda slid into the rear seat. There was a second man in the front passenger seat. He was talking on the cell phone and was armed with a rifle. The driver assumed his position and the vehicle was underway.

The passenger looked at the driver.

"Avoid the highways for a while. Let's not make their job too easy."

The driver took off on a back road he was driving as fast as he dared. After he had driven for a bit, he could see some lights on the side of the road ahead. He slowed the SUV a bit so as not to draw the attention of local police. As he got almost on top of the roadside sign, an orange Jeep came bursting out of the parking lot onto the road right in front of him. The driver slammed his brakes in response to the sudden appearance of the Wrangler. It was only directly in front of him for a second and then it was barreling down the road at an even greater speed than he had been traveling. The driver questioned the incident aloud.

"What the hell was that? And what kind of engine does he have in there?"

19

THE COUNCIL ASSOCIATES called a meeting as the outcome of recent events had them concerned. They had been promised a significant move toward their goal was on the near horizon, yet all they were seeing was repeated failure. They were being bested by a single old billionaire and an assumed hitman with a little girl in tow, and now they couldn't even find the billionaire's daughter.

Cornice Felsder was all it said on her nameplate at the table. Sitting around her were other familiar faces, however, there didn't seem to be a friendly one in the lot of them.

Pierce Bins was a consigliere of the Council, it was his role to facilitate and run these group meetings. Despite the daily hierarchy that existed in operations, there was none other than Pierce during these meetings. Tonight, this was his room, and all who were in attendance knew that. He called the meeting to order from a massive elevated wooden chair that was set back from the table; a location that allowed him to see every member. He consulted an agenda that everyone had agreed to before attendance and explained that the purpose was to address issues with operations currently underway.

"I would like to start," a man at the far end of the table spoke.

"Ming Shu Li, it would be our honor to hear your words," Pierce stated in a flagrant showy tone.

"I have concerns that the goals established in this Council may be exposed or worse yet corrupted by our current actions in America. Why have we gone after Mr. Avail and his daughter? They have never stood in our way before, and why are we pursuing some unknown man and a little girl? What purpose does this serve to our end goals?" He already knew the answers, but China was hoping to sow some infighting amongst the Council members to obfuscate their own actions.

There were quiet murmurings that went around the table immediately following these questions.

"I vish to be heard as vell," came another voice just to the left of where Pierce was observing from his elevated position.

"Victor Dubrovic, you may speak."

"I also am concerned with these failures that Ming speaks of. We have poured billions of dollars, and numerous hours, and even lives into creating an executable plan that would bring the vision of this Council to life. It seems recent actions may be jeopardizing that plan."

There was silence for a few seconds and then another voice spoke.

"I request to be heard to answer these questions."

"Cornice Felsder, you may speak, but you should know your words may be used against you by members of this Council."

She shook her head indicating she understood.

"First of all, I would like to say that my actions ALWAYS consider the goals of this Council. That is why I am confident I can answer your questions to your satisfaction. The American was targeted because he was pursuing Mr. Avail and I felt that he was getting too close to our involvement that is running adjacent to Mr. Avail's plans. The young girl was used as part of the initial attack on the American and has been targeted because I felt she has too much knowledge of our existence. Lastly, Mr. Avail is pushing his agenda that could expose or diminish our goals. The daughter's capture was meant to provide us leverage to control him more readily."

Ming spoke without being acknowledged.

"But you didn't kill the man or the girl, and you haven't captured the daughter, and now you've lost track of Mr. Avail. Isn't that correct, Madam Felsder?"

Pierce spoke from his platform. "I would ask that members await being called upon before speaking to the table. Mr. Ming, your question has been heard. Any response?"

This time the Madam remained silent. The table seemed to erupt into a semi-quiet chatter, with small group talking amongst themselves. Only one was left to sit by herself and await the decisions made by the Council.

———

THE DOOR SWUNG OPEN, and Harlem was staring at Elsy's beautiful eyes. He was so happy to see her. The moment was shattered when Elsy snapped at him.

"You gonna stand there, or help me with my bags?" she asked.

Harlem jumped from his trance and reached for the larger of her two bags.

"I'm sorry, I was just caught up in your physical presence, it's been too long since I saw you last," he said apologetically.

"Yeah yeah, whatever. I'm glad I'm here too," she said with a grin.

She leaned forward and kissed him; he pulled her in close in an enveloping hug, she hugged him equally tightly.

He was right, she thought, *it has been too long.*

They stood and hugged firmly for several minutes before they released each other and moved farther inside of Harlem's house. They put the bags down in the bedroom and returned to the kitchen. Harlem offered her food, but she declined.

"So why is your friend Derrick coming here?" Harlem asked.

"I'm not sure, he didn't say. All I know is that he said he had something important to show us," she answered.

Harlem drummed his fingers on the counter. "So when will he be here?"

Elsy wrinkled her nose. "That part I'm not exactly sure about, he ran into some trouble in Florida and is driving here from there."

———

THE SUV that Linda was riding in had slammed on its brakes when the Jeep cut it off. It was then that the driver noticed the shape of a car behind him, but no headlights were on. The guard started to accelerate, and when suddenly the lights came on behind him, he accelerated more. It wasn't long before he overtook the Jeep and passed it. The Jeep driver gave him an evil stare and reduced his speed. This was beneficial to the SUV driver, as it placed another car between him and the car that was now obviously following them. He watched in his mirror as the chase car caught up to and passed the Wrangler.

"Damn, no buffer," he mumbled under his breath.

Linda noticed that something had changed about the atmosphere in the SUV. The guard in the passenger seat was checking his weapon and the driver was now driving at an accelerated speed.

"What's going on, gentlemen?" she inquired.

"Ma'am we're being pursued, I need you to keep your seatbelt firmly secured and your head down, okay?" he instructed her.

Linda complied without question. After all the day's events, she knew they only told her what she needed to do to survive.

———

DERRICK WAS surprised by the SUV that almost hit him as he left the diner parking lot. He was more surprised when they overtook him on the highway. He first thought that they were another hit squad, so he slammed on the brakes as they pulled alongside them, but they kept going. Then out of nowhere, a second vehicle turned its lights on directly behind him. Derrick instinctively reached for one of the weapons he liberated from the two men in the diner parking lot. The second car sped by him. He turned to Trina, who he had told to get down.

"Well, I guess it's our lucky day, it's someone else's turn to be chased today," he said, somewhat surprised.

Through the windshield, they both watched as the second car caught up and pulled alongside the SUV. Derrick could see tiny flashes of light exchanged between the two vehicles.

"What the—?" he didn't finish his question due to Trina sitting beside him. As if on cue, Trina finished his sentence with, "Hell?" The cars collided and the SUV went into a slide, flipped, and landed on its roof. The car sped off the road at full speed and slammed into a dirt bank about forty feet off the side of the road. Dirt collapsed from the bank, covering the passenger compartment of the car.

Derrick stopped the Jeep about a football field's length from the SUV. He drew the gun and carefully approached the vehicle. He had no idea what he was walking into. As he reached the vehicle, he saw the front seat passenger partway out the window. There was a large pool of blood creeping across the pavement—the man's face was almost nonexistent. It appeared that he had suffered several bullet wounds before his head was slammed into the pavement at high speed.

Derrick slowly walked around to the driver's side. The airbags were blocking his view inside the vehicle. He pulled the airbag by the driver's window out of the way and a hand grabbed his arm from inside the SUV. The driver was covered in blood and could barely speak, though his plea to Derrick was clear.

"You must protect her."

The guard let go and closed his eyes, and the gargling sound he was making while he was breathing abruptly stopped.

Derrick pulled the airbag by the back seat aside. There was a woman hanging upside down by her seatbelt. He couldn't tell if she was alive. He tried the door, and to his surprise, it released and opened slightly. Derrick had to use his body weight to open it all the way, forcing it passed some bent metal, and the top of the door scraping on the pavement. He carefully released the woman from the seatbelt and absorbed her weight as she fell onto him.

He crawled from the SUV and dragged the woman to a safe distance away. She started to stir. Derrick observed her as she began to wake, her face illuminated by the partial moon and the Jeep lights a hundred yards down the road. As she brushed her hair from her face, Derrick's eyes widened, and his hair started to raise on his arms and neck, he felt a lump rise in his throat.

"This can't be—what are the odds," he exclaimed.

"The odds of what?" came a voice from behind him.

Derrick whipped around to see Trina standing there.

"Nothing. Help me get her up, we have to get out of here."

The irony of saving the life of a person you were plotting to kill yourself is immeasurable. Derrick almost laughed as they poured Linda Avail into the back seat. He had been sure that the Avails were the ones trying to kill him, a theory that now seemed to be incorrect. He looked around; they needed to get out of there.

"Trina, get in we need to go," he ordered.

Trina complied as Derrick went around to the driver's seat. They sped away from the scene.

———

AFTER WORKING the lock on the trunk, he was able to pop it open. He pushed the body of the tall man off of his own and crawled out. His head was still spinning a bit. He was pissed that he let himself be succumbed by a rear naked choke so quickly. He looked at his partner. His face was badly injured, he wasn't sure if he was even alive. He reached in and checked for a pulse—faint, but still there. He would need to regroup and get further instructions from their handlers. As he stood up, he heard the distinctive sound of guns shots somewhere down the road. It was more than one engaging another. He slammed the trunk.

There may still be time to save this operation after all, he thought. Who else would be involved with gunfire but their target?

He put the car in drive and headed out down the road. He drove slowly. He wanted the gunfight to be over when he arrived. He came up over a small crest in the road and saw the SUV on its roof in the road. He pulled up just close enough so the headlights shined right on the overturned vehicle. He could see a man lying out the window of the overturned SUV. He got out and walked around the SUV. Two dead men and a rear door forced open, but the orange Jeep was nowhere to be seen.

"I guess I drove too slow," he said to the dead men.

He rounded the SUV and noticed two taillights off the road on the other side; he took a step toward them. Before he could identify the lights, he heard screaming coming from his car.

He ran back, and as he got closer to his car the screaming became louder.

"Where are you? Get me the hell out of this trunk!" came the tall man's voice from inside.

"Give me a second, I have to get the keys," he responded.

He shut off the car and used the keys to pop open the trunk, his partner was pale like a zombie.

His face was disfigured and covered with blood and mucus. Some of it dried and some still oozing, his eyes and nose and lips were all swollen.

The tall man reached out for assistance to get out of the trunk, a tattoo with the number forty could be seen on his hand. The shorter man extended his arm to assist him, the number forty-three became visible on his hand.

"Aaahhh, my face is killing me! What's going on? Where are we?" Forty shouted the words, producing a spittle of blood while he talked.

Forty-Three recounted the story from the time he awoke until now, including the taillights he was about to investigate.

Forty climbed into the passenger seat. "Let's drive up to it, we can use the headlights better that way."

They repositioned their car to illuminate the other vehicle. They realized the car was half-buried, but they couldn't see any movement. Forty-Three had found a rifle on the ground next to the SUV; that was the only gun between the two of them. He used the butt of the rifle to smash the back window. The interior was still full of smoke that slowly seeped out of the opening he created. There were two men in the front seat. They were dressed just like he and the tall man were.

Forty-Three called into the car, "Hey, can you hear me?"

Neither man moved. He tried to open the rear door. At first, it wouldn't move but after several violent yanks, the door gave way and flew open. He crawled into the back seat and slowly checked each man's neck. No pulse, both were dead. He searched the best he could he found their wallets and a cell phone on the passenger. He climbed out and returned to the car, where he shared the find with the tall man. The IDs were fake just like the ones they had been carrying. He checked the phone.

"What the hell?" Forty-Three questioned.

"I think this was the other team we were going to meet," Forty surmised.

Forty-Three held the phone out to Forty—the phone number last called was the same number that gave them their orders. Forty grabbed the phone and dialed the number. The call was answered with a question.

"Did you get her?" the phone probed.

"No, this is Forty I'm here with Forty-Three, we were in pursuit of the man and girl, and came across this phone at an accident scene, all parties deceased."

After a moment of silence, the man responded. "Uh Forty, you're the tall one, right? Did you get the man and girl? Is there a woman who is one of the deceased?"

"No on the man and girl, and no on the woman, just two dead men in each vehicle. There was lots of blood and gunfire was exchanged, she may have been hit." Forty informed him.

"Okay received. You stand by; we're sending a clean-up team," the voice said.

Forty knew what that meant, but he wasn't sure he wanted to stand by based on his injuries. He turned to inform Forty-Three and found himself staring down the barrel of the rifle. One loud bang and the red mist hung in the air, even as his body fell backward to the ground. Forty-Three left the body where it fell, grabbed the phone, and went back to the car. He must find that Jeep.

20

AFTER SPEEDING away from the ambush, Derrick drove for a few miles and then started turning off on side roads. He found a little dirt road and turned off onto it, he pulled the Wrangler off the side a bit to keep it hidden. Linda Avail was starting to regain consciousness.

"Can you hear me?" he asked.

Linda looked around, she realized she was neither in the car nor with the men she started the trip with.

"Who are you?" she asked.

"I'm the guy that rescued you. Why were those men trying to kill you?" Derrick questioned her.

"I don't know for sure, I'm very wealthy and my dad and I have made lots of enemies. I was attacked earlier and those men in the SUV were part of a company that was hired to protect me and get me back to my father."

"That's not going well, is it?" Derrick said, kind of sneering.

The sarcasm was thick in Derrick's voice. Linda appeared hurt by it.

"Why would you be so sarcastic about something like this?" she asked, unaware of who he was.

Derrick's face lost all expression, his eyes became dead and ice-cold.

"You don't even know who I am. You don't understand how lucky you are to still be breathing. Yes, you and your father have made enemies, and

I am one of them. I'm sitting here wondering, for what purpose did fate just dump you into my lap?"

Linda watched the change in his demeanor, it wasn't until right then she noticed the gun in his hand, slightly waving while he spoke. A small tear dropped from her eye, running down her face, she wiped it away with her sleeve.

"I have done many bad things. I'm sorry if I wronged you somehow, but please, I have changed. I am only headed to meet my father because of the attack. We were no longer talking; I wanted a new life."

Derrick was having a crisis of conscience. He wanted to raise the pistol and satisfy half of his promise to Shannon, another part of him wanted to believe that a person could change after doing such horrible things because that would mean he might be able to resume his life when this was all done.

He lowered the gun. Trina let out a loud sigh when the gun was put away.

"Wow, that was intense. Lady, you must be a bad person to make him want to kill you too," she blurted out.

"I was," Linda replied honestly.

Derrick started the Jeep. He wanted to get to Virginia Beach by morning. Elsy would definitely be surprised now.

———

PAULA NEWLY SETTLED into her new office. The President had sent boxes of files for her to review and investigate. She needed to get some help. She picked up the phone and called her old office and spoke to two agents. She offered them both the same options to come and work for her in a special investigation, both accepted and promised to be there by the next morning.

Looking through the first layer of reports, Paula understood that this was going to be a very complex investigation. She needed a little more help and only thought of one person. The President had given her the latitude to select her team from anywhere, including outside of the FBI. That's what she was planning to do next.

———

TINKER HAD COMPLETED ALL the benchmarks given to him by Barry Klinger, except the final one. He was looking for vulnerabilities in the AI access that his crew had hacked. It was then that he noticed something he hadn't ever seen before. His code was slowly rewriting itself. The AI seemed to be quietly defending itself by recoding what Tinker and his group installed. Tinker thought at first it was the Chinese doing it, but as he watched the code, it became apparent that it was being written from the inside. He hacked back into the system in under thirty seconds, and he had full control in less than a minute.

"That was way too easy." He was alarmed that there was no obvious defense to his repeated intrusion.

He explored the system and inserted some code to make sure both this intrusion and any that followed would be completely hidden; however, he was unsure if his code would hold.

Deidra appeared at his office door holding a cell phone.

"There's some guy on the line here, who says he needs to talk to you. Sounds important."

He extended his hand for the phone, and she entered and gave it to him.

He looked at the phone screen and then held it to his ear.

"Hello, who am I speaking with and why?" Tinker demanded.

"Tinker, It's Barry Klinger. You need to take a low profile for a little while. Some unexpected and dangerous people seem to be after Mr. Avail and myself. Stay on track, just don't make waves, okay?"

"Sir, your project is complete and ready for the last part," he said, unsure if it was an accurate representation. "You should know the Chinese are trying to intervene in the same systems as well."

Barry contemplated the report Tinker had just given him.

"Thank you for that information, we'll let you know when we want you to activate the final piece."

Tinker was perplexed by the need to go dark for a while, and the subtle reference to Mr. Avail being hunted. He had always known the Avails to be the apex predators, never the prey. This was a curious turn of events that concerned him.

AS BARRY HUNG up the phone with Tinker, it was ringing almost instantly again. This time Eric Forsythe was calling.

"Eric, I'm hoping you're calling to tell us everything is okay?" Barry said quizzically.

"I am afraid that this call contains no good news. Mr. Avail's daughter was taken. We lost two more agents and three of theirs were down. Linda is nowhere to be seen."

"What happened?" Barry interrogated; his tone immediately changed.

"It appears as though they were ambushed. A car drove up alongside them and opened fire, after the exchange the vehicles collided and the SUV with your daughter in it flipped over and landed on its roof. The other car went off the road and struck a bank and was partially covered, the occupants dead from gunshot wounds." Eric informed him.

"I see. Any leads on her whereabouts?" Barry continued.

"Not currently. We're shooting in the dark here. We surmise she may have been picked up by a good Samaritan. I have men spread out all over the area, and we're monitoring local police and hospitals. So far there has been nothing."

"Let me know the second anything changes," Barry said. "I will inform Mr. Avail."

Barry stood still for a second after the call ended, thinking, "This must be the worst-case scenario for Mr. Avail."

———

FORTY-THREE KEPT DRIVING, searching for the orange Jeep. It was a long night and not one sighting. As his eyes started to creep shut, he decided it was time to pull over and rest. He pulled off the shoulder of the municipal highway and shut his car down. He was sure his prey was long gone, and he didn't need to crash without finding it. By morning he would be replaced, and most likely they would kill him for failing. All he had was the rifle with a few rounds left, but he refused to go down easy. He rested his head and nodded off quickly.

———

THE SUN WASN'T OFFICIALLY up yet, but the sky was brightening. Derrick had been driving all night. He was looking at the taillights in front of him when he realized they were from a parked car. He swerved the Jeep back onto the road, nearly missing the car. He wasn't sure if the driver even knew how close he was to a violent awakening. Trina woke due to the rapid lane change.

"What the heck was that?" she asked, concerned.

Derrick smiled sheepishly at her.

"That other car was going way too slow," he said sarcastically.

"You were falling asleep. I told you I could drive," she said in a motherly tone.

"You're not old enough, and you don't have a license," he reminded her.

"You have a lady in the back that you want to kill and will probably say we kidnaped her if we get pulled over. I don't think traffic laws are your biggest issue right now," Trina said, trying to defuse his argument of her driving.

He smiled at her again.

"Are you sure you're not just a mini lawyer?" he asked jokingly.

She laughed at that.

"I'm hungry, can we stop somewhere? You could probably use a coffee anyhow," she said, matter-of-factly.

Another voice chimed in from the back seat.

"I could use some breakfast myself, I haven't eaten in a while, and coffee sounds great," Linda added in.

Derrick stared in the mirror at the woman he had spent so long wanting to kill. She wasn't the person he had originally imagined her to be. He realized that to keep his initial promise to Shannon, he would have to strip away his humanity to accomplish it. Secretly, he was now hoping Elsy would come through on her plan. Up ahead the lights of a town started to illuminate the sky as they approached. There were several places to eat along the road.

Trina spied one she had been to before. She pointed it out.

"Oooh let's eat there," she suggested.

Derrick complied by swinging the Wrangler off into the parking lot. They were a strange sight as they walked into the restaurant. Derrick was wearing shorts and a tropical print shirt, and Trina was wearing a similar outfit, but her hair was wild. Linda was wearing jeans, a flannel shirt and black combat boots and her hair was as wild as Trina's. They sat and ordered breakfast. Derrick looked at the map he had in his pocket, trying to figure out where they were now and how much further they need to go.

He noticed Katrina and Linda having an actual conversation.

Linda turned and faced him. "What did my father and I do to you? I can see it was terrible."

Derrick met her stare with the same cold eyes she had seen the other night.

"You don't want to bring this up. Please let it go," Derrick said, fighting back the rage that would come with the memories.

Derrick knew that if she made him recount the murder of Shannon, that would probably be enough to push him to fulfill his promise to her.

They ate the rest of their breakfast in silence.

———

PAULA NEEDED a few more people on her task force, so she made another call.

"I hear you're in Virginia Beach. I'm sorry I couldn't help with your last request, but I have a case I can use your help on. If you're interested, you would have an official consultant status with the FBI."

Elsy listened to the sales pitch. She knew Derrick would probably be there sometime today.

"I have something else going on right now, can I call you later and let you know?" Elsy advised her.

Paula had expected a more direct answer.

"Uhh yes. Don't wait too long. I need to get this up and running. I think it's going to be part of the President's re-election campaign as well," Paula said.

"I will let you know, as soon as I know something," Elsy replied.

Elsy hung up, leaving Paula more perplexed than ever. She spoke to herself in a low tone.

"What has she gotten into? Is she still pursuing the social media tampering? Damn, that could be very dangerous if it's real," Paula questioned quietly to herself.

———

GEORGE WAS WATCHING the morning news. The battle in Milekistan was going full-bore. Russia and China were siding with the Royal General. Military equipment from both of those countries were being operated by the royal forces. It was clear that the rebels were utilizing a mixture of ol' Soviet weapons and more modern US and other weapons harvested from the fighting. They were holding their own for now. Every day the Royal General would become more violent in the way he dealt with them. George expected the televised beheading of captured soldiers to start soon. It was the trademark intimidation the General had used when he took power.

Barry walked into the room quietly and sat down across from George, using the remote to shut down the TV.

"Sir, I have some news. It's not good. Linda is missing, her escort team were all killed. There are currently no indicators as to where she is," he stated, his concern evident.

George stared back at Barry,

"Do you think she is alive?" George asked.

"All indications are that she fled the scene," Barry said.

"Okay, we will operate on the assumption that she is alive and trying to hide. I can be satisfied with that. Linda is a smart girl," George said stoically.

"Sir, I think it means there is still room for hope," Barry said realizing how corny it sounded,

George took a sip from a drink on the table next to him. "I guess this is partly my fault. If I hadn't tricked her, she would be here with us."

Barry was surprised at how calm he was taking this news.

———

THE COUNCIL HAD ADJOURNED their meeting. The decision was made that Madam Felsder would no longer be seated as a member. Her body was rolled up in plastic before it was hauled away from the table; only one person knew the secret that otherwise died with her. Mr. Bins oversaw the removal and cleanup himself; the Council had very uncompromising expectations for cleanliness in the chamber.

As a result of the meeting, the attack on the Avails and the man and child had been tabled. Field agents were ordered to suspend their assignments regarding both sets of targets, this order was to be sent immediately.

———

FORTY-THREE AWAKENED SUDDENLY as if his car had been shaken. He saw taillights in the distance ahead of him. His eyes were still adjusting to waking up. As the lights disappeared, he checked his watch. Almost morning, the sky was already lit up awaiting the full display of the sun. He decided to grab something to eat and resume his search for the Jeep. He pulled off into the first restaurant he saw that was serving breakfast. As he walked in, he looked up at where the sun was just peeking out over the horizon. Something caught his eye down the street a bit.

"It couldn't be," he said aloud to himself.

He walked back to his car and drove down to another parking lot. There weren't a lot of places for cover, but he found a small spot between his car and some dumpsters that gave him a great place to set up and watch. He checked his rifle—four rounds left. He'd make them count. The order said, "Alive, *if possible.*"

"I'm afraid that won't be possible." He laughed as he said it. The phone in his pocket vibrated, but he ignored it. No time for distractions; he wanted to finish his assignment for a chance to survive himself.

———

"COULD I PLEASE USE YOUR PHONE?" She asked.

Derrick watched Linda while he sipped his coffee. The woman in front of him didn't match the evil villainess he had pictured in his mind. He reached into his pocket and handed her the burner he had purchased. She took the phone and grabbed his hand at the same time as if conveying her thanks for him saving her.

"Thank you. I just need to let someone know I'm alive," she said quietly.

Derrick was sure he would regret this, but continued with his coffee.

Trina smiled at him.

"You are the best human I know," she said, her face glowing.

After that, she lowered her head and continued with her breakfast. She was eating slowly for the first time in a long time.

———

"HI, father. It's me, I'm still alive," Linda almost cried into the phone.

"I'm glad you're okay, where are you?" George asked.

"I don't know exactly, somewhere almost to Virginia Beach," she advised.

"You're coming here?" he questioned.

"I didn't know you were there, it's just where we're going," she replied.

"Who are you traveling with?" he asked.

"I don't know, a man and a girl. They've been quite accommodating, but I think the girl might have something to do with that," Linda told him, leaving out the part about Derrick wanting to kill her.

"You be careful, please. Call me when you get here, Barry and I will come to get you," he advised her.

"I still love you, Father," she said emotionally.

"Me too," he replied.

As Linda was walking back to the booth, a noise sounded like someone slammed their hand against the pane of the glass window. Linda went to take another step, but her weight seemed too much to bear, and she collapsed onto the floor. Her chest felt like it was on fire, she grabbed at the pain with her hand, there was a hole in her shirt. Her hand was bright red even under the lights of the restaurant.

People were screaming and ducking to the floor around her. Did the man shoot her? She looked around, he had pushed the girl under the table and was coming to her side. He was there for her? This didn't make sense. Who shot her, if not him? Why would he care if she died? She realized that he was a good man.

"I'm sorry for what I took from you." Blood tinged her lips as she spoke.

"I forgive you. Lay still. Conserve your energy." Derrick felt strangely different after uttering those words, almost lighter.

Linda lost consciousness. Derrick weighed his options; he knew there was nothing he could do for her now. He ran back to the booth and grabbed Trina by the hand.

"Come on, let's go out the back, this can only get worse if we stay."

Trina looked back as they headed out, and she saw Linda lying in a pool of blood.

———

FORTY-THREE WATCHED as the lady went down with a single shot. He was proud of himself for his marksmanship. Unfortunately, he allowed his two other targets to slip from sight as he mentally patted himself on the back. Forty would have harassed him for that; he was glad he killed him. *He was always an ass,* he thought. He searched through the scope. *Where are they?* He saw several people run from the diner; one older obese man was semi-waddling toward his car. This irritated Forty-Three, he leveled the scope on the man's back and fired. The man went down like a wounded animal, collapsing mid-run in a cloud of dust as he struck the ground.

Forty-Three returned to his search, mad at himself again for succumbing to distraction. He pressed his eye close to the scope trying to get a better view. Wait—he heard something next to him. He rolled over just in time to see a foot coming down on his face. There was no time to react; the foot struck his face with immense force, fracturing his nose and his left eye socket. Everything went black.

21

SIMON HAD HIT a dead end at first, then he started hearing of an attack on the Avail's island villa. He knew George was still in the US as of right now, but his daughter hadn't been seen. There were additional reports of other attacks that didn't make sense as well, including an attack that left two unidentified males dead in Florida that was cleaned up professionally before major police involvement.

Just now he was handed a report about another incident involving the Blackheart group and two more unidentified males. The report indicated they were looking for a woman that matched the description of Linda Avail. He looked over the report twice. "Barry would never leave George Avail's side if his daughter were in trouble," he thought. He picked up the phone.

"Have the plane fueled and ready to go to Virginia Beach. I think we're about to find our fugitive."

———

THE AMBULANCE CREW called for a life flight helicopter, there was no time to transport by land. They had started large bore IVs on the patient and were biding time for the inevitable if she didn't receive surgery very quickly. The police had the whole area shut down. The shooter had been found unconscious and tied up by his vehicle. The police assumed it was another incident of a "good guy with a gun" that had foiled what was now often referred to as 'an attempted mass shooting', but out here they were not interested in the assigned politics of the crime they were investigating.

The helicopter landed in the parking lot. Dust and small debris blew all over the place. People outside turned away and attempted to cover their faces from the turbulence. The medical crew exited the restaurant with the patient, meeting the life flight crew halfway across the parking lot. They relayed what little information they had, and the flight crew loaded their new patient into the helicopter and lifted off toward the closest trauma hospital.

———

DERRICK FINISHED the drive to Harlem's house without incident. He swung the oversized Jeep into the open spot in the driveway. Trina hopped out before he could even tell her to wait. He was sure she was reading his mind.

Elsy ran from the house, expecting to see Derrick first. The sight of a young girl with toussled hair and a bit of dirt on her face was a big surprise. As Derrick rounded the Jeep as well, she stared at him. She could see the pain on his face and knew he was going through something, then she noticed he had blood on his clothing.

"Are you okay, and who is this?" she asked, equally concerned and confused.

Trina didn't wait for Derrick to respond.

"I'm Katrina, if you're my friend you can call me Trina. Are you Derrick's girlfriend?"

Elsy laughed out loud.

"Oh my, definitely not," Elsy said, still concerned about the blood.

Derrick scrunched his face up.

"*Definitely* not? That's hurtful," he said.

Harlem emerged from the house.

"So, this is Derrick the dead. Who is this young lady?" He asked.

Elsy jabbed Harlem for using the 'Derrick the dead' term. It was her secret name for him. While they had conversed on the phone and were both aware of each other, this was the first time Derrick and Harlem ever met. Harlem had reservations; he was pretty sure Derrick had previously killed two hitmen in separate unsolved cases.

Derrick turned to Elsy.

"Can we go inside? We need to talk," he requested.

They all went inside, and Harlem got everyone drinks, including soda for Trina.

"My guess is we're gonna need these, even though it's still early," he said as he passed them out.

Derrick started to relay the whole story, starting in Florida with Trina and continuing through the diner where Linda was shot.

Elsy sat in silence listening to the story unfold. How a trip for vengeance could end up with Derrick attempting to save one of the people he had sworn to kill was almost unbelievable.

Harlem decided to ask the million-dollar question. "So, who's trying to kill you both, if it's not each other?"

———

SIMON'S PLANE TOUCHED DOWN. As it was taxiing to the terminal, he received an update regarding a shootout on the highway not too far away. He also received info on the restaurant shooting, he read over the email, the woman's description is what caught his eye.

"Could this be Linda Avail?" he questioned aloud.

As he was ushered to an SUV, he instructed the driver to head to the trauma hospital instead. The scene of the incident was not going anywhere. He looked over the file twice; nowhere did it describe her condition, it only said she was flown out. *That's usually not a good sign,* he thought.

———

DANIEL WRIGHT FOLLOWED the trail from the cars off the road to the shooting site at the restaurant. He cycled through the IDs he kept with him; he came up with an agency called the DES. The Department of Extra Services. It was completely fictitious, but he had found that when using an official-looking badge, one that people don't recognize, they would rather comply and look like they were already aware of your existence than appear as though they were unknowledgeable of other agencies in their field. He found the officer in charge and flashed his badge.

"Sir, I promise we are not here to interfere with your investigation, we would like to offer our assistance in any way that we can."

The officer studied him for a long moment of silence.

"What can you do for me that my department can't do itself?" he asked.

"Well for starters, I understand that you have a suspect in custody, but you are unable to identify him. We have access to databases that you probably do not," Daniel informed him.

The officer eyed him up one more time and pointed to a cruiser.

"He's over there. See what you can find out. His weapon is in the trunk, the officer will let you see it if you want, just use proper evidence techniques, we're not all backwoods here," the officer stated with a bit of obvious contempt for federal law enforcement.

Daniel pulled several of his men to gather as much evidence as possible. He went over to the cruiser, and an officer opened the door for him. The man in the back seat said nothing. Daniel took his picture and sent it away via his phone. He asked the man who he worked for; the silence continued. Daniel looked down as his phone pinged with a reply. His eyes widened at the reply to the photo. He looked at the man in the cruiser, then he reached in and grabbed his wrist. A forty-three was tattooed on his hand. Daniel went back to his phone. "It's confirmed. The tattoo was present, number forty-three."

Forty-Three was conscious enough to understand he was now compromised. He had a tooth in his mouth that was slightly higher than the others, he bit down as hard as he could and ground his teeth, the tooth broke releasing its hidden contents. Daniel noticed a brief sweet almond smell and then the prisoner was convulsing in the back seat. Seconds later, Forty-Three was dead.

———

ALEXANDER CORTEZ HADN'T HEARD from anyone in a while. As elections were drawing closer, he was hoping for another cash infusion for his campaign; unfortunately, it seemed he was on his own. He sat in his campaign office reviewing the latest poll numbers. He had won the primary and was now leading against his opposition, but only narrowly. He was hoping for some more financial assistance. His phone rang and he answered it quickly, praying it was the answer to his wishes. The call was an answer, only not from whom he expected.

———

THE COUNCIL HAD VOTED on their new leader. He was going through the entire office that was previously assigned to the now-deceased Madam Felsder. Jeac Pastil was much younger than the Madam had been. He considered himself to be more agile, both physically and mentally. He shuffled through the documents she had opened on her desk. He called in the aide she had almost killed in their last encounter.

"So, you're the one who gave her bad news?" he asked the aide.

The young aide was petrified. "I'm sorry, yes that was me."

Jeac smiled. "Good, you've got balls. You will be my new primary aide," he stated as fact.

"Uhh yes sir. Thank you, sir," the aide stammered.

"You're welcome. Go out there and empty that desk, tell whoever is sitting there to come see me. By the way, what is your name?" Jeac asked.

"Denler Faulk, sir," the aide answered.

"Okay Denny, go get 'em for me," Jeac ordered.

The new assistant disappeared from his office. He was replaced shortly by the person who was occupying the same desk he told Denler to take.

The arrogant employee stood before him. Jeac could see the entitlement that was built into his personality.

"I am going to say this once. You will vacate your desk; you will report to assignments, and you will go where you are told without protest. Any deviation will result in your immediate discharge. I am assuming you know what 'discharge' entails?"

The aide shook his head up and down, though he remained silent.

"You are dismissed. Follow your orders," Jeac stated.

The aide turned and left the office. He couldn't help himself but run to the little covey of his fellow workers who shared his feelings of entitlement. The new boss took note.

———

SIMON RUSHED into the emergency room. "Who's in charge here?"

"I am," came a reply from behind a counter area in the center of the room. A young woman stood up from behind the counter. "And who are you?" she asked.

Simon flashed his Federal Marshal credentials.

"My name is Agent Little. I must find a woman that you just flew in here."

The nurse knew who he was referring to.

"I can't give you that information unless you have a warrant," she said firmly.

"Ma'am. She is in grave danger; she wasn't shot by accident. I imagine that places whoever is around her in danger as well. It is both of our jobs to help this victim, we just do it in different ways," he said, trying to be diplomatic.

Simon saw the change while he was talking; he knew he had her.

"She's upstairs in surgery. She's not in good shape! Should I notify security?" the nurse said, obviously shaken.

"No, that might make things worse. My team will handle this," Simon assured her.

Simon gathered the specific location and doctor's name from the nurse.

"Thank you for all your help," he shouted back as he ran for the elevator.

He had a plan forming and would need help from the hospital and others to pull it off.

———

THE NEWS of the shooting reached George Avail. He staggered a bit as he heard that his daughter had been shot; even Barry sank into a chair as the news was relayed.

"My plan is falling apart and now my daughter has been shot, someone is going to pay!" he shouted.

Barry listened quietly. He assumed George would want to go to his daughter, so he called Eric Forsythe.

"Eric, we need a mobile team at the safe house. We need to go to the hospital that Linda was taken to."

———

SIMON WORKED FAST; he had team members at the office pulling files on everyone in the operating room. Before the surgery was over, he had everything he needed. Now it was up to Linda to survive. He stood patiently awaiting the end of the procedure. When it was complete, Simon's team made sure no one left the room.

"Ladies and gentlemen, I need a minute of your time before you continue with your day," Simon stated.

The surgeon was the first to respond. "Who the hell are you? How did you get in my operating room?"

"As of right now, this is my operating room. My name is Agent Simon Little. The patient you are operating on will be in great peril if she survives, that is why I need your assistance now," he advised.

There were gasps from almost every person in the room as Simon relayed his plan. The surgeon erupted at Simon's announcement. "Are you crazy? We did not just go through hours of surgery to allow you to put her in more jeopardy."

"I'm sorry Doc, she's not going to be safe here. The only way to protect her and the people around her, is to do what I say," Simon responded.

"Doc, when can we safely move her?" one of Simon's team asked.

"It will be several hours before we even know if she'll survive," the surgeon responded.

"Okay, we need a secure section of the hospital to hold her in then," Simon pivoted.

"We're a hospital, not a prison, we don't have a secure area like that," the surgeon said incredulously.

Simon was thinking on the fly. He had to find a way to protect Linda so that he could lure Barry and George out into the open. A new plan started to emerge. Before it could be put in motion, an alarm sounded from Linda's monitors, and the doctors and nurses responded immediately.

———

BARRY HAD all he could do to keep George still until their transport security arrived. As the van pulled up into the driveway, George walked out to meet it.

"Let's go," he yelled as he climbed into the van. Barry followed him out and jumped into the van as well.

"Okay gentlemen, we are headed to the trauma hospital. When we get there, we need to protect Mr. Avail but also his daughter. We will assist or replace hospital security if they are not up to the task. We do have to get there safely, so eyes up and be alert, whoever is targeting this family has a lot of reach," Barry ordered.

22

PRESIDENT HARRINGTON WAS CONSISTENTLY LEADING in every news poll as the cycle turned to almost full-time election coverage. The news of the processing plant fires and other questionable accidents that could put the country's food supply in jeopardy were pushed to the way back of the reporting cycle.

He was hoping for some news of his own regarding these issues, but the task force he initiated was hitting roadblocks just getting staffed. He read some files on his desk; a security brief indicated there had been some suspicious activity regarding the AI integrity of several social media outlets in the United States, so he read further. These social media groups had been implicated in previous elections for controlling what users could see related to candidates and certain news stories. Would someone be foolish enough to try and use the same tactics to manipulate voters again?

The committee that reviewed the event stated that it was beyond the current level of tech to individually target users to achieve a specific outcome. The President had his doubts as he weighed these seemingly benign incidents in his mind. The events preceding the last election had started out benign at first, as well.

———

DESPITE NOT HAVING an answer from Elsy yet, Paula's task force had taken shape. She now had thirty agents working for her. The President had made a call to the Director and simply said that agents were needed to assist with an investigation at his request. Office politics being what they are, agents started lining up to assist; most hoping to gain favor for future benefits. Paula was now tasked with sifting through a mountain of data and evidence that was being collected from the various scenes.

So far, there was no direct connection that they could find, other than the similarities of the fires and the way they started. On their own, each fire was simple and easy to explain as accidental. The rapid-fire spread was easily attributed to the nature of the businesses. Once you considered the number of fires that had occurred all in the same fashion, the level of coincidence rose to more suspicious. The only problem was every location that had surveillance cameras, seemed to have a camera malfunction seconds before the fire. Paula made notes on the reports, *send agents to collect Fire Marshall reports and speak to investigators.* She didn't want to leave anything out of her investigation. She was baffled by how there could be so many similar fires and seemingly no evidence of anything suspicious.

———

GEORGE BOLTED from the vehicle the second it stopped in front of the emergency room entrance. He ran up to the desk like a man on fire.

"Where is my daughter?" he demanded from the nurse at the desk.

She looked at him unfazed. She had dealt with too many irate and emotional family members in her career to be bothered by these incidents.

"Sir, please calm down and give me some information. I can help you if you help me."

Barry and the guards entered while George was having his exchange with the nurse. She saw the armed men and immediately changed her demeanor. Guns in the ER were not new to her, but men in military-style uniforms carrying rifles were outside of her comfort zone. She stopped talking and just stared at them.

George snapped her out of it. "Forget them, look at me. Just tell me where my daughter is."

The nurse abandoned all the hospital protocols, trembling as she spoke.

"Sir, your daughter is up on floor seven. She was in surgery last I heard. It wasn't looking good."

George processed that information. *It wasn't looking good.* He should be with her. George and the entourage shadowing him all headed for the elevator. They pushed the button for floor seven and waited.

———

SIMON GOT a text on his phone as he waited. *"On their way,"* was all it said. He alerted the others.

"Showtime, everyone be ready."

They all watched the floor indicator on the elevator as it rose, nearing their location. The elevator stopped on the floor and George Avail burst past the armed guards who were there to protect him. He slammed his hands down on the floor nurse's desk. A male nurse turned to see him. Two more guards and Barry stepped from the elevator, and as they did all three were instantly subdued by federal agents. George realized they had walked into a trap.

"Has my daughter been shot, or was this an elaborate rouse?" he demanded.

He yelled at the man at the nurse's desk, who responded calmly in an almost caring tone.

"I'm sorry Mr. Avail, but your daughter truly was shot, she did not make it," the man advised him.

George was stunned by the news. "I need to see her," he demanded.

"That won't be possible right now, you'll be coming with us," the man told him.

"There is no way I am leaving without seeing my daughter. Let me see her and I'll go calmly and answer your questions."

Simon was elated to hear that; this is what he had been hoping for.

"Mr. Avail, I will accommodate your wishes, but please understand, it is not a pretty sight. You may wish to retain the vision of her you have right now," Simon warned.

George looked unfazed, the tone of his voice was calm and even.

"What happened to my daughter? Do you know who killed her?" he asked.

"That part is still under investigation. We hope to have some answers soon," Simon told him.

———

SEVERAL OF SIMON'S agents went to the shooting at the diner to gather evidence. They ran into the Blackheart employees impersonating federal agents. Rather than make a scene, they found the one in charge and let him know he would be facing federal charges if he didn't assist them and share what they had learned. There was no argument; Daniel Wright offered everything his team had uncovered. When they learned of the international assassin involvement, they made a call to the FBI as well. The local sheriff was not happy to find out he now had to wait for FBI agents to show up before he could move the bodies or release the crime scene. The agent Simon had tasked with investigating the shooting was the one to call him.

"Sir, this is kind of weird, the person who killed Linda Avail was known to be part of an international assassin group. His only identity is a number, Forty-Three," the agent relayed.

Simon listened to the report—this kept getting bigger. He was now certain he had enough to officially take George Avail into custody as well. He made another call before he escorted the senior Avail to the hospital morgue to view the body.

"We'll be down shortly. Are we all good?" Simon asked.

"Yes sir, everything is what you asked for," the agent with the body responded.

Simon smiled. "This might work."

———

GEORGE WASN'T ready for what he saw, despite the warning given by Simon. His mind just couldn't comprehend what he was looking at. It appeared that a bullet had torn through her face, it had flapped open the skin around her eyes, like a big, red-soaked cauliflower. He tried to look for more ways to recognize her, but as bile erupted into his throat, he didn't even have time to turn away. It burst from inside him, covering the viewing window in front of him. The vomit fell to the floor around his feet, causing him to lose his footing and fall to the floor into the puddle of his own stomach contents.

No one reached down to help him up. He knew he was now out of power. Almost everyone had either turned on him or been taken from him; it seemed it was just him and Barry from here on out. No more waiting to initiate his plan—he would tell this agent enough to buy his freedom and implicate others, then he would use his scheme to control them all.

———

JEAC PASTIL READ the reports from their various operations. Each one was the leg of a bigger plan, centered on bringing America to her knees on the world stage, and creating a financial opportunity for the Council members that would be greater than anyone had ever seen.

He read *The Plant Report,* as it had been dubbed. It related to the enormous success they were having in limiting supply through America's food processing plants by simply burning them down. Their cohorts within the American government had done a wonderful job of downplaying the disturbing similarities and circumstantial evidence of each incident. As a result, the first wave of inflation had been started in America. Certain food prices were going up, and to add to that, now social media was blaming a very popular President for allowing this inflation to creep into an otherwise stable economy.

Jeac smiled, and he set that report aside for another; *The Global Currency Initiative* was his next read. China and Russia were pushing this agenda, and many small countries like Milekistan were joining. Some larger countries like India refused to join, but instead switched to their own countries' currency for all transactions. China had been working mostly unnoticed for decades nibbling away at the countries that America assumed would always use the dollar for its back up currency; that was also changing. "America is in for a big surprise," he thought. Jeac was now concerned with reading the third report; the first two had been so positive he was afraid of the third. A folder labeled, *Social Media Manipulation and Standing,* lay closed in front of him.

"Ahh, the document that got George Avail in trouble," he quietly stated aloud as he opened the document. As he read, he became concerned—not at what he was reading, but what he wasn't. There was no mention of the interference that George had been accused of by Madam Felsder, in fact, it only stated that there had been a successful infiltration by an unknown hacker. This concerned him, since he had been led to believe George Avail was responsible.

While social media in America had always been skewed to push the agenda of socialism to children and young adults, their goal was to broaden the scope of psychological manipulation to include as many users as possible. The latitude and power of modern AI would allow them to tailor their approach to subtly guiding each user. Russia had spent decades perfecting its psychological user manipulation tactics, and happily supplied its research to be utilized by the Council in this plan. Jeac set aside the last report to consider its ramifications, and switched the news on. The war in Milekistan was fierce, and images of dead civilians and the burning bodies of soldiers played across the screen; this was even worse than he anticipated.

———

ELSY COULDN'T HELP but love Trina. The girl was incredibly smart, and she seemed to draw out the best version of Derrick that anyone had seen for a long time. After the long story that brought them all to her, Elsy relayed her own information to the group.

"So, I have been monitoring the hacker that started this all for me ever since he dropped off during the Popolous case. Recently my team identified some very peculiar activity from him. We found that he was hacking into the AI programming of most of the major US social media companies," she took a breath and looked at everyone to see if they were keeping up, then continued.

"We haven't identified their end goal, but it must have something to do with elections, given who we're dealing with. Here's the odd part, I took this to Paula Newly, and she said she is currently barred from looking into it. She was afraid that it might be a partisan push within the FBI, but was afraid to speculate any further. Also, the President put her on some new case, which is top secret and compartmentalized. I don't know what that's about at all," she finished.

Harlem had taken a call from work while Elsy was talking.

"Okay, it seems that Linda Avail was flown to the trauma hospital here in Virginia Beach. It's unclear if she survived her injuries or not. An officer at the scene said she was listed in post-op recovery in critical condition and then was changed to deceased. I should probably get down there."

Derrick leaned over to Elsy.

"I would like to go with him, if you could watch Trina?" he asked.

"Sure, I'm sure we can entertain each other and only find a little trouble to get into," Elsy winked as she said it.

"Oh yeah, I'm an expert trouble finder," Trina laughed.

Harlem kissed Elsy, and Trina gave Derrick a big hug.

"You come back here safe. I like you," Katrina said to Derrick.

Elsy smiled at Harlem and said, "Ditto."

———

SIMON GREW tired of the George Avail show. He ordered two of his associates to pick him up and cuff him. Reluctantly, the two agents grabbed the man now covered in vomit and forced him to his feet, they stripped his coat off because it contained most of the contamination and dropped it to the floor.

"See if we can find him a shower and some clean clothes before we get out of here," Simon ordered.

A third agent disappeared to try and accommodate Simon's wishes. In the meantime, they sat George on a metal chair in the hallway outside the morgue.

"Who did this to your daughter?" Simon asked him.

George gazed at him with a blank stare. "How would I know?" he gasped.

"Come on Mr. Avail, you said you would tell me everything if I showed you your daughter. Help me find the people responsible for her death," Simon pleaded.

George rested his head in his hands. Simon gave him a minute and then started again.

"George, every second you delay lets them escape responsibility for this," he prodded.

Quietly through his clasped hands, he made a statement.

"It's the Global Council, they did this. I don't know why; I think it has to do with Milekistan."

Simon was excited and confused all at once. The tie-in to Milekistan was what he had been waiting for. The reference to some *Global Council* as George called it, was entirely new to him. He had a hard time assuming there was some rogue global agency he had never heard of, but at the same time, he did not doubt the veracity of George's statement.

Simon realized and then said to himself, "This could get very interesting if it's real."

23

PAULA REVIEWED the notes from her agents in the field. It was looking like there were more parallels to these cases. While there were still no direct links between any of the fires, small similarities were detected. In several of the smaller communities where these fires occurred, local people remembered the presence of "out-of-town folks" days before the incidents. In each place this was reported, they were always gone the day after the fire occurred. Each agent reporting this had been sent a Bureau sketch artist. Paula would have to wait to see if there were similarities.

———

HARLEM FLASHED his badge when they got to the hospital.

"Damn, sure are a lot of you folks here today."

Harlem responded to the receptionist, "What other folks?"

"Don't you police types talk to each other? We've had local police, FBI, Federal Marshals, even some private military I presume."

"Okay, where am I going?"

"That depends, do you want to walk into the Federal Marshal's trap or stay out of his way?

"Let's go with staying out of the way right now."

"Then I'd go quietly to the morgue, you might find it interesting down there."

Harlem winked at the older lady and said, "Thank You."

"Anything for you and your beautiful friend, sweetie."

Harlem gave Derrick a poke with his elbow.

"When you're ready, I got you."

Despite the current circumstances, Derrick chuckled.

"Yeah alright, won't be soon."

They headed down the stairs to the morgue quietly.

The smells as they descended brought back memories for Derrick. He was torn about how he felt thinking they were going to look at Linda's body. It was not the satisfaction of revenge he hoped he would have. He had forgiven her as she lay dying on the floor, then he left her there. She was no longer a target for him—she had somehow become a victim he failed to protect.

They approached the door that opened to the morgue. Harlem went through first, and Derrick hung back for a second to collect his thoughts. He didn't want to be an anchor for his partner. Harlem stopped before exiting the stairwell door. Derrick almost bumped into him as he exited the stairs. They could hear voices and a man quietly speaking while crying, though neither could make out what he was saying. There was another voice telling someone else to find him a shower and clothes.

Both men carefully crept toward the voices, hoping they could find a place to observe and listen without being detected. They quietly moved into a dark office that, luckily for them, had an observation mirror. They were able to watch without being seen. The trade-off was they could no longer hear the conversation. There was an intercom on the counter that could have allowed them access to whatever was being said, but the risk to activate it was too great.

Derrick immediately recognized George Avail from the pictures he had been studying for what felt like an eternity. He reached down and felt the pistol tucked in his waistband. Once again, he was conflicted. While he had spent so much time planning his demise, in this instant, the opportunity to watch him tormented over the death of his daughter appealed to him. He thought it was almost more fitting to let him live.

Harlem noticed Derrick pat for his weapon. He quietly whispered, "There won't be any vigilante shit while I'm here. I'm still a cop."

Derrick turned to meet his stern gaze.

"No, there won't. I'm good," he lied. He still wanted to unload his pistol into George's face.

Both men returned their attention to the glass.

———

SIMON WAITED with Mr. Avail next to his daughter's body until his assistant returned with clothes and a towel. "There's a shower in a room upstairs you can use." George was reluctant to leave. The realization that this was the last he would ever see of his daughter caused him to lock up in anger. George needed to do something, anything. He felt a furor he had seldom experienced. He reached down and snatched the sheet from the lifeless body that was lying so close to him. Simon wasn't prepared for this reaction, and could only watch as George threw the sheet to the floor. He didn't want the violence that had occurred to be obscured. It was time for him to reclaim his power and destroy everyone who had wronged him. Simon looked at him and then at the agents that were around him.

"Get him up to the shower. We need to get this underway."

The agents complied and took him away as ordered.

Simon bent down to grab the sheet and tossed it haphazardly onto the body.

"Thank you for your assistance," he mumbled to the corpse.

———

HARLEM AND DERRICK watched the scene unfold through the glass. Harlem used his phone to take some pictures for facial recognition later. It was clear, the unknown man was in charge, and he wanted George to move. They watched as George reacted almost violently. None of this was a surprise to Derrick, he had felt this emotion himself. The surprise is what he saw when the father pulled the sheet from his daughter's body as he fell to the floor. Derrick almost gave away their position.

"What the fuck?" he gasped.

Harlem shot him a look saying, "Be quiet!"

Derrick pulled closer to Harlem.

"That's not Linda Avail. She was shot in the chest, not the face.

Something strange is going on here. We need to find out who this guy is," he stated.

Harlem took a second to process this information. All he could think was, "Not again."

Derrick moved into the autopsy area to get a closer look at the body when everyone had gone.

Harlem cautiously followed the unknown man upstairs to where they were getting George Avail cleaned up.

———

DERRICK DIDN'T RECOGNIZE the body on the table, but the absence of a face was the first clue that this wasn't Linda Avail. The rest of the body was a close match from what he could remember. The image of her on the floor of the diner while he said he forgave her was seared into his memory. He could see it like he was holding a photograph. He slowly compared the body in front of him to that image.

Small differences emerged that fully convinced him this was not the body of Miss Avail. The color of her fingernails was different than Linda's had been in the diner, and why hadn't the color been removed in the prep for autopsy? Dark roots in the hair—in his memory, these did not exist. As he continued his methodic review, he found other minuscule differences as well. After he finished, he covered the body. He was convinced that Linda was still alive somewhere in the hospital.

———

HARLEM WATCHED from a waiting area that had a view of the doorway to the room that they had George Avail in. Several people were in and out over the time he was watching. He wasn't deterred from his observation duties when Derrick sat down beside him and started to share his suspicions about Linda. Harlem was just starting to turn toward Derrick when both men noticed a tall man being walked down the hall by two others on either side of him.

The tall man was handcuffed in front, but had been afforded the kindness of a shirt draped over the top of the handcuffs. Harlem snapped a picture of the new man while pretending to answer a text. Rather than wait to get back to the precinct, he forwarded the pictures to Elsy. He knew she could run them faster and through a much larger database than he could without a warrant.

———

PAULA STARTED GETTING the sketch artist drawings delivered by her agents. The same face started to appear repeatedly. Dark hair, dark complexion, brown eyes, thin and short, maybe five foot six inches tall. "This is something," she thought.

She ran the face through an AI program the FBI had started using, and then through facial recognition. Normally the program could match similar faces in a matter of minutes and a specific face in about ten minutes. After forty-five minutes, she was still waiting, even though she had access to one of the largest databases in the world. Images the government had been secretly collecting not only from driver's licenses and other government IDs, but from public camera systems all over the US.

It was justified as a tool to expose and fight terrorists. Their new artificial intelligence system would compile these images and then track the individual, building a profile and ID for each one. It ran nonstop; the database grew every second of every day. All this data, and still no hits on their image. Paula looked at another report. At first, she thought it had been sent to her by accident. As she read it, she was suddenly overtaken by a sense of dread.

"Perhaps the President is only seeing the tip of the iceberg," she thought.

She picked up her secure office line and dialed a number she had been given.

When the voice picked up on the other end, it knew who she was already.

"Good evening, Agent Newly, how can I assist you this evening?"

"I need to see the President. It's regarding the assignment he gave me. I have some news he needs immediately," Paula explained.

"I will send a car for you straightaway; it should arrive in twenty minutes. Be ready," the voice replied.

Paula was not expecting that kind of response. "Uh okay. That's fast.

I'll be waiting. I'm here at the…"

The voice cut her off. "I am well aware of where you are, Agent Newly. Please be ready."

Paula hung up. She was impressed by how serious the President seemed to be taking this, and yet a little creeped out by the tone of the person on the phone.

She couldn't help but wonder, "Were they watching me?"

She glanced out of her office window as if she might catch someone looking.

———

TINKER HAD LOST all contact with Barry and George Avail. He had obtained the access to the artificial intelligence used by the world's most popular social media sites but wasn't sure what the next step was. He called Deidra to his office.

"Hey, we're at a standstill with the AI stuff for our client until I hear back from them. Why don't you quietly poke around in the code and see if you find anything interesting?"

"Anything specific you're looking for?"

"I'm not sure, all of this was to gain access to some subroutine that was planted years ago. I haven't been told what it does or its specific location in the system yet. It would be great if we can stay ahead of what they want."

"Alright, I'll get right on it."

Deidra disappeared as fast as she has shown up. Tinker sat back in his chair.

"Where are my contacts?" He said aloud, tapping the computer screen.

———

BARRY WAS TREATED like a true enemy of the state. He had been apprehended like an ordinary criminal, tackled without warning when he accompanied George to find his daughter. Now he was led through the hospital, handcuffed and escorted by two agents on either side. While they attempted to hide his status with a jacket over the cuffs holding his arms together in front of him, anyone that had ever watched any cop show would recognize his predicament.

They led him down the hallway and he saw agents outside the door of a room. He wondered if it was George with Linda. The agents swept him right passed the room and to a stairwell. They carefully descended with their prisoner and exited to a waiting van. The side door slid open as they approached, and Barry was partly assisted, partly stuffed inside. As soon as he was buckled into the seat, a set of earmuffs and a blindfold were positioned on his ears and eyes, Barry knew what this was—he had used it before himself. He would stay calm and see what happens next. He knew he wasn't with the FBI; this was a different alphabet agency.

———

ELSY STARTED RUNNING the pictures that Harlem had sent. The first one to pop up was easy, *George Avail*. The random ones started to take longer. The next was one of the agents with the tall man. He came back as William Nans, Army Ranger retired, no further info. Elsy had seen this type of file before; she was quite certain he was a government operative. That would explain the time and difficulty of identifying the others. She wasn't sure why the man in handcuffs was a challenge though. "He can't be an agent," she thought.

She punched a few keys on her computer to refine her search. She focused it on the databases that contained the difficult-to-access files. The search was on autopilot, so she decided to take a minute and talk with Katrina who had been left with her.

"So, what's your story?" Elsy asked.

Katrina turned from the iPad she had been playing on.

"How long do you have?" she inquired back with a smile.

"I have all day," Elsy told her.

Katrina jumped up and joined Elsy at the kitchen island where she was working.

"How far back do you want me to go?" Trina asked.

"As far as you want to," Elsy said.

"Well, it was a few years ago when my mom died, then I went to live with my aunt. She was hooked on drugs and tried to pimp me out to pay for her fix, so I ran away. I've been taking care of myself ever since then. I lived in a homeless camp for a while and those people looked out for me like I was their daughter. Eventually the city came to move them out, so I ran again," Trina took a breath.

"My God, you have had it hard," Elsy empathized.

"Wait, I'm getting to the good part. So, I started learning how to use people for money, sometimes like a gift, or pickpocketing, I even learned how to boost cars. I wouldn't sell drugs or be a prostitute though. I ended up meeting Derrick because I was hired to participate in a charade that was supposed to lure him out so they could ask him some questions, instead, D kicked the guy's ass, because he thought the man had hurt me."

"If that's all true, how did you end up traveling with him?" Elsy asked, a bit concerned.

"Oh, it's all true. I ended up with him because they found me and brought me to his room and used me to get him to open the door. I know he told you the rest, so I won't repeat it. For whatever reason, he chose to protect me too."

Elsy looked at the little girl, who was too old for her actual age.

"Well, you're safe now," she reassured Trina.

"Thank you, I only want to know where I'll end up when this is all over," Trina asked.

Elsy smiled at her. "When the time comes, we'll all figure it out together," she promised.

24

SIMON ARRIVED at the building they were using to house their 'guests'. His driver pulled into an open garage and the door closed after them, when the door had completely shut, he exited the car. George Avail, who was seated beside him, was assisted out on the other side. Simon led the way as other agents assisted George to walk behind him. George was led into a brightly lit, small room with a small table and two chairs on either side. He was placed into one of the chairs. He just gazed ahead as Simon sat down across from him.

"George, we're going to play a little game of *Simon says*. You are going to do what I say and answer what I ask. Do you understand?"

George looked at him sheepishly, but was secretly defiant. He wanted to throw Simon off the roof.

"I understand, what do you want to know?" he asked quietly.

Simon was sure George was planning to give wrong or misleading answers to his questions.

"Who is Barry Klinger to you?" He asked.

"Barry is a facilitator for me, he is also a long-time friend," George confessed.

Simon was shocked by the forthrightness of his answer. He looked over his shoulder to make sure the cameras were recording.

"Okay, a little tougher question this time. What was Barry doing for you in Milekistan?" Simon continued.

"Oh, that's a good question." George baited before answering. "Barry was trying to orchestrate the revolution and the General's response so it would provide alternate news coverage, that way other things might be pushed to the back as far as the public saw."

Simon was sitting on the edge of his chair; he had never anticipated this level of honesty from George Avail. Quite frankly, the man's reputation had led him to believe he might be unbreakable.

"Are you in this alone for your purposes or are you working with anyone else?"

George did not answer this question immediately. He contemplated the ramifications of answering honestly. What would government involvement do to his plan? It was obvious Simon didn't understand the waters he was fishing in. He thought of his daughter and how she turned her back on him and the business—she was taken before he could change her mind.

"Okay, I'll tell you what you want, but you'll have to realize that everything that happens after this, is your fault for asking," George warned.

Simon wasn't sure if that was a threat or a warning. Somehow though, he felt it was very real. "Hold on a second. We'll do this instead." He reached around and switched off the cameras. Then he took out his phone and started recording. "Okay, go ahead," he urged his prisoner.

George started slow and methodical.

"There are people all over the globe who have tried to infiltrate the American government for decades. Some for financial purposes, some for more nefarious reasons, and the most dangerous are the nation-states who hate the US and seek to destroy it from within. The American government is now riddled with both corruption and agents of other interests, who are acting against the securities of the American people. Your agency alone is littered with them; don't worry though, it's not just your agency, it's all of them. It's the House and the Senate, its state and local governments, it's prosecutors and judges, and they won't stop till they have a President.

This has been going on for a long time, and people were content to let it happen. We are now at a culmination of these actions and subversions.

Large global players are getting ready to put their plans into action. I admit I had been an outside player in this, making my moves for access to power and money. Now my interventions have been stopped for the facilitation of the larger actions. Agent Little, you better get moving or America might cease to exist as we know it. I guarantee even President Harrington is oblivious to the magnitude of the plan against America. It might already be too late," George said, with a bit of arrogant pride.

"Is that all? I want names, places, and actions they are planning. I need more than this nice little dark fairytale," Simon demanded.

"Mr. Little, if either of us is still alive tomorrow, I'll be shocked. Bring Barry in, I'll tell him to cooperate, you'll see," George assured him.

Simon stepped out of the room, turning the cameras back on before he left.

Would Barry also corroborate George's tale? he wondered. He headed for where they were keeping Barry.

"This should be interesting."

————

AN INTENSIVE CARE room had been set up hastily on the maternity floor. Doctors and nurses from somewhere other than the hospital had been brought in to staff it; the only exception was the surgeon who had saved her life. The maternity ward was restricted access already, so it worked perfectly for the safety of the patient.

It had been about eighteen hours since the emergency relocation they had performed at the request of the Federal Marshal. The patient was recovering under the watch of specialists brought in for the sole purpose of keeping her alive and getting her talking. A nurse checking her meds was the first to see the change. Linda opened her eyes; she was still intubated and unable to speak due to the tube protruding from her mouth. She tried to move her arms, but was too weak to do so. The nurse looked at her understandingly and softly said.

"It's okay. You've been through a major surgery. You're lucky to be alive. Let me go get the doctor."

Linda remembered being shot, she remembered the man who tried to save her twice and forgave her for some atrocity she had committed against him. He was all she could think of.

The doctor hastily entered the room and grabbed Linda's medical chart from the door.

"This is very good, you're recovering nicely. Ms. Avail, please give me a moment, and I'll have someone extubate you shortly. We need to closely monitor your breathing as we do it, due to the location of your injury," he informed her.

In her mind, Linda wondered why no one would refer to her wound as a gunshot. They all kept calling it an *injury*. "Maybe I'll ask that when I can talk again?" she thought.

———

BARRY'S GUARD had left the room before Simon came in. He had a very important errand he needed to run as he ascended the elevator to the main floor and left the building. He didn't swipe out, even though it was policy whenever personnel were entering or leaving. He jumped into his car and drove about ten minutes away before stopping at a convenience store and buying a disposable phone. He pulled a number scratched on a small piece of paper from his pocket and dialed the number.

"Hello, who is this?" came the voice from the number he dialed.

"You don't know me, but Barry needed to send you a message. I'm here to relay it. I must be quick, so please record this and don't interrupt. Are you ready?" the guard asked.

After making sure the call would be recorded, "Yes, please go ahead," the person on the phone said.

"An additional payment should be in your mail today; it's been encrypted for your crypto account. It's on a thumb drive; along with it is the actual data George needs you to uncover and collect. This is dangerous information, so be extremely careful. A twenty percent increase has been added to your pay because of the danger. Please acquire and retain this information as soon as you can. That's it," the guard finished reading and hung up.

"Deidra, we need to check the mail right now," he called out from his office.

———

JEAC PASTIL HAD CALLED another meeting for the members of the group he led. While they were referred to commonly as the World Council, it was a name given to itself by its members. Officially they had no name, nor did they exist. That being what it was, he still had the responsibility to run the day-to-day operations that would achieve the cohesive desires of the group. A few problems were popping up that he would now have to deal with. The US President was not controlled by the association. He was quietly investigating issues that were supposed to have been dismissed. Reports were indicating the FBI team he appointed to investigate might have found a small bit of evidence that could allude to the true intent of those incidents.

Also, George Avail, a man who had been working alongside their group for years, now was seemingly working against them. Intelligence from the group's assets was indicating he was now cooperating with the US intelligence community. This could be very bad, as George knew quite a lot about the Council's operations.

Lastly, it seemed an elite hacker group had accessed a manipulative code that they had embedded in most of the social media platforms used around the world, predominantly the US. These issues would be discussed in length tonight and resolutions would be decided. He called his assistant.

"Mr. Faulk, is everything ready for this evening?"

"Yes sir, everything is secure, and all your requests have been confirmed. All invited members have also verified their attendance," Denler reassured him.

"Good, I'd like you to be there as well," he informed his assistant.

"Me, sir? I've never attended one of these meetings before," Denler responded.

"No worries. I have assigned you to Mr. Bins, he will show you the ropes, so to speak. Enjoy yourself and soak up as much knowledge as you can. This is my gift to you for being a loyal and effective assistant," Jeac said.

Denler was shocked and honored. "Thank you, sir, I won't disappoint you."

"I know you won't, Mr. Faulk," Jeac said as he turned away.

———

HARLEM AND DERRICK had split up at the hospital. Harlem took the car and followed the vehicle that took George Avail from the hospital. The driver was cautious and made it hard for Harlem to follow without being detected; he would drive slowly, then fast, and slow again, he changed lanes when possible, and made unpredictable turns. Twice, he stopped for no apparent reason. Harlem was aware of these tactics and kept as much room between them as he could.

After about thirty minutes of driving, sometimes in a big circle, the van pulled into an industrial park. The driveway was gated and guarded. Harlem wouldn't be able to follow them inside. Unfortunately, there were multiple buildings within the park area and Harlem had no way to determine which one they entered.

While Harlem was tracking George Avail, Derrick was charming the nurses looking for information on Linda. He was convinced that she was still alive and most likely still in the hospital. He spoke with the head ER nurse and lied a little bit.

"Hi, I'm writing a hospital thriller. If I wanted to secure a patient in the hospital that needed serious care, is there an area here that I could do that?" he asked.

The nurse looked at him quizzically.

"Well, I guess you could use one of the operating areas on the seventh floor, but that would shut them down for surgery," she answered.

"Is there somewhere I could go that would not disrupt daily operations, or at least minimally?" he continued questioning.

"I know they would never do it, but the only other place I can think of would be the maternity floor. It's already secure, entry only with ID. I suppose they could take over one room without any major effect on normal operations," the nurse surmised.

Derrick smiled; he knew this was the right information he needed.

"Thank you so much, you've been an incredible help," he said.

Derrick consulted the hospital directory. Maternity, Floor 5.

He headed for the fifth floor. Derick got off the elevator that led directly to a waiting room. Two older folks were waiting; he presumed they were grandparents awaiting news on a grandchild.

He took a seat behind them where he could look down the hallway through the small windows in the door. Occasionally, a staff member would walk through, and Derrick would have the opportunity to look down the hallway without the door as an obstruction. Almost at the end of the hall, something caught his eye. A man dressed in a suit sitting in a chair in the hallway. He watched for quite a while. Every time the door swung open, Derrick would intentionally look. The man in the suit was still there.

He smiled to himself. He was now positive Linda Avail was alive and that she was still here in the hospital.

25

JEAC WATCHED from a small room aside from the meeting hall where the attendees were gathering. There was a very large table in the shape of a circle at the center of the large room. He was expecting sixty-five members to attend tonight, comprised of the wealthiest and most powerful people on the planet. Presidents and Prime Ministers of several countries as well as billionaires from around the globe, including from America. CEOs of social media companies as well as mainstream media.

All the attendees had a purpose to the Council despite their expectations of why they were given membership. Failure to fulfill that purpose could cause them to be removed from the Council. He looked out and saw his assistant working feverishly to make sure each member's needs were met, and Pierce Bins quietly directing the show like a silent conductor. Jeac observed until the second-to-last seat was filled.

Everyone was here. He stepped out and moved to the last empty chair at the table.

"Good evening members, we have some troubling issues to discuss tonight and to develop resolutions for. Let's get started."

———

THE CAR PAULA had been waiting for took much longer than she had expected. She was notified that a few things had come up and would be delayed, but they never said how long. She decided to risk it and took a quick shower and changed before she would meet with the President. As she stepped from the bathroom to her office, she found that more information had been delivered to her email. She read the reports and was troubled by what she found.

First, she was notified that the sketch artist had been killed in a motor vehicle accident just a few hours ago and that the agent who uncovered the similar features of their possible suspect had gone missing. Paula picked up the phone and called the local police where the agent was last known to be working. After a brief discussion, the officer she spoke with assured her they would locate her agent and get back to her.

As Paula was trying to understand these occurrences and if they could be related, the gate called.

"Ma'am, there is a car here for you."

"Thank you, let them in and direct them to my building," she informed the gate guard.

She grabbed her things and headed outside. Being assigned to a field office instead of her new role in Boston was like being a field agent again. She remembered what she loved about the job. She hopped into the back seat and the car started to move again, out through the gate and headed toward DC.

———

DERRICK GRABBED a cab at the hospital and headed back to Harlem's house. He couldn't wait to share the news with anyone but didn't want to risk the phones—it had taken some serious pull to accomplish what had been done with Linda. As the cab pulled up in front of the home, he realized that Harlem's car wasn't back yet. *Is that good or bad?* He wondered.

Inside, Derrick found Elsy and Trina chatting away. They got quiet when he approached them.

"Did I interrupt something?" he asked.

Trina jumped at the chance to mess with him.

"Of course you did, that's kinda your thing," she giggled.

She couldn't contain the big smile when she said it. Derrick realized she wasn't just talking about their conversation. He smiled back.

"I guess it is. Have you heard from Harlem yet? I have some interesting things I discovered at the hospital," he teased.

Elsy answered him, "Yes, he called seconds before you came in. He followed them to an industrial park and said he would be back soon to fill us in."

Derrick thought about everything he had learned in the last few hours. They were dealing with some powerful people; he just didn't know who or why yet.

———

HARLEM CAME THROUGH THE DOOR, as if on cue. He wanted to get up to speed and see what they were dealing with.

"Hi, sorry I'm late apparently," he playfully apologized.

Everyone was sitting at the kitchen island waiting for him. Derrick had poured bourbon for Elsy and himself and had an empty glass waiting for Harlem. He noticed the glass Derrick was holding and the bottle on the table.

"My Eagle Rare, really?" Harlem complained.

"I think we're gonna need it, Besides I'll buy you another if it's a big deal," Derrick offered, not selling Elsy out for it being her idea.

Harlem smiled. "I'm just messing with you, it's here to be enjoyed."

"Good because you're not gonna enjoy what you hear next," Derrick warned.

Derrick took a sip and shared his story with the group. He started with his suspicions in the morgue and continued from there to his talk with the ER nurse, finishing with his observations in the maternity ward.

"So, I was sitting there, and every time the door opened, I could see the same guy in a suit sitting by the door. No nurses even went down the hall there, as far as I could tell. I'm positive Linda Avail is alive in there. I know that seems like a leap, but I'm telling you, this has all the earmarks of a government cover-up. George Avail has been fooled into thinking his daughter is dead, my guess is to cause him to share information he absolutely wouldn't otherwise."

Derrick took another sip and swished it around in his mouth. He could feel the flavors seem to separate into distinct parts as he swallowed. Harlem was silent in thought for a moment, and Elsy decided that was her cue.

"Okay, well on the note of big government interference, the faces you sent were very hard to identify. Most still have no names. The couple I was able to find, are questionable at best and have special ops ties," she said as she handed out the printouts with the pictures, most of them without IDs. "That's all I have so far. It seems we've jumped into the deep end again."

Harlem now sensed it was his turn. "I followed the SUV with Mr. Avail and his captors. They went to an industrial park that is guarded better than most military bases. There were armed people everywhere. The entrance to the whole area is gated and the limited access blinds you to which building they might have chosen to enter. I drove around a little bit before I came back. There is an office building being renovated about a half block away. While the building doesn't provide a good view, they have a crane set up that would allow us to see every building in the park, I think."

They all conversed for a second, then Trina spoke, "I could get in there."

All eyes turned to her.

"Yeah, I don't think so," Derrick responded almost immediately, his protective instincts obvious in his tone.

"No really, listen. If they are police or government agents, they'd be bound by law to turn me over to someone. You guys could pretend to be child services and be escorted right to me," Trina encouraged.

Now suddenly everyone was looking at Derrick.

"Wait. Is this somehow my call? We are all in this together now. I'm not sure I'm comfortable allowing Trina to be placed into such a potentially dangerous scenario," he stated.

"You know I'm good under pressure, and I'm smart. You know I can do this," Trina begged him.

"You're also only thirteen. I truly believe you *can* do it, that doesn't mean you *should*," Derrick reminded her.

The whole room was silent for a second, then Katrina spoke again.

"Tell you what, if you come up with a better or even equal plan, I'll stay home and be a good girl, otherwise, my plan is the safest so far," she said with authority.

No one spoke, they seemed afraid to admit she was right.

Finally, Harlem said, "I think that's a fair deal."

Derrick shot him a hard stare, then swallowed the remainder of the bourbon in his glass and reached to refill it.

———

TULIA AND DILLON had been keeping tabs on Tinker since Elsy left. It had been quiet for a while, and now suddenly there was a ton of data being sifted through on multiple sites. Each location was managed by the same AI formats that Tinker had already hacked. There was no evidence that the Chinese were involved at all in this data collection. Rather than try to understand what Tinker was doing, the pair decided to mirror his actions and collect the same data. When their stream started, they had some catch-up to do to have a complete cache of the information that was being stolen. They couldn't go too fast, or they'd compromise their invisibility. It was time to update Elsy.

Tulia grabbed the phone.

———

THE PHONE RANG SEVERAL TIMES, finally on the sixth ring it was answered.

"Yes, what is it? I said not to be disturbed right now."

"Sir, I'm sorry, I thought you'd want to know. She's awake."

"Is she talking?"

"No sir, we've kept the room sealed except for her doctors."

"Alright, keep it that way until I can get there. I must finish up here first."

Simon went back into the room with George. This time he brought him a pitcher of cold water and a glass.

"Mr. Avail, you have been forthright with us so far. I hope you will continue to do so," Simon said appreciatively.

"I have no reason to lie. I have no reason to do anything anymore." George allowed his voice trail off for effect.

"Sir, you have the chance to get justice for your daughter's death, and you have a chance to help America, instead of only yourself for a change."

George almost smiled; there was a part of him that still wanted to play with Simon. The taunt was so obvious it demanded a vicious response, but instead George responded quietly.

"Mr. Little, I have made billions of dollars off the greed and manipulation of Americans. I have stolen from my adversaries, killed those who stood in my way, and manipulated the easily swayed, for more years than you have been alive. You are not equipped to try and play me, so please do not. Ask your questions and I will answer, but if you try to treat me like I am inferior to you again, I will end this conversation. You are on the verge of my sorrow turning to anger, that will not be good for either of us, I imagine."

Simon felt the sting of the rebuke. He changed his tactics accordingly.

"Tell me more about these people who have infiltrated our government. Who are they and what is their goal?" he asked.

"I do not currently have their identities; their goal is simple. To remove America from the top of the world power food chain. They want to force America to her knees before every other nation. The concept of self-rule is contrary to almost every other form of government in the world. America has been pulling away from it naturally for decades. After all, those "in power" only want to keep and expand their power. That's why I've found it so easy to manipulate some of these politicians. I can give you a few names. There are people I have personally cultivated for my own interests.

They are not the problem you face, though. You face a much larger group with far deeper pockets than mine. They do not operate solely on financial transactions either. They create scenarios with which to blackmail their embedded candidates. Every opportunity to ensure complete compliance is exploited by them. I believe that is why my daughter is dead. They probably didn't mean to kill her, just injure her to force my compliance."

Simon was suddenly concerned. His initial goal had been to tie Barry to the manipulation of the war in Milekistan. Now he was onto something much darker and extremely larger in scope than he anticipated. George had just corroborated everything Barry had said as well. He wasn't sure what to do with the pair now. They were no longer his big fish; they were his informants.

———

AS WITH ALL THEIR big meetings, Pierce Bins stepped forward to call the gathering to order. He announced the ground rules and then graciously turned the control over to Jeac Pastil.

"Fellow, members. First, thank you for the trust you have shown by bestowing this position on me. Thank you truly. I will do whatever it takes to reach our end goal. The demise of the cowboy culture of America."

Cheers and clapping erupted from the group seated around the table.

Jeac held his hands flat and gestured down in a way to suggest stopping the platitudes.

"As I am sure you are all aware, my predecessor had her own agenda and that was dangerous for all of us. My only agenda is *our* agenda," he said, like a politician fishing for votes.

Again, clapping and cheering ensued. This time he waited for it to die down on its own.

"The Council is closer than we have ever been in reaching our objective. With the US presidential election on the horizon, we have a candidate that will assist us from the highest position in their country. Our social media algorithms have produced wildly successful results in both causing separation between parties, but also in sowing disinformation to a whole new level." As he paused, there was applause again.

"This all brings us to why we are here today. Three aspects of our plan are in jeopardy of exposure. The first is someone who we have for years called a friend. Unfortunately, actions taken by my predecessor have turned him against us. He is now in a very dangerous position as a prisoner of the CIA. George Avail is now a threat to the Council, and I'm asking you to consider the appropriate action to resolve this threat. The full details are in the first of the three folders in front of you."

As he paused, he could hear and see the other members shuffling through the files he had prepared for them.

"Number two. Over decades, we have been slowly acquiring farmland in the heart of America, the goal has always been to control the food sources that could easily sustain their nation even if it was cut off by war or embargo. In a second wave of action, my predecessor once again chose to act without Council approval and started to destroy American food processing plants. This action was contained, for the most part, by enforcing limited media coverage and utilizing assets in positions to minimize its true nature.

Unfortunately, President Harrington was not as easily distracted from these events. He recently appointed a special FBI task force to investigate. Based on the latest information we have received; they have possibly tied the two events together and are looking deeper into the questions. This is another dangerous scenario for us. You will find all of this is in folder two."

This time Jeac did not wait for the rustling of paper to subside.

"Finally, we have had extreme success in manipulating Americans with both social media and the mainstream outlets that we control or work with. This has been so effective due to our integration with AI platforms. It has come to my attention that these AI platforms are under attack. The hackers are extremely good and have been elusive to our cybersecurity teams. As of right now, the hack is preventing us from deploying the next round of manipulative code that will help push our candidate into the presidency.

As you all know, President Harrington has the highest approval rating of any US President running for a second term. For our plan to stay on schedule, this must also be handled. Please take time to discuss these issues amongst yourselves. You should return to discuss solutions in exactly ninety minutes." Jeac returned to his seat. A murmur swept across the room as members were already discussing the issues with those seated next to them. Pierce stood up and dismissed the room for ninety minutes.

26

GEORGE WAS NOT EATING. He and Barry had been moved to slightly better accommodations. It was a nice room, but still built inside an industrial building; there were no windows, and only two doors. One door led out of the room and was locked, the other led to a bathroom. George thought of his daughter. He wondered how his business would suffer with her the loss of her. Barry sat at the small table directly across from him; the recessed light directly above them somehow made the food look less desirable. Barry ate it anyway. He had been trained a long time ago when you are a prisoner, always eat, you never know when you'll have a chance that you'll need strength to take advantage of.

Barry tried to read George's mind. "George, I know you're hurting, trust me, I am too. But we need to get out of here to avenge her. You need to eat."

George fixated on one part of his statement. *Avenge her.* That would be the justification for everything he would do from here out. He looked up at the face across the table. He knew Barry, his long-time friend, would have his back no matter what he chose to do.

"I told him everything," George whispered.

"What do you mean?" Barry asked.

"I mean I told him *everything*. The political assets, the corrupt media, the voter manipulation, even the World Council. I mean everything," George said matter-of-factly.

He focused on his plate and started eating. Barry just sat in silence and watched him eat. He could feel that George had a plan, he just didn't know what it was yet.

————

THE DOCTOR CAREFULLY EXTUBATED LINDA. As he pulled the tube from her throat, he gave her instructions.

"Breathe in slowly and deliberately, dn't try to talk for a few minutes. Let your lungs get reacquainted with the effort of breathing."

Linda nodded and did as she was told. After a few minutes of breathing as directed, she tried to talk and was surprised at how much effort it took.

In a quiet raspy voice, she asked, "What happened to the other people I was with? Did they survive?"

The doctor just looked at her quizzically.

"You were the only one transported to us, I don't think there were any other survivors. I'm sorry to say, I heard an officer saying that there were two dead bodies transported from the parking lot."

Linda let out a moan. Her heart rate jumped dramatically on the monitor.

The doctor forced her to lay back and said, "That's enough for today."

Tears welled up in Linda's eyes and ran down her face as she thought of the man who put his hate aside to help her and the beautiful little girl who was so much more than she appeared. In her imagination, she could see their lifeless bodies lying in a pool of blood in the parking lot of that diner. This was her fault; she led the killers right to them. She started to count those who died protecting her; by the time she reached Derrick and Trina, she felt sick. She vomited over the edge of the bed rail as a nurse walked in.

"I'm so sorry," she said wiping her mouth on the sheet.

"No worries sweetie," the nurse replied. "I'm going to get you all cleaned up."

————

SIMON WAS on his way back to the hospital. He felt that Linda would need to be protected, as well as a valuable tool to use against her father. He had no problem detaining her as an uncooperative witness. He called his agent watching the door.

"What's the status there?" he asked.

"Nothing new, sir. The doctor removed her breathing tube, she asked about some people she may have been traveling with and the doctor told her they were killed in the parking lot."

"What? What people? We don't have any information that she was with anyone else. Make sure she doesn't get any more visitors."

"Well, the nurse is in there now," the agent replied.

"Let her finish, then lock it down till I get there," Simon ordered.

THE COUNCIL HAD CONCLUDED their meeting, and Jeac had received the direction he wanted. The hacker would be tracked and removed, the President would be handled by their assets in government, and George Avail would be sanctioned 'in a manner befitting his betrayal'. Mr. Pastil was excited to return to his office today. Things were about to heat up.

THE GROUP at Harlem's had worked on the plan most of the night. Despite her age, it was obvious that Trina's plan was better than anything else they came up with. Harlem already had a government car from the city, and he and Elsy could easily pass as Child and Family Services employees. Derrick would provide overwatch from the crane Harlem had discovered. Harlem and Elsy headed out in Harlem's car, with Trina and Derrick in the Jeep. They needed to identify where Trina could get inside unnoticed, and which building contained the prisoners. It was a weekend; they were praying the construction would be off that day and the crane would be accessible.

The construction site was empty when they drove up. Derrick picked the lock on the gate so quickly that anyone watching would have thought he had a key. Harlem wasn't sure what to think; he was still trying to form his own opinion about Derrick. Inside the gate, they hid their vehicles amongst the building supplies and went inside. They found most of the building on the lower floors were still intact, it was the upper floors that they were actively renovating. They headed up to the top floor. From the windows, they could see most of the buildings in the industrial park; however, not all the entrances.

They decided to eliminate the buildings that could be easily seen from their current position. They headed up to the roof, where there was a temporary walkway that led to the crane. Derrick grabbed the radio that Harlem had gotten them all and headed up with a set of powerful binoculars. They would need to identify the location quickly. Derrick was barely in position when he heard a loud bang from a door slamming at a building in the industrial park. He started to scan and saw a short man moving from one of the buildings. He was the same man Derrick had seen in the morgue with Mr. Avail.

He chirped into the radiom "That was easy."

"You found it already?" Harlem asked.

"I hope so, that same dude from the morgue just exited one of the buildings. He looks upset," Derrick relayed.

"Text us the building number," Harlem advised.

"I don't see a number on that building. It's right between seven and eleven but I do not see an eight, nine or ten. It looks like Trina can get through a small opening off Deagle Street, behind the smoke shop."

Elsy and Harlem gave the direction to Katrina. Harlem had acquired a surveillance setup from work and wired her for sound and video, so they would be able to monitor her as she went. They had been so intent on discovering where the men went and who they were, no one considered what would happen when they found out.

———

THE NURSE MOVED to close the door to Linda's room, and the guard outside watched her, concerned by her action.

"I need to clean her up a bit, she still deserves privacy," she explained to him.

The guard seemed to understand and just nodded his head. With the door closed the nurse approached Linda, she leaned down close to her face and whispered.

"You are still in grave danger, former friends of your father and government agents are actively trying to use you. If you can trust me, I have friends ready to get you out of here."

Linda watched the nurse's eyes, for some reason, she felt she should trust her. She nodded her head yes. The nurses acted as soon as she received Linda's confirmation. She pulled a small radio from her pocket.

"It's a go."

———

A TEXT WENT OUT to the staff of the maternity ward. *Seven seven seven,* flashed on the screens of their phones. The hospital staff started locking down each room on the floor. The guard in front of Linda's room noticed something was wrong, he stood up and knocked on the door.

"Is everything okay in there? I need to come in," he said.

"Yes, give me one more second," the nurse called out.

"I'm sorry, I need to enter now," he stated as he turned the handle to enter. The door pulled away from him as he was pushing it in, and an agitated nurse stood in front of him. His attention was drawn to Linda who was now dressed in street clothes. As he focused back on the nurse, he noticed a needle in her hand. Sensing something wasn't right, he started to draw his weapon. The nurse instinctively sank the needle in his neck and grabbed at the gun he was raising. She redirected his motion and prevented him from raising the weapon.

His mind registered the small prick in his neck, but almost immediately the room started to spin, and he lost his balance and fell to the floor unable to move. The nurse wiped the needle off and dropped it on the floor, then she reached down and pulled the guard's body into the room.

"Four minutes," she said into a radio.

Two additional men in ambulance uniforms showed up at the door with an ambulance gurney. They moved the guard's body out of the way and unplugged Linda from all the monitors.

"Ma'am, this is gonna be a rough ride, but I promise we're getting you to safety," one of the men said.

They carefully lifted her from her bed to the gurney and then headed for the door.

"Two minutes."

At the end of the hall, they took the maintenance elevator. It was tight for the gurney but was better for concealment. They arrived at the ER entrance. Linda was pushed out to a waiting ambulance. All three of the people escorting her jumped in and it started to drive away into traffic. The driver had to slam on the brakes, causing everyone inside to bounce around against each other, due to an SUV that was driving like crazy and almost hit them as they exited.

———

SIMON WAS EXCITED to talk to Linda. The idea that there may be others he could interrogate about this global agency excited him. He felt like he was on to the largest case of his career. His driver swung into the emergency room entrance at a high rate of speed, almost striking an ambulance as it was leaving. Simon made eye contact with the driver who looked a bit agitated over the incident. "I would be too," he thought. The SUV stopped and Simon leapt out and half-ran, half-fast walked to the elevators. He pushed the button for Floor 5, Maternity. A lady behind him tried to offer some helpful information.

"They moved the babies off the floor, they're on floor four right now," she offered.

"What are you talking about?" Simon questioned.

"Maternity, they were moved temporarily, because of an irate parent on the floor, I heard," the lady informed him.

As the door opened on five, Simon sprinted past the nurse's station, and down the hall to where his agent was missing. He knew something was wrong. He threw the door open and immediately noticed that Linda was gone. His agent was propped up in the corner. He was barely stirring, but right now that was not his biggest concern. Simon was in shock for a second, "Who could do this?" he didn't mean to say it aloud, but he did.

A little girl stood in the doorway of the room across the hall. She was holding a little blue teddy bear close to her chest.

"It was the nurse," she said quietly.

Simon took a step back to see who had answered him.

He saw a little girl, evidence of fresh tears still wet on her cheeks.

"What was the nurse, sweetie?" he said quietly as he kneeled to her level.

"You asked, 'who could do this?' It was the nurse," the girl answered.

"You saw her?" Simon asked, excitedly.

"Yes."

"Why are you up here alone?" he wondered aloud.

"They made us move, but they dropped my new little brother's bear. I came back to get it," she answered.

"Okay, you can call me Agent Simon. What's your name?" He asked.

"My name is Charlotte."

"Alright Charlotte, it's nice to meet you. Let's go find your parents," Simon encouraged as he grasped the little girl's hand.

Simon reached back and pulled the door to what was Linda's room closed. It was now a crime scene. He called other agents to come to secure it as he returned his new friend Charlotte to her parents. During the elevator ride, he questioned what else she might have seen.

———

TRINA FOUND the hole in the fence without any issue. Then with the oversight of Derrick, he led her to the building they were assuming was their target. As Trina got closer, she noticed guards were patrolling.

"I think this is the right building, there are guards everywhere," she whispered.

Harlem used the microphone on his radio to respond. "If there are too many guards, get out of there."

"I got this," she quietly responded.

She adeptly slipped past the guards and right into the building through a door that someone had propped open to facilitate the occasional cigarette. Inside, Trina stopped and listened. Her time on the street had taught her how to survive in dangerous situations; awareness was key. Even at thirteen, she was as proficient at avoiding danger as any seasoned soldier. She edged into a small room as two men approached her location—they continued by unaware of her presence. She listened to their conversation.

"I'm surprised he let them back together, I would have thought the goal was to have one turn on the other."

"Either way, he got something he wanted from them. His whole attitude changed after he interviewed that Avail guy."

Trina smiled and said quietly. "I'm in the right place. I'm gonna try and get a closer look."

Derrick responded first this time, "No Trina, just follow the plan, your plan, it was a good one."

Trina didn't respond. Harlem watched the video as Trina nonchalantly walked down the halls of the building. She found a set of stairs and according to the information she gathered from eavesdropping on the men in the hall, she needed to go down one level. She reached the platform outside the lower level and could see guards stationed up and down the halls.

"This could be a problem," she mumbled, forgetting she was being monitored.

"What is it?" Harlem and Derrick asked at the same time.

"Lots of guards, lots and lots of guards," she replied.

"Get out. We know where they are now. We can come up with another plan later," Derrick pleaded.

"Wait, give me a minute," she responded.

Katrina started to think. She headed back towards where the guards had been smoking. She moved like a ninja. Picking up the pack of cigarettes and a lighter off the table where they had been left, she sprinted up two flights of stairs and lit a cigarette in the stairwell. She blew on it to make sure it was lit and smoking and then tossed it on the steps. She listened for guards and then quietly ran back down the steps to the floor below. Now she waited behind a stack of boxes on the landing.

Within a few minutes, a piercing noise erupted from speakers throughout the building. A few seconds later, guards from the floor where Trina was waiting ran out the door past her and headed upstairs. As the last guard ran past, Trina slipped out and grabbed the door. She was in.

27

LINDA FELT tired as the ambulance ride took her away from the hospital. She had moments where she wondered what was happening to her, but mostly she wanted to rest. The ambulance finally came to a stop, the doors in the rear opened, and Linda was removed. They pushed her up the ramp and into another hospital, not a real hospital, but it would serve as one for Linda's recovery. A doctor met them on the way in. "So, this is Ms. Avail?"

"Yes, it is," the nurse answered.

"Well, I hope this works, we'll be on their radar soon." Disapproval was evident in his voice.

They took her inside and moved her to her new room.

Linda had started to awaken from her nap.

The doctor spoke to her. "Hello Ms. Avail, I am Dr. Cartwright. I will be your attending doctor during your recovery. Please feel free to ask any questions when you're ready."

———

TINKER HAD ACQUIRED the thumb drive he was sent. The key to the cryptocurrency accessed all the money he was promised plus more; also included were the instructions on what to do with the backdoor he created. He logged into all the AIs he had targeted; he started the subroutine that Mr. Avail had identified for him. Almost immediately data started to download. He didn't know the value of this information, only that it was important to his employer.

As the data started to come in, he recognized hundreds of documents and other materials, such as names and images that had been collected as well. When he noticed certain financial information start to pile in, he called Deidra. "Can you write a quick program that sorts all this information by the person or entity it ties to? I would like to clean this all up, so I know what we're downloading from these servers."

———

PAULA'S TRIP TO see President Harrington didn't quite go as expected. The car didn't take her to the White House; instead, she was taken to a large townhouse just blocks from Pennsylvania Avenue. The car stopped in front of the ornate steps leading to large double wooden doors with leaded glass inserts. Paula followed the direction of the driver and headed up the stairs to the doors. Before she could knock, the doors swung open.

"Agent Newly, please come in," she was greeted.

It was the booming southern drawl of Senator Alvin Heller who stood before her. Heller was known to be a confidant of the President and one of his trusted advisors. Still, Paula was uneasy with this unexpected turn of events. She followed the Senator into the home. Inside, she couldn't help but stare at the grand staircase that swept down the left side of the large foyer she was standing in.

"Come this way, please," the Senator instructed.

Paula followed the request of the Senator. He led her out onto the covered porch in the rear of the townhouse. It overlooked a beautiful, manicured garden and landscape and a small lap pool, attributes that were unheard of in this area of DC.

"Can I offer you a drink? Ice water, tea, a mint julep? I feel I need to work to keep up my reputation as a southern gentleman, after spending so much time here in DC," he joked.

Paula waved her hand to decline the offer.

"No sir, I'd like to know why I'm here. I have a meeting at the White House," she informed him.

"Agent Newly, I'm sure you understand the President is running for re-election right now. So, here is the problem. He is on the campaign trail today. If you had reached him, he would have cancelled his campaigning to meet with you. We need you to stop with this distraction nonsense. Just inform him the original reports were correct and there is nothing to his concerns," the Senator suggested strongly.

"Senator, with all due respect, why would I do that? I am not at liberty to discuss the case with you, but just say that there is evidence not yet reviewed," Paula said, a bit angered by the Senator.

A bead of sweat broke out on the Senator's face, he started to tug at the collar of the shirt he was wearing.

"What evidence have you found?" he asked, his voice having lost some of the evident confidence he had initially.

"Sir, I will save my findings for the President himself, as per his direction to me," Paula stated firmly.

Senator Heller stared at her for a few seconds.

"Why do you need to be so stubborn? This is for Estephan's own best interest, even if he doesn't know it," Heller said.

Paula knew a BS line when she heard it.

"Senator, it's been nice to meet you, but I need to meet with the President. I must bid you goodbye," she said as she stood.

"Sit back down," Heller ordered.

"Excuse me?" Paula asked incredulously.

"You will sit back down and finish hearing me out or greater measures will be put in place," Heller threatened.

Before she could respond, two men appeared in the doorway. They did not make any movement towards her or even any adversarial actions, they just stood at the door making sure it was blocked.

Paula stared at the men and then the Senator. She was confused by this turn of events, but the only thing she knew for sure was that her case was now about much more than just some burned-down food processing plants.

———

SIMON HAD a full forensic team going over the room. While he was troubled that his agent was assaulted, he was more particularly upset that he lost Linda Avail. Who could have known she was alive? He had every member of the hospital that knew she even existed detained for questioning, but he didn't expect much. Whoever pulled this off had skill and support. He knew Linda would need medical care; he would start with that.

"Analytics," was the answer to his call.

"Hi, it's Little. I need a list of medical products that would be used to build a recovery room for a seriously injured person, then I need to know if they've been sold to any individual or corporation," he requested.

"Yes sir, we'll get right on it," came the reply.

Simon knew a pushback would be coming. He was way outside of his jurisdiction now. Even his temporary Marshal credentials would not cover his actions much longer. He needed to act fast and find answers before his superiors pulled the plug on his operation and turned it over to the FBI.

———

TRINA TIPTOED DOWN THE HALLWAY. She was certain there would be more guards still down there. She could hear two men talking, so she pressed her ear to the door.

"If we don't find a way out, they will make us disappear," a voice said.

Trina took a chance; she swung the door open.

"Ta-da. You old guys ready to leave?" she asked, like a magician pulling a rabbit out.

In her ear, Trina could hear both Derrick and Harlem yelling. "What are you doing? Those men are dangerous, and their captors are more dangerous!"

She ignored the comments and looked at the two men.

"Come on guys, it's now or never," Trina prodded.

Both men stood up.

"It's now," the tall one said.

Derrick scrambled down the crane as fast as he could. Harlem and Elsy were already in the car driving to the alley behind the smoke shop. They were sure this was about to blow up.

Trina led the two men to the stairwell; she could hear the guards above them, all complaining about whichever one thought it was okay to sneak a smoke in the stairwell. She almost giggled. The guards were being ordered to head into a large conference room for a quick reminder about the rules on the site.

As the door closed behind the last guard, Trina motioned for the two men to follow her.

"Do you think it's wise to trust this child?" the older man asked.

"Shhh. And yes, unless you have some better option," Barry whispered back.

Barry smiled at the little girl's attitude.

"Besides, I like her," he said to George. Outside the building, they moved quickly toward the fence. Before they were even close, Trina realized the opening she came through would not accommodate these men.

"We're gonna need a bigger hole," she said into the microphone in her button.

"On it," Harlem responded. He already had the bolt cutters from his trunk and was cutting fence links. Trina came around the corner and ran towards Harlem. The orange Jeep pulled in as she was slipping through the fence. As Derrick exited the Wrangler, Trina wrapped her arms around him in a hug.

"I told you I could do it," she bragged.

Derrick hugged her back.

"I knew you could too, I just didn't want you to," he reassured her.

The two men Katrina had freed slipped through the fence.

Derrick watched as the man he had left home to kill emerged before him. As he looked into his eyes, he saw a look he was worried he'd end up seeing in his own mirror. George Avail's eyes were cold and emotionless.

———

AS TINKER and Deidra started to categorize the information they were collecting, Tulia and Dillon were doing the same. Dillon was the first to recognize what they were archiving.

"These are all big names; I think this is a blackmail list these AIs have created on high profile people," he speculated.

Tulia's eyes widened, and the hair on her neck stood up. This was incredibly dangerous information; they needed to let Elsy know what they'd found.

They reviewed the information again, and Tulia suggested. "We should encrypt all of this as we store it, just to be safe."

"You're right, that is an excellent idea." Dillon agreed.

With a few strokes of the keyboard, the information was now saved as just a bunch of random ones and zeroes. The key was put on a thumb drive and copied to a second. He handed the second one to Tulia.

"We should both have access until we can turn it over to Elsy," he said.

———

BARRY WASN'T sure what was happening when they exited the fence. The little girl was working with a group of adults, but he was sure that no official action would ever put a minor in harm's way. He knew he was free of the CIA blacksite though; it was time to move.

"I do not know who you are or why you rescued us, but we need to move now. This little girl's stunt will not fool them for much longer," Barry advised.

They divided up into two vehicles. Despite their wishes, Barry and George were separated into different vehicles. Barry was sensing a bit of hostility in the group, but wasn't sure if it was toward them or each other. It was clear that George was not going into the most conspicuous vehicle probably on the road; unfortunately, that meant he was.

Barry got into the Jeep with Derrick and Katrina. When Derrick turned the key, the engine's roar startled Barry.

"This is not stock," Barry half-stated, half-questioned.

Derrick laughed. "No, it is not."

He punched the accelerator and they rocketed away from the smoke shop, Harlem right on his tail.

———

THE AGENTS who were guarding George and Barry did not even realize they were gone right away. It was about twenty minutes after the fire alarm that they realized the two men were extremely silent. When they searched the room and did not find them, they put the entire area on lockdown. It was a little too late.

After they had searched every inch of the facility, they were forced to admit they had lost their prisoners. The lead agent who had enjoyed yelling at the other agents for smoking in the stairwell now realized he would be the one on the hook with Agent Little—after all, he had been the one who told the others to leave the prisoners while they investigated the alarm. Today was going to be a bad day.

———

JEAC WAS STANDING in a large room full of people on computers. He traveled sixty minutes by train to get there, so he was not in a good mood. He was talking to a young analyst who looked as if he were twelve.

"You said on the phone you had info on our hacker. Why did I need to suffer an hour on the train to get this information?"

"Well sir, I did not believe it would be safe to share this information on a phone line. We have identified the potential hacker. It is a nation member of the Council."

Jeac was not expecting this information. This was going to get ugly quickly. After all, the Council had just authorized extreme force if necessary to avert the interruption of their data stream.

"Which member?" Jeac asked.

"Sir it appears to be China," the analyst said.

"Are you very certain? Like, if your life depended on it?" Jeac asked harshly.

"Yes sir, the coding is unique to the Chinese Cyber Military," the analyst confirmed.

"Thank you, for the information and for your discretion. Make sure this does not leave this room," Jeac advised.

Jeac was swearing under his breath as he headed back to the train. Instead, he stopped and called his assistant.

"Denler, get me a helicopter, a fast one. I need to go to a few places on the way back, and that will be the best way."

Twenty minutes later, he was sitting in the passenger compartment of a small but fast helicopter. He gave the pilot his destination. The pilot waited for his passenger to be secure and spoke into the microphone on his helmet. After a lengthy reply from assumably the air controller, he gave Jeac the thumbs-up sign and they lifted off.

———

LINDA WAS awake and alert when they came in to replace her IV bags.

"Where am I?" she asked.

The lady she recognized as her nurse gave her a kind smile.

"You're safe, we are a group of Americans dedicated to keeping our country alive as the last bastion of freedom in the world. We call ourselves 'The Gray Americans'. You're lucky we found out about you in time. There are some seriously bad people in very high positions in our government, and it seems they would like you and your father to disappear."

Linda was not able to comprehend everything she said.

"Okay, I caught *bad people* and you're *The Gray Americans,* what does that mean?"

"Live and fight in the shadows, my dear. That's where you are trapped right now. Covert agencies are trying to kill you, maybe American, maybe foreign, we're not sure yet," the nurse answered cryptically.

"Ummm, okay, let's try another question. When I was shot there was a man and a little girl with me, are they dead?" Linda inquired.

"Linda, is it alright if I call you Linda?" the nurse requested.

"Yes, please answer me."

"Linda there were only two bodies found outside the diner. One was some poor sap who was targeted as a distraction, and the other was the shooter himself. He was found alive, but committed suicide on scene," the nurse informed her.

"No man, no little girl? How about a bright orange Wrangler?" Linda asked excitedly.

"Not that we know of," the nurse replied.

Linda relaxed a bit. "I hope they escaped."

28

BARRY AND GEORGE were brought to a house Elsy had found on the Internet. She used a couple of shell companies to rent it through a vacation stay site online. They pulled up to the front of the house. It was well off the road, so hiding Derrick's Jeep wasn't as big of a concern right now. They guided the two men inside. Harlem and Katrina made a grocery list and headed back out, though Harlem wasn't sure he wanted to leave Derrick unsupervised with the man he wanted to kill. The irony of fate was pushing Derrick to choose a path.

Derrick looked at George Avail. In all his imagined meetings, he always envisioned a smug arrogant man so full of himself he wouldn't be afraid of his impending death. The arrogance was missing; instead a very charming and sociable man stood before him. *A man quietly playing the game for his own benefit,* Derrick thought, though it was a passing feeling. Derick wasn't sure of the man he had villainized in his mind. He started to walk away to consider his impression of George Avail.

George hadn't forgotten the call from his daughter just before she was shot. The man she was with had been looking for them—they had wronged him. George put the pieces together as Derrick was observing him. He realized he needed to play his role as a more affable human, at least for now. He couldn't help but think how had karma put him squarely in the sites of a man who hated him and expected that man to help him? *Fate has a terrible sense of humor.*

———

SIMON GOT the call while still attempting to understand who took Linda.

"Sir, the prisoners escaped. We have a team searching the area for them."

He let out a breath. His feeling that he would finally end this chapter of his career dissipated like he was deflating as he exhaled. He didn't yell, he quietly told them, "Continue the search. Check in with any updates."

He hung up. He lowered his head and his shoulders slumped; he walked in to see the forensic lead.

"Anything?" he asked quietly.

"No sir. We'll be taking the needle for analysis, maybe we'll get something there."

Simon nodded. "Damn, this day went to hell quickly."

———

PAULA LEFT the Senator's townhouse and found there was no car waiting for her. She started walking in the direction of the White House. A black car pulled up alongside her as she was walking; she hadn't reached the end of the block yet. The passenger side window rolled down as the car matched her walking speed. Paula leaned down a bit to investigate the car, but kept moving forward.

"Agent Newly, I'm here to give you a ride."

Paula stopped and cautiously walked over to the car. She was still pissed about being hijacked by the Senator.

"Who sent you?" she asked.

"My dispatcher said go to this address and look for the lady in a pantsuit walking. She gave me the name, 'Agent Newly', and I assumed that was you. You look like an agent," the driver told her.

Paula was slightly suspicious of the young man driving, although he seemed to be telling the truth. She got into the car herself as he was exiting the driver's seat to assist her. He jumped back in.

"Where to, ma'am?" he asked.

"First of all, you can call me, Agent Newly, agent, or Paula, not ma'am. Let's head to the White House," Paula ordered.

"The White House it is," he responded.

Paula sensed something in the way he repeated her destination. The car picked up speed as it moved down the street toward the federal buildings. As they approached the Center of American Politics, the car suddenly veered off on a side street. It stopped in front of another townhouse. Paula already knew another 'let it go' speech was coming, but not who was going to deliver it. It was time to find out.

PRESIDENT HARRINGTON SPOKE in front of a crowd of one hundred and eighty thousand supporters. It was crazy the number of people who showed up for his political rallies. At the podium, he addressed the crowd.

"I have been honored to be your President; I hope to continue that honor for the next four years."

The crowd erupted into a deafening applause. It lasted several minutes.

The President gestured for them to quiet down so he could continue his speech.

"Now the other party is only offering a social media influencer up as their candidate. A man whose only claim to fame is reposting other people's work and commenting on it. That seems to sum up what their party has been doing every time they get power; taking the profits of other people's work and using it for their own gain."

Again, the exuberant cheers flooded the air. They were loud enough to make his ears ring.

When they quieted down, the President continued with the points of his speech. All designed to work the crowd up in support of himself in the name of patriotism. It was working. According to others, Harrington didn't have to worry about re-election; the polls had him way up compared to his challenger. The polls had been wrong before—that's when he became President. He still put in the work, because that's what he always did.

"Ladies and gentlemen, thank you for your support, it truly means the world to me. God bless you and God bless America."

He knew the papers and news shows in the morning would concentrate on little of his speech but call him anti-whatever for saying 'ladies and gentlemen'. As he walked off stage, an aide stepped up and handed him his phone.

"Sir, Agent Newly for you, you said put her through as soon as we could."

The President took the phone from the aide.

"Agent Newly."

There was no response. The President listened to see if there was an open line. He could hear talking in the background.

"Who told you to take me here?" he heard Newly's voice.

"I can't say, please go in, they're not going to hurt you, they want to talk."

The President understood the situation as Agent Newly being taken against her will to some unknown location. While he was contemplating what to do, the phone in his hand received a text as well.

I've been taken to an address in DC, presumably another politician to ask me to stop this investigation. I'm sending my coordinates in case I don't get back to you soon.

Harrington read the message. He looked at Air Force One as he was being led towards it.

"Tell the Captain, there's been a change of plans. We're returning to Washington," the President ordered.

———

PAULA WAS LED up the steps of the townhouse by an employee of the residence. She wasn't sure what their title would be. Inside, she found herself in a larger version of the Senator's house. As she wondered how any public servant could afford this type of residence anywhere, let alone in the middle of DC, another house employee approached her.

"Ma'am if you could wait in here, the Senator will see you shortly."

Paula complied; she was now extremely curious about which Senator could afford this lifestyle. She didn't wait long to find out. The double doors that had been closed behind her when she entered burst open as a short woman exploded into the room.

"My dear Agent Newly, I am so sorry for these heavy-handed tactics and theatrical nonsense. I want you to feel at home here. I'm sure after you met with Senator Heller, you're aware of why you've been summoned," the woman stated.

"Summoned? Is that what this is? I think misdirected, maybe even kidnapped would be a better description," Paula retorted.

"Kidnapped? Oh heavens, no. You are free to go at any time," the woman admonished.

Paula stood up.

"Any time after we talk, that is. Please sit back down." The change in the Senator's tone was swift and evident. This was not a social call.

"So, what is it you want me to do?" Paula assumed it would be the opposite of what Heller had suggested.

"Let me start with who I am. I am Senator Irma Waterstein, I am also the chairperson for the Democrat party, and more importantly, I sit on a committee overseeing your agency. What I am about to ask is not a favor, it is a request you will be expected to follow through on, otherwise, you might not see a comfy office again for a long time," the Senator threatened.

"Senator, get to the point. I'm tired of all this BS I've had to deal with today," Paula said, agitated.

The Senator acted shocked someone would dare talk to her in such a tone.

"Well, I thought we were civilized women chatting here, I guess I may have been wrong," she stated as if hurt.

"Senator, you threatened my job if I don't do what you ask, there is nothing civilized about this chat. What is it you want me to do?" Paula questioned, tired of the games.

"Straight to the point? Okay, here it is. You need to take this file and submit it to the President. It details the real reason behind those fires you're investigating, and it even includes info on large land purchases by foreign sources. It's all in there."

"If this is so complete, why is it you have it, and the President doesn't?" Paula queried.

"Well, agent, when you read it, you'll probably understand, but this file implicates several of my elite donors. I didn't want it to get out," the Senator said, acting like the victim.

None of this sat right with Paula. She was suspicious of the timing of the two Senators, and still felt like she was being played. The Senator turned to pour drinks for them, and she tucked her Bluetooth earpiece partially into her chair. She had an idea. She declined the drink.

"I think I need to review these files before I hand them to the President. I will be going now," Paula said.

The same employee who had shown her into the sitting room came and walked her to the door. Paula sat outside for a bit and she put her phone to her ear like she was on a call.

She heard talking, but only one side of the conversation.

"I don't know, I think she'll believe it when she reads it. It covers all the bases and indicates why it was covered up." A pause, presumably while the other person was talking.

"Senator we both know this isn't a partisan issue, it's a paycheck issue. I brought you in a long time ago, you can't start standing up for the flag now. You had to choose between red, white, and blue, and green, and you chose green. You don't think it is all documented somewhere? Get real, we're in this together, and we're not the only ones."

There was silence for several seconds when Paula realized they hung up. She acted as if she hung up as well.

Another black car pulled up; this one had a Presidential Seal on the door. The driver got out and opened the door for Paula, who got in without hesitation. As the car pulled away, Paula saw the Senator in the window and thought, *well, the office was nice while it lasted.*

———

DERRICK AND ELSY chatted with their temporary guests. Derrick had made the whole crew promise not to tell George that his daughter might be alive.

"Who was it that took you, and why?" Derrick asked.

Barry answered, "We've done a few things and it finally caught up with us. That was the CIA, You guys are probably now fugitives as well. Aiding and abetting, I think they call it."

"No worries, we've been there before. So why specifically were they after you, what is involved here?" Derrick questioned.

George had been just sitting with his head hung down, he lifted it and looked up at Derrick.

"You're the man that was with my daughter when she was shot." It was more of a statement than a question.

Derrick stared into the eyes of the man he had vowed to kill. There was nothing there; maybe the evil, war-mongering, power-hungry villain that he imagined he was hunting had been destroyed by the idea his daughter was dead—or maybe this prey was more cunning than he imagined. Part of Derrick was wondering if Linda's presumed death had even affected George at all. This wasn't a cat and mouse game; it was predator versus predator.

"Yes, that was me," he answered.

"Did she say anything?" George asked, hoping she had reconsidered her anger at him.

"She said she was sorry," Derrick shared.

"Sorry? For what? It was all my fault," George said with a calculated tone.

Derrick knew what she was sorry for, and he had chosen to forgive her in that moment. George wouldn't understand. He offered a false narrative to the man who caused him so much pain.

"Sir, maybe it was something else, she was sorry that she wouldn't get to see you again?"

George was content with that idea.

"Yeah, I guess. Do you know who killed her?" he asked Derrick.

"The man that shot her was left for the police. Last I knew they had him in custody," Derrick responded.

"Custody? He must die," George growled.

Derrick saw the predator, and he turned to Barry.

"So, what's your name? We haven't even introduced ourselves. I'm Derrick."

"I'm Barry. I do work for Mr. Avail, who it seems you know already."

"I do. What type of work do you do, Barry?" Derrick asked.

"Let's say I'm a fixer, can we leave it at that?" Barry asked.

"We can for now, thank you for your honesty. So, the CIA had you, What for?" Derrick continued to question.

"We might have started a war in a small country overseas," Barry informed him.

Derrick hadn't expected that answer. "You did *what?*"

"Listen, Derrick, we're appreciative that you got us out, but real big things are going on here. You guys are putting yourselves in grave danger."

Elsy had been listening quietly until she had the urge to ask one question.

"Do you know where Tinker is?" she asked.

Barry whipped around to face her. "How do you know about Tinker? What do you know about Tinker?"

Barry's face had turned red, and George had suddenly become alert as well.

Derick smiled; Elsy hit a nerve.

"So, this *Tinker* is your man?" Derrick queried.

"You can't talk about Tinker. He is our get-out-of-jail card. If anyone finds him first, they will kill him and take the information he's gathering," Barry cried.

"What information would that be?" Derrick asked.

"Names, hundreds of names. Names that indict people who will kill to not be revealed," Barry said. George shot him a look like he should shut up.

As the questioning went on, Elsy got a call.

"That is perfect," she responded to the call. "Keep it encrypted. I think I know what it is. And use caution, I think this could be extremely dangerous information."

Elsy called Derrick over as Harlem and Trina returned from shopping. They brought each other up to speed with their guests.

29

THE REPRESENTATIVES from China and Russia were asked to the special meeting with Jeac and a few other select members of the Council. China was seated alone.

"What is the meaning of this?" the Chinese delegate questioned. "Why am I seated by myself?"

He knew the implications of such a seating arrangement.

"You must answer questions for the country you represent. We have some very serious concerns about actions being perpetrated by your country's Cyber Army." Jeac replied.

The Chinese representative became quiet. He realized he might not even have the answers they wanted.

"I will answer what I can," he said quietly.

The Russian delegate stood.

"Why am I here?" the tone of his voice jumped from the normal bark of an angry dog to the screech of an owl.

"Sir, the current ties between Russia and China are well known to us. You are here to share what you know as well," Jeac told him.

———

PAULA TOOK a nap in a small room at the White House. The President was flying back from Ohio ,where he had attended a rally for his re-election. The was a knock on the door that awoke her; the door was opened slightly.

"Sorry to disturb you. The President has returned and is asking to see you now." Paula scrambled from the small cot she was on, briefly blinded for a second when she flipped on the light. She looked in the mirror that hung on the wall and did her best to straighten up while the aide was waiting just outside for her. Satisfied that it was the best she could do, she grabbed her things and headed for her meeting with the President. She reached his office and was asked to wait outside for a moment. The aide went inside and informed the President she had arrived.

"Send Paula in please," he stated.

LOOKING at his reflection in the mirror, his thoughts were assaulting him. He had lost the daughter, his prisoners, and his lead on the larger global threat. If his goal was truly to protect America, he was doing a piss-poor job. He leaned down and splashed water from the running faucet onto his face, then dried off with a towel. He needed a break, anything to get him back on track.

The vibration of the phone caused it to slide across the counter by the sink. Simon caught it just before it fell. It was a familiar number.

"Please tell me you have something?" He pleaded.

"Boss, we scoured every camera we could access in the area. I think we found what you're hoping for. I'm sending it to you now."

The phone chimed as it received the video. Simon clicked on it and watched as an orange Wrangler sped from an alleyway behind a smoke shop. Through the windshield, He could see a man and what looked like a young girl in the front. There was another passenger in the back. Due to the angle, no face was visible, but Simon could make out one pair of long legs crunched up at an angle.

"We need to find that Jeep. That must be Klinger in the back seat. Put out an APB for the orange Wrangler, mark it *just for questioning*. I don't need local cops or even our agents thinking they're dangerous and killing them before we can get Klinger back," he ordered. His mind immediately wondered, *Is that the same Jeep from Linda's attack, and where is George then?*

————

LINDA WAS RECOVERING a bit each day. She was now able to sit up a bit and eat light foods. The people who had *rescued* her came and went in shifts. She was slowly learning their names. Patsy Hurt was the nurse she had met in the hospital—she continued to be Linda's primary nurse. The doctor who oversaw her care was Dr. Farley, she didn't have a first name yet. There was another guy who was there frequently, but she hadn't learned his name either. She talked to Patsy a lot, but still hadn't learned much about their organization.

They were taking good care of her, though. All the medical equipment they used looked brand new. She was surprised by that. She had asked for a TV and was waiting to see if they would get her one. There were books and magazines, but she had trouble turning the pages. Her arms were still quite weak.

She wondered about her scarring and if she'd ever be able to wear a bikini again.

————

AS THE QUESTIONING CONTINUED, the Chinese delegate realized that Jeac wasn't just fishing, he knew the Cyber Army's actions. He needed to make a call.

"Mr. Pastil, I need to contact a superior to answer more of your questions. May I have a phone and a twenty-minute break?" the delegate asked.

Jeac nodded and directed an assistant to get a phone.

"I will grant you the request, but you must stay here," Jeac responded.

The delegate dialed the international number. He asked for his superior.

"This is an urgent matter, wake him up," he barked into the phone.

A few seconds later he was speaking to the person he needed to.

"They know about the hack, they know everything, I need permission to share our intentions with them or our membership will be in jeopardy," the delegate pleaded.

"Are we speaking privately?" the delegate's superior asked.

"No sir, we are on speaker with Mr. Pastil and others. I need your permission,now," the delegate responded.

Silence ensued for a few seconds.

"Sir, are you there?" the delegate questioned.

Still, it was silent.

"You have permission. Inform Mr. Pastil he will hear from the People's Leader soon," the superior said.

The delegate and his superior disconnected.

As questioning resumed, he shared all the information that he knew.

"The purpose of the hack was to imbed new psychological conditioning we have mastered. Our goal was to ensure a more positive outcome with the direction of American social media users and to disrupt their ability to have meaningful discourse among differing opinions," the delegate confessed.

"Why not bring them to the Council?" Jeac questioned.

"Our people do not always want to be managed in our dealing with America. Like the Council, we also have an agenda for our people," the delegate admitted.

In some ways, this made sense and made the hack less of a threat. Jeac considered all the delegate's answers carefully.

"You may leave this room now; I ask the other delegates to stay to discuss this," he said dismissing the Chinese delegate.

The Chinese delegate was escorted to the door.

"Please do not leave the building until we have finished and you have been informed of our decision," Jeac reminded him.

———

TINKER HAD GATHERED ALMOST eight terabytes of information; this was all the data the imbedded programs had gathered to date. He shut the program down and disconnected from his hacked access. He had no instructions on what to do now that he had acquired this data. He knew it had to get to Mr. Avail, just not the how or where it would need to be delivered.

"Deidra, this data is kryptonite, we need to encrypt it and move it to a portable drive."

"Okay, give me about forty minutes. Are you okay?" she asked, noticing his change in demeanor.

"Do it as fast as we can. Suspend all other system work until this is done. This information needs to be able to go where we do, from now until we can deliver it to Mr. Avail, and yes, I'm fine. I just think we might need to be a bit more cautious as we move forward," he advised.

JEAC DELIBERATED China's actions with the invited board members. "The major issue here is not what China did, it's how they did it. They went behind our backs to accomplish something we would most likely assist them with. Now the question is, can we trust them moving forward?"

The Russian delegate spoke first. "They didn't want to deal with your predecessor, things always took too long for approval. I'm sure that is the reason they did not seek consent."

Other members nodded in agreement with the Russian's statement.

A member from one of the Mexican cartels spoke. "We have long held our silence at these meetings. Our goals have always been aligned in that we all wish to see the downfall of America's superiority. I do not feel that China's actions in any way compromised that goal. I only ask that they provide us with the actual code they installed, and the AI's system logs while their upload was occurring. As an American President once said. 'Trust, but verify.'"

"So, I will call for a vote, those in favor of no sanctions and no punitive actions but a complete recounting of their actions including data streams, say Aye," Jeac stated.

It was unanimous. The Chinese delegate was brought back in.

"Here is our decision..." Jeac proceeded to inform him of the final decision of the group and what China must submit to the Council.

GEORGE WAS TALKING with the others in the kitchen, discussing who it was now pursuing them. Without thought, he looked at Derrick and said, "You know, I used to have the power to make a call and have minor inconveniences like this eliminated," and then he chuckled.

Before anyone could react, Derrick leaped over a chair and had George pinned to the floor by his neck. Derrick squeezed with both hands and a strength he didn't know he possessed. He became oblivious as George's face turned bright red, and then started to slowly get purple. He didn't feel Barry and Harlem trying to lift him from his prey.

Till the debt is paid, was running through his mind like a marquee sign.

George's eyes were turning bloodshot, he was clawing at Derrick's arms and then slowly stopped, his hands dropping away.

Derrick was unaware that Trina was right in front of him, jumping up and down and crying. He couldn't hear her; his rage had blocked everything out. Then he could see Shannon's face; she looked upset with him. He let go, suddenly aware of his hands and his victim, and then staggered to his feet. Trina pulled him away from George's body and led him to another room. Harlem and Barry quickly assessed George to see if he was still alive and breathing. Derrick slowly regained his composure, as he thought about his actions, he felt nauseous. He ran outside and vomited in the bushes. Wiping his mouth with his bare hand, he turned his head up to the sky and asked, "Shannon. What have I become?"

He sat down in the middle of the driveway; the sun had beaten on the asphalt all day and it was still warm now. The sky was clouding over, and small drops started to fall. Derrick sat there as small drops turned into larger ones. He felt a hand slip inside of his. Katrina sat next to him and held his hand in the rain.

"Thank you," he whispered to her as the raindrops tried to drown out his words while hiding his tears.

She smiled softly at him and laid her head against his shoulder grabbing his arm with her other hand.

"I got you."

———

AFTER ABOUT TEN MINUTES, Mr. Avail had recovered enough to get up off the floor and move to a chair. His voice was raspy when he tried to talk.

"What in the hell was that about? Who is that psycho and why did he just try to kill me? He needs to get locked up," he questioned and demanded.

Elsy looked at the man who had ordered her execution as well.

"Well Mr. Avail, like you said, *you've done some bad things.* Unfortunately for you, we're some of the people you did those bad things to."

George's face lost color this time.

Barry stood up and spoke. "It's obvious there's lots of unknown history here," he motioned out at Derrick in the driveway. "I'm sure it's even well deserved, but if we want to stay out of jail and more likely just survive, we'll need to set it all aside and work together. They'll figure out who we are and where we are in a short amount of time. We're going to need to move soon."

———

PAULA STEPPED into the President's office.

"I hear you've had an interesting day?" the President said, half questioning, as he welcomed her.

"Sir, many politicians are trying to get me to stop looking into this. I have just had two agents die and I suspect that it has to do with this case. Now out of the blue, two high-ranking politicians from both parties try to encourage me to stop," Paula recounted.

She needed to stop for a minute.

"Sir, Senator Waterstein gave me a file she said had all the answers. It's all bullshit, if I can say that in front of you," Paula divulged.

The President laughed.

"These walls have heard a lot worse. So, what is it the report and where did it come from?" the President queried.

"It is a security report, supposedly put together by her team of investigators on the security board. It's just all too neat. Every little thing is tied off in a little bow, I don't trust it, sir," Paula responded.

The President held his hand out for the documents. Paula reached into her bag and produced them for him. He laid them on his desk and pulled a pair of reading glasses from the drawer.

"These blame everything on some fake meat extremist group. Is that even a real thing?" he asked.

"Unfortunately, yes, it's a real thing, they call themselves the 'Future Food Apostles' and they get together and hold rallies to try and convince people to move toward synthetic and plant-based meats, all in the name of saving the planet. They get very confrontational at times," Paula informed him.

The President took another look at the document.

"You don't believe this? It seems thorough. It's also a bit inconvenient for Senator Waterstein, considering how much fundraising they do for her," he probed.

"Sir, imagine how big the truth must be for her to sacrifice this group like that," Paula warned.

President Harrington contemplated her words of warning.

"Paula, I think we need to rethink this. Thank the Senator for her help and send most of your agents back to their previous assignments. Then use a small crew to follow up on what you have uncovered so far, but do it quietly. Here's my direct line number. From now on no more intermediaries, you call me directly if you find anything, otherwise, keep it quiet."

The President stood and so did Paula. He shook her hand and pulled her close.

"I believe you, but this is getting out of hand, and I can't risk going all in and being wrong," he confided.

Paula stood close to him for a second and the looked warmly at each other. She drew away first and thanked him for his time and trust in her, and then she left the Oval Office.

———

THE YOUNG ANALYST from the Council's Cyber division came bursting through the doors in an almost full sprint. Denler stood to try and intercept him, but it was too late. The analyst slammed into Jeac Pastil's office like a bull ramming through a gate. He stood in front of Jeac waving a hand full of papers while trying to catch his breath.

"Sir, sir, I'm sorry. I'm sorry to disturb you, to burst in like this. I feel it is most urgent. You must understand about the hack."

Jeac stood, taking a moment to regain his composure after the explosive entrance. He glanced out the door at Denler, who held his arms in the air.

"Young man, you better have a damn good reason for this intrusion," Jeac said.

"I do sir, I have found something buried beneath the Chinese code we were given to review," he answered.

"What kind of *something?*" Jeac demanded.

"Well, it seems someone was harvesting terabytes of data and using the Chinese programming to hide it." The analyst stated.

"Was it the Chinese? What data were they harvesting?" Jeac questioned.

"That's it, sir. We don't know who it was yet, only that they stole what appears to be the identities of people associated with the Council. There was an underlying program already present that was had been collecting this data. Whoever is hiding behind the Chinese code knew where to find and activate it. We are working feverishly now to uncover the source of the code and who accessed it. Unfortunately, the incursion has wiped much of the data away while trying to hide their actions. If they had backups of what they were doing, we could get a better picture." The analyst relayed.

Jeac's face turned bright red. Perspiration was building around his neck. This was the worst possible news.

"Denler, get in here," his voice squeaked a bit as he called him.

"Yes sir?"

"Get the Chinese delegate here. Right now. Take no excuses," Jeac ordered.

Denler turned and went back to his desk to fulfill his boss's command.

Jeac turned back to the analyst.

"Who else knows about this?" he asked.

"Just me and my team, and you, sir," the analyst answered.

"How many are on your team?" Jeac inquired.

"It's me and three others," the analyst replied.

"Get them all here, now. There is a computer annex one floor below us. I will have everyone moved from there immediately. There are also accommodations on that floor. You will now all be sequestered here until we get the answers we need. Go down and see if there is any additional equipment that you will need. Say nothing to anyone. If anyone asks, tell them to contact me directly," Jeac stated.

Denler returned with news.

"Sir the delegate was on a plane at the airport. He is being removed as we speak and brought here," Denler said.

Jeac looked over the papers the analyst had handed him. "This is not good at all."

30

PAULA HAD NOT EXPECTED President Harrington to cut her off like that. By herself, she would have little to no hope of collecting all the evidence she would need to find out what was truly going on. The President had told her to keep the report given to her by the Senator.

She started to review it while awaiting her ride back to Virginia Beach. She was amazed at how thorough the document was, despite the feeling that it was all made up. She did notice something interesting, though. They had the same picture of their suspect that she did. The problem was *she* had that picture drawn. It couldn't have been from a previous investigation.

"How stupid do they think I am?" she wondered.

Paula stuffed the folder back into her bag. Her car was pulling up outside.

As she slid into the back seat, she instructed the driver.

"Straight back to my office, no detours, I don't care who gave you orders," she demanded.

"Ma'am? I have no orders, where is it you want to go?" the driver asked.

Paula felt almost embarrassed, she gave him the address and they headed out.

———

THE WEIGHT of the information they had collected felt like a mountain weighing on his neck. Tinker knew that whoever possessed that information would be in grave danger very soon. He called in specialists to fortify his offices. He wanted a very hardened location. He even had a specialty drilling company come in and drill a shaft down from his office into a city maintenance tunnel that ran underground near his building.

This wasn't the only change he made. He also added an enhanced alarm system controlled by an Artificial Intelligence system personally designed by him. Soon it would have access to lethal countermeasures as well. Poison gas, caustic liquid, suffocation, and automatic weapons were all being added to his lair's defenses. He loved this location and would fight to keep it. He didn't know who was coming, but he knew he wouldn't make it easy.

———

BARRY KLINGER PACED BACK and forth in the living room.

"Can I get a phone for a second?" Barry asked when he saw Derrick.

"Who do you need to call?" Derrick questioned.

"The hacker you referenced earlier; he has some information we will need if we want to stay alive," Barry replied.

"What does he have that could be so powerful or important?" Derrick asked.

"That, I cannot say right now. You should trust me though," Barry appealed.

Derrick let out a laugh. "Yeah, okay. Trust the people who once tried to kill me and others. The same ones who killed many people to try to gain political leverage in an election. That ain't gonna happen."

George heard his reply and almost hissed at him. "What do you know about that? We were not involved with any of that."

"Oh, Mr. Avail. I know more than you could possibly want me to. You should stay quiet like a good little boy and let the men talk, or you could easily meet my dark side again," Derrick sneered.

George Avail felt anger rise inside. *Who was this man to speak to him like that?* The loss of Linda obscured by his arrogance.

"Mr. Dunn, If that's your real name? I will speak when I choose. You obviously don't know who I am," George challenged.

Harlem heard this verbal exchange as it was heating up. He ran from the other room to play referee.

"It doesn't matter right now," he said as he switched his view amongst the participants.

Derrick was seething, with the hatred of George Avail still burning in his eyes.

"It always matters, this man better get himself away from me, or I will finish what I promised," Derrick nearly shouted.

Harlem turned to Derrick put his hands on his chest and gently started to push him back towards the other room. Derrick was not ready to be handled.

"Harlem, you're a great guy and I know Elsy loves you. Take your hands off me right now, or you'll have to wipe your ass with a nub," he said.

Harlem wasn't afraid of Derrick, but he wasn't stupid either. He backed away.

"Come on Derrick, we don't have time for this right now. Like it or not, we need them until we find out more about what's going on and who was trying to kill you and Katrina," Harlem pleaded.

The mention of Katrina worked like a special pill for Derrick. He de-escalated and backed out of the room.

"You deal with him then; it won't work out well if I do," he called over his shoulder to Harlem as he exited the room.

———

ELSY HAD BEEN STANDING in the other room watching this whole episode unfold. She was only there a minute when she was joined by Trina, who had heard the commotion. The two of them watched as the tension erupted in the room, unsure how large the explosion would be. Elsy was nervous that Harlem put himself in jeopardy to alleviate the problem.

As they watched the tension start to unwind, both she and Katrina were surprised that they each played a part in the reduction of hostility that was occurring as they watched. As Derrick entered the room they were watching, both girls rushed to him and threw their arms around him.

Elsy spoke first. "I'm so proud of you for resisting that urge."

In a quieter voice, Trina spoke in a way that was like an autonomous escape from her mind."I love you."

Derrick responded from his heart without giving his brain time to react."I love you too, little girl."

The three of them looked at each other and easily realized the profoundness and intensity of these statements. Elsy chimed in also.

"I love you both as well."

———

THE ESCALATION at the World Council continued. The leak from the Chinese hack was now a full-on disaster. Some delegates from the Council were calling for the Chinese delegate to be sanctioned, and others wanted him removed. Jeac Pastil was running damage control at the highest levels. Russia had once again sided with China over the Council, and asked for the issue to be dropped against China and that the real culprit be pursued and terminated. Jeac was now in the foulest of moods.

Another file had been laid on his desk. It had a picture of a man and a young girl. The top folder was stamped with 'SUSPENDED'. He briefly skimmed the contents.

"Denler, come to my office."

The young assistant appeared and Jeac proceeded to give him directions.

"One, reactivate this," he tossed the file he just viewed. "It seems like a liability. Two, pull a team together and have them on standby for this hacking nonsense. This needs to be resolved quickly and all data must be recovered or destroyed. Three, we will need a group ready for whatever resolution is decided for China."

Denler carefully took notes. It would be up to him to decide who went where, but his decision would be scrutinized if there were any complications. He reviewed the first file. These two had escaped a very seasoned team already. He put a star with a four on the folder. He would send a four-man team of the best they had after him—no more mistakes.

He then evaluated his options and decided the data recovery and elimination group should be an eight-man crew. He didn't know how large the hacker crew was, or what resources they would have. He continued to work on his final order, deciding what would be appropriate given the potential for extreme violence if this went badly.

———

PAULA RETURNED to her office building and sat in the cubicle office area. She felt oddly exposed in her corner office with windows on two sides. She compared her notes to the file she was now supposed to pretend was accurate. The more she looked at it, the more she realized that the new report had been designed to answer any questions that were not satisfied by her current investigation. The Future Food Apostles were the scapegoats for this fake investigation. She did have to admit it was quite tidy and convincing. Even the back story by the Senator about why it was not released upfront was believable. She threw the folder at the wall. Papers separated from the folder while in flight like parachutists leaving the plane. Every piece seems to choose its direction. She hung her head in her hands.

"This is not an investigation, it's a show and tell," she thought aloud.

"Excuse me?" said a strange voice behind her.

Paula swung her chair around and came face to face with a short but muscular man sitting in a cubicle behind her. He had rolled his chair out to the opening and was looking at her.

Paula immediately noticed his Federal Marshal credentials.

"So, what has you so flustered?" he asked gently while pointing to the papers strewn around the floor and cubicle now.

Paula blushed a little for her impetuousness.

"I'm having a bad day with a worse case," she explained.

"Did you lose your witness to the potentially biggest case you've ever had?" the agent asked her.

Paula glanced at him with uncertainty. "No."

"Well, I did, in fact, I lost three in the same hour. You don't see me throwing shit around," he joked.

Paula smiled; it wasn't his words as much as his tone that made the statement seem funny to her.

"So, you lost three high-profile witnesses?" she questioned.

"Oh yeah, That's why I'm here. Traffic cam database," he said.

"Can I help?" Paula asked. She wanted to do something other than the 'pretend-a-case' that she was now assigned to work on.

———

THE NEWS CONFERENCE was called by Senator Irma Waterstein. Every major media outlet was set up to capture whatever statement she made. There was a podium set up on the steps of the capitol building. At ten a.m. sharp, most channels interrupted their normal programming for a 'special news alert'. Irma stepped up to the microphone, and several of her colleagues stood behind her.

"Ladies and gentlemen, and others who may choose different pronouns, I must confess to the American people. Over the past few years, there have been numerous fires in buildings used by a specific industry in America. The President called for an investigation, but due to my own personal interests, the results of the investigation were hidden, and the President was given false information.

I must now come forward and admit that when the results were found, I was concerned because the group responsible was likely to incriminate similar groups for no other reason than their similarities. I thought I was acting in the best interests of all by sheltering the President from the facts, but I was protecting a group of criminals based on nothing more than my personal desire to protect the little person and the marginalized American. I apologize for these actions and humbly ask for forgiveness from my constituents and all Americans. Thank you."

Immediately, the media crowd erupted into questions. The drone was indiscernible at first. Every agency spokesperson trying to get their question answered. The Senator turned and headed back inside. No questions were answered.

———

TINKER HATED the crews entering his 'lair', but he knew it was necessary to achieve the level of security he wanted. He released his lower-level hackers to work remotely. He had told them it was for their security, but

Tinker knew that would make them more exposed and vulnerable. They would be his danger canaries. If they were attacked in any way, it would be his indicator to lock in and be ready. There was no debate that Deidra would stay with him, though. She was too valuable to risk like those others. With the data now secured onto the proper portable drives, they were waiting for another contact to tell them where and when to meet. He was getting up to chase his daily pizza when his phone rang.

"Hello?"

"Tinker, It's Barry. We need the information you collected as soon as possible."

"Where do you want me to send it?" Tinker asked.

"Oh no, you can't send it. You must bring it to us," Barry informed him.

"That will not be happening. I know that I'm in danger for as long as I possess this data. I have taken measures to fortify my current location. I will not be traveling anywhere."

"Do you have someone you would trust your life to?" Barry asked him.

Tinker's mind instantly ran to Deidra. While he wanted to pretend there was no one he would trust his life to, he knew he would with her. He also knew he couldn't let her be in that kind of danger.

"I have someone," he replied.

"Good, get that information to this address in Virginia Beach." Barry said, and texted him the address.

"I'll have him leave right after lunch." Tinker informed him.

Barry was about to say something about not delaying for lunch and realized he was hungry himself.

"Deidra," Tinker called.

She entered his office and said, "What's up?"

"Do you know where I can find Pauly Turk?" Tinker asked.

"That's easy, he just stopped in to pick up some files," Deidra informed him.

Tinker called Pauly up to his office.

"I have a job for you of extreme importance." Tinker told him.

"What is it, boss?" Pauly asked.

"I need you to get this drive to Virginia Beach. I'm renting you a car. They will drop it off in thirty minutes."

———

THE LEADER of the hit squad studied the pictures. There was very little information regarding the two subjects. He wasn't even a little bothered that one was a young girl. He had removed entire families before; this would be nothing. After deciding their starting point would be in the Virginia area, he called in the rest of the four-man team.

"These are our targets," he said holding up the photos. "If anyone has a problem with the kid let me know, you will be replaced."

The other three all responded, "All set, I'm good," almost in unison.

The leader continued, "We'll fly into Virginia and check out this diner." He pointed to another picture on the table in the center of them.

"This was their last known sighting. They were driving in this bright orange Jeep. I don't think it should be too hard to locate," he pointed to another picture. "This should be a quick, easy job. The pay is top tier, so we'll all get to have a nice vacation after this one," he chuckled a bit as he finished.

The men started packing their equipment into black duffle bags. It would be a long flight from California to Virginia, but sneaking across the border from Mexico meant they did not deal with Customs and could bring their own firepower with them. A chartered private plane would fly them to their desired location, no questions asked. The group leader expected an easy payday on this one.

———

BACK IN THE ROOM, Nurse Hurt was checking on the IV and medication of her patient. Linda watched her as she did so. "What's the weather like outside today?"

The nurse smiled. "Is that the best you got?"

"When do I get a chance to go outside?" Linda asked.

"Well, that's a better question, I just don't know the answer. You'll have to ask Dr. Farley," the nurse replied.

"That man says nothing when he's in here. It's like talking to the wall," Linda complained.

A snort and a giggle came from the nurse. "He is quite the conversationalist, isn't he?"

Both women laughed.

"Seriously, when can I get going? I have a life I need to repair," Linda moaned.

Patsy looked at her with a calm and kind demeanor.

"Sweetie, the life you know is in great peril. You have been caught between two formidable forces and you would not have survived this long if we didn't intervene," Nurse Hurt reminded her.

Almost on cue, a loud crashing sound occurred at the front of the house. Both ladies turned toward the door as they heard footsteps slapping the floor and coming at a fast pace down the hall.

A young man Linda had never seen before slid into the doorway grabbing the jamb to keep himself from falling over.

"Pack up, we have to leave now," he shouted.

"What's the emergency?" Linda asked.

Patsy, who knew better, said, "I will get you ready to go. When it's time, we don't ask. Delays get people in trouble… or dead."

Within minutes, Linda was strapped back into an ambulance gurney and pushed outside. This time it was a white panel van with blue lettering. Something about a fish caught her eye before she was pushed up into the back of the truck, where it strangely resembled a modern ambulance. Patsy jumped in beside her and grabbed her hand.

"Hang on dear, I think we're going to leave quickly."

31

THE TEAMS WERE IN MOTION. Team One had been sent after the man and child, and Team Two was on standby. Jeac looked at the report from Denler again.

"Do we know where the man and girl are yet? Do we know who they are?" he asked.

"Sir, their location is still unknown, as is their identity. The team is on the ground and tracking. We know the male was deemed a threat to the Avails, but his identity is still unknown. We tried facial recognition, but it keeps coming back to a dead police officer. Our current theory is that he may be tied to the hackers. Only they would have the expertise to change his identity in facial recognition."

"And what about these hackers, what do we know about that?" Jeac questioned further.

"The Chinese provided the information we asked for, and we are working to separate their code from the hackers. The Cyber team is deep into it, and we hope to have a target very soon," Denler informed him.

Jeac was satisfied with Denver's report. He dismissed him and went to the window. He gazed out over the city and the people moving below him. He mumbled to himself.

"They have no idea how the world works these days…"

————

THE PANEL VAN pulled up into the diner parking lot. There were still areas sectioned off by yellow crime scene tape, but there were no longer any police officers watching the area. TL, as the others called him, exited the van from the front passenger side. The side door slid open at the same time and Three and Four moved to the opening to see. Two remained behind the wheel. TL walked into the diner. A waitress casually greeted him with, "Good morning, how many of y'all are there?"

"Only me."

"Oh, I saw that big van pull up, I thought there'd be more of y'all."

"No," TL said forcefully, he realized this was another reason he hated Americans. The way they all talked, making up their own words.

"I need to see your security tape from the shooting," he stated forcefully.

"I'm sorry dear, but the police took all that. Who'd you say you were again?" The waitress asked.

"I didn't. Do you know where they took the victims?" He continued his questions.

"Oh, that's easy. They flew her to Virginia Beach General Hospital. That's the closest trauma hospital," she stated, happily answering his questions.

"Her?" TL asked, looking for clarity.

"Yeah, the lady was shot. She was with a man and girl that took off, they didn't even wait to see if she lived." The waitress blurted.

"Well, did she?" TL pushed.

"I heard she died, but I don't know. There was a rumor that some top-secret government stuff was going on with the whole thing," she whispered.

"Thank you you've been most helpful." TL reached into his jacket; he pulled out a small black case. He flipped it open, removed a hundred-dollar bill and placed it on the counter near the waitress. "Four black coffees please, to go."

The waitress disappeared for a brief second and returned with a cardboard tray with the coffees tucked into it. She rang him up and handed him the change from the large bill.

"Keep it. Thank you for your help," TL said, leaving with the coffees.

The smile on the waitress's face was as large as it had been in a long time. This made her day. TL returned to the van.

"Virginia Beach General Hospital," he instructed the driver.

———

THE CYBER TEAM was able to separate the Chinese code from the hackers. They also noticed another small stream that seemed to be embedded in the hacker's code, but they were not concerned by it. Their job was to identify the hackers.

The lead Cyber tech was feverishly tapping at his keyboard. He was combatting an active code that was working to destroy his system while simultaneously protecting itself. He called over to two other members of the Cyber team to assist him. The three worked as a single entity against the hacker's code. Their progress was slow, but undeniable. They knew it was only a matter of time before they found him.

Six hours later they broke the code, and they found the location of the hacker.

———

ALARMS WERE GOING off on multiple screens around Tinker's desk. Despite his best efforts, his location was compromised. It wasn't his exact location, but they still knew he was in Boston. The site to which his IP was attached was also part of his upgrade plan. It had been engineered as a trap for any person or group that might be looking to harm him. It had a floor plan that was designed to lead the possible attackers into areas designed to contain, and if necessary, eliminate them.

"Deidra!" He yelled from his office. There was no reply.

He began to sweat, and his heart rate spiked. Fear was starting to set in quickly. He was not designed to be the prey of someone else. He jumped up from his desk and set out to find his assistant. He searched several rooms until he opened a door to find Deidra curled up in a sleeping bag. She had been working so hard for him, and he never even thought to get her a hotel room nearby.

He stood in the doorway. The light from the hallway cascaded around him and fell onto her face. He absorbed the image in his mind. He had feelings for this girl. It was the first time since he was a kid that he had allowed himself the opportunity to care for someone else. Now he was afraid he had put her in danger.

"Deidra," he gently called to her.

She started to wake.

"What's wrong?" She said with a harsh-sounding voice.

"We are in trouble; they bypassed my security program. They will know where and who we are soon. These people are very good," Tinker warned her.

Deidra sat straight up. "I can't go to jail. I have family that need me."

Tinker looked at her solemnly. "I don't think jail will be an option."

Deidra's eyes widened. "Oh."

Tinker offered her a hand. She accepted it, and as she stood Tinker's eyes caught her body. She was only wearing a T-shirt and her underwear. He started to blush and turned away.

"You should get dressed first," he said.

Deidra saw him blush. "Good idea. Guard the door for me."

She threw on the clothes she had stacked on a chair. As she finished tying her sneakers, she watched Tinker, who was still facing the hallway.

"I'm decent, you can look at me now," she said.

Tinker cautiously turned. In his mind, he could still see her without the clothes she was now wearing.

"Marty, snap out of it," she encouraged.

Tinker released the image and looked at her eyes. She was ready for a fight.

"What's our plan now?" she asked.

"We sit tight, for now but be ready. Do you know how to use a gun?" Tinker inquired.

"Hell yeah, I grew up in Texas," Deidra informed him.

Tinker had never known this about her. "Texas? I would never have guessed that. Why didn't that show up when I vetted you?"

"Because I'm a great hacker," she smiled and winked at him when she said it.

Tinker turned and led the way back to his office. On the back wall was a large picture of Ronald Reagan. A picture that Deidra liked, but always thought was out of place. Tinker reached behind and flipped a switch. The picture slid aside, revealing a heavy metal door. He held his thumb on a small pad and the door popped open. Inside Deidra could see stacks of cash and several weapons.

"Come here, pick one you like and feel comfortable with. We're going to stay here for now, at least until the other site is breached. Then I have an escape route we can use," he informed her.

———

AFTER CLEANING up the folder she had thrown and helping the Federal Marshal search traffic cams, Paula was exhausted. She could feel her body screaming to just lay down for a few hours. She tapped the marshal on the shoulder.

"I'm going to head out and get some overture sleep. I can't look at any more videos and camera stills," she let him know.

"Give me ten more minutes, please. Then I can give you a ride to wherever you want, you'll probably wait that long for a ride anyways," the agent begged her.

"Okay, ten minutes, not a second longer," Paula gave in.

She sat back down and re-opened a folder on the computer. She selected another video. She watched as a dark police sedan left an alley. She was about to skip to another when she got a clear view of the passenger in the car.

"Elsy, what are you doing there?" she said to the screen.

She searched for any other videos in the area and couldn't find any. This was from a red-light traffic cam that the police officer had driven through as it was changing to red.

"Hey, what exactly are we looking for again?" Paula asked the agent.

The Marshal turned around. "Evidence of who took my prisoners. Did you find something?"

He spun his chair to look at her screen.

"I'm not sure," she said.

She showed him the image of the car but was careful not to show Elsy's face. She wanted to question Elsy before she was implicated in anything. She had come to realize that in DC, the story was built to fit the need. Facts were dismissed, so the narrative would be right.

The Marshal printed the image Paula had shown him and added it to a folder.

"Alright, it's time for the ride I promised you, where to?" he asked.

"The Grand Regency Hotel," she informed him.

She gathered her things as he pushed the folders he had into a briefcase.

"Ok Miss Newly, let me get you to your hotel," he offered.

She was about to respond with *thank you*, and realized what he never told her.

"Hey, you never told me your name, only that you were a Federal Marshal," she said quizzically.

"I'm sorry, I guess I've lost my manners being all wrapped up in this case. My name is Simon." The agent responded.

———

"Sir, we strongly advise that you drop the investigation completely. This will be used against you in the news cycle and could weaken your chances of re-election. As senior members of your party and ranking members of both houses, we ask that you accept this report and stop all other actions regarding this topic. It is in your best interests that you accept our suggestions. Also, the agent that you assigned to this, should be removed. This is a very delicate time in politics and this issue is not one we should attack at the present time."

PRESIDENT HARRINGTON RE-READ the letter a third time. He slammed it down on his desk. There were eight names on the letter, Senators and Congressmen who were supposed to be his closest advisors. Now they were advising him to abandon what he had set out to do when he was elected. He couldn't clean out the corruption if he became part of it. He had already reduced the size of the investigation to Agent Newly and a handful of others, and now someone thought she should be removed entirely.

"Why was she such a problem for them?" he wondered.

He looked up at the news flashed on his TV monitor. The TV channels had been replaying the news conference that Senator Waterstein had given. From their perspective, she was a saint for coming out with her revelation. He couldn't help but notice the man standing behind her on the steps. Darton Plank was the man the Democrats had chosen to run against him. Darton had no political experience, and as far as he could tell, no experience with anything, other than being on social media.

President Harrington knew this election would be much closer than people thought. All his supporters would need to come out, because his challenger was the media darling now. He turned off the monitor. He had to make some tough decisions.

———

THE BLACK SEDAN pulled into the seemingly empty warehouse building through the open bay door. It was hard to see the armed guard just inside, who watched everyone enter. It sat by itself for a few minutes before another similar car pulled in, then two more. Soon there were eight vehicles in total parked inside this large empty warehouse. The door closed and the guard stepped outside.

Senator Heller was the first to exit his vehicle. Senator Waterstein was next. Gradually the other six also joined them at a table set up in the middle of the floor area.

"Well, aren't we a bunch of mangy hounds?" Heller said, trying to lighten the mood.

Waterstein shot him an evil stare. "Alvin, we do not need your southern outlook on what amounts to treason if we get caught."

Her blatant and open acknowledgment of what they were conspiring to do caused the others to gasp and whisper amongst each other.

"Oh, come on now. We are trying to get the 'do-gooder' out of office. We all know what we signed up for. Every one of us is already guilty of insider trading and other crimes. This is not even the most serious for some of you," she recounted.

"Let's just get this meeting over with," Heller said.

They all sat down at the table. This left one seat still empty. A few seconds later the door opened again, and a small red sports car drove in. The last guest had arrived. He walked over like he was a king greeting his subjects. As he approached the table, no one stood like he had been hoping they'd do.

"No, please stay seated." He wouldn't let them feel like he wasn't the one in charge.

"Mr. Plank, so wonderful you could join us in such a timely manner," Heller said, the obvious disdain heavy on his voice.

"Well thank you, Mr. Senator. That means so much coming from you, you are working so close to the current President and all." Darton was good at verbal sparring. He even enjoyed it. He savored how his words cut right into Heller.

Waterstein told him to be quiet and sit down. He complied.

"This is the only time we will ever meet in person as a group. We each must know who the others are to allow us to trust each other moving forward on this issue. The only way we will defeat Harrington in this election is if we stick to our plan. We have financial backing from global interests and the full support of ninety percent of the media. Our only issue now is to move this plan into the media and get the President on defense," Waterstein informed them.

She laid out their entire plan, lightly touching on their foreign investors and what they sought in return.

She wrapped up with, "If Harrington wins, it is likely that we will all be put in jail. His 'clean the gutters' initiative will end our extracurricular money flow and make us criminals. We must succeed for our own benefit."

There was no clapping, just quiet conversation between attendees as they gathered their notes and headed back to their respective cars. Heller turned to Plank. "You leave last."

Darton wanted to be smart in his reply, but the look on Heller's face made him hold his tongue. He headed for his car. Heller and Waterstein stopped to have a private conversation.

"Was the note delivered?" she asked.

"Yes. I don't know if he'll follow through though," Heller replied.

"I'll talk to the foreign investors, if he doesn't remove her, we will have to, and they can help," she reminded him.

"You mean we should put her down like and old dog?" he asked.

"We will do what we must," she said.

They moved to their cars and the doors opened. Cars were directed out in varying intervals about three minutes apart. Darton wasn't allowed out until last.

32

THE AIR OUTSIDE was warm but dry for a change. Derrick sat outside behind the house on the deck. He had a bourbon over ice on the table and was smoking a cigar. He wasn't celebrating anything, this was how he let go of stress. It was his magic pill to unwind. He had been out there for a while when Trina came out to check on him.

"Are you okay?" she asked.

"I'm fine. There are just a lot of things I am being forced to deal with right now. Sometimes they get the best of me." Derrick smiled at her.

"Can you tell me about her?" Trina asked.

Derrick was caught off guard by her question.

"About whom?" he questioned.

"The person you lost because of that man in there. I know you're not a killer, but I see the hatred in your eyes when you look at him. I know I'm young, but I have seen a lot already," she said softly.

He contemplated her question.

"Her name was Shannon; she was my everything. We were building a great life and had lots of plans. That man in there sent men to kill us, they only killed Shannon," he informed her.

Trina stood up and moved closer, she wrapped her arms around him.

"I understand what you think you need to do. Just remember there are others in your life now that want you around to make plans with," she whispered in his ear.

Her statement hit him like a truck. The bourbon and cigar were not enough to overcome the emotion that Katrina had just slapped him with. He squeezed her tight in return.

"Where'd you come from?" he asked. He wasn't really looking for an answer.

———

TEAM THREE WAS TASKED with the hacker, they were another four-man team of mercenaries. They followed the same original route into the US as Team One; they had been on standby at a corporate property owned by members of the Council. Now they had an initial destination: the team was headed for Boston. They drove a van that looked like the cliché plumber's van. It was labeled and had ladders and pipes on the top. The numbers on the side were 800 numbers and went back to the corporation that had harbored them after their illegal entry into the US. A receptionist there would usually discourage any caller or tell them they were booked full and recommend another plumber in their area. They had the remainder of a two-day drive still in front of them.

———

TEAM ONE, had uncovered a couple of leads. They now had a vehicle description and a probable direction of travel. If the woman they were with went to the hospital, it was likely they went there to check on her. TL found a little motel in the area they needed to be in. It allowed him to pay cash for rooms without any ID. He got four rooms. He didn't like to share a room with anyone, so he treated his men the same way. They had a job to do, and no one should be unrested because they had a roommate that kept them up.

"Two and Four, go check out the hospital and see what you can find out about the woman. See if the man and child checked in on her. Let's get some names for all these people."

TL then went into his room and set up a laptop. He used a cellular data connection to avoid being compromised on public Wi-Fi. He sent an encrypted email.

In the area. Hope to have eyes on by tomorrow. Plan completion is expected by the end of the week.

That was all he sent. With the time difference, he did not expect a reply until tomorrow anyhow. He was hopeful Two and Four would return with useful information.

———

IT WAS time for another round with Barry and George. Derrick cleared his throat and announced his presence to the two of them. "I'm here to talk." George immediately took the offensive.

"Are you here to kill me now?" George asked.

"Mr. Avail. Let's just table the whole 'kill you' thing for now. I agree that for the present we need to work together. That will start with you telling me everything. No holding back. Do you understand?" Derrick replied.

Barry nodded in agreement. George just stared at him.

"Why exactly would I show you my cards? Intentionally give you the upper hand. What's in it for me, for us?" He corrected himself as Barry stared at him.

"We're not sure who is after us, or why we're being chased. I need to know where the danger is coming from and who's bringing it," Derrick stated.

Barry started first. "We were involved in the coup in Milekistan. It was coming anyway, so we nudged it to allow us to pull some strings while the media was preoccupied. Unfortunately, there is a larger group at play here. They refer to themselves as the 'World Council' however they have no actual name. They are comprised of the richest people all over the globe and they have one goal: to defeat America.

For over a decade, they have had no real plan but just buy politicians and use them to enact policies that undermine the Constitution. A plan that we used for our benefit as well. In the last election, despite all the money they pushed, and the media influence they paid for, they still lost to Harrington. This caused a change in their plan. It seems to have forced them to escalate and now push for the collapse of our way of life."

George nodded in agreement to everything Barry said. "It was then that George saw an opportunity to act against the Council. We secretly commissioned a hacker—the one you asked about before—to collect data that we could use to expose these Council members and the pawns they've purchased in our government."

"Why would you want to switch sides now?" Derrick questioned.

George thought for a few seconds. He chose his words carefully. "I have become exceedingly rich because of this country. If the Council has its way, I could lose all of it in a second."

"Well, it's time to choose sides, Mr. Avail. You can no longer play the middle hoping to pick the winner to hold on to. We can't let these people win. We need that list. Where is it?" Derrick interrogated.

"Hopefully it's on its way here. That was that call I needed to make," Barry chimed in.

"You gave out the address where were hiding from our government over the phone?" Derrick was aghast at their foolishness, especially Barry, who was supposed to be good at this stuff. "Are you trying to get us caught?"

"Once we get the drive, we can move. I have houses all over the world. Most are owned through shell companies with no direct ties to me. There is one within three miles from there, and the view is nicer too," George offered.

Harlem and Elsy had been listening. Elsy asked Derrick into the kitchen. She sat down at the island. "I've been monitoring Tinker the whole time, and my employees are also in possession of the same list that they were waiting for. We have a backup, and no one knows it."

Harlem took her hand. "I'm glad you're so smart, but this information will get people killed." She understood how dangerous the information was, she had been a target before.

"I will send an encrypted message to Tulia and Dillon. I want them to be prepared for possible fallout," she said.

———

THE DRIVER WAS LOOKING at the GPS. Twenty-five minutes to go. He had done some crazy things for Tinker before, but never played a multi-state delivery driver before. This was all new to him. Not to mention he would get to meet Tinker's client. "I wonder why Tinker isn't making this trip," he asked himself. It was a common occurrence for Pauly to speak to the mirror. "Maybe he just wanted some alone time with Deidra," he answered his own question. "Yeah, I bet that's it, that dirty dog."

"Right turn in one hundred feet. You have arrived at your destination," the GPS sang out. Pauly stepped out in front of a poorly kept house. He wasn't sure if he had the right address. He checked the address Tinker had given him. This was the place. He carried a small bag under his arm and approached the house cautiously. He knocked on the front door. An attractive lady with a big smile opened the door and invited him in. Once inside the door was quickly shut behind him. The mood instantly changed. The woman stood back, her smile was gone, and two men had guns pointed at him. He felt nauseous.

"Take it take whatever you want, just don't hurt me," Pauly said.

"We're not going to hurt you, we're just gonna pat you down to make sure you can't hurt us, okay?" Elsy informed him.

Pauly nodded okay. For once, he had no words for the situation.

Harlem stepped up and patted him down quickly. Nothing suspicious was found. Pauly held out the bag.

"This is for whichever one of you is George," he offered.

George walked in and took the bag from him. "Tell Mr. Brennan that his payment will be in his account tomorrow. Plus hazard pay."

"Wait, hazard pay? For what?" Pauly questioned.

"For the hazard associated with his job. Just tell him, and he'll understand. You should go now," Barry shared.

Pauly glanced around the room. "You don't have to tell me twice," he turned and bolted for the door like someone would be chasing him. He did not look back.

———

A PHONE RANG on the kitchen island. It slid around as it made the standard *bbrrrppp* noise on the hard surface. Elsy stepped over and answered. She had assumed it would be Tulia or Dillon. "Are you okay? I said don't use the phone unless it's an emergency."

"Elsy is that you? It's Paula."

Elsy wrinkled her nose; she hadn't meant to invite Paula into their situation. Her phone greeting would draw questions she'd have to answer from Paula now.

"I'm sorry, my neighbor's kids are house-sitting back in Boston and keep calling about the TV channels," she hoped the off the top of her head explanation would suffice to keep Paula's investigatory side at ease.

"I need to see you as soon as possible, tell me you're still at Harlem's," Paula informed her.

"I am, what's up," Elsy asked.

"Like your warning, I can't say over the phone. I'm already on my way, I'll be there in about ten minutes," Paula shared.

"You're coming here?" Elsy asked loud enough to get Harlem's attention.

"Yes, ten minutes." Paula said.

"Uhh, we're out right now. We'll head back that way and should make it home about the same time as you," she lied.

She hung up the phone. "This is unexpected. Harlem, we have to go home right now. Do you think we can leave Derrick alone with these two?" she asked.

"They won't be alone," chimed in Trina, who seemed to always go without notice when people were talking.

"Okay, it seems this is important. You'll need to be alert for anything. Where's Derrick now?"

"He's actually in there looking at the hard drive with those two."

"Okay, we have faith in you," Elsy encouraged Trina.

———

THE RIDE across town to get back to Harlem's house was at lightning speed. They did not want to keep Paula waiting and have her start looking around too much. Harlem swung the cruiser into his driveway. No Paula yet. As they started to exit the car, another vehicle with a government plate pulled up and Paula exited the car. She stepped up and gave them hugs.

"It's good to see you, but I have some disturbing questions to ask you, can we go inside?"

"Sure. Pardon the mess. We didn't clean before we left," Elsy joked.

"It's not that kind of visit," Paula warned.

Elsy knew Paula well; she was on the verge of sharing bad news.

They got situated in the dining area around the table. Harlem played host.

"Do you want a beer or something?" It was a test to see if this was an on-duty official visit or not.

"Do you have something stronger? I think I'm going to need it," Paula requested.

Harlem pulled out the bourbon that Derrick had taken the liberty of opening.

"This, okay?" he asked, holding up the bottle.

"That will be perfect. Straight up, please," Paula indicated.

With the drinks all around, Paula started right in.

"I met a man who said he was a Federal Marshal the other night. After a bit of discussion, I learned that he was looking for two escaped prisoners. He was searching for traffic cameras in the area, and he asked me to help him," she shared.

"Okay, Paula. How does that concern us?" Elsy asked her.

"This is how," she unfolded a printout from the video, clearly showing Elsy in the passenger seat of the same car Harlem had outside.

"Care to explain this?" She asked after presenting the photo.

Elsy scanned the photo and then turned to Harlem.

"So, remember when I told you about the hacker still messing with things related to the election?" Elsy questioned in response.

"Well, I was wrong about his intentions. It is so much bigger than that now," she continued.

Paula looked at her quizzically.

"How so? And did you break two prisoners from federal custody?" Paula interrogated.

"Well, if I tell you and you don't act, you'll be an accomplice," Elsy reminded her.

"I'm not worried about the legal implications. I pulled some strings, the 'Federal Marshal' is actually CIA. He lawfully can't detain anyone or even legally operate on US soil. What's going on?" Paula demanded.

Harlem and Elsy gave each other a look that said, "Should we bring her in?"

"Paula, if we tell you what's going on, you'll have a legal responsibility to pursue it. We are still trying to piece things together ourselves," Elsy warned.

"Spill it, we've been down this road before," Paula blurted.

"Paula, this is bigger than the Waller case," Elsy said.

Paula thought about that statement. That couldn't be possible—that was the biggest case since JFK was assassinated.

"What is bigger than the Speaker of the House trying to assassinate the President?" she asked, confused.

"How about a global cabal that has infiltrated our government and is trying to destroy our country from within?" Elsy teased.

"Are you for real, what are you involved with?"

Neither Harlem nor Elsy said another word. They just waited for Paula to realize they were telling her the truth.

"Holy shit, how deep does this go?" Paula questioned.

"We don't know yet, we just received intel we haven't had a chance to review yet. We believe we have a list of names."

———

THE BLACK VAN pulled up outside the house. The occupants could see three people in the house. They watched from the street for a bit; they wanted no surprises. They double-checked their weapons and TL gave the signal. They moved silently from the van toward the house, walking in a rehearsed formation. Each member was always aware of the others. They didn't have to look, they had practiced these moments thousands of times. Two moved to the front and two moved to the rear.

———

THE PRESIDENT COULDN'T SLEEP he tossed and turned, the words of the letter still bouncing around in his head. *Agent Newly must be removed.* He sat up. When he read the letter in his office, he thought they meant she needed to be removed from the case. He now realized they meant *removed,* as in permanently. He leaned over to the phone on the nightstand. He pressed a button.

"Good evening Mr. President. How can I assist you?" was the switchboard operator's standard greeting when that line ran through.

"Get me FBI Agent Newly on the line, now," he ordered.

"Yes sir, stand by." They had agent Newly's number on hand because the President had called her frequently. "Here you go, sir."

The operator's voice disappeared and was replaced by the sound of a phone ringing.

"Hello, this is Agent Newly," Paula answered.

"Paula, you're in danger," he shouted into the phone over her talking.

"I'm not available right now, but leave a message and I'll get back to you," her voicemail greeting continued.

He waited for the tone. "Paula, you're in danger right now, get ready."

"Shit, shit, shit." He hung up and pushed the button for the operator again. "Get me someone from the FBI Cybercrime unit."

Again, he was told to wait briefly.

"Mr. President, how can I help you?" The phone was answered by an agent.

"Can you identify a phone's location?" The President asked.

"Yes sir, but we need a warrant." The agent replied.

"We don't have time for that. I need you to tell me where this phone is right now. It's life or death."

"Sir, I would need authorization. I can't just..." the agent started.

"I'm the damn President of the United States. That is all the authorization you need. Do it now or I'll find you a replacement that will."

"Sorry, Mr. President. Yes sir, give me two minutes."

The analyst was back in less than a minute and produced the address associated with the phone's location to the President.

"Thank you, sorry for yelling," the President said. One more time he pressed the operator button.

"How can I..." the operator began.

"Listen," he said, cutting her off. "I need you to connect me to the Virginia Beach Police Department immediately."

The desk officer at the PD almost hung up because he thought the call was a prank.

"Listen closely, this is not a joke, and I am President Harrington. There is an FBI agent at the following address," he spoke calmly but with a sense of urgency. "That agent and anyone with her are in extreme danger. Dispatch a SWAT team to that location to protect them all until I can arrange secure transport for them. Do you understand?"

"Yes, sir," the officer answered.

"Good, then do it now," the President ordered.

33

THE BOX TRUCK had been on the road just driving for a while. It made a turn into the parking lot of an old department store. They drove around to the rear of the building and backed up to the loading dock. The dock door opened simultaneously with the rear truck door. Several people were standing there to greet the occupants. Most had weapons except for one, the doctor who was treating Linda. He stepped into the truck to check on her.

"How long has she been out?" someone asked.

"Not long, maybe twenty minutes," the nurse answered.

The doctor noticed blood soaking into the sheets of the gurney. He lifted her to see where it was coming from.

"Damn, some of her sutures came out. We need to get her inside right now. Nurse Hurt, grab me IV bags and meet me in the surgical setup."

They rushed Linda to the room they had set up as a surgical/recovery room. They hadn't expected to use it, but built it to be safe.

"She seems to have lost a lot of blood. Her vitals show borderline shock. Bolus these IVs into her. I need to close this up before it gets worse."

Medical assistants arrived to assist with the operation being performed.

All had the same goal. *Save Linda Avail.*

THE SWAT TEAM raced across town to get to their target. The location was a fellow officer's home. The only information they had was that the occupants were in imminent danger from an unknown external force. They didn't use their lights or sirens though; they just drove exceedingly fast. The surprise might be what would give them the advantage. Captain Koenig was monitoring their approach from his office. The residence belonged to one of his best detectives, and the President of the United States had requested the SWAT Team be activated for someone there.

THE ASSAULT TEAMS moved into position.

"On my count." The leader said.

"Three, two, one," he counted down with his fingers.

They started shooting from outside through the windows. The targets fell or leapt to the floor—it was unclear through all the shattering glass and smoke and flash from their weapons. They moved towards the doors, two in front and two in back. They entered simultaneously. Both pairs moved toward the kitchen where their targets had been observed. They reached the kitchen and they found blood, but no targets. As they started to look around, the lights went out. Three guns were fired at almost the same instant. Three bodies jerked backward, each from a round striking their head. The team leader turned to his teammate to point toward the direction of the fire, and found he wasn't there.

The lights came back on. The assassin was staring at the wall where the contents of his partner's brains now were splattered across the surface. He turned around and started to raise his gun he saw two guns pointed at his head. The third fired and the bullet struck him just below his knee, shattering his tibia and dropping him to the floor like a bag of sand.

ELSY GRABBED PAULA; blood was covering the left side of her face. She had taken a round right through the ear and out the other side. The ear was hanging loosely in a grotesque manner. She was spitting out blood as it ran down her cheek into her mouth.

"Sit down, we have to look at that," Elsy ordered.

Harlem kicked the gun away from the man bleeding on the floor and removed several other weapons from him. As Elsy tended to Paula, they heard more commotion outside. The front door burst open; several armed men burst in.

"Police, lay down your weapons," the lead man ordered.

All three complied. Harlem set his gun on the island but pushed their attacker to the floor with his foot at the same time. "Don't you move."

He then addressed the SWAT officer, "I'm Detective Harlem Posada. This is my house. The attackers have been subdued."

The sergeant in charge of the SWAT Team kept his gun pointed at him. "Do you have ID on you?"

"Yes sir, please take custody of this man here first. He and his former associates just tried to kill us. Also we need a medic for Agent Newly, she's FBI," Harlem requested.

The Sargent heard the name Newly and his attitude changed abruptly.

"Get a medic in here now," he ordered, then asked Harlem again, "You got that ID?"

Haley carefully removed it from his pocket and showed it to the man.

The team of officers moved through the house clearing the residence, they returned saying all was clear. Captain Koenig had arrived as they were removing the single living attacker. He was handcuffed to the stretcher and had three officers surrounding him while the EMTs packaged his injury for transport.

His search by officers before his treatment had uncovered nothing other than the weapons Harlem had removed from him and numerous magazines for those weapons. He had come prepared for war, just not for his victims to be trained and ready for him. The only thing he said at all before he stopped talking was, "Where is the little girl?"

––––––––

ANOTHER DARK SEDAN was parked at the end of the street. The occupants were bewildered by the attack on their target. The driver picked up a secured satellite phone.

"Is there more than one team assigned to this?" he asked.

The line was silent for a second.

"No, this is supposed to be highly classified and off-book. Are you telling me you failed to remove the target?"

"No ma'am, I'm saying another team was here when we arrived, they were also trying to remove the target, and they did not succeed."

"Then stay on assignment. The target must not be allowed to continue their interference."

———

THE PHONE RANG LATE at night. He rolled over and looked at the caller ID. "What the hell does she want?" he said while reaching for his phone.

"Are you secure?" Irma Waterstein asked.

"Yes Irma, I am always secure when you call. What the hell is so important you need to ruin my sleep?" Heller replied.

"Your crack team was interrupted by another group attacking our target," she informed him.

"What are you talking about? I authorized one team. One team only. This is the kind of trash that will put us in prison, or worse," Heller moaned.

"You don't think I know that? That's why I woke your ass up in the night," Irma fired back.

"Okay, let me make some calls. This is going bad quickly. Did the other team get our target?" Heller asked.

"No. If they had, we'd have just walked away without any involvement. You'd still be sleeping," Irma reminded him.

"Damn, okay. Are they staying on assignment?" Heller inquired.

"Yes, it will be harder now, I think. She'll be on alert now," Waterstein surmised.

"Unfortunately, that will be the case. It means this will likely be less surgical and a lot messier," Heller warned.

"Let's hope we stay clean," Waterstein wished.

"Let's hope the President doesn't figure this out," Heller corrected.

"It might be time to start pointing this at him," Irma suggested.

"Yeah okay. Good night, Irma."

"Good night, Alvin."

———

WHILE HARLEM and Elsy were away, Derrick made the effort to play nice with his guests.

"We need to see what's on that drive."

Barry pointed to the laptop on the counter. "Bring me the computer, we'll look together."

George gave Barry an apprehensive look. "Are you sure we should share this?"

"We're all in this together at this point," Barry replied.

George walked up to Barry and handed him a paper with an address on it.

"Give that to him," he said pointing to Derrick. "That's where we can go when they get back."

Despite how hard he was trying to suppress it, the urge to kill this man stayed ever so close to the surface. He pulled up a seat on the other side of Barry rather than be right next to George.

They inserted the drive into the computer. A program auto-loaded and then stopped, asking for a key to continue. The three men looked at questioningly each other.

"What friggin' key?" Barry blurted.

He searched in the bag the courier had given him. Nothing else was in there. He shook it upside down without success. No one had any suggestions.

Someone started knocking on the door.

Derrick drew his weapon. "Could someone track us by turning that on?"

"I don't know, maybe. They would have had to be parked outside to be that quick," Barry replied.

Derrick peered out the curtain towards the door. The guy who brought the drive was standing there.

"Did you forget something?" Derrick asked as he opened the door.

"As a matter of fact, I did. I was supposed to give this envelope to Mr. Avail as well."

Derrick snapped the envelope from the kid's hands. "Thanks," he said as he slammed the door in his face and rushed back into the other room. George tore the envelope open, and a USB drive fell out.

"Hopefully this is the key," Barry said as he plugged it into the laptop. Nothing happened. They tried several times, complaining louder each time.

Trina awakened by their noise joined them and asked what they were doing.

"Just trying to open this drive," Barry said.

Trina watched as they fumbled around.

"You just need to remove both drives and start over. If the second drive isn't accessed within a few seconds, the main drive will lock and stop looking. That's all," she said like they all should have known that.

The three men just stared at her.

Barry followed her directions.

He reinserted the cable for the drive. It ran its program again and then asked for the key. He inserted the USB, the screen changed, and a long string of numbers started scrolling up the screen. About a minute later, a page with a search engine screen showed up.

'Enter your query' appeared on the screen.

———

"SIR, Team One has failed to check in." Denler informed his boss.

He didn't take the news well. Jeac grabbed an object from his desk and threw it at the wall. The triangle crystal paperweight stuck into the wall like a tomahawk.

"Send another team, make it bigger, more men. How hard can it be to take out a man and a child?" He was spitting while he yelled, his face was bright red. "I want this settled. We have more pressing issues to resolve," Jeac yelled.

"Yes sir, sending a bigger team," Denler acknowledged.

Denler searched through the assets they had in the US already, then at assets that were available through members in the US. He dialed the number for a cartel delegate. This would have to be outsourced to get there as fast as possible.

———

AFTER A TRIP to the hospital under the protection of the SWAT Team, where Paula had her ear stitched up, Harlem, Elsy, and Paula all went down to the police station for debriefing and questioning of the suspect. It seemed that the intent of the gunmen was already known, though. The remaining gunman had refused to talk and was being treated at the local ER under police supervision. Captain Koenig walked into the conference room where his detective and the two others were waiting.

"Ladies and detectives. I'd like to thank you for ruining a perfectly good night. I am glad you're alright though," he greeted them.

"Captain, we honestly don't even know who those men were or why they attacked us," Harlem responded.

"I'm aware, Harlem. We're pretty sure it was an attempt on Agent Newly's life." The captain informed them,

"What? My life? By whom? When did I become someone's target?" Paula gasped.

"That's a lot of questions, Agent Newly. This is what I know. Earlier this night, the President himself called our dispatch and said you were in extreme danger. He ordered the SWAT Team to respond and protect you."

"The President called you?" Paula questioned.

"Yes, Paula—if I can call you that? He was very concerned and stated we were to keep you safe until he could provide for your security," Koenig replied.

Paula was about to ask another question when her phone rang. She held it to her good ear.

"Paula, are you safe?"

"Yes, Mr. President. Thanks to you. Your message was relayed at precisely the right time," she said.

"I have a team of Secret Service on their way to take you to a secure location," the President told her.

"I'm sorry Mr. President, but I have friends that will protect me and that I know won't betray my location. I don't think I should trust a government agency with my safety right now. Can you make this right with the agency?" Paula pleaded.

"Yes, I will. You be safe. If you need anything you call me directly, you have the number."

"Thank you, Mr. President."

———

THE SEDAN SAT in the public lot across from the police department. The occupants took turns watching for their target while the others ate or slept. They were hoping they might have a shot at their target before it meant engaging in a shootout with the police. Their existence had been erased, and none of them would talk if they were captured, but they were not afraid of justice because they were under orders. This was different from where they normally would operate.

Killing a traitor FBI agent would be a patriotic act as far as they were concerned. They didn't care for politics, but they loved the USA and hated anyone who betrayed her. Especially an FBI agent, like the one they were sent after. The briefing told it all—she was found to be colluding with Russia to make the President look bad and to assist China with gaining access to files that would have caused political harm to several high-ranking members of Congress. Their orders came directly through a Senate Special Committee on Terrorism, which oversaw their team's operations. It was signed by the Chairman of the committee himself, Senator Alvin Heller.

———

FOUR OF THEM huddled around the computer screen. They had entered their query and now watched as the results accumulated across the screen. They typed in just one Senator's name, and the data started to accrue. Crimes and bribes, bank accounts, numerous recorded transactions, conversations, and more. Just this one query was enough to guarantee the removal and likely incarceration of the Senator they searched for.

"Why was all of this information in one location?" Derrick asked.

"It wasn't, it was held across the servers of every major social media platform we have access to. I had convinced the manager of the Council that she should use the AI to collect and catalog this information in case she ever needed it to save herself," George was amused with himself because of this.

"So, she collected all of this and then just gave you access to it?" Derrick asked.

"Oh no, she doesn't know I gained access to it," George bragged. "That's why no one has come to kill us yet."

George typed another name into the query.

"Wait I know that name," Derrick said. "He's a drug cartel leader."

"Yes, Mr. Dunn, I wanted you to see why the Council is so dangerous. These are not just rogue politicians seeking to harm America. Some very dangerous criminals have an equal say in the direction the Council takes."

Derrick just looked at George and then at Trina. He knew his only concern in that room was her. He would die trying to keep her safe if that's what it took.

34

"I HOPE it's alright that I join you guys. I didn't even ask before I told the President I'd be safer with you," Paula apologized.

Elsy smiled at her. "Sister, you know I always have your six, and Harlem has mine. So, let's get out of here and get you safe. We need to tell you a few things as well," Elsy assured her.

They collected their weapons back from the PD. Captain Koenig signed off on Harlem officially being part of Paula's protection detail.

"Just keep me in the loop whenever you can do so safely," the captain said.

"Yes, Captain," Harlem answered.

As an official safety detail, Harlem went to the armory before they headed out. He collected three M4 long guns and three nine-millimeter pistols, three combat belts, three bulletproof vests, and a few other items he thought might come in handy. He also loaded up enough magazines and ammunition to supply a small army. He dispersed the items into three bags equally, except for the vests. He set those on top. He carried the bags out one at a time and handed them off to Paula and Elsy.

"Put the vests on now, no sense taking chances," he said.

"What did you say?" Paula feigned not hearing him as she held her hand up to her uninjured ear.

Harlem was ready to repeat himself when he caught her pointing at him and smiling.

"Just put it on," he urged.

They grabbed the bags and headed out to the parking lot. The President had arranged an armored SUV for their use, and it was waiting for them there.

———

AS THE TRIO stepped from the building, the man assigned to watch for them, started waking the others. "They're coming out."

Soon the men started checking their weapons.

"Are we gonna do this here?" A man in the backseat asked.

"They're here and we're here, seems like the right time to make it happen," their leader answered.

"What about the cops? I'm not a fan of killing cops just doing their jobs," a team member voiced his opinion.

"I agree, but collateral damage is sometimes necessary to accomplish the mission. Preventing this traitor and her allies from divulging secrets to our enemies is our primary goal. Our orders are to eliminate the target at the first opportunity we get, this is it."

The talking ended and the men prepared to exit on their leader's orders.

"Let's get them."

———

THE GUNFIRE FLASHED across the parking lot. A bullet meant for Paula struck an unlucky officer in the head, dropping him next to his personal vehicle at the end of his shift. The sound of the gunfire put the building on lockdown and mobilized the officers inside. Many of them drew their sidearms and moved slowly towards the gunfire, while others sought larger caliper weapons from the armory to better repel any attack. Captain Koenig opened the public address system in the building. *"All Officers, Defend Detective Posada and Agent Newly. They're in the parking lot."*

Officers moved to the exits that serviced the front and sides of the building. The four-man assault team reacted and tried to force them back inside.

"If they come out to engage, we must treat them like hostiles," the leader ordered.

Bullets ricocheted off the pavement and the sides of cars. A whirring noise could be heard as they spun past, dangerously out of control.

Harlem grabbed the rifle from his bag and put on the combat belt already loaded with magazines. He stayed low between cars. He had counted two attackers, but knew there were more than that. When he felt he had moved sufficiently to the side, he popped up and found a target. He opened fire. His bullets narrowly missed, and the return fire was swift and accurate. Harlem took two rounds to the chest and fell backward. It was hard to breathe—he just laid there for a second. He tore at the velcro holding the vest in place, ran his hand under it and then looked at his hand—no blood.

Despite the pain, he replaced the vest and got back in the fight. The vehicle he was behind was now taking sustained fire. He was trapped and was sure someone would be moving on his position.

———

THE HIT SQUAD kept moving toward their target. Agent Newly was their primary; they needed to remove her.

Working in pairs, they cautiously but methodically moved to pinch Agent Newly in. There were now several officers that had joined the fight against them, and they were no longer trying to spare them. An officer stepped out and fired his service weapon at one of the assault team men. The assault member crumpled to the ground. His teammate fired three rounds, all striking the officer. The last round struck him in the face—the officer was no longer a threat. The attacker checked on his partner, who was swearing.

"You good?" he asked.

"Yeah, vest stopped it. It still fucking hurts," his partner swore.

"Shake it off, we still have a job to do," his teammate ordered.

They resumed their push forward. This time Elsy leaned out from behind a car; she was almost laying on the ground when she appeared to them. She fired the M4 at one then the other. The first round struck the first one in the thigh. In seconds bright red blood was pushing from the wound. He tried to scramble behind cover while reaching for his tourniquet. He knew he had only a short time before he would bleed to death if he didn't stop the bleeding. His partner leaned down to help him. This gave Elsy a clear shot at his head. The back of his head exploded from the force of the small round as it entered and then expelled its force as it exited, covering his teammates face with a mixture of blood and brain matter.

His lifeless body fell forward onto his partner, who was still trying to get to cover. The weight of his partner and the loss of blood were severely limiting his ability to escape. He realized that he probably wouldn't survive and decided to make the traitor's friend pay. He grabbed his gun and scanned for a target. He saw her lying on the ground under the rear of a truck. As he brought his sight up toward the target, he felt the impact of a bullet just below his jaw, striking his neck. The bullet traveled through the soft neck tissue and struck his spine. The gun fell from his hand, and his face dropped to the pavement. He couldn't move, his mind raced, and he wasn't able to draw a breath. Even though his mind had seconds left, his body was gone, his vision clouded, and it all went black.

The team leader saw his men go down.

"Fuck this bitch," he growled to his remaining partner. "She has to die now."

He moved quicker and with less caution than he originally had. He moved through the middle of the parked cars which provided them with the best cover as they moved forward. Windows exploded into fragments as bullets flew in both directions. Members of the SWAT Team had exited the building from the side and were moving as a unit up toward the fighting. They were hoping to flank the attackers and stop the attack on their department.

The assailants moved quickly through the parked cars, firing, and striking several officers with their bullets. They sensed a chance to get their prey. They were only one row away from where Paula had made her fight position. The leader lay on the ground and rolled to his side. He could see her knee where she was taking cover behind a cruiser. He took the shot. Paula screamed at the bullet struck her knee and pushed pieces of shattered bone down through her calf. As she fell to the ground the team leader fired again, this bullet was on target and struck Paula in the right armpit. It entered just above the vest and traveled through her chest.

"I got her. I don't think she'll survive that. Let's get out of here," the assault leader said.

The two started their tactical withdrawal, something they had practiced so many times before. They wanted to collect their fallen brothers, but there was no time. If they were to escape, it would be now. They carefully stepped backward, taking turns shooting, taking cover, and reloading. They reached their car even as the SWAT Team was moving forward to their position. They both flipped the switch on the side of their weapons. They laid down fully automatic fire, which caused the SWAT Team to dive for cover.

They jumped into their car and took off, even as gunfire followed them down the empty street.

———

PAULA LAY ON THE GROUND; Elsy was the first to make it to her. "Are you hit? Where are you hit?"

Paula tried to speak but blood just spit from her mouth. Her breathing was quick and shallow.

Elsy screamed, "Someone help, I need a medic, we need an ambulance."

Harlem joined her in a second. He could tell that this was bad.

The SWAT medic appeared and made Elsy and Harlem move. He checked her wound and immediately started working on her. His partner showed up a second later.

"Start an IV wide open, I found the entrance, there's no exit." The first medic relayed.

Elsy remembered enough from her basic first aid when she went through the police academy that this was bad. She resisted the urge to ask if she'd be okay. She knew the medics didn't have a crystal ball and that they would do everything they could to help her survive.

As they waited for the ambulance, the SWAT Team cleared the area once more. Several officers were being treated for a variety of injuries and at least three officers had been killed. Two others were in similar conditions as Paula, and had been rushed to the hospital by fellow police officers in patrol cars.

The ambulance showed up after what seemed like an eternity. Harlem checked his watch, it had been three minutes since they called.

Paula was loaded inside and the medics who were working on her climbed alongside to continue her treatment en route.

Harlem pulled Elsy aside. "Grab the bags, we need to go."

———

BY MORNING, the shootout at the police department was all over the news. Not a single channel reported the story correctly. One was saying that a rogue FBI agent started the shootout with the police and that she was killed in the shootout. One channel said that the police, under the direction of the President of the United States, tried to protect a known terrorist from agents who were sent to take her into custody. And then one small channel known for conspiracy theories claimed it was a black ops team sent by members high within our government that attacked the police department to silence an FBI agent that knew too much.

Elsy and Harlem had returned to the house where the others were still seated around the computer.

Upon hearing them arrive. Trina shouted, "Hey we're in here."

Elsy shuffled into the living room where they were gathered. Trina let out a shriek when she saw her.

"Are you alright? Are you bleeding?" Trina cried.

Elsy hadn't even realized she was covered in Paula's blood.

"It's not my blood, it's a friend's," Elsy said quietly.

Derrick jumped up from the computer. "What happened? Are you guys alright?"

Harlem just pulled his shirt back to reveal the bullets still lodged in his vest.

"What the hell happened out there? I thought you were meeting an FBI agent?" Derrick asked again.

"We did, and apparently she had a hit team after her," Elsy shared.

"Maybe two," Harlem corrected.

"Oh yeah, maybe two hit teams," Elsy updated.

"We need to move. We can talk all about this in the next place," Derrick informed them.

"Do we have another place?" Harlem asked.

Derrick pointed to George and Barry. "They say we do, and we don't have any other options right now."

Once again, they divided into two vehicles. Just to be safe, the hard drive went with one and the key went with the other. The occupants remained the same as on the first trip.

———

"OH NO, this is huge and terrible." The Cyber tech jumped back from his desk as though it was infected. "This can't be."

His teammates all turned to stare at him. He turned to his team partner. "Check my work, please tell me I'm wrong," his teammate slid his chair over and started to scroll through the code. As he did his face turned pale. A sweat broke out across the back of his neck. As he finished scanning the code, he turned and looked at his partner.

"I'm afraid you are spot on. There is no error," his coworker said.

"God, this is gonna kill us all," The tech exclaimed.

With that outburst, the other six members left their seats to come see what was found. One by one they covered their mouths in horror, one or two just collapsed to sit on the floor.

"What do we do now?" was the common question being asked by all.

"It's a good thing you found it, you're the boss," one member said.

"That is no comfort to me," he responded back.

———

THE PHONE RANG on Denler's desk.

"Hello, this is Faulk. How can I help you?" he answered.

"Denler, it's Conner in the Cyber division. I need to see you in here now," he stated.

Denler pulled the handset from his ear and stared at it like it was scrambling the words.

"You need me in there?" he asked.

"Yes, I must show you something of extreme importance," Conner repeated.

"Ok, let me get Mr. Pastil," Denler offered.

"NO. I need you to see it first. Do not say anything to Mr. Pastil yet," Conner pleaded.

Denler was confused. He had no authority; he was only an assistant; he only did what he was told to.

"Okay. I'm coming, you'd better have a good reason for this," Denler warned.

"Oh, it's a reason you'll understand," Conner prodded.

Denler hung up. He knocked on his boss's door.

"Come in," Jeac answered.

"Sir, I just wanted to let you know I'm stepping away from my desk for a minute. I must check on something," Denler warned him.

"Very well, be quick. We're still awaiting more info from the Cyber department," Jeac advised him.

Denler went to the floor the Cyber guys had been relocated to.

Conner was waiting for him at the door. As Denler followed him into the darkened room, he noticed all the team members were standing huddled together and whispering in the corner.

"What the hell is so important? And why isn't the rest of the team working?" Denler demanded.

The team lead pointed at the computer monitor.

"Sit down and look at the data," Conner pushed.

Denler absorbed the information from the computer screen, realizing what the information was, he understood the gravity of the situation. He slowly stood up and turned towards the door. His face had a blank look.

"I must share this information with Mr. Pastil. This changes everything," Denler said as he turned to leave.

35

TWO VEHICLES PULLED up to the beautiful sprawling beach estate. The car in the lead reached out and punched in a code on a small stand. A gate that was blocking the driveway slowly moved from their path.

Both cars passed and headed up toward the main house. As they got closer, the driveway split. To the left it entered a circle drive directly in front of the estate, to the right, the drive went behind the main house to a multi-bay carriage-style garage. Both cars went to the right.

George pointed to the two end bays. "Those two should be empty."

Elsy hopped out and entered through a door on the side. Lights came on automatically as she entered. She found the buttons and opened both doors. The sedan and the Jeep pulled into the garage and the doors were shut. They looked around at four other vehicles in the garage.

"I think we should swap into those," Harlem said, pointing to a black Range Rover and a gray Audi RS Q8.

"That's a really smart idea," Barry said. "These vehicles aren't known to anyone, and they're not registered to us. They're registered to a shell corporation."

They decided to quickly make the switch before heading inside.

Harlem and Derrick chose to flip a coin to see who got which vehicle.

"Heads, I get the Range Rover, tails you do," Derrick said as Harlem prepared to flip the coin.

Harlem tossed the coin up, it landed on the concrete of the garage and bounced and started to roll. Barry squashed it like a bug with his foot as it started to roll by him. He pulled his foot away. "Tails," he stated. The discussion ended. Each vehicle was loaded per their agreement.

With the cars swapped and loaded, it was time to head inside. Elsy started to head towards the door she had entered through.

"No, no, come this way," George called to her and the others. Near the back of the garage, there was a stairway that led down. This was a surprise, given how close they were to the ocean. The group followed George and Barry as they headed through the tunnel that came back up inside the estate house. At the top of the stairs, Barry flipped a small toggle and a panel slid away releasing them into the pantry. They all entered the kitchen from the pantry.

"Oh, I hope it's all stocked," George exclaimed. He walked over to a large commercial-style fridge and opened it. Inside it was fully stocked with fresh food.

"Did you tell someone we were coming here?" Derrick asked him.

"No, I pay to keep all my safe houses always stocked with fresh food. The food gets sent to the local shelter when a new order is delivered." George answered.

Most of the group couldn't imagine the kind of money that would allow him to do that.

Barry perused the refrigerator. "I'll make us something to eat. We should all talk about what's coming for us," he said, pointing to a large island in the kitchen area.

"You guys talk, I'm gonna explore. This place is like a mansion," Trina burst out with.

Derrick nodded and she disappeared as fast as she could. They could already hear her surprise as she made discoveries throughout the house.

Four of them sat down at the kitchen island, George and Derrick on opposite ends.

"We need to hear the rest of your story about Paula," Derrick said.

———

THE NEWS MEDIA had suddenly latched onto the story that had President Harrington responsible for ordering a team to attack a police department and try to kill a witness that could undermine his presidency. Senator Waterstein watched the newscast with excitement.

"They're pushing this narrative quite well," she said to her guest. "Your position should start to grow just in time for the elections."

"All I can say is thank you, Senator. I wasn't sure I'd have the slightest chance when you asked me to put my hat in the ring for President. After all, President Harrington has the best approval rating of any President in recorded times," Darton responded.

"All of those polls are temporary; all you need is the appearance of a scandal and people flee. Voters are so fickle these days," Senator Waterstein said.

"Do you think I have a legitimate chance to be elected?" Darton asked.

"Darton, I would not have chosen you if I didn't think you had a real chance. As I said, voters are fickle, not smart. They love you and that's what they'll remember when they're voting. Rationality has nothing to do with how most people vote anymore, that's why it's so important to keep them agitated against the other side."

"I get it." Darton acknowledged.

They sat and watched the rest of the news broadcast while sipping tea. Irma was pleased with all of it.

———

THE OBJECT he had thrown at the wall was still embedded there. He was looking at how the light seemed to fracture when it hit it, sending different pieces of itself out in various colors across the wall. There was a quiet knock at his door.

"Denler, that better be you," Jeac said firmly.

The door opened slowly.

"It is, sir. I come with news; it is not good," Denler warned.

"What could be worse than the news we've already had this week?" Jeac asked tentatively.

Denler continued walking toward Jeac's desk, a bundle of papers in his hands.

"This," he said as he dropped the stack onto the desk.

His boss sifted through the papers, at first it didn't make much sense, then he realized what he was looking at. Detailed dossiers on members of the Council and the people they used to accomplish their goals.

"What the fuck is this?" His face was red, and his anger was apparent.

"It is exactly what it looks like, sir." Denler replied.

"Who authorized this?" Jeac demanded.

"Sir, that's the info the hacker acquired," Denler stated flatly.

Jeac just collapsed into his chair.

"This isn't bad, this is catastrophic. Why would all of this be available on our servers?" he questioned.

"Cyber says this is an AI instruction authorized by this office. The information was fragmented across multiple servers that are used by our social media partners; it was initiated several years ago. Sir, the data is complete on every current and past member and asset we have or have had. The hacker now has all of this."

"This will get every one of us killed if this info gets out. Does the Cyber team know who the hacker is yet?" Jeac asked hopefully.

"They expect an address today, they are very close," Denler advised.

"Contact the team headed there, and tell them about a change in orders, we need all targets alive for interrogation," Jeac ordered.

————

PRESIDENT HARRINGTON SCHEDULED A PRESS CONFERENCE, he needed to get out in front of this hatchet story playing in the news. Senator Heller stood in his office.

"Sir, I told you about this issue with the FBI agent would go badly. I just didn't expect this," Senator Heller stated.

"Alvin, Cut the shit. I have no doubt you were involved in this. When I can prove it, I'll have you hanged as a traitor on the front lawn," Harrington replied.

"Well, Mr. President, good luck trying to make that happen. Without my help and that of others, you will probably only be President for a few more months," Heller warned him.

"Get out. Consider your appointment to my Council ended," the President almost yelled.

The Senator just gave him an evil smile. "Whatever you say, Mr. President," he turned and walked out.

His Chief of Staff entered. "Sir, Senator Heller is a bad person to make an enemy."

"I didn't make him an enemy, his actions did. Get me the FBI Director, I need to see him now, and get me an update on Agent Newly's condition." The President ordered.

"Yes sir." The Chief said.

Estephan sat down behind his desk and poured himself a glass of tequila. He took a swig and paused as it burned his throat going down. He whispered to himself, "President or not, someone will pay for this betrayal and this attack on Paula."

———

THE DOCTOR WAS SATISFIED that he had repaired the bleed caused by the tearing of Linda's stitches. They would just have to wait a bit for her to respond to the fluids and medications. This was a setback, but they would overcome it. He exited the sterile room and went to the kitchen area that was set up inside the structure they were housed in. In fact, like the warehouse they had been in previously, a whole home plus specialty rooms were erected within this building. There were more members of their group here now.

"Why the abrupt move?" he asked one of the armed members.

"We had intel that we were compromised. One of our assistants informed us that feds were going to move on that location," The member informed him.

"We must try to keep her more stable. We can't afford another move for a while if we want to keep her alive," the doctor replied.

"Why do we need her?" the member asked.

"We are hoping she will lead us to her father and the information he is believed to possess. If our intelligence is accurate, that info will uncover corrupt many politicians in our government," the doctor replied.

"Where was this info supposed to come from? Why would her father have it?" the member queried.

"That part we don't know, we are still learning as we go," the doctor answered.

———

TEAM TWO RECEIVED their updated rules of engagement and a physical address. The eight-man team reviewed the information they had on the address. It was a warehouse mostly set off by itself. There were several industrial buildings nearby, but most if not all appeared to be deserted. This was ideal for their purposes. Limited witnesses and buildings could be used for cover on approach and surveillance. The team leader, named Raouf Nile, was a former SAS member and now employed by a drug cartel. His team all operated by call signs only—he was Nitelite. He laid out the plan to approach and infiltrate.

"This is a hacker; we expect high-tech surveillance and maybe electronic countermeasures to suppress the entry. Once inside, there should be limited opposition," he pointed to the schematics they had been sent related to the location.

"We'll go in two teams of four. There seem to be two entrances, here and here," he pointed to the building blueprint, then kept going. "I'll take Team One with Gripe, Charley One, and Dover. Flash, you'll take Paydirt, Guns and Loader to the second entrance. I will call entry on Channel Two." The men all shook their heads in understanding.

Paydirt raised his hand like he was in school. "Sir, what if we receive hostile resistance, are we cleared to engage?"

"If it's hired help, lethal is authorized. If you have any doubt that it could be our target, non-lethal only. Is that clear to all of you? We must take the hacker alive for questioning. We need the name of his client and any other information we can gather."

Nitelite ended his briefing. "Let's load up."

———

THE PRESIDENT ADDRESSED America from the Oval Office while sitting behind the resolute desk.

"My fellow Americans."

It was a cliche opening, but seemed appropriate for the moment.

"Recently, the media and some members of government have deemed that it is appropriate to try to implicate me in the recent tragic events that occurred in Virginia Beach. First, I'd like to offer my sympathy and condolences to the officers, and family members who were injured or killed in this heinous attack," he paused for a moment.

"I want all Americans to know unequivocally, that I had nothing to do with this attack. The agent who was attacked had been working on a case at my request. It seems she may have found information that left some very high-ranking politicians scared of what was being uncovered. I am currently working with the FBI Director and other law enforcement agencies to uncover the truth. Rest assured, I will not tire, I will not rest, and I will find the answers. Those who are truly responsible will be held accountable and pay for this atrocity. This is all I have for now, but I will keep you, the citizens of this great county apprised as we move forward. Good day and God bless America."

The cameras were turned off and several members of his staff told him how great it was.

He looked for the FBI Director.

"How is she? Any word yet?" He asked?

"She is reported to be in critical condition. *Touch and go* is how they described it," the Director replied.

"If she becomes conscious, I want to know immediately," the President said.

"Yes sir. Do we need to discuss what she was working on?" the Director inquired.

"Not yet. There are a few people I need to speak with first," the President informed him.

————

THEY ALL SAT at the large dining room table eating the meal Barry had put together. As it turned out, Barry was an excellent cook. He had made a batch of linguini and clam sauce.

Trina wrinkled her face when she saw the little clams in her sauce. "What are those?"

"They're called clams, just try one," Elsy encouraged her.

She carefully dug one clam out with her fork and spoon and put it slowly in her mouth, after a second her face lit up.

"Whoa, these are really good." Everyone laughed, it felt like a quick minute of normalcy.

While waiting for Barry's meal, they had started a list of politicians that were in this file. In a short time, they had compiled over a dozen names of officials who were compromised or outright traitors.

Derrick had folded the list and pocketed it during their meal.

———

DENLER AND JEAC were searching through the Council's database.

"There has to be some record of who authorized this," Jeac hissed.

"Sir, if it's here, we'll find it. Why aren't we getting the Cyber department to help us?" Denler questioned.

"Denler, listen to me very carefully. There may come a time when the Council will move to silence anyone who knows of this. You've proven your allegiance to me, but those poor Cyber guys are all dispensable. Let's not get caught up in that."

Denler stared right at him. "Alright sir, just you and me," he went back to the computer screen.

36

SIMON HAD EXPLORED every option he could think of, so he made a call again.

"Hey buddy, I need another favor," he asked over the phone.

"What the hell, you still owe me like ten," was the reply.

"I know, and I'll pay up. Check your email, I need help with that satellite program you run."

"Simon, I can lose my job and my clearance for this, maybe even go to prison," Deacon replied.

"Not this time," Simon pushed. "This is national security related. Did you open the email?" he asked.

"An orange Jeep? What do you need?" Deacon's curiosity peaked.

"Look at the time stamp and location on the image. I need you to tell me where it went," Simon instructed.

"Okay. I'll get Betty on it; she should have an answer in about half an hour, provided they didn't leave the coverage area. I'll have her utilize every ground camera we have access to as well," Deacon advised him.

"Great. This is time-sensitive, something big is occurring and I'm falling behind trying to figure it out," Simon confessed.

Simon felt a little better now that he had one last hand to play. He took a breather and turned the news on. There was a special news bulletin being flashed on the screen. He recognized the image of the FBI agent he met earlier; he turned up the volume.

"Channel Seven had learned exclusively that an FBI agent that was shot in the Virginia Beach shootout is in critical condition at Virginia Beach Hospital. Our source says she is under constant guard by Secret Service agents. America's prayers are with her and the other officers."

Simon was shocked by the news; he had just been with her. What was this all about? He logged into his secured company computer. He searched for her name and any information he could find. Even at his clearance level, her file was locked, it was labeled *'Presidential order—Authorized Eyes only.'*

"What is going on here?" How many bad things can happen at the same time?" he wondered.

———

DINNER WAS OVER and not surprisingly, everyone but George helped clear the plates and do the dishes.

"We need to discuss what we're going to do with this information," Barry said as they moved to a large sitting room.

"We need to get it to someone who can use it to remove these traitors," Harlem stated matter-of-factly.

"Do you think that will be as easy as it sounds? As soon as they realize this information is out, they will send everyone for us, and quite frankly, we may find it difficult to find anyone in a position to help that isn't on the list," George reminded them.

"What about the President himself? He wasn't on the list," Elsy asked.

"That's not a bad idea, but think of all the people you'd need to go through to get to him. I bet there's a few of them in here." Derrick chimed in, holding the list of names they were building. "It's just gonna take a while to write them all down."

Trina popped her head into the room. "Hey, you guys should know there's a printer in the big office on the second floor. You could just print everything out and then compare names."

"Why are you so smart?" Derrick questioned her.

"That and looks, I'm quite the prize," she blurted out with a big grin as she disappeared again.

They took the laptop to the office Trina had mentioned.

They plugged it directly into the printer. It started to print. After about ten minutes of printing, there were hundreds of names, but the printer was blinking, *out of paper.*

"Shit, anyone notice extra paper around here?" Harlem asked.

Cabinets were thrown open as everyone searched for the one thing keeping them from a complete list.

———

DEACON DIDN'T HAVE to wait long for Betsy to complete her search. Only a few people knew he called his supercomputer Betsy—Simon was one of them.

"Hey buddy, you owe me two for one on this one. I can tell you where that wrangler is at right now," Deacon bragged.

Simon almost dropped his phone.

"Tell me you're not fucking with me," Simon pleaded.

"I'm not fucking with you. It's at an estate right on the beach. That Jeep pulled into a garage there a few hours ago. It was following a black sedan, if that means anything to you. The only thing is it seems they stayed in the garage. I double-checked no one left the garage that I could see."

"Oh god, I needed this. You're my hero. Send me the address," Simon rushed him.

———

"DID YOU SEE THE NEWS? She is still alive," Senator Heller asked.

"Yes, do we risk sending another team?" Senator Waterstein responded.

"That's why I called. We're kind of already in this way down the well," Alvin replied.

"Is that southern for *deep* or *over our heads*?" Irma asked for clarity.

Alvin chuckled, "Right now it just means deep, let's hope it doesn't come to the other. I was thinking more of an independent contractor."

"Do we have access to those?" Irma asked.

"Irma, don't play coy with me. I know for a fact you've used them before; all that stuff goes through my office. I have the documents with your signature," Alvin admonished.

"I guess this is where mutually assured destruction comes from. You know I have documents on you, too," she warned.

"Okay, if we're done posturing, we need to make a decision," he stated flatly.

"I say send a man in. Let's make sure any evidence she has dies with her. She is already almost dead; it shouldn't be too hard to finish this," Irma pushed.

"I agree. I'll send someone," Alvin promised. "Just know the President already suspects foul play."

———

ESTEPHAN CALLED his Secret Service Director into his office.

"I want to move Agent Newly to Bethesda as soon as she can safely be moved. Until then, I want security that would put mine to shame. No one is in or out without vetting. I have asked for some of Bethesda's medical staff to relocate to handle her care. Every doctor, nurse or attendant who goes into her room should have been cleared before any attempt to enter. Anyone who tries and isn't cleared should be detained and investigated."

"Yes sir. I can make that happen right now. When should we expect the team from Bethesda?" the Director asked.

"They're already en route. Your agents should expect them within the hour," the President informed him.

———

LINDA STARTED to open her eyes; her head was pounding. She began to look around, but her vision was cloudy.

"Go get the doctor, tell him she's waking up," she heard, but couldn't tell who was talking.

She felt like going back to sleep. A hand gently rubbed her shoulder opposite where she was shot. "Please stay awake, Ms. Avail. The doctor will be here shortly."

Linda tried to open her eyes again. She tried to talk but her mouth was very dry, she tried to point to her mouth by lifting her arms. *What happened to me?* she wondered.

A slight panic was starting to rise within her and the person with her noticed her heart rate start to elevate.

"Ms. Avail, it's ok. Please try to remain calm, you were injured during the move but you're okay now. The doctor will explain when he comes in."

Linda did her best to calm herself despite her growing fears.

"Ms. Avail, It's Doctor Cartwright. We had to patch you up and you were unconscious for a little while. Your vision will return shortly. Your eyes just need to adjust to being open again. The nurse will give you a small amount of water to help with the dry mouth I'm sure you have. I'm glad you're awake. We would like to keep you awake for a little while to monitor your vitals. Let someone know when you think you can talk. I'll be back then."

SIMON ORGANIZED an action team to respond to the address Deacon had sent him. It would have to be a stealth response due to numerous factors. The most important to his bosses would be not interfering with the lives of the affluent neighbors surrounding the estate they were targeting.

He pulled his government SUV up on the curb. He was about half a block away from his target, but he could see the driveway very well. If the target vehicles left, he would be able to follow. The team would be here soon, and he would have his prisoners back, as well as the people who helped them escape.

THE ATTACK TEAMS moved into the building. They entered simultaneously from two separate points. At first there was no resistance. When the doors closed behind them, they heard them lock, flashing strobes went off, and extremely loud music started to play. Nitelite ordered one member of his assault team to find the source and eliminate it. The man disappeared looking for the source of the distraction. The team of three continued towards the office area described in the schematics.

The second team of four made their approach from the alternate entry point. Before either team reached their target, they heard automatic weapon fire. Despite the loud music, Nitelite tried to contact his teammate.

"Charley One. Report," he called into the mic. No response. The gunfire stopped.

"Charley One, report," still no reply. "Team Two, take rear cover. Continue the mission and find Charley One on evac."

"Yes, sir. Cover." Flash replied.

Nitelite approached the office. There was no movement that he could detect. Then there was a flash from inside an office area. It illuminated them for a brief second. All three instinctively dropped to a crouch and watched. They waited for a full minute, there was nothing else.

"Let's go," Nitelite told his team. They moved into the office. They could see the silhouette of a person huddled over a computer keyboard.

"Hands up, don't move," Gripe called as he started to move towards the target.

The music and flashing lights stopped.

"Which is it? Should I put my hands up or not move? Your command is confusing," a voice responded.

Gripe put a single round from his weapon through the monitor.

"How's that, smartass. Put your hands up." Gripe ordered.

The silhouette didn't even flinch, Gripe kept moving forward. On his second step, a concentrated beam of light shone directly on him and he stopped. Before he could react to what came next, it was too late. Automatic gunfire from a small mini gun concentrated on his body. The bullets pierced his body armor and shredded his internal organs. The only breath that escaped his lungs was mixed with blood from his chest as it was torn apart by the thousand rounds per minute rate the gun fired at. Nitelite and Dover watched in horror as their teammate was decimated by an automated weapon. The realization of what most likely happened to Charley One also set in.

"Pull back, pull back," Nitelite ordered. The light searched the room and found Dover.

Before Nitelite could warn him, the desk he was behind exploded into splinters, as the automated gun homed in on Dover's position behind what he thought was cover. The bullets tore into Dover just like Gripe before him. Tearing through his armor and flesh, nearly bisecting his body, Dover fell to the floor lifeless.

Team Two called again on the radio. "Boss, do you read us? Something is moving in behind us. Should we engage?"

Finally, their message got through.

"It's a trap. Automated weapons, Abort mission, retreat, retreat, retreat!" Nitelite yelled back.

He took a chance and fired a short burst from his rifle, striking the figure at the keyboard in the forehead as he moved to cover behind a concrete column just before the unmanned weapon targeted him.

"Should I still keep my hands up?" A taunt from the figure.

Nitelite realized this had been a trap, no one was here. Now he was just hoping Team Two would make it out.

The concrete started to shatter around him. It was only a matter of time and ammunition before the column was no longer protecting him. Then he heard gunfire behind him. He switched his position to see where it was coming from. Team Two had approached from the rear. They had identified several cameras that they believed the system was using to track and target them. They fired on three more cameras, and then on the weapon itself. Finally, all went quiet. They carefully moved to check on their teammates. A quick check to affirm what they already knew to be, that their two brothers were dead, and there was still the issue of Charley One. They would not leave until they verified his status as well. They searched the office and found a single computer screen that was active. There was a single message on it. *"Got Ya."* Nitelite pointed his gun at the message and fired a burst.

"You know that doesn't do anything, that's just a monitor," Flash offered.

"Yeah, but it makes me feel better, there's that." Nitelite retorted.

"Fair enough," Flash said as he looked over at two of his team.

"Loader, you and Paydirt carefully try to locate Charley One. Use caution and if you encounter another automated gun, back out and wait for all of us to attack it."

"Yes, sir." They both headed off in the last direction their teammate was seen in.

———

TINKER WAS WATCHING the mayhem from his office far from the location the team was given. He was sure it would only be a matter of time till he had his real location. Everyone had been sent away, except Deidra. He had asked her to leave but she refused.

"I'll go when you go," she told him.

Tinker had started to develop feelings for her. Even though she was younger than him. She was his kindred soul.

"Alright," he finally conceded. "We will stay here until they arrive. I have an escape route planned from there, we'll be alright, we'll just have to leave when I say, no delays."

"Deidra shook her head in agreement. Then she moved close to Tinker, her face next to his, her mouth next to his ear.

"I couldn't stand it if anything happened to you," she whispered. She grabbed his hand while they talked.

Tinker started to feel weakness spreading to his legs. It had been a long time since he shared feelings like this or intimacy of any kind with someone. He pulled back slightly to look into her eyes. It was mutual, he was sure. He leaned forward and kissed her. She responded by wrapping her arms around him and kissing him back. For a long second, he didn't care what happened next, he would die happy. Then he remembered he now had put Deidra in danger as well. His mood changed.

———

AFTER ALEXANDER CORTEZ lost touch with the Avails, he received another call offering to back him. An offer he readily accepted, now that the Avail money was running out. As a result, he became associated with the rising star of the Democrat party. They were out on the road together campaigning now. He didn't think too highly of Darton as a person, but he was impressed with his ability to market himself to anyone. He was on the plane that the DNC used to ferry their presidential hopefuls around the country for public appearances.

This was their first candidate in a long time that drew huge crowds at his campaign stops. He still hadn't caught up to the number of supporters that President Harrington drew, but the numbers were growing. Tv and social media were pushing him as the 'right man for the job'. It was a slogan that was gaining traction. Today Alexander would step on stage ahead of the well-known influencer. It would be his moment to shine, briefly.

37

HE WATCHED INTENTLY while waiting for his team to arrive. No one in or out from the driveway that he watched. After what felt like an eternity, two black high-top vans pulled up behind his vehicle. He stepped out to talk to the team leaders.

"As far as we know they are still in the garage. Just to be safe, we'll hit the house at the same time. There is a gate at the driveway that needs to be accessed. I am assuming as soon as we do that they will be alerted to our presence. Full speed from there."

The leaders of each team understood their assignments. No lethal fire unless they were fired upon. The goal was to capture all parties alive. Simon needed intel, and they seemed to have a lot of it.

———

ELSY SAT AT THE LAPTOP. "Are we sure we want to do this? Once we do there's no undoing it. We'll have shown our hand."

"Yes, I think this is something we have to do," Barry said with a soft voice.

The others solemnly nodded.

"Wait," Derrick said. "There's something we need to talk about first."

"What now?" Elsy questioned.

"As far as we know they're just looking for Barry, Mr. Avail, and whoever freed them. You and Harlem should take Katrina and get out of here. Go somewhere no one knows. We'll find you when the dust settles," Derrick suggested.

"No way. I'm staying with you," Trina interjected. Derrick looked at her, he had grown very fond of her. It was hard for him to push her away from his ability to protect her, but felt this was the best way to do that.

"I'm sorry, lil' girl. This is the best plan. I will be more efficient if I'm not worried about you every second. Harlem and Elsy will protect you," he said.

The adults talked it over and decided that Derrick's plan was the best. They would wait to hit 'enter' until the trio had left the premises.

George decided to break his normal silence.

"Out behind the garage, there's a small building. There is an electric beach cart in there, take it and drive down the beach to the south. When you see the stone house on the water, it's another house of mine. In the garage is the sister car to that Range Rover." They grabbed their belongings and one of the bags of weapons. They followed the instructions George gave and disappeared quietly down the beach. Derrick hit 'enter'.

————

ONE AGENT carefully approached the gate and disassembled the keypad. He gave the thumbs up to the team. They swung the vans into position. Simon was riding in the lead van. "We'll take the main house, Team Two take the garage."

The gate opened and the first van raced toward it. The driver's anticipation got him to the opening before it was large enough for the van. He struck the gate with the left side of the van, knocking the mirror off and sending some sparks into the air. He didn't slow down. They wouldn't need that mirror. The second van slowed up with the side door open for their teammate to jump in.

They sped down the drive as fast as they could, slamming on the brakes when they reached their targets. The agents left the vans in a quick and orderly manner, spreading out into positions to breach the build they were assigned. As he approached the main building, Simon could see movement inside the house.

"I've got movement," he called out. He smiled a bit. He knew he had guessed right.

———

THE ASSAULT TEAM backed out of the warehouse that was a trap for them. They found Charley One with a severely wounded leg and a broken radio. He had placed his own tourniquet to prevent himself from bleeding out. His pants were drenched in his blood, and he had left a trail from where he dragged himself to cover. He had shot out the cameras he saw once he realized he was up against a computer-controlled weapon. His teammates were relieved to find him alive, but were still distressed about leaving their fallen comrades behind. Nitelite had them regroup at their vehicle. "I need to let the home office know what we encountered." He pulled a satellite phone from the truck and dialed in. The news of their failure did not go over well with those on the other end of the call.

"Stand down for now and patch up your team. We expect to find the actual address shortly based on the connection you established with the computer there," the voice informed him.

"Yes, sir. Standing by," Nitelite complied.

"Load up, let's get Charley some Medical attention while we're waiting," Nitelite ordered his own men.

———

THE FIRST STATION TO air the story was a small conservative internet station. It was always labeled as a conspiracy theory site, but had broken several major stories that had come true despite the label.

"Breaking News. America's News Network has just received evidence that several politicians have taken bribes or been blackmailed to work against American interests. ANN has evidence and supporting documents to show the Governor of California, two Senators and a Congressman are heavily involved in corruption and possibly treason. This evidence has been turned over to multiple agencies for them to act upon. Stay tuned for this massive story as it unfolds."

George, Barry, and Derick watched as the story scrolled across the website. They switched over to the television—still nothing on TV news channels. They were still covering the Darton Plank rally, like he was a king slumming with the peasants.

"Will this work? There is so much corruption here. Can we overcome it?" Derrick asked, not to anyone specific. Mostly just to get it off his chest.

Barry moved to the laptop. "Here, let's try this." He typed for a few minutes and then hit 'enter'.

"What did you do?" Derrick asked.

"I just sent the name of the largest network's CEO who is on the list here. That might help encourage the other networks to play a little fairer."

———

THEY DIDN'T KNOCK. They crashed through the door with a ram. Six agents stormed the house to the room where Simon had observed their quarry. The first two agents cleared the hallway and side rooms as the rest advanced. As they burst through the door to the office, Barry and Derrick had taken cover, Derrick had his gun drawn and was ready to fight.

"Federal agents, lay down your weapons," Simon called out.

"You first," Derrick called from behind a large bookshelf.

"That's not gonna happen," Simon assured him.

George just stood in the open with his hands up. He was not as quick as the other two and realized this was his only option. He thought to himself that if they were here to kill him, they would not have much difficulty.

"Listen we want to take you in peacefully, there is no reason to escalate this," Simon called out.

"Yeah, that's what Agent Newly thought too. Look what happened to her," Derrick snapped back.

This caught Simon off guard. He gave his team the hold signal.

"How do you know about that?" Simon questioned.

"I know a lot of things. Look at the news on the laptop," Derrick quipped.

As he glanced over, the TV now had a similar Breaking News alert.

"And now on the TV," Derrick added.

Simon glanced at the TV without giving up his cover position.

"What the hell is going on?" He didn't mean to question Derrick about it, but Derrick answered.

"Our government is full of corrupt and outright foreign agents at all levels. That's why we're gonna need a little show of faith before we stand down," Derrick advised.

Simon lowered his weapon and stepped out.

"My team will not lower their weapons until they know you are not a threat. I am stepping out with my gun holstered. This is the best I can do to show good faith," Simon said as he abandoned his cover position.

Derrick understood. He would do the same. "Okay I'm coming out; my gun is holstered as well."

Derrick stepped out from the bookshelf with his hands up. The weapons of three agents turned to aim at him.

Derrick acknowledged them. "So did I make a mistake in believing you?" he asked.

Simon motioned to the agents by pushing toward the floor with his hand. They all lowered their weapons to a low ready position, not pointed at Derrick but ready if the situation changed.

George still stood, by himself with his hand raised, Barry remained behind the concealment of the large desk.

Simon looked at Derrick as he moved closer. "You look familiar to me."

"I have one of those faces," Derrick responded.

"I don't think that's it. I only remember faces I've dealt with before," Simon replied.

Derrick looked closely at Simon, then he remembered. He had worked a case where the suspect ended up being an international arms dealer. Simon was a CIA agent posing as a Federal Marshal that showed up to take custody. Derrick realized why Barry and George were of such interest to this man.

"Well, I haven't dealt with anyone in a while," Derrick lied.

"So, what is this breaking news that I'm seeing, and how are you involved with it?" Simon jumped back to the current issue.

While Derrick was still trying to judge if Simon could be a friend or foe, George just belted it out.

"It's just a few names of corrupt politicians and others who we accidentally stumbled across. We are willing to share it if you stop treating us like we're the bad guys," George pleaded.

Simon considered the plea from Mr. Avail.

"Why can't I just take it from you? If you have it, and I now have you?" Simon reminded him.

"Because you don't have the key," George said triumphantly.

"But obviously, it's here somewhere because you just used the information," Simon chided him.

George sneered back at him. That is when Derrick knew this had all been a ploy to slow Simon down—making him search the house for the key, instead of looking for the three that left.

————

HE WALKED around the hospital for eight hours, getting his bearings and watching the men who were standing guard. He didn't help anyone or do anything, but no one cared enough to notice, as they all had their own specific duties to attend to. The guards never approached him because he did not try to access the person they were there to protect. A small high-definition camera in his pocket recorded everything he needed to be able to review tonight. At the end of his reconnaissance, he headed out like any other employee ending their shift. Today was a success by any standards.

————

NEWS of the names being released to the media outlets had the Council on edge. Members requested an immediate meeting. Many were concerned that their assets were outed, and therefore their access would now be diminished. Some were outraged that their names were mentioned. Most were just concerned that they might be next, and were curious how this information was obtained.

Jeac was extremely concerned about how to share the current situation with them. The fact that somewhere out there, a single person had enough information to burn every one of them.

"Denler, do we have an address for that hacker yet? A real address this time?" Jeac asked.

"Sir, they've narrowed it to a three-block radius, and they believe they will have an actual address very soon," Denler replied.

"Send the general area to the team, have them stand by ready for their address. We need to have the hacker in custody before the start of this emergency session or we might not be around to see this end."

Denler knew this was not an idle threat. "Yes sir, as soon as I hear the team will know."

Normally Jeac would expect to be the first to hear news like this from Denler. Today he was fine with being second.

"Just let me know when they're on the way," Jeac asked.

TWO LARGE SEDANS pulled up on the street edge behind an SUV that was parked there. One person got out and investigated the SUV. Government plates, no one around. He gazed toward the driveway.

"We might be late," he said to the men in the first sedan. He was speaking Spanish.

"Doesn't matter, we have a job to do," was the reply.

"Looks like a fed car, do you think he went to the FBI because of the last attack?" the first man asked.

"Maybe, so what? We'll kill whoever is in there," was the reply.

The man hopped back in the car. They pulled out slowly and headed for the driveway. As they turned in, they killed their headlights. They were surprised to find the gate open.

"That's a help. Let's go. Don't give anyone time to call for backup." The two sedans sped down the driveway. They saw a van parked in front of the house.

"There may be a team here already. Kill shots, make them count. We are not bringing any of you home wounded, so don't get hit. Got it?" They pulled their masks up over their noses and mouths and ran toward the house. Four men went to the obvious front door that was partly busted from its hinges. The second team went to the side entrance. Neither team noticed the second van parked to the side of the garage.

As the first man burst through the door, he saw an agent walking in the foyer and he opened fire. The agent went down almost immediately. Gunfire erupted from a room just beyond the foyer, and the first attacker's head erupted onto the face of the man behind him as the bullet passed through, narrowly missing him as well. The remaining three paid killers stacked around the door and returned fire. The second group pushed through the side door at the sound of gunfire. They saw another agent moving toward the foyer. Three of them fired their automatic weapons at him.

While most of the bullets missed their intended target, four of them hit their mark. The agent went to the floor writhing in pain. An attacker stepped in and fired a single round into his skull. It resulted in a large red splatter across the white tile of the foyer. The attacker was unfazed by the grizzly sight. They pressed inward to assist the group under fire.

38

SIMON HEARD the gunfire and drew his gun on Derrick. "Who else is here?" he demanded.

"If that's not you, chances are they're here for all of us now," Derrick answered.

Simon called to his agent who left the room as the first rounds fired. No answer. Nothing from the agent in the foyer as well. He looked at Derrick. "Can I trust you not to shoot me?"

"As long as that rule goes both ways," Derrick advised.

"It does," Simon assured him.

Simon turned towards the gunfire as Derrick drew his pistol again. George moved to better cover and Barry grabbed a rifle, magazines, and other weapons from the bag Harlem had left for them. It was time to fight or die.

The three of them left George alone with the laptop and the drive.

"Stay hidden until one of us comes back for you," Barry told him and handed him a pistol.

Simon just glanced at Derrick. "He won't fight?"

"Not with guns, he uses others for that," Derrick sneered.

They moved down a small staircase that was a second entrance to the office, as he came to the doorway at the bottom of the stairs, they encountered the first attackers that were in the hallway. Simon hesitated to make sure it wasn't his team. Derrick did not, and fired a round striking the first man straight through the chest.

The man didn't fly backwards like some movies make it seem, instead he just collapsed to the floor. A large section of his back was gone with the forty-five-caliber bullet that passed through him. It severed his aorta, pierced a lung, and shattered his spine on the way out. He lay on the floor bleeding as his life drained away with the blood exiting his body. Rounds suddenly were flying everywhere as the other attackers fired their automatics in the direction of Derrick and Simon. The attackers pushed forward as Derrick and Simon dove for cover.

The team passed the door that their prey had exited from and never bothered to check it. The first attacker crouched behind a concrete statue on the floor as the hallway widened and stopped to reload. The second and third stopped in a staggered pattern behind him. The third man stepped into the doorway near him to seek cover. He only felt surprised for a second when a large hand grabbed him across the mouth and face. It was followed by the blade of a combat knife being inserted at the base of his skull and pushed to the hilt. His lifeless body was lowered quietly to the floor by the giant who had slayed him.

Barry re-sheathed the knife just as quietly and brought his weapon up on the second attacker. As he fired the weapon, the door jamb all around him turned into splinters. The fire came from across the foyer as the first attack team closed in on their location. Barry felt a burning in his arm as he was struck with one of the bullets. He changed his position and laid down fire to draw them away from Derrick and Simon. Simon caught the second man out in the open, turning towards Barry. He fired several rounds at the man's legs, the only clear shot he had from his cover. He struck the attacker in the knee, causing his leg to fold in the wrong direction and the attacker to fall to the floor. Simon fired again, striking the attacker in the throat. He heard a gargling sound as the man tried to scream. It ended very quickly as Barry put another round into his head.

The attacker that had forced Derrick and Simon to cover had positioned himself behind cover also. He was calling his teammates for assistance and relaying the number of people in the house. The team that entered the front was down a man, but still felt confident they could overtake the remaining forces.

———

SIMON'S second team heard the gunfire from the main house. They had been searching Derrick's Jeep and the last communication said that Simon had the men in custody without incident. The automatic weapon fire surprised them. *Had these men suddenly attacked Simon and the other agents?* They moved to the door as a team and headed for the house in a staggered formation when they hit the open. Each man maintained an open field of view and fire. When they saw the additional cars in the driveway, they knew their party had been crashed by another hostile force. They used cover and concealment as best they could as they rushed to their teammates, who were obviously under fire.

———

TEAM One of the killers pushed across the foyer. They split up as two more agents appeared at the top of the stairs above them, and opened fire. One of the killers pulled another gun from a bag he was carrying. The agents recognized the weapon as it was brought up and aimed at their location. The killer opened fire with a belt-fed machine gun. The sustained fire was like small explosions as the bullets ripped through almost everything they hit. The railings all but disintegrated, and the agents retreated for cover.

One of the agents made it into a room at the top of the stairs. The other was struck in the arm, leg, and shoulder while trying to crawl to safety as they fired on his position again. He was struck numerous times, he stopped trying to move. The other agent watched as his teammate fell and was fired on without mercy. He could see his still open but lifeless eyes.

———

BARRY INSPECTED HIS WOUND. He reached around and found an exit.

Well, it's not all bad, he thought. He wished he had his first aid kit he always carried when he expected trouble. He checked his weapon—half mag in weapon and three full. He pushed his injured arm against the door frame and looked down the sights at the doorway the second group had fired at him from. He couldn't see anyone. As he scanned, he saw the end of a shoe protruding from behind a statue. He signaled to Derrick who was prone on the floor behind a large square planter. Derrick nodded that he understood.

Barry pressed the trigger and sent a single round into the toe he could see. A short scream of pain and then the head of the attacker was clearly in Derrick's sights. Two rounds left his gun in rapid succession, both were on target, striking the man in the forehead and then the left cheek. A mixture of blood and brain matter soaked the statue. Barry leaned out to check the doorway again and was caught in gunfire. This time the bullets were on target. Barry felt the searing pain as a round tore through his other shoulder and neck. He dropped his gun and collapsed onto the floor. He could still breathe, but he couldn't move his right arm. He tried to reach across his body to draw his pistol—he had fallen onto it and couldn't roll off. He was out of the fight.

Derrick watched Barry go down.

"Barry's down. It's just you and me, and hopefully those other two agents," he was unaware of their status at the moment.

Simon nodded. They moved a bit to change their perspective. Bullets struck the area around them. They were safe for now, but effectively pinned down. They needed a miracle. A small object came rolling at their position. "Cover," Derrick yelled as he recognized the grenade land close to him. Derrick instinctively grabbed it and pulled it beneath him to shield Simon. He waited for the end, and nothing happened. After what seemed like an eternity, Derrick inspected the grenade. It was still intact the pin hadn't been pulled yet. He racked his brain for why someone would throw a grenade without pulling the pin. He realized it was a gift from Barry.

Derrick looked at his angles without putting himself in the line of fire. He realized Simon had a better line to the attackers' position, but it was much narrower and could potentially land on Derrick if Simon messed up the throw. Simon seemed to understand his thoughts.

"Toss it over here, I got this," Simon encouraged him.

Derrick tossed him the explosive like a softball. Simon checked his angles and pulled the pin.

"Here goes everything," he said as he hurled the grenade at their enemies. As the device left his hand, the spoon released from the handle activating the timer fuse. The explosive landed in front of the intended target and rolled down the hall at them. Before they could find cover, it exploded, sending pieces of pre-fragmented shrapnel into them like multiple gunshots hitting them simultaneously.

Some of the pieces punctured them like bullets, piercing vital organs, others acted like a sharp mini shovel gouging at parts of their flesh and tearing it away. The physical damage from the blast was more than they could survive. Both died nearly instantly, surviving only long enough to endure a moment of excruciating pain. Derrick and Simon pressed ahead. They could hear sustained fire from a large caliber weapon coming from the foyer.

As the hallway opened completely to the foyer, they could see a two-man team firing at the door to a room upstairs. Before they could move into position, the gun turned towards them. Once again, they were both diving for cover to avoid the massive firepower being trained on them. The walls turned to dust around them, the wood of the trim was turned into splinters. The air was filled with dust, blood, and smoke. Derrick and Simon exchanged glances, and each understood this time they would be lucky to survive.

From behind them came more gunfire. They couldn't turn without exposing themselves to the heavy gun. The gunfire wasn't trained on them, though—it was on the two attackers with the belt fed. The exchange of fire went on for a few moments while two of Simon's teammates engaged them. The other two had found their way up the office stairs and to the foyer, where they had an advantage over the killers with the machine gun. Below them, two men were lying prone in the foyer shooting down the hall. The two agents called out quietly.

"Left."

"Okay, right on three."

"One. Two…"

They both fired at the same time. They never said three, they just fired based on the timing.

Headshots ended the reign of terror by these two hired killers.

Quietly and carefully, they tended to their wounded teammate and searched the house for additional attackers. No attackers were found alive in the house. Simon's team had lost three members and one was wounded, along with Barry who was in bad shape in the stairwell. The agents checked for life signs and searched for the attackers. They found one who had something interesting on him, and they brought it to Simon and Derrick. Derrick just stared at the description of his Jeep and of Trina and himself.

"Why was an eight-man team of what appears to be cartel hitmen sent after you? And who is the girl?" Simon asked.

"I don't know," Derrick only half lied.

———

DENLER TOOK the information right from Cyber and called the team. They finally were able to find the address of the hacker.

"He's at this location. He owns the entire building, so which floor he's on is unknown."

Denler relayed all the information to them while he was talking to the team leader.

"Sir, we need you to take this hacker into your custody. As soon as possible. His information may save our lives. In the file is information on someone who may be able to give you leverage."

The team was inside the block for the address. They moved towards their new target.

———

JEAC SAT in front of the largest gathering of Council members in twenty years. He was uncertain of how this would go and chose to play the offense from the start.

"We have been infiltrated by some of our own, and we have been attacked by an external force, members of the Council, we are at war."

There were murmurings and outright talking that occurred.

"War with who?" an unseen delegate shouted from the back of the auditorium they were all seated in.

"Our enemies are not yet fully known. We have operations in play right now around the globe to bring us closer to an answer," Jeac responded.

"So, who betrayed us?" the Russian delegate asked.

"Several members made this happen. It appears the former chair, Madam Felsder started the ball rolling, then the Chinese in their effort to obscure their own actions, allowed another entity to access the systems we use most frequently. Dominos, if you will, began to fall, and now, seriously harmful information about the existence of the Council is in the hands of men who have proven they will use it. The information currently exposed has been of positions we are not currently using. However, the backlash against that will come may cause more substantial problems. The biggest issue is the quantity and quality of the data that has been revealed about every member of this organization. We are all at risk of exposure."

"Unacceptable. All involved need to be eliminated and the data recovered before it falls into the wrong hands," a cartel member shouted.

"It's already in the wrong hands, you buffoon," came a reply from the crowd.

"Come say that to my face. I'll cut your tongue out and make you eat it," the Cartel member sneered.

"Gentlemen, gentlemen," Jeac shouted above their raised voices. He watched the members who were stirring uneasily with the news he shared.

"We are here to find solutions, not attack each other. We will have targets to attack very shortly. Make no mistake, this is warfare, we will have to win to survive. All of you may be called upon to participate."

A tall thin man stood up in front, "I'm the CEO of *Facester*, a social media platform, how can I help in a 'war'?"

"I am so glad you asked. My team has a project just for you, as soon as we have a better understanding of who has our data, your platform will start a game of hide and seek. You will post pictures of our targets and ask your readers to post sightings and information about their whereabouts. In essence, we will have the world's largest investigatory service looking for our targets. That, sir, is how you'll help." Jeac turned back to the audience now staring intently at him.

"All of you will be contacted with what we need from you. Be patient as your time will come," he advised.

Jeac gathered his things. The room erupted into questions being shouted at him from everywhere. He held his hand up and the noise quieted a bit. "I will answer questions when I call you for assistance. Until then, I must return to attend to ongoing operations. Good night, gentlemen."

39

BARRY'S CONDITION worsened on the way to the hospital. He was still losing blood and couldn't move his right arm. He lost consciousness en route to the ER. Derrick and George were cuffed next to each other in the back of Simon's SUV. Simon had carefully collected the laptop and the drive, and placed them on the front seat.

"If you two want to avoid jail time, you'd better start talking," Simon encouraged them.

Derrick smiled in a way that unnerved Simon.

"I'm guessing you don't want us to talk too much..." Derrick baited.

"What do you mean?" Simon countered, but it was evident he knew exactly what Derrick meant. In terms of crimes, using a CIA assault team to detain Americans on American soil was a huge crime. If word got out, he would probably face more time behind bars than Derrick or George would—if he could even prove they committed a crime other than trying to stay alive in the face of a corrupt government. "Okay. Let's play nice then," Simon proposed. He hopped out and opened the back door and uncuffed the pair. "Let's start with that. Now it's your turn," he slammed the door and locked them in to prevent either from just walking away.

HARLEM, Elsy, and Trina drove for a while in the Range Rover. Elsy decided she might buy one when this was over. Trina was sleeping in the backseat, and they were trying to figure out where to go.

"Let's get out of the country," Elsy smiled as she presented her idea. "I know a small bungalow in St. Croix we can use. It's my uncle's friend's but he always said, 'Just drop in.' I even know where the key is hidden."

"Okay, so how do we get there?" Harlem asked.

"Easy," she grabbed her phone and dialed. "I need a private plane from a small airfield, anywhere south of Virginia to take us to St. Croix. Can you make that happen? Oh, and no paperwork."

From the other end, "Uh yeah, but that last part makes it a bit more difficult and a lot more expensive."

"No worries, just send me the bill. You know I'm good for it. And as you might imagine, this call never happened. I guess I'll owe you a new phone too," Elsy said lightly.

"I'll text you the details as soon as I know. That'll be the last thing we share," the other person relayed on the phone.

Five minutes later, Elsy got the details of their flight. An airport and the plane's tail number. They headed for a small field in North Carolina. They pulled into the parking area as Trina stirred in the backseat.

"Where are we? Have you heard from D?" She had taken to calling Derrick 'D', and it was no secret that she would rather have stayed with him.

"No Trina, we're headed someplace safe for now. Derrick will let us know when we can send for him or go home. Until then, we have two jobs, keep this key hidden and keep you safe." Elsy informed her.

The plane lifted off, its twin engines pulling it effortlessly into the air. All three of them looked out the windows—each with their concerns for the ones left behind.

———

HE GLANCED AT THE TAG. *Dr. Avril Kind.* "What kind of doctor's name is that?"

He knew it was a real person—that was the only way to get him clearance that fast. He was also aware that Dr. Kind was having a very bad day somewhere else. He entered the doctor's locker room like he owned the place. Other doctors in there just nodded as he walked by. They were either coming or going, and didn't have time for him. He found an empty locker and undressed from his street clothes. He switched into a pair of blue scrubs and clipped his name tag to the waist. *Dr. Avril Kind, Bethesda Naval Hospital* was displayed for anyone to inspect. He placed a small caliber pistol inside the metal clipboard. With the suppressor attached, it barely fit diagonally.

He closed the clipboard and left the locker room. He walked with purpose and straight up to the guard who was guarding the room. "Dr. Kind," he said as the guard asked what his business was. "I'm here to check on our patient, by orders of POTUS." The guard checked his name tag, and then scanned it for verification. Lastly, he compared the name to a list of those with pre-vetted access approval. Dr. Kind was on the list. It had been so easy to fool the guard, it almost felt like a trap. There she was, just lying there, machines monitoring her heart rate, her respiration, and her IVs.

This was like taking candy from children. Something he enjoyed doing just to make them cry. He pulled the clipboard out from under his arm and opened it up. He removed the small pistol from its hiding place. He walked closer to the bed. The door burst open and he hid the weapon, expecting to need it to get out of there, instead, the guard entered and said quietly. "I need to use the restroom and my relief isn't here, are you alright by yourself for five minutes?"

"I think I'll manage." He smiled as the guard disappeared. He walked over to her bedside and opened a drawer in the cart that contained several monitors on the top. He shuffled around a bit and found what he was looking for. It was a sixty CC syringe. He opened it up and then screwed it into her IV line. Slowly he injected the whole syringe as air into the line. He undid it and repeated it a second time, to be sure. He unscrewed the syringe and opened the IV wide open. It would only take a minute.

He left the room. He had just finished changing back into street clothes when he heard the alarms going off, a little faster than he hoped. Whatever secrets they were afraid she knew, they were dying with her. He left the scrubs and the name tag on the floor and headed for the stairs to exit the hospital. As he descended the stairs, he bumped into a janitor mopping the stairs. "Sorry," he said as he tracked through the liquid the janitor had just spread across the landing.

———

THE PHONE RANG on his nightstand. He was still awake, though. He rolled over and answered it on the second ring.

"I hope I didn't wake you, sir. You were right. They tried to kill her. We have agents on the man right now. How do you want us to proceed?" The agent asked.

"Follow him and see if he meets with anyone. Make sure you have full electronic surveillance in case he contacts them, through call or text. I want to know who authorized this," he ordered.

"Yes, sir. We're on it. Everything is all in place, AG Lemmer signed off on all of it," the agent informed him.

"Sir, do you still want the gallows relocated from the Smithsonian exhibit?" the agent queried.

"Oh yes, most definitely. I made a promise that I will keep if this goes how I think it will," the President said.

"Very well, sir. It will be done," the agent said as he hung up.

Harrington rolled over, a big smile on his face. He sat up and put on his robe and slippers, then headed for his study. He sat in a chair that had been occupied at one time or another by almost every President that ever graced—or disgraced—the White House. He poured a full three fingers of bourbon in a glass. Tonight, he wouldn't need ice. He wanted to savor every flavor, just as he would when the news of who was betraying him and this country would be revealed.

———

THE MAN LEFT the hospital quietly. He was satisfied that he had accomplished his task. He walked for about two blocks, carefully making sure he was not being followed—there wasn't a soul to be seen. He stopped at the compact car parked on the side of the road and looked around once more. Satisfied, he got in and pulled away. He constantly checked his mirrors for any car's headlights that might suddenly appear, but it was all dark. When he reached the highway, he felt he was confident he was clear without entanglements. He dialed a number.

The phone was answered without a word.

"My task is complete. Full removal accomplished," he said flatly.

"Very good. The remainder is on its way." The call ended.

————

"DID WE GET ALL THAT?" The Secret Service agent asked the tech analyst.

"Yes sir, and I already have the recipient of the call," the analyst stated.

The tech guy printed out the information and handed it to the agent.

"Oh my. This is huge," the agent whispered. Then he reminded the tech guy, "This is classified at the highest levels. If you breathe a word of this to anyone, you know what will happen."

"Yes sir," the analyst admitted.

The tech guy wasn't sure what he was admitting to knowing when he agreed. His mind raced with thoughts, ranging from imprisonment to disappearing. He just knew he should never tell anyone about tonight.

————

SENATORS WATERSTEIN and Heller watched as two Senators were escorted from their offices by federal officers. They had seen the news and were shocked by the amount of evidence ANN had released to the public. These fellow Senators would be destroyed by public perception well before they reached the courtroom. Their bigger concern, however, was that these two Senators knew enough to bring down several others with them. They stood on opposite sides of the hallway, but gave each other concerned glances now and then. The officers paraded their suspects right past them. The detainees never moved their heads as they were led by. They just stared at the ground.

Senator Heller's phone was ringing as he made it back to his office.

"Hold all my calls," he said to his secretary as he walked in.

"Sir, I can't hold this one, it's the President. He sounds angry."

Heller forced himself to be composed for the call. He had no idea what the President wanted, but the timing made him nervous.

"Mr. President, how can I help you?" Heller inquired.

"Alvin, the agent I had working for me died last night. I just wanted you to know," the President lied.

"I am so sorry, Mr. President. I know you were close to her." Alvin continued the charade.

"I'm not calling to get your sympathy, Alvin. I'm calling to let you know I'm setting up gallows on the lawn of the White House," the President pushed.

"Why on God's Earth would you do that in an election cycle, Mr. President? That's crazy," Alvis asked, sounding concerned.

"Crazy or not, I made you a promise and I intend to keep it." The President hung up.

Heller wasn't used to being cornered by people with more clout than he had. He started to sweat. He reached into his desk drawer and retrieved a bottle of Japanese whiskey that an ambassador had given him as a gift a few months back. He cracked the cork and poured a glass. Though it was meant to be sipped and enjoyed, Alvin drained the whole glass in one gulp. The burn reminded him he was still alive. For now.

PAULA WAS CAREFULLY MOVED to Bethesda Naval Hospital at the direction of the President. She was placed in a secure ward where the staff was now sequestered with her. The benefit of a naval hospital was that they were all soldiers, all under the direction of the Commander in Chief. The hospital staff was doing their best to keep her alive. They had placed her in an induced coma to help her recover. It was a long shot, but one of the many they were trying to care for this agent and friend of the President.

SIMON PULLED up in front of a large hotel in Alexandria. He let his *guests* out of the car and made sure they stayed right beside him the whole time. He walked past the front desk and right to the elevators. He pulled a card from his pocket and held it against a little black pad in the elevator. He then pushed two numbers at the same time, and the elevator ascended.

When the door opened, no numbers were on the wall indicating the floor. There were guards stationed in the hallway and Simon went and checked in with one sitting behind a desk. Derrick noticed the man's hand was below the desk the whole time Simon checked in, until his identity was verified. Derick guessed there was a gun aimed at Simon during the process. Simon turned and ushered them down the hallway. The laptop was still under his arm, and the drive protruded from his pants pocket.

It would soon be time to bring the CIA up to speed. First, he hoped Simon would check the database for names at the CIA just to avoid drawing anyone right to them. They set up the laptop and tried to access the database again. *Enter Key* appeared on the screen.

"Did you close the program?" Derrick asked.

"Yes, of course, I didn't want it to be damaged during transport," Simon admitted.

"Shit, we're out of luck for now. We don't have the key," Derrick confessed.

"What do you mean you don't have the key? Where is it?" Simon demanded.

"Well, we…" George started to talk, but Derrick cut him off.

"We don't know it; only Barry knows it," Derrick lied.

George just looked at him. He realized that Derrick didn't trust Simon any more than he trusted him. He realized something else as well—Derrick just motivated Simon to do everything in his power to keep Barry from dying. He smiled a little bit to himself. Simon caught him.

"What so funny, old man?" Simon was becoming angry.

"I just realized that you are now in the same boat as we are. Until you have the list, there is no way to know who you can trust and who will kill you," George said triumphantly.

———

THE TEAM PULLED up in the street before their target building. They expected the same type of deterrent or even greater at this location. They spied a couple of guys selling drugs at the rear of one of the buildings. Nitelite grabbed one of his team.

"Come with me, we need decoys," he stated.

He grabbed a small black duffle from the rear of the car and headed over to the men he saw. As he approached, they got ready to run, he pulled a silenced pistol from his jacket and fired a couple of rounds at their feet. They stopped in their tracks.

"We're not cops. I have a business proposition for you," Nitelite informed them.

"Why would we help you? You shot at us," one of the men replied.

"But I didn't kill you, did I?" Nitelite reminded them.

The men just looked at him.

"I need you to dress up for us and go knock on a few doors. We need to shake up the occupant. If you're okay with that, I'll pay you each a thousand dollars."

"Is it dangerous?" one asked.

"Well, I'm not going to lie, that depends on how he reacts. But most likely not," Nitelite lied.

"Then we want two grand each, hazard pay and all," the second one chimed in.

Nitelite reached into the back and tossed two banded bundles of hundreds on the ground by their feet.

"Deal."

40

THE TWO DRUG dealers followed the directions they were given. They headed into the lobby and started pressing intercom buttons for every tenant. Whenever someone answered, they declared, "We're here to collect for the hacking." Every button pushed resulted in the same response, the person they contacted just disconnected the line.

What they didn't know was that every move they made was being observed from below their location. Multiple cameras surveilled their every move. After about fifteen minutes, they had pushed every button with no response. They left the lobby and returned to the man who paid them.

"Good job, now go try the rear entrance," Nitelite ordered.

"That'll cost extra. You never said we had to do two entrances," one of the men tried to renegotiate.

Nitelite raised the pistol above the window edge.

"I think we had an agreement. You're not trying to go back on it, are you?" he queried.

"Oh no, never mind we were just kidding." They hustled off to the rear entrance.

Inside, they found no entrance at all. It was painted dark and had ornate trim and fixtures. It was like something they had seen in comic books. They searched all around, but found no interior doors.

"This is weird."

"Yeah, I'll say."

Without warning a panel slid away revealing a hallway. They looked at each other. Should they enter, or just go tell the guys in the car what they found?

Curiosity outweighed what little commonsense they possessed. They entered the hallway, and the door slid closed behind them.

———

TINKER WATCHED HIS SURVEILLANCE CAMERAS. He now knew a team was staged in cars outside waiting on what these two dumbasses told them. Now that the two canaries were in the hallway, he could choose what to do with them. He pressed a button on his computer, and a gas dispensed from small orifices in the wall. The two men started to cough. When they realized what was happening, they tried to cover their mouth and nose with their shirts. A few seconds later, they were unconscious on the floor. Deidra had walked in without him noticing.

"Did you just kill them?" she gasped.

He looked up to find her eyes wide open and her face pale, staring back and forth between him and the screen.

"No no no, I just put them to sleep. They'll wake up with a headache, but they'll be fine."

"Oh my god, I thought you killed them."

"No, lethal force is reserved as a final measure. Only after they've chosen that course of action. Mostly my AI chooses the reaction based on what she deems the threat is. A few seconds later, the screen changed to a different camera. The three men moved toward the rear of the building. They were carrying gas masks. Their weapons were not drawn. They entered and searched the area where the wall had opened for their pawns. They found a switch and the panel slid away. Tinker watched as they located the biometric locks that he installed to access the hallway to the elevator.

"This will slow them down for a while," he said triumphantly.

"Let's hope. Should we start leaving?" Deidra asked.

"No, we have time. I'm starting the shutdown procedure. Care to help?" he asked confidently.

"Sure, what do you want me to do? You never showed me any of that." Deidra asked.

"I've never shown anyone any of it," Tinker informed her.

He wrote down a string of letters and numbers fifty-six characters long. "That's the password to access the system. You'll need that to shut down the servers. There is a keyboard and monitor in the server six cabinet, it's the control server. Tear that up and throw it in the incinerator trap when you're done." Tinker told her.

"Okay. I got this. What are you doing?" she inquired.

"I'm transmitting my remote system controls," he replied. "That way we can re-establish connection from wherever we land."

"You don't have a set escape location?" Deidra asked, perplexed.

"Oh hell no. That's how you get caught," Tinker said with a grin.

She smiled at him. He soaked it in like sunshine. She was the one. He could feel it.

"Let's get this done. They're moving quicker than I expected," Tinker called out to her.

She came running back into the office. Just slightly out of breath.

"Okay, Houdini. How do we escape this now?" She asked.

"Follow me," he said as he took her to the closet.

He stood up and went to the back of his office, and stepped into his closet. "Care to join me?"

"We're gonna hide in a closet. That's your big escape plan?" Deidra asked.

"Just get in here," Tinker said.

Deidra complied. Tinker reached down to the floor and pulled a panel up with a suction cup he pulled from a shelf. There was a hatch below. He punched in a code and the hatch opened. Below them was a long ladder leading down.

"You go first. I must replace this," he pointed to the floor.

From above they heard an explosion, the office lights shook just a bit.

"Well, I guess that's one way in," he climbed down enough to pull the hatch closed and let the flooring fall back into place. He followed Deidra down the ladder. They were almost to safety, and the intruders would have no idea where they went.

———

THE GALLOWS ARRIVED and were being assembled on the lawn of the White House. Reporters were having a field day. *Did the President lose his mind? Does he intend to hang people his enemies on the White House lawn? What type of country are we in?*

Another station took a different stance. *It's about time we had a President willing to follow the law and hold traitors accountable. This should serve as a warning to every traitor still hiding in the shadows—when we find you, you'll swing too.*

But on social media, there was little talk of the gallows. Everyone was involved in the game of hide and seek. Right now, there were only clues, but soon they were promised pictures of people who were hiding. *Whoever finds the Hidden Crew will also find themselves five million dollars richer. Come play hide and seek. This is a global venture, and the Hidden Crew may run and hide wherever they choose.* Most people were talking about the chance to become a millionaire, not about anything happening in politics.

———

SIMON WAS PISSED. George and Derrick were right; he believed their story of massive corruption and he didn't trust his Director at all. He was a holdover from the past President. Harrington had chosen not to replace him, and Simon always thought that was a mistake.

He was pacing back and forth when Derrick asked him a question. "You guys collected everything from the house, right?"

"Yes, of course. It's all evidence," Simon advised.

"Where is it now?" Derrick asked.

"It's on its way to our office at Langley," Simon assured him.

"Can you get it back here?" Derrick questioned.

"Why would I do that?" Simon responded.

"We were in the process of printing a list. It didn't finish, but maybe there's a chance it can give you names to be wary of," Derrick informed him.

Simon's mood brightened. He picked up a phone and called the driver directly.

"Where are you? Okay. Turn around and come back to the hotel. I need something from the evidence. Yes, I'm sure. This is dire. Get here as soon as you can," he hung up.

"You'd better not be fooling with me," Simon warned therm.

"I'm not," Derrick assured him.

Derrick sat in a metal chair; he leaned it back on its two back legs against the wall, he was wondering about Trina. He hoped she was safe and not too worried about him. He imagined her playing with Killer outside the cabin in the tall grass. A strange thought invaded his mind. *I need a lawnmower if I survive this.* It made him smile just a little, and then he remembered what was going on around him. "What a stupid thought," he chastised himself for letting his mind wander. He needed to always stay focused. They were in constant danger, even if it didn't seem like it.

"Simon, when you get the list, I want my gun back," Derrick said firmly.

"Yeah okay, you want a pizza with that?" Simon quipped.

"As a matter of fact, I am hungry. So yes," Derrick played him.

Simon looked at the two men. George as usual was silent and scheming.

"Alright. I'll get us some food but you're not getting your gun. I'm not that stupid," Simon conceded.

———

AT THE BOTTOM of the ladder, she stepped off into something wet and squishy.

"Fuck, what is that?" Deidra asked.

"Are you alright?" Tinker called from above her, still descending the ladder.

"Yeah, I'm fine, I'm gonna need a new pair of shoes though, are you almost here?" It was pitch black and she couldn't see him. She wanted to use her phone as a flashlight, but knew better.

"Almost there, I think," Tinker guessed.

"Well hurry up. It's creepy down here. Where are we, anyway?" Deidra asked.

"It's a city utilities tunnel. They abandoned it a long time ago. I resurrected it for my escape tunnel." Tinker replied proudly.

She heard him do an evil laugh like, "Mwahhaha."

"You're a weirdo," she replied.

"Yeah, I know, that's why you love me," he toyed.

Deidra didn't say anything.

Tinker finally hit the bottom. His feet squished around in whatever Deidra had screamed about.

"We must walk this way. Put your hand against the wall. In about thirty feet, we'll trigger the light and then we won't be blind anymore."

She let him lead the way and put her hand on his shoulder.

———

THE PRESIDENT'S phone call had put him on edge.

He made a call. "We need to meet. Something is going on we seem to be in the dark about."

"Okay. Where and when?"

"Now. In the normal place," he responded.

The normal place was code for their emergency destination. A place they saved for when they felt they might be followed or eavesdropped on. Twenty minutes later, they stood across from one another.

"So, what's so important that we have to play this cloak and dagger game?" Senator Waterstein asked.

"I'm pretty sure the President knows we sent the assassin that killed his friend. He called me at my office and implied he's going to hang me in front of the White House. He's having the gallows from the Smithsonian exhibit moved," Heller warned.

"He is just trying to push you to act brash. You know, like meeting your supposed enemy in the middle of the woods. You're being played and may now have put us both in jeopardy," Waterstein rebuked him.

"What about the news leaks for those other guys? We all have taken money from the same group. Do you think that is a coincidence?" Heller queried.

"No. I researched a bit and found that the Council is scrambling. Someone stole a bunch of data with hundreds of names and documents, blackmail files on every person that the Council uses or who is a member," Waterstein replied.

"That could put every one of us in jail or worse. What are we supposed to do?" Heller panicked.

"Keep a low profile, you know the status quo," Waterstein encouraged.

There was a noise in the woods and the two became silent, listening.

Bright lights suddenly illuminated them from every direction.

"Police! Freeze, don't move, keep your hands where we can see them," an officer ordered.

"Do you know who we are? You officers are making a big mistake," Heller barked.

"No, Senator, *you* made a big mistake. You are both under arrest for attempted murder for hire," the Officer informed them both.

Attempted murder. Those words echoed in his head. "He failed," Heller murmured to Waterstein.

"I knew he played you," she hissed back.

———

TINKER CAREFULLY WALKED down the tunnel. He had moved along slowly, not wanting to rush and fall. After a minute of his cautious pace a dim light flickered on, then another, and another. Soon the tunnel was illuminated, showing a golf cart wrapped in plastic sitting in the tunnel. Tinker turned to Deidra and spoke.

"I love it when a plan comes together." A line from a show he remembered from watching reruns as a child.

Deidra just stared at him—there were tears in her eyes.

"I'm sorry," she whispered.

"Hey what's up, why are you sorry? Why are you crying?" Tinker questioned.

Two men stepped out of the darkness with their guns drawn.

"Mr. Brennan, you need to come with us," one said.

Tinker moved to stand between Deidra and the men.

"Okay. Take me, let her go," Tinker offered.

The men started laughing.

"You don't get it to do you? How do you think we found you? She traded you up for cash."

The effect of those words on Tinker was visible. He seemed to shrink right in front of them.

He looked at Deidra. She was crying. "I'm sorry."

"Take the cart, your cash is in the bags on the back. Do you have the password?"

Deidra handed him the paper Tinker had given her to shut everything down.

"Go now before I change my mind," the man ordered her.

Deidra wasn't told twice. She pulled the plastic from the cart and double-checked the bags. She flipped the switch and headed out down the tunnel.

Tinker was defeated. He just didn't care; everything had been taken from him. He now understood what it felt like to be the target.

"What do you want to know? I'll tell you anything." They bound his hands and then escorted him to their cart hidden in the tunnel. They pulled away a tarp and made it blend in with the walls in the dimly lit area. Tinker was strapped in. One of the men sat beside him while the other drove, they headed for the surface. As they neared the increasing light from the end of the tunnel.

One of the two men asked him a question. "Who did you hack our servers for?"

Tinker abandoned any loyalty to others. "A man named George Avail."

"Do you know where he is now?" the questioning continued.

"No. I haven't heard from him since I delivered the drive," Tinker answered.

"Where was that?"

Tinker readily told the man the address. Then he noticed the man's gun start to raise toward him.

"Wait, Wait, I can track the drive," Tinker shared.

The man lowered the gun. "You can track the drive?"

"Yes, but only if I'm alive," he bartered.

They exited the tunnel, and his captors took him to a car parked on the street.

Three other men joined them in the car behind them.

———

THE BOX WAS HAND-DELIVERED. It was full of papers just tossed into it; it was obvious that whoever collected it didn't realize the value of the documents. Also in the box was a pistol. Simon hadn't decided that he would give it back to Derrick yet, but he felt like he could trust him for some reason.

Simon shuffled through the papers looking for specific names of people he worked with or for at the agency. It didn't take long for the first name to show up. It was the DC liaison officer that he had worked with many times. It made a lot more sense now how some of the targets managed to just slip away before they were apprehended.

"Son of a bitch," he said as he came across another name. One of the agents he had used in Milekistan was on his list. He continued to skim through the names—he was still looking for a particular one.

"Well, maybe I was wrong," he said to himself as he neared the end of the printouts.

The man he was expecting didn't seem to be there.

An agent walked into the room with a single piece of paper. "Sir, we dropped this one on the way up. Sorry."

Simon snatched the paper from him like it was candy. He scanned the names. *Robert Holden.*

There it was, in black and white.

"Fuck, I was right," Simon blurted aloud. "We're in trouble now, boys. My boss and a few others are on here. Derrick, here's your gun."

As he started to hand the weapon over, another agent walked in carrying files. He stepped between Simon and the weapon handoff. Simon looked through the file and then turned sharply to face Derrick.

"Why aren't you dead? Because all this paperwork says you are," Simon looked hurt by the news.

Derrick realized that Simon probably ran his fingerprints through a much more thorough check than his friend Paula had been able to scrub.

"Derrick Driver, Boston PD. Killed in an accidental gas explosion. That's what my file says."

"And yet, here I am. So, what now?" Derrick asked.

"Well for starters, why have you stayed dead? What are you up to that required you to remain a ghost?" Simon interrogated, afraid of thee answer.

Before Derrick responded, George made the connection.

"He's been waiting to kill me," he exclaimed.

Simon spun to face George. "For what?"

"He blames me for the death of his lover. That's what," George stated.

It was Derrick's time to just sit quietly as George continued.

"My daughter told me that a man was hunting me before she died."

Simon was confused, he assumed that George had arranged for her removal from the hospital.

"Okay, just stop for a minute. You don't know that your daughter is still alive? Who took her, then?" Simon questioned.

"You said she was dead," George shouted. "What do you mean who took her? Where is she now?"

Once again Simon felt like he missed something big right under his nose.

"I don't know who has her. I didn't look too hard for her because I figured when I found you, I'd find her," he stated simply.

Derrick stood up and walked over and nonchalantly took his pistol from Simon's hand. "Thank you."

Simon just nodded, his mind struggling to wrap everything together.

George was now even more agitated.

"The Council must have her; they will use her as leverage to try and make me turn over the drive. Then they will kill us all."

Derrick had loaded his magazines from a box of ammo he found on a shelf in the room they were in. He placed a round in the chamber by hand and then released the slide. The sound of it slamming into place caused the others to look up at him. He ignored the attention and then inserted the magazine into the weapon and holstered it.

"Do you still plan on killing him?" Simon questioned him.

"I'm not sure yet. He deserves it. If anyone else dies or gets hurt because of this man, I won't have a choice," Derrick said, as if it was a given fact.

"Well, I still need him for information," Simon advised.

"Why do you think he's still breathing?" Derrick responded.

41

GETTING the girl to turn on him was far more effective than any torture he had ever inflicted on someone. Every question they asked, he answered. Now they were returning him to his office to track the drive. They were wary based on their encounter from his decoy spot. They knew the kind of defenses he could have in play. They also knew if he was close enough, he would be their protection. They went to the rear entrance, and when the wall panel slid away, there was no sign of the two delinquents that they had stranded in there.

Tinker disabled the security and they all descended to his office. At his desk, he punched in the code that he had foolishly shared with Deidra. He thought of her momentarily, and a tear formed and ran down his face. The computers started to hum. Flashing lights and the sound of small fans could be seen and heard from the server room as well. After a few minutes, Tinker looked up. "All set. It's tracking now. Give it thirty seconds."

The man looked at his phone. *No service*. "Do you have a phone that works down here?"

Tinker lifted the handset from the phone on his desk. "This one."

His captor stepped over and took the phone from him. He entered a number by looking it up on his phone and keying numbers a few at a time.

A few seconds later the phone was answered. "Do you know what time it is? I haven't slept in two days and now you wake me up in the middle of the night. This better be good!"

"Kid, shut the hell up and take this down. You're just an assistant and if you want the chance to be more, don't ever talk that way to me again," the man shouted into the phone.

Denler realized it wasn't one of the Cyber guys. "Oh man, I'm sorry, I thought you were someone else."

"We have coordinates on the drive containing the lost data," the man informed him.

"Oh great. Will you be able to retrieve it?" Denler asked excitedly.

"Not great, it is already in the hands of the CIA. We have no idea how much they know or have been told—we have to assume everything. I'm transmitting the names and coordinates now." Tinker displayed them in an email and then forwarded them to the address he was given.

"Now we wait," the man said as he hung up.

Tinker sensed an opportunity. "Can I ask how you managed to corrupt my favorite employee?"

"It was a little harder than we imagined. At first, we just offered the cash and then she refused. It wasn't until we showed her pictures of her mom and little sister that she agreed to comply," the man grinned as he answered.

The fire alarm went off in the building above. All the men instantly drew their weapons.

"Don't worry, one of my tenants repeatedly smokes in the stairwell. This happens several times a month." Nitelite calmed down, as did the others. They didn't notice the small screen that Tinker had displayed in the corner of his monitor. It showed the tenants all exiting the building. They had all been informed on what to do if that alarm ever sounded.

"So, you made me feel like the one girl I fell for, maybe ever, betrayed me—when in reality, you gave her an ultimatum between me and her family?" Tinker inquired.

"Yeah, that's pretty much it," Nitelite answered.

"You know who the most dangerous men are?" Tinker asked him flatly.

"I don't know. Probably assassins like us," he laughed, and so did his men.

"No. It's men who have nothing to live for..." Tinker pushed the enter key. A series of small *pops* could be heard from up above. Then they continued and started getting louder.

"What did you do?" There was uncertainty in his voice.

"You might say, I sealed our fates," Tinker said.

The *pop* had turned into explosions and the ceiling started to cave in. The men ran towards the elevator and were covered with chunks of concrete as the building started to collapse on top of them.

"Nothing more dangerous than me," Tinker said, smiling as the ceiling collapsed onto the men around him.

———

HE NEEDED to speak to his boss before he ordered a hit on the CIA—actions like that were far above his pay grade. He had been sleeping in a room off the back of his office. He didn't know if Jeac would be in or not. He strolled past his desk. He was wearing sweatpants and a t-shirt, but didn't think this information could wait.

———

SENATOR HELLER WAS ESCORTED to a police station in DC, but no one spoke to him. He was off limits until the FBI got there. Senator Waterstein was fair game, they said. Two young detectives tried their interview skills out on her.

"So, what do you know about the Senator's involvement in the murder for hire of an FBI agent? The first detective asked.

"I'm afraid I don't know what you're talking about," Waterstein replied.

"Why were you with him in the woods this evening?" the second detective inquired.

"He called and asked me to meet him. That's how many negotiations get done in DC, dear," Irma replied, unfazed.

"Did you know he was under surveillance?" The detectives took turns asking questions.

"Why would I know that?" Irma questioned back.

"Are you aware that a member from a clandestine assault group named you as one of their handlers?"

"Again dear, why would I know that? I have several agencies whose teams are managed by my office, but that doesn't mean I directly handle them. I have people for that," the Senator deflected.

"Senator, would you have reason to want FBI Agent Paula Newly dead?"

"Oh Heavens, why would I want that?" Irma asked in a motherly tone.

The detectives realized that a seasoned politician would not break easily or even slip up.

"That's all for now. We'll be back."

———

THE HOUSE WAS SMALL. It had two bedrooms and two bathrooms, a kitchen, and a small dining area. It had a huge, covered terrace that overlooked the sea from where the house was perched. The weather was perfect, and the key had been right where Elsy thought it would be. They needed to get some supplies and some clothes. Luckily, there was a whole tourist shopping area not too far from the home. They went shopping and Elsy paid for everything with her card. She knew it was a risk, but hoped no one was looking for her specifically. She bought three prepaid phones as well, one for each of them. After buying the essentials for clothing, food, and hygiene, they headed back. Trina was still feeling anxious about Derrick.

"I hope he's okay," she moaned.

"I'm sure he is dear," Elsy said an an attempt to be more endearing.

"Elsy, I like you too but don't use that *dear* BS on me, it's just a way of trying to placate my feelings," Trina said defiantly.

Elsy laughed at her vocabulary. "Okay, deal. I'm just trying to figure all of this out as well."

"What happened to D's woman?" Trina suddenly asked.

"Oh, that's a long story. One you'd better ask him," Elsy deflected.

"I tried; he wouldn't say anything," Trina continued.

"I imagine because it's still painful," Elsy offered.

"But why?" Trina kept at it.

"Because she died," Elsy said finally.

"Oh, that makes more sense why no one wants to talk about it. Sorry for asking," Trina apologized.

Elsy opened the prepaid phone and dialed a number.

"Hello?"

"Don't say my name. Are you guys still okay?" she asked.

"Yes. How about you? Where are you?"

"I can't say right now. Do you still have that package?" Elsy inquired.

"Yes of course. We both have a copy," Tulia answered.

"Oh, even better. Lock one in my office safe and always keep the other with you. Is there still a copy on the system?" Elsy continued to question.

"Oh yes. We forgot to erase it," Tulia confessed.

"That's okay. I'm gonna remote in and I'll erase it when I'm through. You guys be safe, okay. Use the company card for anything you need to stay safe," Elsy informed them.

"You stay safe as well. Bye," Tulia offered as she hung up.

———

THE GALLOWS WERE ASSEMBLED ACCORDING to the President's order. Now he had called a press conference in front of them. Cameras were set up and the talking heads were all giving the paid opinions of their respective networks. Many were almost verbatim with the network next to them, yet somehow the public never noticed.

The President stepped out of a protective trailer surrounded by Secret Service agents. He walked out to the podium waving to citizens who had gathered outside the fences. He stepped up to the microphones.

"Never, in the history of our country, have so many enemies of our Republic been actively working against the ideals outlined in the Constitution from within our own government. It is a sad day that brings me to stand here, in front of this form of justice used by our forefathers, to deal with treason within this very institution. As many of you have seen and are following, our very own government has become infested with corruption at the expense of the citizens of this great nation. Therefore, as President of these great United States, I make you this promise, If the allegations are true and if these alleged traitors are found to be so by a jury, they will face this punishment set forth by the Constitution as a warning to those who may yet be discovered. Stop your actions, do not give solace to our enemies, and follow your oath of office. If you do not, we will find and uncover your deeds, and then may God have mercy on your soul—this government will not."

As expected, numerous reporters jockeyed for the first question. "Mr. President, are you condoning the death penalty again?"

"I'm telling you treason will be routed out and dealt with according to the Constitution," the President responded.

"Sir, how many of these so-called traitors are in your opposition's party? Isn't this a form of election tampering?"

"When you have a real question, come back. Next," the President admonished.

"Sir, how many names have you uncovered so far?"

"I would have to refer you to what's been leaked already, any others would be considered ongoing investigations," the President hinted.

"So, you are investigating others?"

"No comment," he knew in this scenario, that *was* a comment, but that's what he wanted.

He stepped away from the podium and a staff member took his place. "No more questions. We will have a press release as more information becomes available. Thank you."

———

THE COUNCIL MEETING had been tenuous. He was still alive and in charge, so that was good, but they wanted blood. If he couldn't give it to them, they would want his. The information from Denler was both good and bad. He now knew where the data was, but not to what extent it had been shared. The only breach they could identify for sure were the names released to American news channels. The identities of a few American politicians and one CEO would not hurt them in the long run. He had the names and now faces of the men who would have requested the data. George Avail was known to them, as well as his fixer Barry Klinger. They would be released to the social media partners for the 'game' they had created. Soon, he would know where all the players were.

"Denler, where is the team and this hacker now?" Jeac asked.

"I'm unsure sir, we lost contact right after they transmitted the information to us. There is a report on the local news of a building explosion at that same address. They're reporting the building owner as missing and presumed dead."

"And our team?" Jeac inquired.

"Sir, they were with him. The media wouldn't know that," Denler responded.

"Get me another team then. We need to secure or destroy this drive before it's too late. That gives me an idea. Get me Connor McNeely instead."

"McNeely, sir?" Denler asked with trepidation.

"You heard me. Make it happen."

———

SOCIAL MEDIA WAS a buzz now that pictures had been released of the 'Hiding Crew'. The reports started almost immediately. The initial ones were all fabricated by people just hoping to throw off their competition. The AI used by the sites had already been programmed to authenticate the veracity of every claim for the probability of accuracy. Most were found to have less than a one percent chance of accuracy. The highest rating so far was half a percent. Each platform was responsible to tabulate and forward the information to the Council. They were to report anything that exceeded a twenty percent rating. So far, none of them had anything to report.

———

GEORGE WAS GETTING nervous just sitting in one place. "How long are we going to stay here?"

"It's the safest place we can be," Simon answered.

"Do you really believe any place is safe?" George questioned.

"I believe there are a hundred agents from various agencies here in this building, most of them are armed. There is an armory to arm the rest should the need arise. There is high-tech surveillance that is monitored twenty-four-seven. I think we are in the safest place we can be. Besides, no one knows you're here."

George laughed. "You keep telling yourself that. I guarantee they already know what floor we're on."

Derrick just listened. He knew George was probably right. He also knew Simon was partially right. His real concern was what kind of force these guys could send to get them. If it was up to him, he'd head back to New Hampshire where he'd have an advantage and his dog.

He realized he hadn't checked in on Killer in a while. He felt bad about that, and hoped his canine buddy was doing okay.

"Simon, what kind of weapons do you have in the armory?" Derrick asked.

"I don't know if I should tell you, now that your intentions toward Mr. Avail are out in the open," Simon admonished.

"Seriously? If I was going to kill him so recklessly, I could just do it right now. I wouldn't need a weapon and I'd probably enjoy it more," Derrick conceded.

Simon shook his head, and George just gave him a look. "Go ahead and try it."

"We have everything you could want. I think there's even a Humvee with a mounted mini gun in the garage."

"We should get the keys for that ahead of time," Derrick warned.

———

SHE SAT up in bed by herself. The nurse was amazed, her recovery was now going much faster than anticipated.

"Ms. Avail, you are doing wonderful. How are you feeling today?"

"I feel good. I'm ready for a walk," Linda quipped.

The nurse laughed. "Oh, we're not quite at that point yet, despite how you feel."

"I need to leave this room; can't you even take me for a wheelchair ride?" Linda asked.

"Hmm. Let me check with Dr. Farley. I'll be back in a minute." The nurse said, and disappeared.

True to her word, the nurse popped back in with the doctor in tow.

"So, you want to go sightseeing? Let me give you a quick once over and I'll decide. Is that fair?" The doctor bargained.

"I guess it'll have to do," Linda agreed.

The doctor checked her vitals, her wounds, and the stitches. He was pleased with the rate of her recovery.

"Fifteen minutes. Okay? Let's start slow and see how you tolerate it. It will be more exertion than you think it will," The doctor granted.

"Thank you, doctor," Linda accepted.

Linda was excited to leave the room.

The nurse and another helper eased her into the wheelchair. There was some pain when they moved her, but she kept that to herself.

"Let's go," she encouraged.

"Just a minute we have to hang your IV, then we can go," the nurse informed her.

A second later she was being ushered down a hallway that didn't resemble her room at all. After that, she could tell she was in an abandoned store of some type. There were makeshift stations where people were typing on computers and an area surrounded by dividers where several people were gathered and talking quietly. She recognized Dr. Brody and tried to wave. A sharp pain forced her to withdraw her arm quickly.

"It's probably a little too early to spread your social wings, honey," the nurse warned.

She was pushed by the enclosure without being noticed. They made a lap of the floor they were on, and Linda got the lay of the building. She was hoping they could go out a little longer tomorrow.

42

"THE PRESIDENT IS RACIST. *Why else would he allow gallows to be displayed at the White House?*"

"*Didn't you listen to his speech? This isn't about race. This is about corruption and treason.*"

"*Yeah, that's what he wants the fools of his party to believe. Seems you're fitting right in.*"

"*You're losing with the facts, so you resort to name-calling. Seems about right for your political affiliation.*"

"*You're one to talk, you seem to be fine with the President telling black people their history of hardship means nothing to him.*"

"*Where do you make this stuff up? Do you do it yourself or is it in the party handbook?*"

The President shut off the TV. These talk shows had become just people arguing nonsense. Even the ones who supported him frequently sounded like fanatics just supporting a blind cause. It was quite tiring. He wished he could go back to the days when both parties just wanted to follow the Constitution and the divide was over *how* to follow it, not *if* we should follow it.

———

THE MEN WERE DISCUSSING the latest intel they had received. They knew where the drive was, and that it contained the evidence they needed to correct the path of our government.

"Sir, we do not plan on storming a CIA safe house, do we?"

"No, Peter. That is not an option we'll consider. At some point, the hard drive and Linda's father will have to move to where the drive can be entered as evidence. That is when we will hopefully utilize Linda and get her dad to help us. I do not want to fight other Americans. That is not now, and Lord willing, never will be our goal. This opportunity is the biggest and best chance we have to get the corruption out of our government at all levels. If the intel is correct, we can bring down multiple sources around the world who are behind this. We need that drive if our goals are to be accomplished."

Peter had another question. "Will our contact be able to tell us when they're going to move?"

"That is uncertain. I hope so." The group went back to studying the plans for the building. Getting schematics for a classified building wasn't easy. Luckily their numbers had grown, as more and more Americans saw the benefit of their group. The Gray Americans spanned across the country, with members in every state and at different levels of government. They didn't shift policy or combat Constitutional issues, they just observe and report, trying to weed out the corruption that has infested politics.

———

A SHORT MAN that resembled a leprechaun stepped into his office.

"Connor McNeely, your reputation proceeds you," Denler said trying to be friendly.

"How the fuck would you know? I don't know you at all. Now where's that little shit you call your boss?" McNeely thundered.

Denler walked over and knocked on Jeac's door. Connor just pushed him out of the way and stormed in.

"Jeac, You miserable opportunist. What have you screwed up this time?"

Jeac stood up from his desk.

"Connor, you haven't changed a bit. How's the cereal business?"

Connor didn't laugh. Very few people could even survive saying that joke. Jeac just happened to be one of them.

"Marshmallow shortage I'm afraid, I'm here to get yours," he said making a scissor motion with his fingers. The two men embraced and then sat in more comfortable chairs in front of Jeac's desk.

Connor mentioned the object that was still embedded in the wall. "Nice art, but a little too small for my taste."

"Bad day." Jeac excused it as.

"That, I understand. I have a live grenade stuck in my wall. I just leave it there as well," McNeely admitted.

"I need your skills. Do you have time?" Jeac asked.

"For you, my friend, I'll make it," Conner promised.

Jeac proceeded to tell him what was going on and what he needed to do to end it.

"So, you want me to take on the CIA?" McNeely questioned.

"Well, not exactly. Just do what you do to make my problem go away. I can give you any size team you need. The Chinese said they are willing to send an elite combat team to help clean this up. They have culpability in how it happened," Jeac informed him.

"How many guys?" McNeely inquired.

"They will send up to forty," Jeac replied.

"Yeah, that won't be easy to hide. The media can't spin it. It's an act of war," Conner stated as fact.

"Trust me, I've come to believe the American media can spin anything," Jeac surmised.

———

DARTON PLANK WAS SURGING in the polls ever since the gallows appeared at the White House. Talk of racism and Gestapo tactics were prevailing on the news. The evidence of corruption was buried amongst the opinions of newscasters who were more concerned with the optics they could rile their viewers with. It was working—viewership for most news networks had increased since the President's news conference.

Regardless of what viewers had tuned in to find, they were being fed a steady video diet of a recorded message. Multiple networks shared the exact same message as if it was given to them. *How do we know the*

President isn't just trying to frame his enemies? Why would this information be released just before the election, if it wasn't meant to sway voters? What's the likelihood that these politicians are truly corrupt? They haven't had a trial yet, so we should give them the benefit of the doubt. Do you think a governor would violate the Constitution, his oath of office and his loyalty to America, just for money and influence?" These were the questions that each network seemed to ask verbatim.

For Darton, they were better than he could have hoped for. He copied them and played them on his website on a loop. On the web, people logging in for the popular influencer were inundated with the propaganda of his party.

———

TWO WEEKS till Election Day and the President was declining in the polls. He met with his advisors to determine the best course of action.

"Mr. President, you need to remove the gallows. Tell the American citizens it was just a warning in response to the revelation of the traitors who were uncovered by the press. Thank them for their assistance in keeping the government free of outside influence and encourage them to keep vigilant in this goal."

This recommendation was met with agreement from most of his Council.

"So just let the traitors off with a warning? I don't think so. We arrested two more traitors last night while most of you were sleeping. They conspired to kill an FBI Agent, and we have insurmountable proof. These are two more Senators in addition to the ones already uncovered. They are in interrogation right now. We will find out who is behind them and remove them as well." The President thundered.

The President was adamant that the gallows would not only stay, but they would also be used.

His advisors could see no way to make this a positive for his campaign. They just hoped his record and his following were enough to overcome the bad press he was receiving daily.

———

PEOPLE HAVE BEEN SAYING for a long time that the true power in America was the power of media.

Gordan Darkley knew this was true. He was the CEO of one of the 'Big Four'. His company routinely ranked number one across all platforms for news broadcasts. He had been given a script for his news broadcasts and followed it explicitly. He knew what he was doing, and he knew there would be consequences if he was ever found out. He wasn't worried even a little bit.

Now as he sat in his office in NY, he had a view of most of the city. Two walls of glass gave him a panoramic setting that many people would kill for. The room had a modern feel to the décor, the floor was a stained concrete that was popular now, the walls that weren't glass were adorned with his accolades over the years and the three diplomas he had, indicating his Ph.D. in public communications. He didn't use the term *doctor* at all, even though he had earned it. He looked at his latest statistics. The stories his network was running were working. People were starting to question the motives of the President, which polls had said was unbeatable just a month ago. The spin was effective. He would buy a new beach house with the payout he would receive if this all went as planned. "Screw politics, media manipulation is where the real power is at."

He poured himself a drink from the well-stocked bar in the corner and then walked over to the window. "Thank you, little people, for being so easily manipulated. You are making me so very rich," he laughed as he looked down on the city below.

———

"TWO WEEKS? You expect us to stay here for two more weeks? I need a few more amenities than this place provides," George demanded.

Simon considered George's statement.

"Well, it does have the added advantage of keeping your ass alive, that's quite an amenity, isn't it?" Simon countered.

"For now, maybe. We might not know when they'll come, but they will come, and then you may be just overestimating this place," George warned.

"Mr. Avail. What is it that you are not getting right now? I'll see what I can do to accommodate you, but it will be at this location," Simon rebutted.

"Well for starters, I'd like better sheets and a private room—you guys snore too much. Second, the food is terrible, can't we at least order out from some of the nicer restaurants in the city? I'll even pay if the government can't afford it," George offered, hoping to get his way.

"That's reasonable, I can make that happen. You will both have personal rooms tonight, the doors are alarmed though so don't try to stroll around after ten p.m. Find a restaurant of your liking, and we'll order there tonight," Simon finished.

Derrick kind of agreed with George. Two weeks would feel like a long time to be sequestered in this hotel on a floor with no windows.

"What else can we do here to pass the time?" he asked.

Simon pointed to a box of papers. "I don't know, let's see who else you have here on this list. Maybe we can ruin some people's careers that deserve it."

Derrick was okay with that. He pulled up a chair next to Simon and started reviewing names. The first few pages were people in state or low-level positions. The first person they found to uncover and ruin appeared on the third page. Simon found his boss's name. "The CIA Director is on here, but it doesn't give the specifics or any evidence. Why is that?"

"Well, we didn't finish printing all the names. We only printed about twenty percent before we ran out of paper."

Simon looked at the stack of papers he had already. "This is only twenty percent?"

"Yup," Derrick assured him.

"How will we know who else is on it, if Mr. Klinger dies?" Simon questioned.

"I'd say we won't. How's he doing?" Derrick asked.

"He's stable. They've moved him to the intensive care unit," Simon shared.

Simon decided he would make a trip to the hospital. If Barry regained consciousness, he would need that key.

"I am going to check on Barry. You two will need to stay here until I return. I will have guards posted at every exit from this floor. Don't even try," Simon warned.

———

THE CHINESE SOLDIERS were jumping from a commercial airliner that had been specially fitted with a compartment in its belly. The plane was flying during the night so darkness would help hide their unscheduled exit. Twenty advanced combat soldiers waited for the small green light that would tell them to jump from the jet. They all carried their weapons and ammunition. Several small cargo boxes with additional supplies would be dropped as well.

Their target was on the east coast of the US, so they chose to drop in on the coastline near the North Carolina and Virginia line. The plane's Captain warned the unsuspecting passengers of a bit of turbulence. A yellow light came on alerting the group that it was time to prepare. They stood up almost in unison and donned the masks that provided oxygen. The light turned orange and the small sealed area depressurized. A door slid open, and the jet started to vibrate a bit due to the turbulence. The soldiers moved to the door and crunched up as they were sucked out into the night.

———

FLYING COMMERCIALLY under the fake surname of Neely, Connor landed and cleared customs without incident. With the help of the Chinese government's cyberwarfare service, his images had been scrubbed from global servers, thereby defeating the facial recognition that was deployed in every airport around the globe.

He exited, collecting his bag that contained only his clothes, an encrypted satellite phone, and a paper map with the location of his rental house in Virginia. He had a rental car in long-term parking waiting for him. He located the car by the description and plate number he had been given. The blue Ford Edge had the key tucked inside the gas cap. He retrieved the keys and headed to his destination.

———

DURING THE NIGHT, the media friends of the Council had prepared another assault against President Harrington. A young black man was found hanging in West Virginia. The Police were still on scene investigating, but the media was preparing a full-scale assault to blame the President over the incident, citing, *the gallows in Washington DC were propelling America back into its racist past and Americans should not tolerate this.*

Once again, the media created the news before any facts were even known. The President would wake to a media storm that had been manufactured to do nothing but enrage Americans and attack his poll position.

43

THERE WAS a light rain falling on the beach as dark images emerged from the sky and landed one by one. As the soldiers touched down on American soil, they were essentially committing an act of war. If they were discovered, the American government would be fully within its rights to declare this incursion as such and retaliate.

They quickly retrieved their gear and headed towards several cargo trucks that had been left just a short distance from their landing position. They moved quickly and efficiently to accomplish this. With their squad loaded up into their trucks, they headed for a location they had been given in Virginia.

———

SEVERAL MEMBERS of the group had been assigned the same task: follow a man from his last known location and determine his current location. They all were using advanced satellite tracking programs and were making great progress. They hoped to have the location of their target within the hour. Each member called out the last position they could determine to the rest of the team. This wasn't any type of competition— this was their assignment. They operated as a team and personal gain was not even a consideration.

———

AT THE HOSPITAL, Simon found that Barry was starting to regain consciousness.

"Has anyone been here to ask about him?" Simon questioned one of the guards he had stationed there. "No, it's been quiet. Doctors say he should recover fine. He is already starting to stir, they're expecting him to awaken anytime now," the guard informed him.

Simon was relieved. "Excellent, I needed some good news."

He entered the room and looked at Barry, who was wrapped like a mummy around his arm neck and chest.

"Alright Mr. Klinger, it's time to wake up, we need to talk. I need that key," Simon coaxed him.

He found a chair in the corner and settled into it. He pulled a small tablet from a bag he was carrying. Time to wait.

———

ON THE NEXT round in the wheelchair, Linda was much more alert. She was taking in as much as she could from any conversation she could eavesdrop on. Despite the answers she had been given, she still wasn't sure why she was there, or why they had gone out of their way to protect her. She looked at her chauffeur. "Can we rest here a moment?" The aide was oblivious to her real intent, and parked her out of the way. Linda intently listened to the conversation occurring a short distance away.

"Our guy says they'll have their location today. He also warned that there is a whole squad sent to eliminate them as a threat. At least twenty men, possibly more."

"That's a large force, who sent them?"

"It seems they are a Chinese special operations team."

"A military force, on US soil? That's an act of war if they're discovered. This drive may be more important than we imagined. Why else would they take such a risk?

Before she could hear the answer, her aide resumed their trek. She tried to listen as they moved away, but she was unable to hear the reply.

———

SENIOR STAFF HAD all been called in. The latest media attack on the President was completely unfounded. By the time he had become aware of the media storm being perpetrated against him, the facts had already been released unofficially. The media was continuing with their claims of racism influenced by the President's actions. The facts were already proving the incident to be self-inflicted by the victim. These facts were not being shown on most networks, though. Social media was ablaze with their theories on who and what was truly responsible. Most theories removed the victim's actions from the equation and found blame with others that were more in line with their provided narrative.

"I want action against the networks for this false and vicious attack of lies against me," the President barked.

He slammed his hand down for emphasis.

"I am getting killed out there by straightforward lies being offered as truth. Call this voter tampering and arrest a few of the producers behind this," he suggested to his staff.

Several of his advisors almost responded in unison. "No sir, that would be a huge mistake. They would claim a violation of their First Amendment rights. They'd say you were attempting to silence the press."

"I *am* trying to silence the press, silence them from outright lies designed to mislead American citizens!" the President fired back.

"Sir, trust us, it won't play that way. It will get even worse," his press secretary advised him.

"So, I am just supposed to tolerate them tearing down my image with lies?" Harrington asked.

No sir. We will reveal their lies by releasing the facts, we will build a competitive narrative that shows your history that is contradictory to their claims," the press secretary offered.

"Well, get on it. My lead in the polls is almost gone. They are winning the image fight right now, and my competitor stands for absolutely nothing. It's disgusting," the President moaned.

As the meeting drew down, a man in a suit walked in. "Sir, I need a minute with you."

The President dismissed the remainder of the staff and spoke with the suited man.

"Sir, I have some disturbing news for you, I have a close and trusted friend within the CIA. He has informed me that he has proof that the CIA

Director may be compromised and working against the interests of our country," the man informed him.

"That is a very strong accusation. I hope you can back it up. He has held that position for two presidents now," Harrington reminded him.

The man handed the President a piece of paper. The President looked it over—it wasn't complete, but the implication was very bad.

"This is real?" the President asked.

"I believe it is, sir," the suited man answered.

"Shit. Just what I need right now. Is there anything else?" the President inquired.

"Well actually, my contact believes this is just the tip of the iceberg. This comes from the same source as the leak that ANN revealed earlier. He says he has a drive with hundreds of names on it along with the evidence to back up the claims."

"Well, that's actually some good news," the President smiled.

"Sir, I recommend keeping this quiet until we know who else is on the list. It seems there are some very big names on the list," the man suggested.

"So how do I remove the Director of the CIA without alerting anyone?" the President asked.

"Sorry, Mr. President. I can't help with that."

———

THE GUARD FINALLY CONCEDED. "Alright you can make one call, but do not give away your location."

Derrick grabbed the landline and dialed a number. It was answered automatically with a beep. He left a message. "Tell Alexandria we need the house key back. ASAP. Hug the little one," he hung up. He knew that since their separation under restricted communications, Elsy would resort to the voicemail drop. He dialed again quickly before the guard caught wind that it was a second call. Same routine, but this time, he keyed in additional messages. "One new message. Hi honey, wish you were here, the island just isn't the same without you." At first, he started to assume the 'island' was New York, but then he heard the calypso music in the background. They were all safe for now.

ONE MAN POPPED from his chair, and in his native language, he called to his comrades. "I have found them, they are in Alexandria, Virginia in the United States. It appears to be a hotel run by the US State Department. We have a positive trail from an estate in Virginia Beach, our satellites observed bodies being removed from the same location."

They relayed the information to their superior. He was happy to send it on to the Council and their troops, who were risking their lives for this operation on American soil. His team had performed ahead of schedule, which would be recognized.

SIMON'S PHONE WAS RINGING. It was a White House exchange. Either his friend was successful in reaching the one person he felt he could trust with the drive, or he was about to be given an ultimatum that would probably end with the disk destroyed and his guests terminated.

"This is Agent Little," Simon answered cautiously.

"Agent Little, this is Estephan Harrington, President of the United States. I will need to see you in person as soon as you can get to the White House. How soon can you make that happen?"

Simon looked at Barry, who seemed like he was about to wake any moment.

"Sir, it will take me a couple of hours to get there," Simon responded.

"Very well. Where are you now?" The President asked.

"I am in Virginia, sir," Simon answered.

The President responded with, "Okay. Send me your coordinates, I will send a helicopter to shorten your commute time."

The call ended, and Simon mused, "I guess he got through."

Barry started to stir, and Simon leaned in close. "Mr. Klinger, I need you to wake up now."

THE ROOM SEEMED VERY bright as he slowly cracked the lids of his eyes. He heard someone talking but wasn't sure who it was. He continued to open his eyes. At first foggy images appeared, then ever so slowly the images began to take shape. He could see the shape of a man leaning over him. Then the face grew more defined, finally, recognition occurred in his mind. "The CIA agent?" he breathed out slowly, like a question.

"Yes Barry, I am. I need the key; do you remember it? I must share the information with the President. I need the key now," Simon pushed.

Barry was more alert now, but still spoke very softly. "I don't have the key; it went with the others."

Simon took a sharp deep breath. This, he was not expecting. The story that Barry possessed the key was so believable at the time he never thought to verify the information. Now he was suffering a setback and did not see any way to get the information to the President on time.

"Shit, why can't this just go right?" Simon muttered as he left the room.

He called to the doctor. "He's awake."

Now he had to find a way to uncover the contents of the drive. He had just enough time to return to the hotel and question the other two before his helicopter would arrive.

———

SHE HEARD the message and smiled. "He remembered; we have a message," she called to Harlem.

"That's good. What did he say?" Harlem inquired; Elsy shushed him.

She listened to the message; she could tell by Derrick's voice that things were heating up.

The third member of their party walked in, looking concerned. Before she could ask, Elsy walked over and hugged Trina. "That was from Derrick, he gave specific instructions to give that to you."

Trina's face erupted into a giant smile. "He's okay then?"

"Yes, it seems so," Elsy said.

Trina let out a sigh and ran outside to look at the ocean that D was on the other side of.

"So, what did he say?" Harlem asked again.

"He needs the key; I am going to upload it to a secure server and give him a passcode. He should be able to recreate the key." Elsy advised.

"Where is he?" Harlem continued.

"Alexandria. That's all he left for us." Elsy finished.

They chatted a little bit about their arrangements there. Harlem walked over and hugged Elsy. The island had been causing him to remember their spring break in college, old feelings crept in over the top of new ones, as he pulled her close, he gazed at her and asked, "Remember Spring Break?"

Her face flashed with a blush and her lips turned up at the corners.

"Yes, I do. But we have work to do right now," she said, smiling back at him.

"I know. I just wanted you to know how much I still love you," Harlem said sincerely.

Now as bright as a tomato she grinned. "I love you too, but you still have shitty timing."

They both laughed and Elsy grabbed her laptop and the key. Time to work.

Forty-five minutes later, she grabbed the phone. She dialed the same number that Derrick had; at the beep she left her message.

"I need an address from you, for the place where it all started. Can you get it there for me? You know the number."

She hung up.

———

DERRICK WAS STILL TRYING to convince the guard to give him access to the phone one more time.

"You don't understand, Simon will need this." Derrick pleaded with the guard.

"Yeah, you can wait till he returns," the guard replied.

Simon walked in mid-sentence. "What is going on here? I know you guys lied about the key. Who else is involved in this?"

Derrick assumed they inevitably would get to this point.

"Sit down, let's talk," he said to Simon.

Simon led him over to a small table.

"You have ten minutes, then I must go see the President. If you don't give me the key, I'm turning you over to the FBI and they can figure out who you are and what you've done," Simon threatened.

Derrick started talking. He refused to give up the others but explained how he hoped he could access the key soon. Simon was a bit upset when he heard the guard gave him phone access.

"So, you sent this message and now you want me to trust you, while you've been lying to me the whole time?" Simon questioned.

"It was only to protect my friends. Everything else besides that was true," Derrick confessed.

"So, where's this key now?" Simon probed.

"I need to use the phone and hopefully I'll have an answer," Derrick stated.

Simon handed him his encrypted cellphone.

"Go ahead, you better have some better answers," Simon said.

Derrick dialed the number and listened to the message. "I know where the key is. I'll need a large capacity thumb drive and a computer."

"Anything else?" Simon asked sarcastically.

"Yes, you need to take me to the President with you," Derrick added.

"Absolutely f'n not," Simon barked.

"You want the key, that's the deal," Derrick said flatly.

Simon looked at his watch. The helicopter was inbound. "Shit, you'd better be telling the truth."

Simon gathered the printout and the drive. He and Derrick entered the elevator and ascended to the roof. They waited behind a closed door in the small lobby at the top. The helicopter swooped in and landed gracefully. The two men rained out and boarded the aircraft as the sliding door on the side was opened for them. An armed man in a dark suit exited and pointed to the empty seats inside. The door slid shut again and they were airborne seconds after they were buckled in.

44

SENATOR HELLER HAD REFUSED to talk; they were keeping him sequestered from everyone and he had been denied a lawyer. He wondered if Irma had given him or anyone else up. The room was small and had a bed, a small table in the corner, and a small bathroom with a shower. They had provided him with a couple of sets of clothes that consisted of t-shirts, sweatpants, and underwear. The clothes he was wearing when he was taken were confiscated shortly after they brought him here.

The longer he remained incommunicado, the more likely he would be deemed a threat by the very people he had chosen to serve over his oath of office. He was still confident they would find a way to protect him and get him released.

———

THE ATMOSPHERE in the old department store was buzzing. Linda could sense it on her trips around in the wheelchair. Her strolls were now delegated to a young aide. She guessed the girl was no more than twenty-two or so. As her attendant prepared to help her move to the chair, Linda decided to test her. "I'm supposed to stand before I go into the chair today."

The aide just looked at her and shrugged her shoulders. She stood there waiting as Linda carefully swung her legs out of bed and used the momentum to assist her in sitting up. She stopped for a second. That was the most physical exertion she had performed in a while. The lightheadedness that came with the action passed quickly. She wasn't sure how strong her legs were, but she needed to find out. The aide seemed to sense her thoughts, and moved in to help her if needed. Linda dropped her feet onto the cold concrete floor. The feeling of the concrete reminded her of the stone patio at the island, where she had a new realization about her life before all hell broke loose.

She pushed against the floor and away from the bed. She was standing. She took a step toward the chair. The aide reached out and stabilized her. A small second step and a spin, and she was in the chair. "Not bad for a day's work," she joked to the aide.

"Not bad at all," the aide repeated. They moved through the facility unimpeded. Linda's ears were wide open. Something big was happening. She could feel it.

———

DR. BRODY WASN'T JUST The Gray Americans' surgeon; he was the founder. In the years since the group was started—a year after the 9/11 attack—he had seen it grow at an unanticipated rate. More Americans than he could have imagined were tired of the corruption that was now evident in all of politics. As a result, he now had a small army of patriots, scattered throughout the US and at different levels of government and corporations, both domestic and foreign.

They were waiting on confirmation of their target and the evidence they needed to prove the corruption that they were trying to expose. If all went well, they hoped the unveiling of such a huge level of bipartisan corruption would reset the American mindset and allow The Gray Americans to push for their agenda of return to the Constitutional concept of citizen authority over government.

———

THE HELICOPTER TOUCHED down on the lawn of the White House. The two occupants were led inside the building where they underwent a security screening. Simon had changed into a suit and tie before they left. Derrick was wearing a pair of tan pants and a black polo. He felt underdressed to meet the President, but his clothing options were quite slim.

After the screening, three Secret Service agents led them through the building to a small conference down the hall from the Oval Office. They were told to wait inside until someone came for them.

"You must give me the key. I promised it to the President," Simon pleaded.

"I told you my conditions. I will keep it," Derrick reminded him.

Simon looked upset. He understood Derrick's position, but it was limiting his position with the President.

"Before we leave, you'd better be able to give it up," Simon advised.

Derrick nodded. "I will."

The President headed to the conference room with two more agents, one in front, one behind him.

The door was opened by the first agent who stood aside for the President.

"Agent Little, I wasn't aware you were bringing a guest. Do you have what I asked for?"

"Yes and no, Mr. President. That is why I brought Mr. Driver with me; he has access to the key."

"Mr. Driver, you are a mystery. My agents informed me that you are listed as dead, yet here you are. I assume you are looking for a deal of some sort?" the President presumed.

Derrick offered his hand, but the President just stared at him.

"Why don't we get down to business before I decide if yours is a hand worth shaking," the President suggested.

The three men sat down at the large wooden conference table, emblazoned with the Presidential seal in the middle.

"So, if I am to understand correctly, you have a drive that potentially contains the names of every corrupt politician in the United States government?" the President repeated.

Simon spoke quietly. "Well sir, It's much more than that. It contains employees, state politicians, corporate figures, and foreign influencers as well. Along with all of that, it contains the proof of each allegation. Sir, no pun intended, but this is the holy grail of corruption."

He slid the papers over to the President. "This is just a sample of what's on the drive."

The Commander in Chief looked through the documents. The names he found were incredible and sickening. He found names of trusted members of his own party and evidence of their actions against the United States.

"This is real?" there was a tone of disbelief in his question.

"Yes, sir." Derrick answered.

"Okay, Mr. Driver. Let's hear what you want to unlock this information," the President prodded.

"Sir, let me start by saying I am a patriot, and the content of this drive sickens me. I am, however, in a predicament that only you can resolve for me. So here is my request. I will present you with the key. In exchange, I would like immunity from all crimes committed, previously, or related to this case, for my three associates and myself, and I would like to be listed among the living again."

"And what type of crimes may those be, Mr. Driver?" the President asked.

"Mr. President, any crimes I speak of occurred either in pursuit of this information or related to the incident that occurred shortly after your election. The incident, which was never told to anyone, the attempt to program Americans through genetic manipulation."

Simon flung his head around to look at Derrick. Even he wasn't fully cleared on that event. "How do you—?" He didn't finish his question.

President Harrington's face went white. "Are you trying to blackmail the White House?"

"No sir. I have no intention of sharing any of this. My associates and I may have committed certain crimes to facilitate that case coming to light, and others in the search and investigation of this incident. I would prefer it if our actions didn't land us in jail, especially now that my existence is becoming known," Derrick assured him.

The three continued their conversation, till they reached an agreement they could all live with.

Derrick, Elsy, Harlem, and even Katrina would have immunity from all previous crimes and any related to the resolution of the drive being exposed. The President stood. He reached out to Derrick, and they shook hands.

"Gentlemen, I have the biggest gun, but you have the ammunition. You have forty-eight hours. I want the drive back, unlocked, and ready for my review. The helicopter is waiting to return you to the hotel. Mr. Driver, you will have your immunity if the drive is unlocked by my deadline."

———

THE VAN WAS SAGGING on its axles. The load was far more than would be needed, but Connor always liked to overdo it just for effect. Several of the Chinese soldiers were applying graphics that made the vehicle look like a dry cleaners' delivery van. He reached inside the van and flipped a switch on the dash. A small air pump started, and the van raised up off its axles. They had installed airbags that hid the indicators of the load the van carried.

"Okay, finish those graphics and make sure they're perfect. We can't afford some nosey perfectionist looking this thing over." Conner ordered.

They were nearly ready. They needed the final schedule of their targets, and they would get the job done. Now, all they could do was wait.

———

AS THEY RODE down from the roof in the elevator, each man had separate thoughts on the meeting they had just left. Simon saw an opportunity for advancement and maybe even a service commendation. Derrick, on the other hand, saw a chance to regain a portion of his life that was taken, and a way to protect his friends from anything they had done to assist him.

"That went well." Derrick said.

"I'm glad you think so. You made me look like a dumbass. You'd better be able to get that key," Simon growled.

Simon led Derrick to a room he hadn't seen yet. It had several computers set up inside. He pointed to one, "Will this work for you?"

"I think so, I'll just need that USB drive," Derrick reminded him.

Simon reached into his pocket and handed Derrick a drive.

Derrick sat down at the terminal and started typing. Elsy had made him memorize an IP address a long time ago. He entered it in the browser screen. A blue page popped up saying, *404: files were not found.* Derrick hit the 'enter' key three times and a log-in screen popped up. He entered a password, and the screen changed again. It asked for another password, which he entered. This time, a list of files populated on the screen. Derrick chose the one labeled *Alexandria.* He did not open it, but gave him a list of choices including copy to drive—he chose that one. A little light on the thumb drive started to flash and the screen indicated twenty minutes to copy the files. Simon would have to wait.

———

GEORGE HAD BEEN GOING a little stir-crazy. He watched as Simon and Derrick returned and walked right on by without so much as a nod toward him. He wasn't used to being ignored. He began pacing, waiting for someone to acknowledge him. A few minutes later, Simon appeared with a small video camera and a notepad.

"Alright, Mr. Avail. It's time to come clean and tell me everything. Right now, I have enough to have you charged with treason. Your cooperation is the only thing that will keep you from death row," Simon informed him.

It wasn't until right then that George realized he was no longer running the game—he was now the pawn. He was aware of all the things he had done against the interests of America. He was willing to tell what he needed to, hopefully to avoid death, and maybe even jail.

"First, I want my lawyer present, I will make a written deal and then you will know what I know," George bargained.

Simon agreed. Due to the potential nature of his charges, he could deny a lawyer under the Patriot Act, but Simon wanted everything as soon as possible.

"Alright, I will get you a lawyer, his job will solely be to verify any deal you can make. That's it. He will not be present to confer with you during your testimony. That's it, that's the deal."

George took a second and contemplated the offer, he knew that he had little bargaining power left.

"Okay, that is acceptable. I will tell you all I know, but I want immunity from prosecution," George added.

"That's a big ask considering the scope of what you've done against your own country," Simon reminded him.

"That's my deal. Take it or leave it," George offered.

"Let me make a call."

———

THE GUARD WALKED down the hall and opened the cell. "Mr. Heller, dinner time."

He handed a tray with food on it to the disgraced Senator, who looked at it with disgust. Meatloaf, green beans, and mashed potatoes. The gravy had been spread liberally on all the items. A cup of premade chocolate-flavored pudding sat on the side.

"You want me to eat this garbage? How about a little respect? I am still human," Heller complained.

The guard turned and left without saying anything else, locking the door behind him.

Heller had put up a good front, but he was starving. In his normal routine, he would eat almost every four hours. It had been almost twenty since his last meal. He sat at a small table and devoured the food with the plastic utensils they included with the meal. He cleaned the plate. Despite his outburst, he was surprised at how good it tasted. He even polished off the pudding.

After his meal, he started to feel tired. He decided it might be time to just sleep. He laid down on the mattress, not bothering to use the bed coverings that were at the end of the bed. The room started to spin a bit, as if he had drunk too much. Then he felt nauseous. He started to get up to head towards the bathroom, but collapsed on the floor. He vomited, and he tried to get up again but felt an immense sharp pain in his chest. The room seemed to close in on him and his vision grew dark—he was having trouble breathing. The realization that he had been poisoned came quickly to him. He smirked as he realized his last meal was meatloaf and fake pudding. "Sons of bitches," he hissed out as his last breath.

———

FBI AGENTS WERE NOW INTERVIEWING Senator Waterstein. They were writing notes as fast as they could. She was throwing names and dates as fast as she could. Her goal was to seem as helpful as possible to garner a deal from the US Attorney General. She had already set that in motion when they first tried to question her. She was making most of it up, but once she had the deal it would be too late to take it back. She could see how desperate they were—her stories were making them drool for more. She had them right where she wanted them.

Another agent entered the room and whispered to one of her interrogators. She couldn't hear what was said, but she could tell by his reaction that it wasn't good.

"Senator Waterstein, we're going to have to cut this short. It seems that your partner in these crimes just had a major heart attack. The AG wants a medical evaluation for you before we continue. Irma's face felt cold, she touched her hand to her cheek. She knew exactly what had happened.

"He was killed. There was no heart attack. Run a tox screen immediately before it dissipates. You'll see," she offered.

The agent turned to face her. "How would you know that ma'am, you're not even in the same building."

"Because I know how they deal with loose ends. You've made us loose ends. They'll be coming for me next," she moaned.

"Who will?" The agent asked her.

"I can tell you, but I must have protection," she pleaded.

45

DENLER STEPPED out of the office for a smoke. On the sidewalk floors below, he lit up and pulled a phone from his pocket.

"It's going down soon. They have everyone in place and have the location. Expect heavy resistance on site."

"Thank you, stay safe."

"Will do."

He hung up and took a long drag on the cigarette. He exhaled slowly, watching the smoke slowly curl up into the air and disperse until it was like it was never there.

———

JEAC YELLED as Denler returned to the office. "Where were you?"

"Cigarette, sir," he tapped his chest pocket.

"You know you can smoke in here," Jeac advised him.

"Yes sir, I just enjoy it more when I'm outside," Denler stated.

It seemed that Jeac shared that sentiment, and let it slide.

"Where are we with the solution?" Jeac asked.

"The solution?" Denler questioned.

"Yes Denler, the solution. That's what it is for us. We wipe them all out, destroy the drive and blame it all on the Chinese. What else would you call that?" Jeac stated.

It was obvious the stress was getting to his boss. "Well sir, I guess solution is a fitting title. Everything is in place. The team is ready to execute. Our mole says they will exit to return to the White House with the data in less than forty-eight hours. He believes he can give us twenty minutes notice when it's going to happen," Denler advised.

"And Avail is there as well?" Jeac queried.

"Yes, sir."

"Let Connor know to be on standby. We only get this one shot without risking the Chinese starting a war," Jeac ordered.

———

THE LAWYER for George Avail arrived and met them in a secure room. He showed the documents from the Attorney General's office. It was not what he was hoping for.

"This says I only have immunity from charges of treason, what about other crimes?" George asked.

"Sir, this is the only deal they would make. They have the drive and from what I've heard, it doesn't need your corroboration. My advice is for you to take the deal and honor your promise to talk." George mulled over the document. At least it removed the death penalty and treason charges.

"Do you have a pen?" he asked.

The lawyer pulled a pen from his briefcase. George hastily scribbled his signature on the documents.

"Let's get this over with," he stated.

Simon activated his camera, and a red light indicated it was recording. George started with his name and the date. Then he dove right into telling all he knew about corruption and the World Council's plans for America.

———

THE COMPUTER BEEPED and the light on the drive stopped flashing. Derrick pulled it from the machine. He called to the man assigned outside.

"Hey, do you have another USB? This one isn't working right," he lied.

The man walked over to another desk in the room and returned with a second drive identical to the first.

"Thanks, keep your fingers crossed," Derrick requested.

Derrick pressed a few keys, and the computer repeated the process. The guard, unaware of Derrick's subterfuge, returned to stand by the door. Derrick quietly pocketed the first drive. He didn't know why, but felt he should have it.

———

GUN CHECKS, run-throughs, and mapping routes were continuously happening with the Chinese soldiers—they were elite fighters. They would not tolerate mistakes or lack of preparation. Downtime only occurred off mission. That would not happen again until they returned home to China, if they did. They all knew this was a non-capture mission. They would rather die than be in the hands of the enemy.

Connor watched their drills. Occasionally, they practiced dispatching their own wounded to prevent capture. He wasn't any kind of zealot. Even during his military days, he couldn't have imagined intentionally dying to prevent capture. He admired their conviction, but it scared him as well. Luckily, his part would not require him to go anywhere near the point of attack. If he did his job right, they wouldn't have to, either. Unfortunately, their plans put them in a dangerous location.

———

THE DOCUMENTS DERRICK had requested arrived from the President as an agent delivered them to him. He quickly looked over the documents. It provided blanket immunity for any crimes committed by the four names he had given. They were free from prosecution, and his name was restored immediately—Derrick Driver was alive again. He pulled out the picture of Shannon he always carried with him. A tear slipped from his eye, betraying his inner thoughts. "Please do not think I'm betraying you. This is just bigger than both of us. I need to see it through, even if it means finding a different resolution than I originally planned."

A voice came from the doorway.

"Who are you talking to?" He turned, and Simon was standing there.

"No one." The computer beeped at the same time. Derrick grabbed the drive and tossed it to Simon.

"My end is upheld," he said.

"So it is. I guess you'll be a free man again, Mr. Driver. Can I ask that you remain here until I leave with Mr. Avail?"

"Where are you taking him?" Derrick asked.

"I will drop him at a secure facility before I drive to the White House with both the drive and the key," Simon informed him.

"Do you want to verify it works first?" Derrick asked about the key.

For some reason, that thought had escaped Simon until now.

"That is the smartest thing I've heard you suggest yet, Mr. Driver," Simon said sarcastically.

Simon sat down at the terminal and plugged in the drive. He followed the prompts and plugged in the key. Just like the first time, the drive verified itself and then revealed its contents. Simon looked at the wealth of information and searched for a few specific names. Several were there, some were not. Either way, the drive and the key worked. He was ready to meet the President.

LINDA HAD MANAGED to walk more than ride today. Her strength was returning, and she felt good. She was off the IVs and was eating normal food, and now she was dressed in what the others called *normal clothes*. By *normal*, they meant fatigues of some sort, but they fit her well and were surprisingly comfortable. She was okay with it for now. Dr. Brody promised to see her today and explain why they had taken her. She desperately wanted to know the real story of why they needed her and if she would be allowed to leave when they achieved their goal.

THE INTERNET HIDE-AND-SEEK game raised the payout for information. Ten million for the whereabouts of the people whose images they showed. George Avail and Barry Klinger's faces flashed across the screen with the announcement. A nurse at the hospital looked at the image on her phone a second time. She compared it with the man in bed in front of her.

"Holy shit, it's you," she exclaimed.

Barry was tired and didn't understand her outburst.

"What's me?" he asked.

"You're the hide and seek guy. I found you," she stammered.

She took his picture and hurriedly left the room. She posted the picture and the location to her social media page with the words, "I found him."

———

BARRY'S LOCATION was relayed almost immediately from the time the nurse posted. Two Chinese soldiers were tasked with solving that portion of their assignment.

The two left their staging area and proceeded to the hospital. It was a forty-minute drive.

———

THE CAMERAS WERE all set up for the President. Reporters gathered, uncertain of what the President had called the meeting for. It was described as a speech of importance regarding national security.

The President stepped out into the briefing room after being introduced by his press secretary.

"Good afternoon. Today I have learned of massive corruption within the ranks of many branches of federal and state governments. This evidence will be made available to all news outlets as soon as it is verified. Many reporters have criticized the gallows I had placed on the front lawn. Today's revelations are why we needed to shake the trees to cause some of the rot to start to fall, and it has worked. I am sorry for those who felt hurt or slighted, this was never the goal of my actions.

As a result of this shake-up, Senator Alvin Heller was exposed for his corruption. Unfortunately, Senator Heller succumbed to a heart attack before interrogation. Senator Irma Waterstein was also uncovered and is currently cooperating. The CIA Director is also implicated, and I have asked for his resignation pending charges. This is just the beginning. The State of California has detained the governor there on similar charges, stemming from the leak of documents detailing his corruption. Others are being apprehended by FBI agents as we speak. I believe this is just the beginning.

Our elections are just a few days away. I encourage all Americans to follow this story as it unfolds and exercise their right to vote. Vote with intelligence and for what is best for America. For too long, we have allowed those among us to sow division based on false issues for their own benefit. We must all come together as Americans and fight this corrupt influence that we have been secretly subjected to. That is all I can say at this time.

Good day and God bless America."

―――――――

THE LATEST POLLS were handed to him, and Darton reviewed them before he recorded his daily blog. Today's were down dramatically. The President's speech seemed to touch base with the voters. He was down to near his original polling numbers in less than three hours. He looked out the window of his multi-million-dollar home. He had become rich for being prominent on social media. His video blogs were about nothing but him looking pretty and talking about silly things. Now, he was a candidate for President.

He still remembered when he was approached and asked to consider it. He had thought it a joke until the campaign money started rolling in. When he won the party nomination by a landslide, even against more prominent party members, he knew there was more than money behind this. He had played a kind of less intelligent version of himself on his blog because modern women loved it, and men didn't feel competitive with it. It was the perfect position to ignite a brand and turn it into cash. If all went as planned, he was now taking it all the way to the White House.

―――――――

THE NURSE HANDED the phone off to a doctor.

"Yes Mr. President, what can I do for you?" he asked.

"I would like to check on the status of Agent Newly," the President indicated.

"Sir, I am happy to report that Ms. Newly is doing much better, she is out of the coma and has regained consciousness. She still has a long recovery ahead of her though."

"That's wonderful news. Tell her to take her time. I will be in touch after the elections are over, either as the President or as a friend," he promised.

"I will tell her, Mr. President. I know as military we are not supposed to be partisan, but good luck on Tuesday sir," the doctor encouraged.

Harrington smiled as he hung up.

"Finally, some good news."

———

THE PHONE RANG at the house. Connor answered it. "Hello?"

"Twenty-minute window starts now," the voice said.

Connor called the Commander of the Chinese forces into the room.

"It's time to deploy, we're in the twenty-minute window," Conner ordered.

The commander took the information to his team. Connor headed for the van. Time for final preparations. A young soldier accompanied him— he would be the driver that placed the van by their target. Connor would monitor remotely from a safe distance. They had already secretly placed cameras around the area to help them identify their target. "Today should be easy in the scheme of things… Damn. Why did I think that? It's bad luck. Stupid brain." Conner argued with himself.

The soldier just stood in silence while Connor berated himself for his errant thought. Connor saw him and responded by lifting his arms and tossing out a, "What?"

The young soldier just stood there silently awaiting his instructions.

———

SIMON HAD COMPLETED his interview with George. He had placed the camera and recording in his briefcase, along with the drive and the key that Derrick had given him. He tossed Derrick a set of keys. "These go to a sedan in the parking garage. I assume you know where your Jeep still is. According to the President, you're a free man, Mr. Driver—don't screw it up," Simon directed.

Derrick took the keys and headed down to the garage via the elevator. The doors opened to the underground parking facility. He hit the lock button and a horn chirped. He added in the direction it came from. As he moved in the direction, he hit it again.

"Getting closer."

———

SIMON NEEDED some help in moving George and other evidence to the transport vehicle. He saw another agent standing around with apparently nothing to do. "Hey, Agent Betterman, right?"

"Yes, that's right." Betterman answered sheepishly.

"Good, I need you to help me get this prisoner down to the transport vehicle. I need to carry this stuff," Simon ordered.

"I uh, no. I'm busy right now." Betterman countered.

Simon didn't care what else the agent was up to. "I'm not asking, agent. Take the prisoner."

"Alright sir, just give me a minute. I need to let my partner know what I'm doing, he's waiting for me." Betterman insisted.

Simon stood at the door while the agent texted on his phone for a minute. In the meantime, Simon received a text of his own. *"Transport delayed, standby."*

"Ok, I can help." Betterman returned.

"It will be a few more minutes, hang tight," Simon ordered.

The other agent's face seemed very distraught for the mere assistance that was requested of him. Simon was more concerned about the delays in getting the data to the President.

———

DR. BRODY WALKED BRISKLY into her room. "I hear you can walk now?"

"News travels fast." Linda chuckled.

"Good, let's walk," the doctor suggested.

Linda grabbed the doctor's arm as they headed out into the main area of the old store. He led her towards the back of the store. As they passed down a hallway, she noticed what looked like cases of guns stacked on top of each other. She kept walking slowly with the doctor. They reached the loading dock area; several trucks and SUVs were being loaded.

"I need you to come with me now. I will explain everything on the way," Brody informed her.

46

DERRICK REACHED the car he was searching for, a typical government car. No frills, dark paint job, not even power windows. He got in and with a twist of the key the car started right up though. He looked around. There was garbage on the floor, old coffee cups and fast food wrappers. It smelled like a boy's locker room mixed with an ashtray and old coffee. It reminded him of a stakeout vehicle from when he was still a cop.

He put the car in gear and started to head out of the parking garage. He got to the street and the smell seemed like it was intensifying in the car. He rolled the window down as he drove. First, he stopped at a roadside mailbox and dropped an envelope in, then he headed towards the highway. He wanted his Jeep back badly. As he started to speed up, a paper started to swirl around the floor. He hadn't seen it before, and guessed it blew out from under the seat.

As he approached a red light, he reached down and grabbed the paper. There was something familiar about it. It was a page from the list he had printed from the drive. He looked at the names. "Why was this here?" One name leapt off the page at him. He studied the name to make sure it was right.

"Damn, how did I miss that?" he questioned himself.

He swung the car around in the road with one fluid motion, tires breaking free and spinning on the pavement, a bit of smoke rising from the surface.

He grabbed for his phone. Gone. Simon never gave it back.

"This is just getting worse," he growled.

———

THE DRY CLEANING van pulled up in front of the hotel. There was a black sedan on the curb, the van pulled up and double-parked alongside it. A single Asian man exited the van and headed inside with several suits to deliver. A police cruiser drove by and looked at the van's parking job.

The two officers looked at each other. The driver said, "Those damn agents think they own this block. If I thought it would matter, I'd ticket their dry cleaners until they raised their prices to deliver here." His partner chuckled. "They'd probably make you disappear first."

They continued past the van with no second thought. The driver checked in at the front desk and gave three room numbers on nonsecure floors. He was cleared to deliver them without question. Instead, he tossed the clothes he carried and the uniform he was wearing in the dumpster behind the building as he exited the rear. He checked his watch —right on schedule.

———

SIMON CALLED for the helicopter again. It would be here at the same time as the transport for George Avail. He decided he didn't want the President to wait any longer than he had to for this vital information. He informed Agent Betterman of the change in plans and instructed him to go with Mr. Avail until he was in the custody of Federal Marshalls. Betterman was sweating.

"Betterman, are you feeling alright?" Simon asked concerned.

"Not really sir, is there someone else that could take him? I'm not feeling well," Betterman admitted.

Simon looked around and found another young agent to replace Betterman.

"Go get checked out at the infirmary, make sure you're not contagious before you leave," Simon ordered.

Betterman shook his head and ran out the door. The new agent took charge of Mr. Avail and headed for the front; the transport should be pulling up any second now. He called to Betterman to hold the elevator, instead he pushed the door close button and watched as the agent and Mr. Avail looked on as the doors closed without them.

———

THE SMALL BLACK car pulled away just as the transport approached allowing the transport to pull right up to the curb. The agents inside thought, *the dry cleaning van gives us extra cover.* The young agent and Mr. Avail headed down the elevator. Thanks to Betterman's arrogance, the transport would have to wait a few more seconds.

———

DERRICK ROUNDED the corner too and could see the hotel a few blocks away. He sped up the street and saw the helicopter landing atop the hotel. *Simon must have changed his plans.* Derrick was not concerned for George Avail. He was concerned, however, for the safety of the data. Traffic was stopped on the street all the way to the hotel. Derrick looked for options to get closer and chose to park two blocks away. He started heading towards the hotel on foot. He looked at the names on the list. Betterman was a spy and Simon would need to know. As Derrick was walking, he saw Betterman speed by in a small car. There was panic on his face. Derrick's first impulse was that he had already been found out. Then he started looking at other clues. The white van, the two dark vans he had passed just down the street. There was a kill team here, and they had a bomb. Derrick broke into a full sprint headed towards the hotel.

———

A DARK GRAY SUV moved slowly down the street. The occupants were carefully observing the building and anything and anyone moving around it. Seeing a man running down the street full speed at the building caught them off guard.

"That's Derrick," Linda said from the back seat. "What's he doing here?"

The doctor quickly told her of how Derrick had freed her father and Barry from the CIA before they were all captured together. Their source says he was given immunity by the President. "But why is he running toward the building?"

They were distracted when down the street they saw two men exit the building—one was her father.

"My father!" Linda exclaimed.

A bright white and yellow flash released from the van; in an instant their SUV was rocked by the blast. It blew out windows and spun the vehicle around. They were three blocks away and partially protected by a building. By the time they regained their senses, the building was hidden by a large cloud of smoke, dust, and ash. The van had disintegrated, leaving a crater in the street. The transport had been thrown through the building and broke into pieces as it was accelerated through the mass of the building.

Those who happened to be on the street between the van and the building were instantly vaporized by the detonation. The rebound wave severely damaged buildings all around the area. However, most of that damage was limited to glass and minor structural damage. People outside less than a block away suffered potentially life-threatening injuries. Those in the two block range were subject to concussive and debris injuries—Derrick was in that group. Luckily, he was forced to avoid a car parked on the sidewalk that caused him to sidestep behind the edge of a building. He was partially shielded at the instant of the blast.

———

AS THE SMOKE and debris settled, the men in the SUV regrouped and looked for survivors they could help. They exited the vehicle with their side arms covered as they moved towards the target. They heard gunfire erupt down the street. Rapid automatic weapon fire could be heard. Men dressed in all black were shooting survivors in the street. Two of these men were headed towards Derrick who was still rolling on the ground. Linda called from the van, "Save him. Don't let them kill him!"

Two of the men drew their pistols and shot the attackers. She exited the broken vehicle and started limping towards Derrick. She was joined by several armed men who surrounded her as she moved forward. They weren't there to stop her, but to protect her.

———

DERRICK LOOKED UP. His head was ringing like it was stuck in a church bell, his vision was blurry, and his hearing was gone. He could smell smoke and felt the burn of fire. In his mind, he was back in his apartment the day Shannon died. Then he saw it, a woman's face peering through the smoke. "Shannon? I'm sorry I failed you; I love you," he let out in a whisper. He tried to reach for his lost love, but she was gone. His world went black.

Linda looked down at him. Blood covered his face. He had been thrown back like a puppet by the force of the explosion. "Pick him up, we have to save him." She acted as if she was in charge. The men did not question her.

Dr. Brody grabbed her under the arm. "We need to go. There is nothing else we can do here."

"I'm not leaving unless you bring him too," Linda resisted.

The doctor nodded, and the men surrounded Derrick's body and lifted him in unison. They rushed back towards their vehicle. The doctor called into a radio, "Vehicle extraction immediately."

As they reached the spot of their broken SUV, another van pulled up. They carefully placed Derrick in the back and then Linda and three of their men got in. "Get them to safety. See what can be done for him." Brody ordered.

The van sped away.

———

THE PILOT SCREAMED into the microphone of his headset as they were lifting off.

"Brace, brace, brace."

Simon knew from his military time what that meant. He grabbed for a handrail. The helicopter lurched in the air and listed to one side. Simon watched as the building disappeared, replaced by a cloud of smoke and debris. The pilot twisted the throttle. The engines did everything they could to combat the sudden turbulence they had to overcome. The helicopter slowly climbed from the cloud and started to regain control. Simon looked at the devastation below.

"Holy shit, they blew up the whole building," he cried out.

"Sir it's not over yet. We have suffered damage. I will need to see us down quickly," the pilot warned.

"Get us away from here first." Simon picked up his phone and dialed the number the President had given him for emergencies.

"Mr. President, we are under attack, I am transmitting the location of the backup data I made. It's with a mutually trusted person."

As Simon was finishing his statement, the pilot made a violent maneuver without warning. Simon saw the missile fly closely by the aircraft. Before he could right the copter, a second missile secured a hit. The tail of the aircraft burst into flames and the copter seemed to linger in the air for just a second before rapidly spinning toward the ground.

———

THE PRESIDENT WAS ALERTED IMMEDIATELY to the attack in Alexandria. The news was already calling it a terrorist attack. He was receiving different information. The reports were that a small militia group was fighting with a group of Chinese soldiers. Members of his staff were rushing into his office; they all came with the same basic message. *"Sir we've been attacked on our own soil. This is an act of war."*

The President was inclined to believe them, but reserved his actions until he had more information.

"Get the National Guard down there now, secure that area. Start rescue proceedings to save who we can. Take everyone into custody. We will get to the bottom of this. This was not a random act."

"Yes, Mr. President. Right away." An Army General saluted and left the room.

"Set up the situation room. We'll convene there in ten minutes," the President ordered.

The men in the room stood, saluted, and went to see to the President's order.

President Harrington sat back at his desk for a minute. He took a deep breath. This was going to be a long day.

"Please Agent Little, get me that drive," he mumbled.

Polls opened for the election in thirty-six hours.

———

THEY DROVE Derrick and Linda back to the Department store. This time, it was Derrick they rushed to the makeshift ER. There was a room full of medical staff waiting for his arrival. A gurney was waiting when they pulled into the loading area. They carefully pulled him from the van, placed him on the rolling bed, and rushed him off to the medical area. Linda watched as they worked on him. They cut away his clothes and moved him to the surgical bed—a place she had spent too much time recently. The doctor carefully inspected his body for puncture wounds from shrapnel. They hooked him up to multiple monitors to watch his vitals. They gently wiped away the blood from his face and head. Then the doctor looked up.

"Good news, no new holes. Bad news, severe concussion. We will need some x-rays to rule out internal injuries. Ms. Avail, I will need you to wait outside."

Derrick's acceptance of her plea for forgiveness had haunted her, she needed him to survive. She felt her soul required it.

———

TWO ASIAN MEN dressed as doctors entered the hospital. They moved right to the room Barry was recovering in. At the nurse's station, two nurses were comparing fingernail polish. They entered the room. Barry stirred a bit. "Who are you?" The men pulled suppressed pistols from their coats. Two rapid shots were fired—the noise wasn't suppressed at all. Both men fell in almost in unison. The agent stepped from the darkened bathroom. "I guess Simon was right." Security came running down the hall guns drawn.

"You're a bit late for the party, fellas," the agent joked.

The agent was smiling at them as the two Chinese soldiers slowly bled onto the gray tile floor.

47

THE MEDIA WAS IN A FRENZY. An attack on American soil, on Election Day. Massive corruption uncovered, with multiple levels of government aided by corporate conspiracy. Every station seemed to lead with a different story. Across the country, polls were open but people were more confused than ever about what to believe. The votes they had been sure they would cast were now in question. For the first time in a long time, no pundits were claiming to know how the vote would tally at the end of the day.

———

PRESIDENT HARRINGTON ISSUED A RECORDED statement from the White House. It stated the following:

"Fellow Citizens, we have suffered an attack on our great nation. This attack was far greater than just the explosion that destroyed a building and killed many of our fellow Americans. It was an attack on our very sovereignty as a nation. This visible attack was just the surface of the intent to destroy us, but the perpetrators will be rooted out and face the justice they so mightily deserve.

I have every confidence that our elections are safe today. Do not refrain from exercising your inherent right to cast your vote. This is not a plea to vote for me, but a call for unity in protecting this great nation.

Our forefathers faced much greater adversity when they crafted this great nation to be resilient in the face of such adversity. Let us all make them proud by standing shoulder to shoulder as we uphold their dreams for a perpetual beacon of freedom for the rest of the world.

Go vote your conscience. Vote for who or what you believe, but please go vote, and let it be an indicator to those who would foster such an atrocity, that we as Americans are stronger than their worst attacks. As your President, I say thank you for your resiliency and your trust in me to lead you through these dark times. America will prevail and be stronger as a result.

God bless this country and her citizens."

————

IN THE SITUATION ROOM, the President asked everyone in there to have a seat, then he held up several sheets of paper.

"If I call your name, please stand," he indicated.

The President called seven names, ranging from senior members of his staff to trusted aides.

Each was uncertain to why they were singled out.

"These people standing here among us are traitors. Whether directly or through conspiracy, they participated in this attack on our nation," the President accused.

Military guards appeared at each doorway as the President spoke.

"Take these traitors from my sight. Lock them up and keep them separately. They will all have very important choices to make soon," the President ordered.

————

JEAC WAS VERY PLEASED. The drive was destroyed, and Mr. Avail was eliminated. The Chinese were being blamed for an act of war against America. There was no evidence that the Council had any involvement or even existed—he would be hailed a hero at their next meeting. China would be removed from the Council. Jeac and the Council were in the clear. He could return to his day job as an advisor to the French President.

He went to pack up the desk and head home. Seven French special police officers were waiting for him when he exited the building. He was immediately arrested for actions detrimental to the goals of France. He didn't know exactly what that meant, but he knew he wasn't as clear as he thought.

———

DENLER MADE a call from outside where he had been watching. "They got him. He's being arrested as we speak."

"Thank you, Denny, you've done a great job. Come home for now. This is far from over," Doctor Brody replied.

"Thank you, doctor, I can't wait to be back home with all of you," Denler said.

———

THE CHINESE EMBASSY in America had been quarantined. No one in or out. It was surrounded by American troops. The President stated that until he had a reasonable explanation of what had occurred on American soil, they would be considered prisoners of war. The American Embassy in China had already been evacuated to prevent further retaliation. Several other countries rushed to play an intermediary between the two nuclear superpowers.

———

AT THE END of the day, the polls were closed, and the vote had been called in favor of the obvious winner. Darton Plank took to the stage in front of thunderous applause from his followers and supporters.

"Ladies and Gentlemen and others, we ran a good fight, we showed up, and made our voices heard. We let everyone know that anyone can find a path to run for President. I thank you all for that. The one thing I've learned through all of this is that we may at times act like angry siblings with each other, but don't come at us, we will fight together. Don't mess with America!"

Again, the applause overwhelmed the sound system he spoke through. He waited for them to quiet down.

"I know that today's outcome isn't what every American hoped for, but I pray we continue this unity in the face of those who sought to harm us. I take this moment to congratulate President Harrington on his second term and ask that he remember the wants and desires of the others of us who didn't vote for him."

Some boos could be heard at the mention of President Harrington, but he shushed them down.

"Let's all just be Americans for tonight and celebrate the truest symbol of freedom: an open election."

Darton knew that his speech would garner more than a million likes by morning. He still was on top of his day job.

———

PRESIDENT HARRINGTON DID NOT HAVE the time to celebrate his overwhelming victory. There was a crisis at hand. Several politicians had resigned in advance of their public removal. The FBI was reviewing all the names on the list that the President currently had. Each person was being detained for questioning until the evidence referenced could be verified. This was the largest shake-up in American politics that had ever occurred. Three incumbents who were re-elected just hours before were also detained. But the big surprise to the President was how many newly elected first timers were already on the list. A new Congressman from Massachusetts was already implicated in treason.

The reports kept coming to his desk. He might not have the hard drive, but the people he could get were talking to save themselves. The list was growing.

He replayed the message from Simon, *someone we both trust.* The President thought of the man who had visited his office. It wouldn't be him. He racked his memory to come up with a name. "Who else could he mean?"

———

PAULA Newly finally was off the machines that had briefly kept her alive. She was still confined to her bed, but she could now sit up and talk a bit. The nurse came in to find her watching the news.

"Oh dear, shut that off. You don't need to get worked up over things you can't control. Let's just concentrate on getting you better and out of here," she smiled gently as she shut off the TV.

"Is that all true? We were attacked by China?" Paula asked.

"I'm afraid it is, dear," the nurse replied.

"Man, you take a nap, and the world goes to hell," Paula joked.

The nurse laughed. "Well, your sense of humor is still intact. That is always a good sign."

The nurse checked her vitals and the bandages on her wounds, replaced an IV bag, and then headed out of the room. Paula snapped up the remote and turned the news back on. She needed to know.

———

THE MEMBERS of the World Council were shaken by the news coming out of America. Some were furious that China would act on its own, and others were just upset it seemed to have failed. Then the news of Jeac's arrest reached them, and they slowly realized the implications of the list.

They all quietly started withdrawing to their respective areas and started to remove the evidence of their involvement in the Council. The Council shrank overnight as members pulled their funds and their people backed out. While not directly attacked, the Council suffered a massive blow. It would take a while to recover—if it ever did.

———

ELSY AND HARLEM watched the video on the news. It was a traffic cam showing the whole blast sequence. They could see a man running towards the building just before the explosion. You could see him struck by the blast wave and thrown to the ground. Then the debris blinded the camera, and the news switched to the aftermath from their crews on the scene. News of a helicopter shot down was also now being shared on multiple networks. Elsy played the broadcast over again.

"That's Derrick, I know it is. Only he is stupid enough to run at a bomb," she moaned.

She was crying, and Harlem put his arms around her.

"He was a long way away. He's probably fine. Just got knocked down and beat up a bit," Harlem offered.

Elsy seemed to like Harlem's rendition of what the video could mean.

"Ok, let's go with that. We need to head back and find him," Elsy stated.

"Do you think it's safe?" he asked.

"As it's ever gonna be. I'll call the plane," Elsy decided.

Trina had been listening longer than they realized. "He is okay, I can feel it."

She smiled cautiously at them. "D is the strongest man I know."

NEWLY ELECTED Alexander Cortez stood with a crowd of people at his celebration. With a loud bang, six federal agents slammed open doors and proceeded directly towards him.

"What is the meaning of this? This is my victory celebration. You have no right—" Cortez started.

The officers ignored his entire statement. One looked at him and spoke.

"Alexander Ernest Cortez, you are under arrest for suspicion of Treason. You will be held under the Patriot Act. Please come with us."

Gasps could be heard coming from the guests that had attended his celebration. Some were moving away and shielding their faces as the cameras started to pop. Suddenly everyone was a journalist with their cellphones.

DERRICK STIRRED IN THE BED. His head was pounding. He didn't know where he was or how he got there. He was wearing a hospital gown and nothing else. His body was bruised all over. He could smell the antiseptic of a hospital, but he couldn't see any windows—the only lights were from monitors he was attached to. His mouth was very dry, and his eyesight was blurry. He tried to rub them and realized he was strapped to the bed. His mind raced. Was he captured by the people he was trying to expose? Was he a prisoner of the Council? Then he remembered. George and the young agent had just stepped out in front of the hotel, then the blast. He had felt the wave hit him as he tried to drop down to the ground. He remembered seeing Shannon, and then nothing. "Is anyone out there?" he shouted as loudly as he could.

He tried to call out again, but his voice was more like a harsh whisper. That was the best he could do for now.

No one responded.

———

IT WOULD TAKE MONTHS, maybe even years to investigate and prosecute most of the people brought in from what was now referred to as *The List*. The President had numerous people looking for the data that Simon had sent to someone before the crash. He knew it would not be the complete contents, but hoped it would uncover more of those who were in positions to harm this country.

———

AS THE NURSE CAME BACK, Paula was sitting up in bed waiting for her.

"I need a phone," Paula demanded.

"We all need things dearie, that doesn't make it happen," the nurse said.

"I know that, but I need a phone or a laptop," Paula continued.

"I'll check with the doctor and see what he says. If he's ok with it, I'll be back with something," the nurse advised.

"Thank you," Paula accepted.

A few minutes later, the nurse reappeared with Paula's cellphone and her computer from her things.

"Doc said it was okay, just don't get worked up," she advised.

"I promise," Paula agreed.

Paula opened the laptop on her legs and started to check her emails. She had hundreds. She started skimming the subject line for anything of interest. As she got to the most recent ones, one caught her eye. From

Agent Little CIA. *Paula, you were the only trusted person I could think of. There is a file attachment. It's unlocked, it contains evidence the President is waiting for. Please forward it to him. Simon.*

Paula clicked on the attachment. As she started to read, she quickly understood what she was looking at. It appeared that only thirty percent of the file he was sending made it through. She wondered what happened. She found the number he gave her in her phone, and she tried to call. It was routed to the CIA main desk, where the cover agency answered. "Stronghold Logistics, how may I direct your call?"

"Simon Little please," she responded.

The person on the other end just went silent for a few seconds.

"Uhm, I ah, well, I'm sorry to inform you that he is no longer with the company."

Paula read between the lines. Simon had died in the attack. She hung up. She dialed a number she now knew by heart.

"Paula, is that you?"

"Yes, Mr. President."

"At this point, I think you can call me Steve like the rest of my friends."

"I can't do that, Mr. President. I have vital information I believe you are looking for," Paula shared.

"Oh, and what might that be?" the President asked.

"Some data Simon Little sent before he died," she informed him.

The President's mood changed immediately.

"Are you still at the hospital?" he asked.

"Yes sir," she replied.

"Don't move. I'll have people there immediately," the President responded.

Two minutes later, two Marines were guarding her door. Both were armed.

48

A WEEK AFTER THE ELECTION, things were still changing in American politics. Multiple laws were proposed to safeguard the system. Or at least, that's how they were presented. Sixty-two Americans were caught in what was dubbed *Operation Wrap Up*. The information from the data that Paula had gotten to the President revealed even more names than he had on his printouts.

A special election had already been scheduled to refill the position vacated by the traitors that were uncovered. The media seemed to have a newfound interest in actual news and set aside their previous habits of opinion-based news. Many of them were nothing but mouthpieces, and they were now working diligently to repair that trust they had squandered.

———

ELSY, Harlem, and Trina returned to the States. Back at Harlem house, they started their search for Derrick. He had disappeared without any word. No one had seen him since they identified him on the news video. Elsy was working on her computer writing software that would search any camera that was near the bomb area and hack the recorded video. Most, as it turned out, had already been confiscated by the FBI and other agencies working on the case. She had to be very careful, knowing they would still be watching. Harlem was on the phone with guys from work. He was hoping they would tell him if they had heard anything. Trina, opting to keep busy, filed through the mail that had piled up while they were gone. She found a big envelope that was addressed to all three of them. There was no return address.

"Hey, I think I have something," she called out.

The two adults joined her on the floor to review her findings. She pulled out some very official-looking documents from the folder. One document for each of them. Harlem lifted the one with his name away from Trina's grasp.

"It's a letter of immunity signed by the President and the Attorney General. One for each of us."

"This means D is alive, right?" Trina asked.

No one answered.

"What does it mean?" Elsy questioned.

"It means anything illegal we might have done up until now can't be held against us," Harlem stated.

"I get that, what does it mean for Derrick? Did he send it before or after the explosion?" Trina questioned.

"There is no way to know right now. We will keep looking."

"Did you guys read this closely?" Trina asked.

"Why? What did you find?" Elsy questioned.

"The way it's worded, sounds like immunity extends until all the traitors are brought to justice. It's like the President gave us a get out of jail free card," Trina blurted out.

Harlem and Elsy scanned their documents.

"Holy shit, the kid is right," Harlem agreed.

Elsy returned to her computer, no longer afraid if the FBI knew they were looking.

"We need to find Derrick," she said, expanding her search.

———

WITH EVERY NAME they had access to, detained or arrested, the President was comfortable with the safety of America from intervention from the group that had called themselves the Council. He was not foolish enough to think the threat of corruption had been extinguished, though. The rest of the list contained names he would not know unless people talked, or another copy of the drive was found.

He was inside Marine One flying to Walter Reed Hospital. A friend of his was being discharged today, and he intended to meet her when she was. Paula had become special to him during the investigation he ordered. When she was gravely wounded, he found that his feelings for her went beyond professional. He was hoping she'd have dinner at the White House with him.

The media frequently referred to him as *the single President*. There were always women eager to change that, but until now he never shared their sentiment.

———

DERRICK WAS RECOVERING NICELY. He was now talking to the doctors and nurses and ready to get out of bed. The concern for any possible head injuries had passed, and many of his bruises had started to fade. He had walked around his room without their knowledge, but didn't think they'd like to hear that.

Dr. Brody stepped inside his room. "So, how are you feeling today?

"I'm doing good, so when can I get out of here?" Derrick asked.

"Ah, the million-dollar question. I think first we need to have a chat." The doctor tossed the immunity agreement on the bed.

"Where did you get that?" Derrick questioned.

"My men found it in an abandoned car a couple blocks from the explosion site." The Doc informed him.

Derrick pondered his words *my men*. Not something a normal doctor would say.

"What are you, military?" Derrick inquired.

"Not exactly. You are quite a resilient man, Mr. Driver. We'd like you to join us." The doctor offered.

Derrick just stared at the doctor. What was he into now?

The doctor laid out who and what The Gray Americans were. He told Derrick he was free to go, but asked that he consider the offer. Before he left, he added one more thing. "There is a woman out here that had been waiting to see you. If it's okay, I'd like to let her come in."

Derrick was baffled by that, who could know he was there? He shook his head. "Sure."

The doctor stood up and as he left, he heard him say.

"Send her in."

When Linda stepped through the door, Derrick was flooded with multiple emotions. He knew she had survived, but never expected to see her again. The desire to see her die by his own hands had left him. Strangely, he felt lighter at the sight of her. He felt… Redeemed.

––––––––

THE GRAY AMERICANS sent out a press release.

> *America has escaped a threat that, if it had run its course, would have destroyed our nation from the inside. From the manipulation of people through social media to direct influence of our politicians by foreign interests, we have never been so close to the quiet annihilation of the freedoms that make this nation great.*
>
> *For now, the threat was diminished. For how long? No one can say. Money and power will continuously threaten the vows of dishonest men and women who seek power to rule over others. The Gray Americans will continue to fight to uncover these traitors who serve their own goals at the expense of the Constitution. Return America to self-rule, shrink the size of government, and live by the document that created this great nation. These are the goals of The Gray Americans.*

It was released on all media platforms. Some speculated that it was some type of threat, others believed it was a call for Americans to be more careful with their vote, and some thought it was a warning aimed directly at them.

––––––––

GORDON DARKLY SAT in a dark corner of the pub, a hat pulled down over his brow. Three other men joined him, who had also made efforts to conceal their identities. They talked in quiet voices.

"Gentlemen, George, rest his soul, is gone. With the Council mostly abandoned, we now have the opportunity to use George's plan combined with our ability to influence to serve our ends. We have proven the ability to successfully manipulate users with the latest generation of our AI platforms. Our users' weaknesses can be uncovered and exploited for whatever means we choose. This current President may think he has won against the corruption in government, but we have an opportunity to seize control while everyone is looking the other way. If we can control our users' actions, we control everything. Brothers, will you join me?"

Their heads nodded in agreement.

"Then let's get rich and powerful beyond our dreams. We will be the Kings of America. First step, the drive, its contents, and those who know of it, must be erased. No one can ever know that we sat on the Council." Gordon stated.

The three men agreed by tapping their beer mugs together. "To the Kings of America!"

―――――

AFTER DERRICK MET WITH LINDA, he left the safe house and returned to the house where his Jeep was. He pulled out of the garage at the beach house estate, driving over the police tape that was blowing loosely across the driveway. It was time to go home. He wanted to see his dog, Killer, and to have a beer with his friends. He wanted to rest. He made a call on his cell phone.

"I'm alive. I'll be there soon, then, I'm headed back to New Hampshire."

Trina cried when she heard his voice, and Elsy couldn't help but join her. Harlem just let out a huge sigh. Once again, they had managed to survive. They made a good team. When Derrick arrived, everyone was hugging and sharing their concerns for him. Harlem disappeared for a minute. He returned with a small box. "While everyone is here." He got down on a knee in front of Elsy.

"Oh my God," Trina exclaimed.

Elsy just blushed with a giant smile on her face.

"Elsy, one thing I've come to realize is that I'm my best when I'm with you. Help me be the best version of me I can be. Will you marry me?"

Elsy opened her mouth, but she couldn't speak. She shook her head up and down vigorously.

Slowly the words came out. "Yes, yes, yes. I will marry you. I love you, and I always have."

They kissed.

After that, dinner became a prerequisite, and when they finished Derrick sat down with Trina.

Elsy had mentioned they'd be happy to take care of her now that they will be a family. Derrick wanted to offer that option to her before he left. As they were discussing it, Elsy took a call on her cellphone.

Trina wasn't sure what to do. She loved Elsy and Harlem now—they were her family. But Derrick was the man who saved her, and she felt safer with him than anywhere else in the world.

"I don't know what to do. I don't want to hurt anyone," she cried.

"It's ok. I'm not really equipped to raise a young girl. I love you, but I'm more the uncle type than a father. I promise I'll come see you a lot. And once you're settled here, you can come visit me," Derrick assured her.

Katrina considered all her options and finally made her decision.

"I will stay, but you'd better visit," she negotiated.

"I will," Derrick promised.

Derrick said his goodbyes and got ready to head for the Jeep.

Elsy called out to Derrick before he pulled away.

"Hey, I need you to pick something up in Boston for me on your way home. It's probably best if you hang onto it for now."

DERRICK HAD a long drive to contemplate everything that had happen since he left. He forgave a woman he wanted to kill, he watched his other target die at the hands of another, and he became the target of a global cabal and the CIA. He met Trina and they saved each other. They helped save America from an internal attack by corrupt traitors, he got his life back, and one of his closest friends was getting married.

"What a vacation this has been," he chuckled to himself. In Boston, two of Elsy's employees met him out front and handed him a box.

"What's in it?" he asked.

"You probably don't want to know. Just keep it safe," Tulia told him.

A LIGHT SNOW had started to fall as he drove the final leg of his trip. Before he headed to the cabin, he figured a brief stop was needed. He pulled into the parking lot and a small group was waiting for him. He shut the Jeep off and headed toward them. There was a streak across the parking lot and a dog almost knocked him over, jumping up and down around him in a big circle. Derrick knelt and absorbed the attack of dog kisses. Killer was happy to see him too. His buddy Nik met him with a bear hug and a beer.

"Missed you brother, where have you been?" he asked.

"Oh, it's a long story. One beer isn't enough," Derrick advised.

———

FOUR SOCIAL MEDIA sites offered the same prize on the same day: *find this man for ten million dollars.* The picture was Simon Little…

- The End -

ABOUT THE AUTHOR

KA Brown is the author of *Programmed to Win*, a political thriller; *The Cost of Killing* is his second novel. Before becoming a writer, KA Brown spent over twenty-six years as a firefighter. He retired at the rank of lieutenant to pursue his passion for writing.

In addition to his career as a firefighter, KA has always been an avid reader and has always had a love for storytelling. When he's not writing, KA enjoys spending time with his family, including his wife, adult children, and grandchildren.

KA's experience as a firefighter gave him a unique perspective on the world and has inspired him to explore complex themes in his writing. *The Cost of Killing* continues the themes and characters introduced in *Programmed to Win*, while introducing a new storyline and delving deeper into the characters themselves.

KA is dedicated to creating compelling stories that will keep readers on the edge of their seats and looks forward to continuing his writing journey.

ABOUT THE PUBLISHER

Tactical 16 Publishing is an unconventional publisher that understands the therapeutic value inherent in writing. We help veterans, first responders, and their families and friends to tell their stories using their words.

We are on a mission to capture the history of America's heroes: stories about sacrifices during chaos, humor amid tragedy, and victories learned from experiences not readily recreated — real stories from real people.

Tactical 16 has published books in leadership, business, fiction, and children's genres. We produce all types of works, from self-help to memoirs that preserve unique stories not yet told.

You don't have to be a polished author to join our ranks. If you can write with passion and be unapologetic, we want to talk. Go to Tactical16.com to contact us and to learn more.

All of Tactical 16's books are available on our online bookstore, T16Books.com. Visit it today to see more books from our selection of authors and to find a new adventure to read!